Also by Lawrence David

Family Values

NEED

Lawrence David

Need

Random House   New York

Library of Congress Cataloging-in-Publication Data

David, Lawrence
    Need / Lawrence David.
        p. cm.
    ISBN 0-679-43433-X
    1. Psychotherapist and patient—New York (N.Y.)—Fiction. 2. Man-woman
relationships—New York (N.Y.)—Fiction. 3. Women psychiatrists—New York
(N.Y.)—Fiction. 4. Marriage—New York (N.Y.)—Fiction. I. Title
PS3554.A9166N44 1994
813'.54—dc20   93-48407

Book Design by Tanya M. Pérez

Manufactured in the United States of America
98765432
First Edition

For Jeremy Laufer

In a study of 285 clinical psychologists:

97.2% reported feeling afraid that a client may commit suicide.

53.3% reported feeling so afraid about a client that it affected their eating, sleeping, or concentration.

45.6% reported feeling so angry with a client they did something they later regretted.

—Dr. Kenneth S. Pope and Dr. Barbara G. Tabachnick, "Therapists' Anger, Hate, Fear, and Sexual Feelings: National Survey of Therapist Responses, Client Characteristics, Critical Events, Formal Complaints, and Training," *Professional Psychology: Research and Practice* (May 1993)

From *The New York Times* (May 4, 1993):

While those surveyed were all psychologists, Dr. Pope said he believed that results from psychiatrists or clinical social workers would have been roughly equivalent. . . .

Acknowledgments

For their support throughout the years, I would like to thank Dr. Kantor, Dr. Miller, Dr. Cooper, and Dr. Pomerance.

January

1

D r. Pamela Thompson calculates that within ten minutes, by the time she's reached the end of this session, she'll be able to afford a new, larger microwave oven with built-in carousel. The microwave Pam currently owns is cheap and small with a dial timer—no digital readings or temperature setting controls. Pam bought the oven for cooking popcorn while watching movies on the VCR, but as time passed, Pam and her husband began relying on the oven more, cooking frozen pizzas and entrées and reheating take-out leftovers. Now, approximately one year after the purchase of the original microwave, Pam's ready to invest in a larger, high-powered appliance, her one purchase this week in the redecoration and updating of the apartment.

Pam gazes across the room at her patient, Joan Dwyer. Joan Dwyer's been Pam's patient for a year, Joan coming to see Pam because she didn't like the way her life had been proceeding. Two years divorced at the time of her first therapy appointment, Joan hadn't yet had one date. A year into her therapy with Pam, Joan has had exactly two dates: one with a man she wrote to from an advertisement in *New York* magazine's personals, and a second with a man she met at the health club she'd joined, the second date so embarrassing Joan that she hasn't returned to the club since, says she hated it anyway, feels old and worn-out compared with those young twenty- through thirty-year-old bodies. Joan Dwyer was glad the second date failed, providing her with a reasonable excuse as to why she would never have to ride a stationary bike again.

Pam thinks Joan's problems have less to do with her finding a man and more with her being severely depressed for the past twenty-five years of her life. The marriage Joan describes, in which she was completely dependent upon her husband and kids for any sense of self-worth, sounds sad, not fulfilling. Pam wishes Joan would talk about her childhood, her parents, how she fills her days; *anything* would be better than to listen to Joan ramble on for the fifth consecutive session in the past two weeks delving into the three-year-old details of the split between her ex-husband and herself. However, whenever Pam broaches the issues of Joan's childhood, Joan resists, thinks Pam is missing the point of why she is here: the divorce and wanting a man in her life.

"I feel guilty for moving all of us, but I couldn't function in the house once he left. That's why I had to move back to the city. I had to put him behind us by selling the house. I hate driving, so it's better being in the city, anyway. And I'm much more comfortable in my parents' apartment."

Pam glances to the brass clock sitting on the windowsill. Five-fifty exactly. Pam finds it interesting that approximately one year ago Joan came to see her and she had just bought her first microwave, and today, one year later, close to the exact anniversary of that date, she is now preparing to purchase her second microwave. She looks to Joan with telling eyes; Joan's time is up.

"Is my time up? No?" Joan checks her watch. "Oh. It is." She wears a sad, anxious expression. She stands up from the chair, picking her long wool coat off the couch.

Pam stands, walks to the door, opening it for her patient. "I'll see you on Friday."

Joan's eyes brighten. "Of course. Friday," she replies. "See you then." And she's out the door, into the waiting room.

Pam closes the office door, hears the outer waiting room door open and close, and she knows Joan has left. She is alone and she sits at her large oak rolltop desk, ten minutes to spare before her next patient, her last patient of the day, is due.

Pam opens Joan's folder, taking out the small composition book she makes her notes in, dating a page, writing a sentence to sum up Joan's session.

The office is a two-bedroom apartment in a large prewar apartment building on Manhattan's Upper West Side, Pam's office being one of the two bedrooms. The second is let out to another psychiatrist, who uses the space for his private practice as well as a study in which to write research papers and conduct an affair with one of his patients. Off the short hallway between the two doctors' offices are the kitchenette, bathroom, and waiting area.

Pam, holding the lease on the apartment, decorated the reception room, furnishing it with three navy blue upholstered wingback chairs, a small coffee table, and two shaded floor lamps. Simple and comfortable. Current issues of *The New Yorker, New York, Vogue, Time, The Economist,* and *National Geographic* decorate the coffee table. A small yet concise selection of periodicals—enough from which any patient should be able to find one to pass the time, however not so many as to be overwhelming. Old issues are discarded no later than two weeks after their cover dates have expired; Pam finds nothing more depressing in waiting rooms than magazines dated from a month or year past.

In the corner plugged into the wall is the sound screen. Standard in most therapists' waiting rooms, the unit sits in the corner on the carpet, six inches tall, eight across, small and circular, like a gray metal cake. The screen's motor spins out a consistent white noise as quiet as the whirring of a miniature fan but blowing no air. As patients wait for appointments, the sound screen obscures the sound of voices that may filter out from the doctors' offices, the soft humming sound all the patients hear as they read magazine articles about serial killers, distant Tibetan lands, government budget expenditures, and makeup tips.

Pam puts Joan Dwyer's folder aside and pushes the button on her answering machine, which silently recorded a message during the past appointment. "Hello. Guess I'll see you downstairs after your last session. Call if things have changed. Love you. Bye." Dennis Perry, her husband. Pam chose not to take his name when they married eight years ago, "Dr. Pam Perry" not sounding too appealing to her ears.

The door's buzzer sounds, and Pam reaches over to the white button by her therapy chair, giving it a push, releasing the lock that lets patients into the office from the hallway. Pam hears the office door open and close. Five fifty-nine, the white porcelain clock on her desk reads. Bill Matson, as usual, is perfectly punctual, and Pam walks to the door, glad to have decided to schedule Bill Matson in after Joan Dwyer for the last appointment of the day three days each week. Bill Matson's fascinating, hectic life is a welcome relief following the unrelenting static of Joan Dwyer's.

Joan Dwyer always drinks one—and only one—vodka martini straight up with three olives after each of her three therapy appointments each week. She always drinks the one martini at the bar in Donnelman's, the restaurant off the lobby of her therapist's building.

Joan takes a sip from the flared glass, her eyes fixed down into the drink, watching the cocktail olives slide along the glass side as it's tipped. She purses her lips, the drink a touch heavy on vermouth, and places the martini on the cocktail napkin at the bar's edge, considering what she has learned about herself from today's session. Joan knows this is not a valid or fair question, knows therapy is an *accumulative* process, but worries over each individual session, trying to see the link between all these many sessions, trying to decipher their code and discover where the doctor is taking her, how the doctor is curing her. Today, Joan notes, Dr. Thompson let her talk nonstop with no interruptions even though she had spoken of events the doctor has heard often before: the divorce and its impact on the family.

"Why do you let me go on and repeat myself?" Joan asked Dr. Thompson early on during their work together, and Dr. Thompson replied, "If these are the things that are on your mind, shouldn't I let you talk them out and try to understand them for yourself? I'm not here to tell you what's important to you. Only through your talking things over repeatedly do we both learn the issues that are troubling you. Only through repeatedly considering these issues can we hope to master their meanings."

Joan sometimes wonders if her doctor truly comprehends her feelings or only feigns comprehension and compassion for her. "After all," Joan asked Dr. Thompson, "how do I know you know what it's like to be dumped by your husband for another woman, leaving you, your kids and moving two thousand miles away?"

"Do you think I have to have experienced that to know how much hurt and anger you feel?"

"No, I suppose not," Joan replied politely, and she shut herself up, silencing the thought.

Dr. Pamela Thompson does not wear a wedding band, Joan has noticed; therefore, she may or may not be married, and when Joan asked the doctor whether she was, Dr. Thompson refused to answer, claiming that Joan is here to examine *herself*; why complicate it by bringing the doctor's personal, outside life into the therapeutic process? What does it mean to Joan whether her doctor may or may not be married?

Joan swirls the cone of the glass, a wave of alcohol rolling to its edge, shivering the olives sitting atop the glass's spine. Joan dips a pinkie finger into the glass, skewering the pitted army green olive on the fingernail, and lifting it, sucking it between her lips. Sometimes she believes that if it weren't for the one martini she allows herself following each session, she wouldn't attend therapy at all.

Dennis Perry locks the door of his basement office and walks up the seventeen spiraling brick steps to street level, facing the back of the prewar apartment building in which his wife practices psychiatry. Dennis's graphic design studio is one block north of Pam's office, the basement floor of a four-story brownstone on West Seventy-third Street, just off Central Park West.

Dennis walks around the block to Seventy-second, approaching his wife's building, meeting her for an early dinner. A quarter after six, and the sidewalks are congested with tired faces returning to apartments for the night. Dennis looks ahead, past dinner and sleep, sorting through the list of items to be accomplished tomorrow. He must: bill out weekly hours to all his clients, review outstanding invoices to vendors, take sample sketches of poster designs over to an off-Broadway theater company, finish a layout for a clothing store's ad for a sales promotion, and begin preliminary sketches on a series of color print ads for a new shampoo product, assigned to him by the last agency he worked for before going freelance four years ago. Going freelance because then he wouldn't have to work with anyone he didn't choose to, could choose his own work hours, would no longer be assigned strictly to one client but could work on many varied, wide-ranging projects. He thought it would give him time to get back to doing the artwork he gave up when he began at the agency, but since going freelance, he's found he doesn't have the desire to draw for himself anymore. He no longer has the goal of one day seeing his drawings hanging in a gallery or his characters in a newspaper cartoon strip. Ad art is still art, Dennis recognizes, and it doesn't matter if it's a dishwashing detergent package or canvas; it's all art, pop or otherwise, and his detergent box, sitting on the shelves of supermarkets everywhere, shown on TV dozens of times each week, is probably as familiar to the public as the *Mona Lisa* and *The Last Supper*.

More than half an hour before it's time to meet his wife, Dennis enters the restaurant off the lobby, walks up to the bar, and sits on one of the high-backed stools. The restaurant isn't crowded as it's the in-between hours when people are either finishing up at the office or bolted behind the doors of their apartments watching the daily news horrors before watching their reenactments during the prime-time hours.

Two businessmen sit at the bar discussing computer printouts over beers. At Dennis's right sits an attractive, stylish, fortyish-looking woman. She watches the news on the small color television perched on a shelf overlooking the bar. Dennis orders a scotch and soda. The bartender fixes the drink, then returns to stocking the back counter, filling plastic bins with straws, napkins, and cocktail onions.

Joan looks away from the television with a loud sigh, lifting her drink, taking a sip, pouring the third olive onto her tongue.

Dennis looks up at the television. A commercial for key chain Mace sprayers. He turns to the attractive woman seated nearby. "What happened?"

She gulps down the half-chewed olive. "What?"

"On the news."

"A shooting. A man and woman uptown. They showed the dead body on the stretcher. The woman's, I think." Joan peers down into her empty glass, aware that her one-martini treat is over. It is now time to return to her empty apartment for the evening.

"Are you okay?" Dennis asks.

Joan shakes her head nervously, brushing her bluntly cut shoulder-length hair away from her face with a hand. She averts her gaze from his. "Just thinking about things." She looks at the bartender, considering having a second drink, considers but decides not to. She sighs with disappointment, her willpower winning out.

"Bad day?" Dennis asks. The woman has a pretty face, approximately his age. Another one of many lonely, middle-aged New York ladies. He picks up his drink.

"No, nothing happened today at all." She watches his hand on the glass. No ring, so he's most likely not married.

"Is that good?" Dennis asks.

"I suppose. My daughter only went back to boarding school a week ago, so I guess I'm just not used to living alone again," Joan responds, letting him know she has kids and is single without having to say it. She feels a rush of nervous energy overwhelming her, a panic attack, and she reaches into her clutch bag for one of the Xanax tablets Dr. Thompson prescribes, her antianxiety medication, gesturing to the bartender for water.

"You have a child?" he asks.

"Two. Sixteen and nineteen. A girl and a boy. You?"

"First I'd like to get married." Dennis smiles, not sure why he's lying, but it feels right, the lie. "I would like to have kids, though. Not right now, but someday."

Mistakenly reading her signal, the bartender has brought Joan a second martini. She takes it confidently, glad to have it, and turns to the bar. She places the pink-orange tablet on her tongue, takes a sip, and swallows. She notices the man watching. "It's just aspirin," Joan says defensively.

"I didn't say anything."

"Of course. I'm sorry." Joan pushes the drink away lest she be tempted to sip, doesn't want to chance mixing the alcohol and antianxiety medication. "I like having a family. The kids are great even if the marriage didn't work out."

"Recently divorced?"

"Three years," Joan answers. "I guess, not recently anymore."

"Well, you're a very attractive, friendly woman," Dennis compliments her. "I'm sure you meet plenty of men."

"No, not too many. Not anyone I've liked." Joan reaches into her purse for her wallet, and Dennis takes out his billfold.

"Let me take care of it."

"There's the one before this, too," Joan warns.

"I can handle it." He lays a ten by her glass. "Is this enough?"

"It's happy hour. I guess so." She shrugs. "Thank you. That's nice of you." And her voice rises, sounding to Dennis as if she were about ready to leave, and Dennis is pleased she might—this attractive, available, lonely woman with the full pink lips—but still she remains seated, staring at the near-full martini glass, a hand reaching into the mouth of her purse.

Joan's eyes fix on the olives, distorted through the glass and liquid, small army green olives, and she sits, numb, trying to decide whether she should bring in a Chinese dinner on the way home or make Shake 'n Bake chicken tonight. What is she hungry for if she does decide to go for the Chinese anyway?

"Can I help you to a taxi?"

The voice comes at her, but Joan isn't listening, and the words float by, garbled by her current thoughts. Perhaps sweet-and-sour pork would be best. Sweet-and-sour pork with extra pineapple chunks.

A hand on her arm: "Do you need help to a cab?"

She lifts the hand away, placing it on the bar, standing, and giving him a weak smile. "I'll walk. Just a few blocks."

Dennis picks a napkin off the stack in front of him, taking a felt-tip marker from the breast pocket of his sports coat. He writes his name and office number across the napkin. She watches as he carefully tries not to tear the soft paper. He finishes and hands the napkin to Joan, and she reads it before placing it in her pocketbook. "Do you want mine? Am I supposed to give it to you now?" The Xanax has loosened her tongue, or maybe it's the alcohol or both. She shouldn't have taken the pill so soon after having the first martini, shouldn't have taken it at all perhaps.

"I'd like that," Dennis says. He hasn't exchanged phone numbers with a woman in years, over ten and a half years, since before he met Pam and was married, and he finds this old routine both refreshing and familiar. He hands Joan the marker, and she takes a napkin from the stack alongside the bar, writing out her first name and phone number.

"Okay, there," she says, leaving the napkin along the bar edge by his elbow, trying to sound casual, and she takes a step away, afraid she'll snatch the napkin back if he doesn't take it quickly.

He holds the napkin in his palm. "Joan," he reads.

"Yes," Joan says. She backs off another step. "I'm going to go now."

He looks at her, amused. "That's fine. Whatever you have to do." And he folds the napkin in quarters, inserting it into the back flap of his billfold.

"Okay, then, good-bye." Joan lifts her hand in a tentative half wave, a muted, embarrassed attempt at friendliness, and heads off and out of the restaurant, onto the sidewalk.

Dennis watches her go, assessing her thin legs, the curve of her hip against the trim skirt. Teenage adrenaline along with the scotch flushes his cheeks. Swapping phone numbers on napkins opens up an arsenal of hopes he hasn't felt in a while: the excitement of the waiting game, waiting to see who will call first, how long it will be until she calls him—or *will* she call him? Or will *he* call *her*? He's married and wouldn't or couldn't, and Dennis realizes that although he may see this as sport, this Joan woman he spoke to was obviously lonely, glad to have someone to talk to and share her thoughts with. Maybe she's really hoping he will call. He's never cheated on his wife before, has thought about it, had opportunities, but never has and doesn't want to—*does he not want to?*—start now.

Guilt, regret, remorse flood his mind, leaving him ashamed for flirting with this woman, leading her on when he's entirely devoted to his wife. Dennis checks his watch. Seven-fifteen. Pam's ten minutes late.

"How was your day?"

Pam turns from her office door, encountering Michael Flanting seated in one of the wingback chairs, *The Wall Street Journal* folded open across his knees. The relationship has been going on for five and a half months, so at this point, months after being introduced and having had numerous conversations regarding the weather, restaurants, and the stock market, Pam knows she still shouldn't feel awkward about speaking to her colleague Jack Briden's lover and patient, but she does, finds it inappropriate no matter how long the relationship's lasted. Pam locks the office door. "My day was fine. How was yours?" She smiles, trying hard to sound casual, not irritated.

"Eh, fine." Michael closes the paper. "Can't complain. Can afford all the therapy I want, so even if something is wrong, at least I can get help for it."

Pam holds her smile and nods. "That's good."

The door at the end of the hall opens, and Michael's eyes instantly flicker away from Pam to meet those of his doctor.

"You can come in," Jack Briden says to Michael, then to Pam: "You on your way out?"

"On my way."

"Have a nice evening. We'll talk tomorrow." And then back to his patient. "Mr. Flanting," Jack calls, and Michael tucks his paper under his arm.

"Nice to chat," Michael says to Pam. "I'll ask Jack about us having dinner sometime. You and your husband, maybe."

Pam smiles, extending a hand for a shake. "Please."

Michael pumps her hand firmly. "Will do. See you later." He is off into his doctor's office.

Pam first saw Michael Flanting as she was leaving the office for the day and he was waiting to be taken into Dr. Briden's for a session: a handsome young man in his late twenties, very well dressed. In subsequent weeks the young man began appearing at the office early in the morning, late in the afternoon, and early in the evening. On one Thursday afternoon she encountered the young man sitting in the waiting room with a picnic basket on his lap, a beach umbrella in his hand, and a sombrero on his head.

Pam took her fellow doctor aside at the end of the day. "The fellow with the big hat? What was that all about?"

Jack Briden placed his coffee mug in the kitchen sink. "Was he disruptive to your patient? I'm sorry. Michael doesn't always have the best sense of others; he gets carried away."

"So this was a social call." Pam left the kitchen, too embarrassed to discuss this face-to-face. She went into the waiting area, straightened out the piles of magazines, aligning edges.

Jack followed. "I'll tell him to behave as is appropriate to an office setting. I will. I'm sure you disapprove of this altogether," Jack went on. "But the boy really doesn't even need therapy, so I'm not doing anything unethical. He's rich, and he pays me to talk about movies. I'll introduce you to him. He's really quite charming." Jack smiled, pleased with himself, with his catch of this young man over twenty years his junior.

Unethical, but who is she to protest at this point, five months too late? Call the APA, the American Psychiatric Association, five months after the relationship began and report her colleague? Michael Flanting is happy and Jack Briden is happy, so who is she to say it's wrong? She should be happy for them. Pam stares at Jack Briden's closed office door, considering what may or may not be occurring within the office. Pam winces at the thought, at how inappropriate it all is, and turns away, heading out of the office.

.   .   .

Having decided during her walk home that she would have the Shake 'n Bake, Joan, arriving home, standing in the kitchen and holding the packet of Shake 'n Bake in one hand and the boneless, skinless chicken breasts in the other, collapses on the floor in a heap, drawing herself into a sitting position, legs tucked beneath her, repeatedly looking from the two chicken breasts to the Shake 'n Bake. Searching for some answer amid this confusion, she bursts into tears.

The packet of chicken breasts drops to the floor with a wet thud, a trail of water seeping from under the taut plastic wrap. The aluminum foil seasoning packet sits in Joan's lap, and she presses the heels of her palms into her eyes, grinding at the soft skin.

Who am I? Joan asks herself. Mother of Andrea and Todd. Ex-wife of Al. Daughter of the deceased Walter and Cathy Robins.

Who is Joan Dwyer when her kids are growing and gone and her husband up and left three years ago for another woman—not even a *younger* woman, but a woman her same exact age? Joan would have understood Al leaving for a young, pretty, lithe girl, but he didn't. Al left for a woman of Joan's same age and not even half as pretty as Joan herself, in Joan's best objective opinion. He didn't leave for a trophy wife. He left for an interesting, intellectually minded, extroverted career woman. An insult not against Joan's face or body, but against her mind and personality.

"Why do you think you're depressed?" Dr. Thompson repeatedly asks Joan, hoping to have her patient consider that her depression is the result of many life incidents, not only the divorce, and Joan's answer varies with the day:

"Because I failed at being a good housewife and mother."

"Because I'm lonely."

"Because I've spent all my life trying to create a perfect family life that I can never have, that I thought I had."

"Because my parents raised me to think I couldn't do anything but be a man's wife."

"Because I hate being who I am but am intelligent enough to know I'm incapable of being anything else."

"Because I have the luxury," Joan answers, angry that her doctor keeps asking.

Last night Joan watched television, eating from a bag of rippled salt-and-vinegar potato chips, watching as the mother on some show, some pretty, fortyish brunette, not unlike Joan herself, sauntered into the living room of her quaint, country-living suburban home, which looked much like Joan's home of the past in upper-middle-class suburbia where she lived her life with Al and the kids, and the actress playing the mother sauntered into the room with a briefcase under one arm and an infant under the other, kissed the baby on the forehead, and handed him to her eldest daughter as she rushed out the door to the office for the day.

Joan laughed at this mother last night, laughing at this working woman's predicament as if her own were not equally—if not more—laughable. At least I'm not her, Joan thought last night, potato chips crunching between her teeth, vinegar and salt burning her gums, but tonight, stranded on the kitchen floor, the kitchen in which her mother taught her how to bake lemon meringue pie, her ex-husband first met her parents, her parents shared so many mornings of their married life, Joan wishes otherwise, wishes she had whatever it takes to wake up in the morning and want to get out of bed and make some kind of contribution to the world. Wishes she cared enough to want to change her life when she only cares enough to face up to what it is not and acknowledge the failure.

"Why do you think you're depressed?"

Joan searches for someone to blame, for some event that puts the depression in focus: "I was an abused child." "I was an abused wife." "I was raped as a teenager." All false. There is no answer. She just is, and she doesn't care why she is depressed so much as she cares how to learn to stop it, but according to Dr. Thompson, without Joan examining the roots of the depression, it will be hard to alleviate it at all.

"Beyond finding a man, what is a goal for you? What interests you? Is there anything you want to learn or do?"

Joan can't remember, doesn't want to remember goals long gone, evaporating when she dropped out of Bennington after her sophomore year to marry Al Dwyer, a graduating senior from Williams, and set up house for her husband in New York. She hadn't even had the chance to declare her major before dropping out. What would it have been? Joan tries to choose, as if she were still in college and has to put it in writing to the dean of studies. Painting? Acting? Literature? A time existed when she did want more than to find a man, although at the present time, Joan finds this hard to imagine. Easier to be a housewife than pursue an artist's career. Easier to stay home with a couple of kids, life happening to her, rather than to decide what to do. Now, without the husband, the kids, the parents, the college education and career, who is she? What is she?

Joan stands, hands on the counter's edge, picking up the chicken, the Shake 'n Bake. No, Joan understands, her eyes fixed on her hands, her thin fingers, her birthstone ring, an opal where she once wore a wedding band, the chicken is a bad idea tonight, a terrible, terrible idea, and Joan puts the soft, moist package in the refrigerator for tomorrow. Tomorrow will be a better day for the chicken. The seasoning packet is returned to the Shake 'n Bake box on the top shelf of the spice cabinet. She looks at the spot on the floor where she sat a minute previous—sitting feeling sorry for herself for being depressed, confused, empty Joan Dwyer—and Joan walks to the short patch of counter where she keeps her purse, address book, and yellow and white pages. The phone is mounted on the wall above, and she lifts the receiver, pushing number nine on the memory panel. The phone dials through its sequence of low tones, and Joan hears a shrill ring. One, two, and three, she counts. "Hunan Chef," a bright Oriental female voice answers.

. . .

"Have you come to any decision on the spare room?"

They undress in the bedroom of their two-bedroom co-op on the Upper East Side, Dennis hanging up his suit and sliding into a navy blue sweatshirt and sweatpants, Pam hanging her skirt in the closet, its waist caught between the hanger's metal clips.

"What about it?" she asks, shaking out her silk blouse, hanging it alongside two dozen other silk and cotton blouses all in various shades of white, cream, yellow, pale pink, and blue.

Dennis tosses his paisley tie over a hook on the back of the closet door. "You don't have plans for it? You have plans for everything else in the house."

Pam outlined her plans for the desired redecoration of the apartment in earnest shortly after they stepped out of the restaurant onto the Upper West Side sidewalk, crosstown from the apartment of which they spoke. Pam proceeded to detail the short-term goals she had for their home. Room-by-room details, running through a list of renovations that would be accomplished over the next several months. December's purchases of the new stereo, TV, VCR, and this coming week's microwave being the first steps toward renovating the apartment, Pam initially purchasing items Dennis would appreciate in order to ease him into the many other redecoration plans she had in mind.

By the time Dennis and Pam emerged from Central Park at East Seventy-ninth Street, the apartment was redone in both their minds according to Pam's elaborate schema. The couple walked east four avenues and north four blocks to their twenty-seventh-floor apartment, Pam planning out the itinerary for the renovations in her mind while Dennis shoved it from his, leaving the entire chore up to his wife to get done if that was what she wanted, she being the one in need of it.

Dennis walks to the door of the bedroom, standing there, scrunching his toes into the deep, soft gray-white pile of the carpet. "Are we redoing the guest room as a bedroom or are we doing something else with it?"

Pam's back is to him, her arms reaching behind her, elbows twisted up into the air, unfastening her bra, letting it fall to the carpet. "What do you mean? Don't you want it to match the other furnishings?" She opens a dresser drawer, reaching for an oversize oxford cloth men's shirt.

"Of course. I was just wondering if we're keeping it a bedroom, that's all."

Dennis stands, hand on door's edge, eyes on brass doorknob, his wife's reflection curling around its polished surface as she buttons her shirt.

At a party given by a mutual friend, a colleague of Pam's from the hospital where she was in residence and an ex-roommate of Dennis's from his days at NYU, they had met. She stood in a corner of the apartment, drinking a rum and Coke. "You're not talking to anyone?" he asked, and Pam smiled, tilting her head, surveying the room.

"I don't think I'm in the mood to be here."

"Then why are you?"

She looked back to Dennis, deciding he was attractive, had a cute face. "I'm trying to give myself a social life. I'm not very good at it."

"Would you rather be alone?" Dennis was completely unsure whether this woman was being coy or was truly annoyed.

"No, not at all." Pam kept smiling, trying to show him that she could be fun.

Dennis sipped his beer. "Good."

"So what do you do?" The most obvious question, but wanting him to see she was interested.

"Art director at an ad agency. Mostly print work, some packaging design. What do you do?"

"A psychiatrist. Finishing up my residency."

Dennis grinned. "Help other people with their lives but too afraid to leave the corner of the room?"

Pam nodded. "I feel safer analyzing people than actually meeting them."

"Even me?" Dennis asked.

Pam laughed. "You I'm not sure about yet."

They dated for a year, lived together for a year, married, and bought the apartment. Pam said she would want kids, a boy and a girl in a few years, once her private practice was well established. Dennis agreed, deciding it would be better for both of them when they were further along in their careers. Two years passed. The boy and girl they had originally planned on became one kid per Pam's decision. "No sibling rivalry," Pam explained. "Just one perfect kid. I've read studies. Only children are the best children." Two more years passed. Dennis went into business for himself. "The timing isn't right for a kid now," Pam explained, and three and one half years passed and the one kid became "Maybe one kid, I don't know," until last summer when Pam confessed, "I couldn't be a good mother. I had a terribly distant mother, and you know generations pass on abusive patterns to their children. God only knows what my sisters do to their kids. And I don't want to be like them or my mother. I won't chance it. The two of us are so busy and set in our ways. We're already happy with just us, so why do we need a child?"

But Dennis won't let his wife off so easy. "I don't understand." He speaks to the doorknob. "What's the extra room for, then? We bought it for when we have a kid. For a nursery, a bedroom for a kid." He uses the word *kid* like a weapon, a tool to bludgeon her with, the word all rough at the edges.

Pam doesn't give him the benefit of her attention. She knows this routine, and she walks into the bathroom, switching on the frosted pink bulbs surrounding the mirror, reaching for the body lotion atop the toilet. "You know I can't have a baby when we both work full-time. You know I can't take that much time off from my patients, and I don't want to. I don't see you volunteering to forgo *your* career for a child, and I won't be some half-assed mother who hires someone to care for her baby. You should admire me for being honest and knowing myself, not like most women, who have a litter of kids, then resent them for the rest of their lives." She rubs the coconut lotion over her neck, inhaling its scent, walking past Dennis at the door. "I'll go check the machine."

The answering machine, connected into Pam and Dennis's unlisted phone line, sits in the guest room on the bureau's top. Pam's arms are folded across her chest, resting on the softness of her breasts. She stands facing the machine, watching its two rapid red blinks. She reaches out a finger and strikes the play button, quickly picking up the message pad and pen on the shelf.

"Hello, Pam. Hello, Dennis. It's Madelaine. Inviting you over for dinner this weekend. Friday or Saturday, whatever's best. Friday would be better for us. Call me tomorrow to let me know when and if you can make it. Bye."

A pause, the click of a phone hanging up, a beep, then a long tone and Pam hears her own voice speaking. "Messages recorded at office to be picked up." Pam's office answering machine set to phone her at home and let her know when messages have been received at her office.

The tape spins, the machine resetting itself to pick up messages and record over the messages played. Pam sits on the edge of the guest bed, crossing her legs, the shirt bunching up high on her thighs, parting over her lap. She picks up the beige Trimline phone and dials her office number. Her outgoing office message plays, and Pam punches in her five-digit code. "Message received at eight-forty-one P.M.," the machine indicates, then: "Dr. Thompson. This is Tim Boxer. I am now at home after work. I will be here all night. I will see you tomorrow at ten o'clock."

Pam hangs up. Pam invited Tim Boxer to phone when he needed to, whenever he's feeling overwhelmed by life. "I'll usually check in at least once each evening."

"I don't want to intrude on your personal life. I couldn't do that, really."

"I'd rather have you talk to me for a few minutes each evening than for you to stay up all night on the edge, in fear."

"I promise I won't take advantage of your generosity. I couldn't abuse it."

"I know you wouldn't, that's why I'm telling you this, but don't be afraid to call if you need me, okay? You promise?"

Tim leaves his doctor messages at night, and Pam phones him back. Some months once a week, some weeks once every other day, Tim calls, making his desperate attempts to remain connected to the world and reinforce an attachment to someone. Ever since learning he has HIV, Tim Boxer has alienated himself from family, friends, and coworkers at his proofreading job to the point where once he leaves his office for the day, he's completely alone, lost in his inner thoughts, afraid to speak to anyone, afraid to leave his apartment. "I feel so ashamed for having this thing. I just wish I would come down with some illness that would kill me or that I would at least have the courage to kill myself now instead of waiting and getting sick. If I know it's eventually going to kill me anyway, I wish it would happen already. This is like sitting on death row."

Pam dials his number, hears a ringing. On the fourth ring the phone machine picks up. Tim, despite the fact that he claims no one ever phones him, still screens the one or two calls a week he does receive.

"This is Tim. I'm not home. Leave a message." Beep.

Pam speaks, "Hello, Tim. It's Dr. Thompson calling you back. If you'd—"

"Hello, hold on."

Seconds of warped, screeching audio feedback, then a click as the phone machine is shut off.

Tim returns. "Hello."

"Things more difficult tonight?" Pam asks.

"Yes, I suppose."

"Anything particular happen?"

A pause, then: "I don't know. Sorry. I shouldn't have phoned. I have nothing to say."

"How are you now?"

A pause. A sigh. "I'm not sure. All right."

"*Are* you all right?"

"I think so. I think I'll be. I'll see you tomorrow anyway."

"We'll talk more then."

"Thanks for calling me."

"You're welcome. I'll see you tomorrow."

"Yes."

"Good."

"Good-bye."

"Good-bye," Pam returns, and there is a pause as Pam waits for Tim to hang up first, letting him have the feeling that he's leaving her, that she's waiting for him to be ready to end the conversation. Tim hangs up the phone, and then Pam hangs up on her end.

The popcorn bag inflates in the microwave, the bag rising as it fills with the popped, butter-flavored kernels. Joan carefully takes the full bag from the oven, pulling at opposite corners, the sweet smell of the corn scenting the air, the steam watering Joan's eyes. She carries the bag into the family room and lies down across the sofa. After dinner Joan had changed into a sweatsuit. The better to relax in. Seafoam green top and matching seafoam and coral bottoms, ordered through a mail-order catalog. Suede, lamb's wool–lined slippers on her feet. Joan places the bag of popcorn on the coffee table, taking up the remote control. The detective show that's currently on is not doing it for her: too violent, too fast, and too little dialogue and plot. Only cardboard for characters and exploding cars and guns. Joan runs through channels two through twenty-eight, then backtracks to nineteen, settling on a movie.

The movie, with only a half hour left, is reaching its climax, and Joan tries to fill in from memory what's come before, having seen this on Broadway years ago, Elizabeth Taylor playing the Bette Davis role. A night out with Al in New York City, Joan taking a train in from New Jersey and meeting Al at his office for a night at the theater and dinner. A baby-sitter hired for the kids. Making love on the burgundy leather sofa in his office, Al needing her so badly they did it right there in his dark office downtown, a view of the Brooklyn Bridge in the distance.

No more nights of theatergoing with a husband, none for three years since Al left, Joan sits in, watching TV alone, no kid's head resting in her lap or strong husband's arm draped gently across her shoulder, handsome eyes under dark brows looking at her suggestively in anticipation of the moment when the children will be off to bed and the parents can cuddle spontaneously. Hugging her knees for comfort, Joan watches Bette Davis sitting comfortably on a sofa, staring at some man as he struggles to drag himself up a flight of stairs, her eyes cold and glassy as the man dies behind her.

After Al's departure, with no man around, Joan wasn't secure living with the children in a house set back from the road behind a forest of trees. "What if someone broke in and tried to get us?" Joan asked Todd and Andrea. "I couldn't protect you. I'm not Wonder Woman."

"That's not going to happen, Mom," Todd replied patiently.

"We're all right," Andrea said. "Nothing's ever happened before."

"Well, we won't be all right if something *does* happen. Of that I am certain. I don't think we're safe here. Not without a grown man in the house."

Six months later, in June, Joan sold the house to a French businessman who'd been relocated to the United States with his family. Joan and the kids packed up their belongings and moved into the vacant three-bedroom apartment Joan inherited from her parents when her mother died one year before.

By midsummer, settled into the city home of her childhood, Joan feared the thought of her kids growing up in a violent city, that her daughter would be raped and her son hit by stray gunfire. After phoning Al and asking him to handle the arrangements, Andrea and Todd were sent to a New England boarding school. "The city isn't a good place for children anymore. You can't play outside. You can't trust anyone. Being in boarding schools helps you get into better colleges anyway."

A commercial for carpet cleaner, a woman shaking and spilling the powder across the carpet with reckless abandon. Harvest Moon scented to cover up pet odors.

Joan wonders how Todd and Andrea are at this moment. Eleven P.M., and it's too late to phone. Andrea would be in bed, and the housemother would only take a message. Todd, if up, would probably be out with friends at a bar near campus or perhaps sharing an intimate moment with Emily, his live-in girlfriend.

She clicks off the TV. The only sound left in the apartment is the crunching of the popcorn between her teeth. Joan places a large kernel on her tongue, letting it sit, feeling the saliva soak into it, turning it to mush before she swallows.

At 9:15 P.M. Mountain Time, they're most likely out to dinner, at a movie, concert, play, or dance. Al and his second wife, Linda Dwyer. Intellectual, cosmopolitan, with two college degrees, and Joan can't help recognizing the irony in the fact that she dropped out of college to marry Al and set up their home as he wanted, yet he left her for a woman with a master's degree in philosophy. Joan takes up the popcorn bag and heads into the kitchen. When Al left, he already had his other wife chosen, had had her chosen two years prior to the marriage's breakup, Joan eventually learned. He'd been cheating on her for two years before he ended the marriage, Al told Joan a year after the marriage ended, hoping to shock his ex-wife into an awakening that he was not coming back to her, that their life together had been long over before it was legally over and he was happier with his new wife and she, Joan, was better off without a husband who didn't love her.

With a husband departed, two children grown and no longer living at home, Joan inventories her world: a rent-free apartment, a monthly allowance allotted by her father's, now her, accountant, and a therapist helping her understand why she behaves as she does so she can change her maladaptive patterns and live a healthier life. To learn to accept herself as she is, not needing others to feel worthy but obtaining self-worth through self-recognition. This is why Joan Dwyer is in therapy, she reminds herself, to better herself, to better her life, to give herself back her will to pursue a happy, healthy life. Joan leans on the kitchen counter, glad her nightly panic attack has come to a tentative conclusion.

In bed, reading. Twin modern black matte lamps stand on each of the matching nightstands flanking the queen-size futon in its unfinished wood frame. Dennis reads *People* magazine. Pam reads a medical journal article on diagnosing infants with schizophrenia. Pages are ruffled and turned. The magazine's pages turn smoothly and quickly as Dennis scans captions under black-and-white photos. The journal's pages turn slowly, bent out of shape, crinkled between fingers as Pam carefully reads the findings. A clock ticks loudly on Pam's large dresser along the adjacent wall, its second hand starting around the clock in short, small broken-second jolts of time.

Winter wind howls around the building, putting pressure on the two large panes of glass that are the windows in the bedroom. The bedroom air, however, is warm. Warm enough so Dennis need wear only blue pin-striped boxers to bed and Pam the loose, oversize white shirt. A small humidifier in the corner blasts a steady stream of moist air into the room, clouds of vapor rising, then quickly disappearing.

Dennis, looking over an article about some lady television sitcom star who has recently recovered from drugs, thinks about making love to his wife, enjoys making love to her, would like to, but doesn't know how to approach her. Every time he touches her, he fears she thinks he is doing so only because he wants her to become pregnant despite the fact that she doesn't want it. She's never said this; Dennis fears she thinks it. Making love to his wife no longer being something he is doing *for* or *with* her, but something he is doing *to* her. And he cannot handle the fact that she may think this is so, cannot handle the possibility that somehow this is, subconsciously, his true intent, so Dennis lies dormant, waiting and hoping she'll reach out to him.

Dennis reads that the formerly drug-addicted star attempted to kill herself with an overdose of laxatives. He lets out a small laugh.

Pam looks up, interested. "What's so funny?"

"Nothing. Just an article here."

"What is it?" She folds the medical journal over her lap.

Dennis turns the page to a new article, fears she won't find it funny but sad, tragic. "Just nothing."

Pam yanks the magazine from him, turning back the page. "Let me see." She reads.

Dennis watches her eyes. Riveted upon every word for a millisecond before moving on to the next, they tick across the page.

She smiles a slight smile, hands the magazine to Dennis. "It's the laxative thing, right?"

"That's right."

"It is funny, although it could possibly have killed her. But I guess it is funny if you don't know that." She picks up her paper, spots her place, and continues where she'd left off.

"A person can OD on laxatives?" Dennis thinks about this, wonders what it actually does to a person. "Have you ever known anybody who has?"

Her eyes look up in thought, and then Pam laughs. "I'd rather not think about it. I have heard about it happening. It must warn against overdosage on the side of the box or you could look at one of my pharmaceutical dictionaries."

A warm, tender moment, and Dennis reaches under the covers and places his hand on Pam's leg, rubbing very lightly. She doesn't brush his hand away, but then she doesn't part her legs either. He feels the soft skin of her thigh, recently shaved, and glances at his wife's hand, bare fingers curled around the journal's newspaper-thin pages.

The gold bands bought and used during their wedding ceremony are kept in separate drawers in the bedroom: Pam's in a small cotton ball—filled white cardboard box in the upper-right-hand drawer of her dresser, Dennis's in a glass ashtray from the hotel where they spent their honeymoon in London, the ashtray shoved toward the back of his underwear drawer and filled with the ring, several buffalo-head nickels, and a broken stopwatch, once his father's. Ceremony props were all the rings were. Props to use symbolically in the ceremony, worn through their weeklong honeymoon, then taken off and put away upon returning to New York.

"I just don't think a psychiatrist should wear a ring. It's important that patients feel I'm completely available to them so they can impress whatever they need upon me. If I were to wear a ring, that wouldn't be possible; a patient might hold back."

"What do you plan on telling your patients if they do ask?" Dennis questioned, more than slightly offended.

"I ask why they're asking, why it's important for them to know, and we discuss that." All said so logically as if Dennis should have known this all along, as if it could be no other way.

Dennis looks back at the magazine, the woman who attempted suicide via Ex-Lax. Her large eyes stare out at Dennis, her lips a thin line of pain, and Dennis is struck with the image of the vulnerable woman sitting alone at the bar, that frazzled, scared woman with the martini.

2

———

Brushed and flossed, Joan ties her hair back from her face with a scarf while strolling toward the kitchen, arranging the pale blue scarf knot at the crown of her head. She takes her clutch up, unsnapping the clasp, shaking an assortment of miscellaneous objects through its opening: book of stamps, compact, lipstick, wallet, plastic vial of Xanax and plastic vial of Tofranil, her fourth and currently prescribed antidepressant, three previous medications—Asendin, Prozac, and Norpramin—having had no effect on her depression.

Joan twists the top off the Xanax and spills one of the pink-orange ovals into her palm, tossing it on her tongue, then rushing to the sink. She cups a hand, letting a stream of cold water rush in, which she quickly splashes into her mouth and swallows. When she turns back to the counter, she notices a wrinkled cocktail napkin caught in the fold of the wallet. She folds the flap of the wallet open and smooths out the napkin, looking over the name and number, examining the print of the handwriting. "Dennis Perry," the confident print reads. Joan switches on the coffeemaker, measuring out enough grounds to prepare a full morning's worth of cups. Dennis Perry. She opens the lower kitchen cabinet by the refrigerator, heaving out the latest white pages and sitting at the kitchen table, listening to the coffee machine as water drips into the glass pot.

Only one Dennis Perry is listed in the book, although there are several D. Perrys, and the phone number on the napkin matches that of the Dennis Perry in the book on West Seventy-third Street, just around the corner from her therapist's office.

Joan closes the phone book, returning it to the cabinet. She pours herself some coffee, black, and sits back at the table. She takes a Xanax to calm herself, then drinks coffee. Joan's eyes scan over the name and number, following the handwritten lines.

Joan's two dates, the only dates she's had since the divorce, left her with the feeling that being alone might just possibly be not only easier but better than being with a man. After two years of seclusion, Joan, hating the prospect of physically venturing out into the singles world, chose to respond to a personals ad. Joan thought that people who advertise in the personals, specifically those who advertise in *New York* magazine, want to meet someone seriously. A desperate, sex-starved man would not waste several hundred dollars on a personal ad if all he wanted was a one-night stand. Joan rationalized that if sex was all a man wanted, he could easily pick a girl up at a bar with less trouble, cost, or wait. Joan responded to an ad for "a middle-aged, slightly used professional" with a recent photo of herself taken with Todd and Andrea in Central Park. Todd stood an inch or two taller than his mother on one side, and Andrea up to Joan's chin on the other. Joan's arms hugged them tightly against her shoulders, keeping them still. Joan wrote her name and phone number on the back of the photo. If he liked what he saw, he could call.

Martin Goldstein phoned and they spoke briefly but nicely. He was a divorced, childless man, editor of law textbooks, Joan learned, and they set a weekend afternoon date—an afternoon, Martin Goldstein recommended, so the pressure and fear of intimacy wouldn't doom the enterprise.

The last question Joan asked was "How will I recognize you?"

When Martin Goldstein answered, "I'll be wearing a long black scarf," Joan became worried. The season was summer.

"A scarf?" she asked.

"Scarf, shawl, security blanket, whatever you like," he replied with a laugh.

They met at a coffee shop. Martin Goldstein ate a tidy club sandwich and fries. Joan sipped at an iced tea. One end of the long, thin scarf was wrapped around Martin Goldstein's neck several times while the other was wrapped around his forearm and tied at the wrist. A loop of the silk fabric dangled in the air below Martin Goldstein's elbow, bouncing as he lifted the sandwich from the plate to his mouth. Joan politely asked her date about his job, and Martin Goldstein took a red pencil from his shirt pocket and scrawled the many official publisher's editing marks across the paper place mat before her. Delete, insert a space, close a space, incomplete reference. Martin Goldstein drew loops around the white paper place mat, and Joan watched his thin hands rather than look up into his eager eyes. "I'm not a lawyer, but I know more about the Constitution than most judges," he boasted. "Than most presidents, I suspect," he added.

Exiting the coffee shop, standing on the sidewalk with Martin Goldstein, Joan declined his offer of a movie, said she needed time alone, said she wasn't sure this would work out. Martin Goldstein looked her up and down, smiling harshly. "I'm sure you think you're better than me, more interesting. I'm sure you do think *that*. I'm *sure* you do." He turned and walked off, the loose end of the scarf waving behind him from his neck, Joan left standing on the sidewalk under the glare of a mid-August afternoon sun, hands deep in the pockets of her wide billowing skirt. Martin Goldstein grew smaller and smaller in the haze until he rounded a corner and disappeared. Joan returned to the coffee shop, sat at the end of the counter by the kitchen door, and ordered a tuna melt, a side of onion rings, and an iced tea.

Date two occurred two months later, one month after she'd joined a neighborhood health club, less concerned with her body—which was fine, she told Dr. Thompson—and more concerned with finding a man.

Joan met a man whose exercise schedule coincided with her own, a man she often found herself riding beside on the row of stationary bikes by the wall. He was in good shape, slightly balding, and usually read *The Wall Street Journal* during his thirty-minute ride. Joan wore a Walkman, listening to cassettes. While stretching out on the mats after the ride, they spoke of their lives. He worked as an independent broker with his own portfolio of securities. He lived in the neighborhood and had never been married. She told him about herself, smiling, trying to appear fun and free-spirited. When he asked her if she'd like to go out for coffee after they showered and changed, she was glad to see she had succeeded in attracting him and took him up on the offer.

Joan wasn't sure if it happened because she was light-headed from exercise or as a result of the caffeine from the coffee, but while having an easy discussion about what it was like to grow up in the city, Joan—watching this man intently watching her, this man listening to every word she said, staring into her eyes—began to panic. The coffee cup rattled as she set it down on the saucer.

"Is something wrong?"

"No, no, all right, thanks." And she had reached for her bag—a reflex response to take a Xanax tablet—when she realized she didn't have them with her, never brought them to the gym, never had any reason to, the riding of the stationary cycle usually relaxing her. Joan leaned under the table, clutching the gym bag, staring at the table's underside, a spot of dirty pink gum in the corner, the man's blue sweatpants, his bare, hairy ankles, her mind racing. "Oh, I guess I

forgot—'' She placed the bag in her lap, holding it for security. The
man looked at Joan, then reached out a hand to her shoulder. ''Are
you feeling okay?'' And Joan lurched back, standing, knocking over
her chair with a clatter, the wooden back hitting the café's tile floor.
''Will you excuse me, please?'' She quickly made her way home and
undressed, collapsing on the bed in a heap, curling into a fetal ball,
knees held tight to her chest, and sobbing uncontrollably.

''Why do you think that happened?'' Dr. Thompson asked the
following day.

''The coffee,'' Joan replied, joking, and then when her doctor
didn't laugh, didn't let her patient off so easily: ''Maybe I'm just
afraid to be close to people. Or maybe I really didn't like the guy. I
mean, I've never let myself be close to anyone before, so it's hard for
me just to be me and let people get to know me. We've discussed
that before, how I can't let people get to know me other than as a
wife or mother. That is a problem with me, isn't it? . . . I don't think
it would have worked out with this man anyway. When I was looking
under the table, I noticed he had a tattoo of Garfield on his ankle.''
Joan shook her head wearily. ''I can't date a man who would mutilate
his body for the sake of a cartoon cat.''

Embarrassed by the scene she'd made in front of this man, the fact
that she had panicked and hadn't even left any money for the check,
Joan never returned to the health club, deciding that she wasn't yet
ready for dating, better off remaining safely on her own. ''I took the
initiative, I took the risk, and it didn't pay off. This is the second
mistake I've learned from. I won't do it again. At least not with
anyone I haven't seen in a shirt and tie first.''

''You haven't dated for a long time,'' Dr. Thompson told Joan.
''It takes patience and practice. Nobody has an easy time with it.
Everyone feels a bit anxious, you and the man, and you, being
someone especially sensitive and feeling things intensely, might have
a more difficult time getting yourself out there. Give yourself credit.
You've made a start.''

Joan stares at the name on the napkin, a dare, teasing her, pressing her to phone, but she resists. It's still too early at 6:30 A.M., even if she'd like to, and she folds the napkin along its sharp creases, inserting it into her robe's side pocket, holding it there in her palm.

Pam, jogging in place in the living room, watches the morning news. Her first appointment is at eight o'clock: Arthur Greene, an unmarried publishing executive in his mid-fifties. Pam expects Arthur will be extremely depressed about the never-ending crush he has on his twenty-four-year-old assistant. Arthur's last session ended with his declaring, "I hired her because I wanted her, and now I want to fire her for the same reason. I'm so attracted to her I'm afraid of her. I'm befuddled around her and don't even have her do some of the more boring things I need done, because I'm afraid she won't like me if I have her do them. Honestly," Arthur moaned, "there are moments when she's taking a letter when I come close to divulging it or letting her go altogether."

At 7:00 A.M., just as the *Today* show comes on, Pam will take a shower and then dress, hurry out of the apartment, and take the crosstown bus to her office. Dennis, never rising before 8:00, makes his way to the studio anywhere between 9:00 and 9:30. Pam never sees him up before she's out the door but checks in with him between patients to see when he thinks he'll be finished with work for the day.

Pam swings her arms up around the back of her head, weight bands Velcroed in place around her wrists, watching a series of bombing images flicker across the TV screen. Beirut—Tel Aviv—Teheran—Cairo—somewhere Middle Eastern, where it's always raining bombs. During her teen years Pam, forty pounds overweight, was the object of ridicule by her friends and siblings and the focus of punishment by her parents. One morning each week, like a pop-quiz master, Eric Thompson, Pam's father, carried the scale down from the upstairs bathroom and into the kitchen as Pam and her two sisters sat eating breakfast. Pam was asked to step on the scale to see if she'd lost or gained over the past week, and then the figure was recorded on a chart taped to the refrigerator door, for Pam to contemplate each time she chose to take something to eat.

Finding her eldest daughter fifteen years old and grossly fat, Cheryl Thompson sat Pam down in her husband's den one schoolday afternoon and faced her across her husband's desk. ''You either have to take control of your body and lose the weight yourself or you'll no longer be able to eat the family's food. That's the way it has to be. You want to overeat, buy your own food. Your father and I won't be a party to it any longer,'' Cheryl Thompson informed her daughter. ''You shouldn't even need us to restrict you like this. We wish we didn't have to do it, but it looks like we do considering the way you're eating. There's no reason why you need to use food as a crutch. None.

''Look at me!'' Cheryl Thompson exclaimed proudly. ''Three children!'' She stood, slapping her hands to her hips, her waist, her chest. ''You can't pinch an inch on me!''

Pam began restricting her food intake to what her parents found permissible, deciding that a thin, fit body would be her revenge, proving to her family that she could be as thin and attractive as they were; she would make herself beautiful, then leave for college and shut them out of her life, only to return home for winter and summer breaks with boyfriends more handsome and fit than either of her sisters ever had.

Thirty to forty minutes of jogging four days a week, outside during late spring, summer, and early fall and inside, in place, for the remainder of the year. Never letting herself decline into the body of the fat teen she was, approximately once a month Pam takes out a picture of herself, age fifteen, focusing on the fat girl for several minutes as a reminder of who she once was and could easily become if she were to slack off from her exercise regimen. Not having seen her parents since graduating college, not having spoken to them for the past five years, once a year Pam sends them a five-by-seven-inch full-figure postcard photo of herself holding a newspaper with the date circled. "Still thin," the only words written in the space for the message.

Pam clicks off the TV and heads into the bedroom, pulling the straps of her black bodysuit away from her shoulders, letting them hang down over her arms.

Dennis, on his side, feigns sleep under the covers, holding an erection in one hand, waiting for Pam to enter the bathroom so he can resume masturbating. He watches his wife through slit openings in his eyes. Pam peels the bodysuit down, and Dennis holds himself stiff, looking over her small, firm breasts, smooth stomach, and she turns, bending over as she drags the bodysuit down her back, over the curve of her ass, kicking it to the floor. A glimpse of pussy hair, and then she's standing, hanging the bodysuit over the closet doorknob. Pam steps into the bathroom, shutting the door. Dennis throws back the covers, jerking off to the image of his wife undressing, her perfect body, perfectly controlled by years of exercise and never becoming pregnant, and Dennis stops masturbating, wondering if perhaps this is the reason his wife won't become pregnant: She fears losing control of her body, of not being able to determine its shape as the baby grows and her stomach becomes rounder, larger.

The shower is turned off, and Dennis draws the comforter over his body, holding its upper edge. A minute later Pam steps from the bathroom, glancing at Dennis, who appears asleep, and confidently strides to the dresser, taking out her undergarments.

Dennis shuts his eyes, listening to the sounds of her putting herself together for a day of work, waiting for her to leave before rising.

Joan wears her bathrobe, ironing the many pleats of the wool skirt with force, making every fold of the fabric stand out sharply along its crease. Joan irons across the dining room table, ironing now being the table's only use. Two large bath towels are spread across the table's maple finish, protecting its surface.

Dennis Perry. Joan obsesses. Take a chance on charming, handsome, kind Dennis Perry. Someday he'd like to get married, he said.
Someday he'd like to have kids, and if she were to ask Dennis out,
she could wear this skirt to see him, or maybe the angora sweater
dress.

Joan chose the pleated skirt randomly, choosing some garment
from her large closet randomly, because she wanted to iron but had
no garment in need of ironing, and unless she wears it out with
Dennis Perry, she has no reason to be ironing the skirt at all, none,
unless she wears it to her Sunday brunch with Todd, three days from
now.

She flips the skirt to the opposite side. A wrinkled mess. The skirt
actually looked better, was beautifully pressed, *before* Joan got her
hands on it. Joan sets the iron on its back end; water sputters through
the bottom holes, drops running down the steel and evaporating into
the air with many hisses. She could call him, should call him—he
offered his number, he initiated the contact, so it is now up to her to
follow up with him. Joan slides her hand between the hem of the
skirt. She should have ironed it on the ironing board, rotating the
fabric as she pressed each pleat.

I don't exist for anyone but myself. Joan sits back in a chair by the wall,
crumpling the skirt in her lap. If she doesn't make the effort to phone
Dennis Perry, she has no one to blame but herself.

"Why didn't you phone him?" Joan imagines her doctor asking
her in therapy tomorrow. "If you wanted to, why didn't you?"

"Because I knew it wouldn't work out, so I didn't feel like
bothering."

"Doomed before you even tried?" Dr. Thompson would ask, and
Joan would have to sit there, pathetic and lifeless, making no effort to
better her life despite paying $375 a week to this doctor to help her
understand herself better. At least if she does phone Dennis Perry and
has a bad date, at least then she'll be able to go into her doctor's office
with proof that her life is doomed, Joan recognizes. There is no
reason to make the effort because her doomed future is inevitable,

inescapable, and Joan tosses the skirt onto the dining room table, a mess of wrinkles and folds. If she gets the date, she'll iron it to perfection.

Orange juice, coffee, a bagel, and *Joan,* that is what Dennis faces at his drafting table in his office before going over the billing. Freshly squeezed orange juice, freshly ground coffee, and a freshly baked bagel, all from the gourmet shop around the corner. He stares at the napkin from Donnelman's, "Joan" printed in small, neat, curvy letters along the napkin's edge. "Joan" followed by the seven digits required to reach her. Reach out and touch her. Dennis wipes his buttery fingers across the napkin, deliberately smearing the name and number, crumpling it and tossing it away in the wastebasket. A temptation best avoided.

"Hello. This is Joan," Joan says, her voice trembling. "You bought me the martinis yesterday?"

"Yes, hello," Dennis replies, his pulse quickening. "Of course."

"How are you this morning?"

"I'm good. You?"

"I thought I'd call to say hello and thank you for the drinks."

"I'm glad you did. I was thinking about you this morning."

"Oh. How nice. I was wondering if you weren't too busy if you'd like to get together for lunch? If that fits your schedule."

"That sounds good."

"Is the Bentley okay? On the corner of Sixty-fourth and Broadway by Lincoln Center?"

"That's fine. But I can't do it till two-thirty, if that's not a problem."

"No, two-thirty is perfect. That will work well for me."

"Then I'll see you at two-thirty. Great. I'm glad you called."

"We have a date, then."

"Yes, good-bye, see you."

"Two-thirty at the Bentley. Good-bye."

Dennis copies the phone number, still legible despite the napkin's stains, on a notepad, leaving off the name, tearing the sheet of paper away, and inserting it into the pocket of his wallet containing his business cards. He is wanted, needed, desirable, and he recrumples the napkin, discarding it in the wastebasket again.

Lunch with Joan. A date with another woman, a woman other than his wife, and he isn't sure why he's doing this or why this setting of a lunch date doesn't feel wrong and deceitful, a betrayal, but it doesn't, and again, Dennis thinks, he isn't sure why.

3

Joan is frustrated with herself for having taken the Xanax tablet when she awoke this morning. Fearful of becoming dependent upon the medication, she allows herself one Xanax a day, even though Dr. Thompson has prescribed enough for her to take three each day, and now, arriving at the restaurant to meet Dennis Perry, she's concerned that with him too she will panic and leave as she did with the man from the health club.

Joan stands in the doorway, waiting for the host or hostess, looking around the large, cavernous restaurant. She spots Dennis Perry toward the rear of the room, sitting by the brick wall. Joan waits by the hostess stand to be led over to the table. She wants this to be over. Walking to the restaurant, feelings of hope mixing with feelings of doom and despair, Joan caught a glimpse of herself reflected in a storefront window. Foolish is how she looked, all dressed and made up for this man, dressed up for rejection. Joan examined her reflection and then behind it, jars of cold cream, bottles of dishwashing liquid, roach traps and blow dryers, and she walked on, her reflection gone as she passed a boarded-up storefront plastered with posters announcing a circus. She can already see herself sitting in therapy tomorrow, depressed, catatonic, defeated by life.

Dennis spots Joan handing the hostess an ankle-length camel hair coat and navy blue scarf. He sips a cup of coffee. His date. She *is* pretty, wearing a slim, pale blue knee-length angora dress. The dress drapes loosely around Joan's figure, touching her body slightly at hips and breasts. She follows the hostess to the table, and Dennis compares the two—hostess and Joan—and Joan wins. Dennis stands, reaches around, and pulls out the chair for her. "Hello, nice to see you." He extends his hand, and she takes it, shakes it lightly, then sits. He sits, and she averts her eyes to the table, noting its arrangement, the knife at her place setting with blade wrong side in. Joan reaches her hand over, flipping and straightening the knife to its correct position. When she looks up, she sees he has caught her, and she blushes, feeling the onset of a panic attack.

"Everything set up okay now?"

Joan laughs nervously, drops her hand to her lap. "A habit from keeping house, I guess. I like things to look nice. I think that's important. Shows how much you care."

"You look very nice today."

"Thank you. I tried," she replies quickly without taking in the implications of his remark. But then she sees him looking at her with a smile that's almost a smirk, and Joan looks to the folded menu at her place, picking it up, flipping it open, shielding her red face. She is a joke to him, a cartoon to be laughed at. Joan reads down the list of salads.

A hand folds over the top edge of the menu, pushing it down below her eye level.

"I didn't mean to be making fun of you." Dennis takes his hand off the menu, glances at his coffee, and wishes he'd ordered a scotch. Joan has raised the menu back before her eyes. Dennis cannot gauge how deeply he has offended this woman, and if he has and has to be this careful when speaking with her, maybe she's not worth it. He isn't up to beginning a romance with a woman he must be less open with than his wife. Maybe Joan is too meek, too weak, too vulnerable, no sense of humor, and maybe he *is* better off with strong, independent Pam and this potentially bad date will show him all he does have with his wife, this date proving how much he loves his wife and that no other woman compares, no other woman is worth risking their marriage over. This is a mistake, an error of judgment, and Dennis signals the waitress—*let's get this over with*—and she holds up a finger, indicating she'll be over momentarily.

Joan, having studied the menu carefully, considering all the possible salad, sandwich, and entrée choices and side dish combinations, having weighed what would be the most appropriate thing to eat on a first date and appear most attractive, having eliminated burgers because they're too unladylike and sandwiches because they can be a mess to handle, returns to the salad selections, choosing the walnut chicken salad in a bowl of greens with sliced seasonal fruits. She places the menu by the edge of the table, smiling at Dennis. He isn't smiling, she's caught him lost in thought, but when he does see her slight smile, he quickly manages to return it. "The waitress should be here any second," he says.

A lull, Joan's anxiety returning, growing. "You know," she says, anything to break the silence, "you never told me what you do."

"I'm an artist, graphic designer. Print media. Posters, ads, brochures." He wonders how she gets her money. Probably from alimony, being divorced. "What is it you do?"

"What does it look like I do?" Joan flirts, delaying an answer.

Dennis pauses, evaluating Joan's appearance. He has no idea and doesn't want to say secretary, the first occupation that comes to mind. "Really, I have no idea." He might just order a scotch. One drink isn't a bad idea.

The waitress appears. "Are you ready to order?"

"The chicken salad, please. And a diet cola."

"Grilled chicken breast sandwich and a side of coleslaw, thanks. Also a scotch and soda."

The waitress leaves.

"So what is it you do?" Dennis asks. "Is it something so awful you can't say?" She's unemployed, has recently lost her job, he speculates.

A doctor, a lawyer, even a circus performer as in the poster is better than answering housewife. "I read. I paint, go to museums, the theater," Joan answers, letting Dennis fill in the occupation for himself. All of this as much of a lie as if she had said circus performer.

"What kind of painting?"

Remembering back to college. Sketching a female nude, painting her roommate, Rochelle, sleeping across the room, dipping a paintbrush in a glass of water. "Watercolors," Joan answers. "Some charcoal drawings too."

His interest piqued, Dennis leans forward. "I'd like to see them sometime. Would you mind showing me? I'd be happy to show you some of my work."

If she says yes, they definitely have a second date. If she says no, she isn't sure what happens, but she can't answer yes, has nothing to show. "I really don't do much anymore. Don't save anything I do. I'm really not very good."

"More of a hobby," Dennis offers, letting her off.

"More of." Joan takes the offer. "But I should do more since I enjoy it and have the time."

"Why not?"

Joan smiles. "I was almost going to tell you I was a circus performer."

Dennis smiles. "What if I asked you what you did in the circus? How would you have answered?"

Joan pictures the poster. "A trapeze artist. That might be fun. Would you have believed it?"

"I'd have asked you to do it for me."

Joan pictures herself performing the stunt. "I wonder how much training that requires."

Dennis shakes his head, amused. "I have no idea."

"Oh, well . . . So where do you work?" Joan asks, putting the weight of the conversation on Dennis.

"Out of my apartment. Over on West Seventy-third. I work out of there."

"Just like me." Joan smiles slyly.

"Excuse me?"

"Me. A housewife. My office is my home too." She smiles at her wit, proud of the joke.

"Very cute." Dennis can't keep himself from blushing, returning her smile. "A circus performer, huh?" And then Joan's blushing again.

Both momentarily between sessions, Jack Briden and Pam stand in the kitchenette, a folding door separating it from the waiting room area. Jack pours a cup of coffee from the pot. Pam skins an apple with a steak knife.

"Good or bad day?"

Pam tosses a handful of red peel in the basket under the sink, then begins coring the apple with the knife. "No earth-shattering, revelatory moments," she answers. "At least not yet. How's yours?"

Jack drops a sugar cube into his cup, stirring, watching it slowly dissolve to nothing. "No one's threatened suicide. At least not yet. But the day's not over. I have two more patients."

Pam checks her watch. "My boring patient's due."

"I schedule my boring patients in the morning. By late P.M., if they're not interesting, I just tune out."

"I have an interesting one after her." Pam lays the knife in the sink, drops the core into the basket, and gently kicks the sink cabinet closed.

"Why don't you refer her to someone else if you don't like her? You have plenty of other patients. You can afford to lose one."

Pam takes a bite of the apple. "She's too vulnerable. Vulnerable and boring and depressed." She takes another bite, thinking about referring Joan Dwyer to another therapist. "I think she's attached to me, finally trusts me. I didn't say I didn't like her. She's just boring. I'd hate to refer her to someone else now." She wishes she'd never mentioned Joan Dwyer to Jack.

"Then don't." Jack places the mug in the sink and shuts off the coffeemaker, the bright orange light going dark, auburn. "Just to warn you, Michael will be in tonight. Prepare yourself to see him as you're leaving."

"I don't need to be warned."

The door buzzer sounds, indicating Joan Dwyer has arrived and needs to be let in.

"Good," Jack responds. "Glad it's not an issue between us."

Pam opens the sink cabinet and tosses the apple away. "If you're happy, I'm happy." She folds open the wood door, and they both step out of the kitchen area into the hallway.

"I'm okay, you're okay." Jack draws the door back across the kitchen entrance.

Pam steps to the door and opens it for Joan Dwyer, easier than rushing into the office to push-button release the lock.

"I did lie to him to a certain degree, but I think he knew and didn't mind. On my way home I stopped in an art store and bookstore, so if he does see me again, I won't be lying but will be doing some of what I said I do. I would like to be reading and painting. I'm not just doing it to please him." Joan watches her doctor for a reaction—good or bad, this turn of events—but her doctor's face remains unchanged, a pleasant, concerned expression.

Observing Joan more excited and hopeful than she's been in all of the past year, Pam can't help considering how weak therapy is to Joan in comparison with the hope of a new love. Joan sits across from her in a heavy cotton dress, yellow with a cornflower pattern, duck boots on her feet. A snowy, icy day. Slush drips off the heel of Joan's boot onto the carpet. By the end of winter Pam will have to have the carpet shampooed.

"This man seems to have really woken you up to some things about yourself. He gave you his number, but you decided to act and phone him and set the date. I think that's a big step," Pam comments. "He's stimulated your interests from college. You have some feelings of hope. What other feelings do you have about it?"

Joan looks at her hands, studying her nails, the smooth, shiny red gloss she so carefully painted around her cuticles this morning. First time in two years she's bothered. Last night she spent an hour and a half trying to paint a watercolor of two oranges. The images she painted came out a muddy brown instead of shades of green and orange, less round than flat and oval-shaped. Joan went through four sheets of the watercolor paper, overpainting and warping each with water and paint before she surrendered for the evening, washing the brushes, and placing the art supplies under the sink. The two oranges were dropped down the garbage chute in the hall, Joan not wanting them in her home, reminding her of this frustration. Joan closed the chute's door and listened to the two oranges bouncing off the chute's steel walls, rattling down sixteen flights to the basement.

Her doctor awaits an answer. Joan notices her doctor's shoes match the belt around Dr. Thompson's waist. Dark brown leather flats. Wide dark brown leather belt drawing in the waist of the navy blue dress. "When I think about the date, I am happy. If I consider that it's not going to work, I become more depressed than before I knew him. I get so angry at myself for raising my hopes when I'm sure I'll end up alone."

"Do you think you truly will end up alone or are you guarding against this new hope you have?'' Finally a step toward some progress with Joan.

Joan thinks the question through, doesn't want to make a hasty response and answer incorrectly and then have to take it back later. ''I think I'm doomed to be alone, so I guard myself against feeling hopeful. Does that make sense?'' Joan reaches over the end table between the chair and the sofa, picking up the red ceramic ashtray, taking it in both hands, feeling its smooth, polished surface.

Pam observes Joan retreating to the safety of her depression, keeping her doctor out. ''Let's not talk about what you fear will happen,'' Pam says, hoping to keep Joan connected to her feelings. ''What is your fantasy of what could happen? If anything you hoped for could happen, what would that be?''

Dennis Perry holding her hand, sitting on the living room sofa staring out at the view of the city, his arm around her, keeping her warm and safe, speaking to her gently, softly, her waking up next to him in bed and he still sleeping, reaching out and touching his cheek, brushing his hair away from his eyes, saying good-bye to him at the door, then spending the day preparing their home for him to return to from work at the end of the day, having him come home to her, loving her, not someone else. All the love of a romance novel without the adventure.

''Joan?''

She's crying and hasn't realized it. Tears in her eyes, and Joan takes a breath, clearing them. She places the ashtray in her lap and pulls a tissue from the box on the end table, wiping it at her cheeks. ''I don't know. I'm not sure.'' The first time she's cried since beginning therapy.

''Does it scare you to let yourself feel this hope?''

Joan shakes her head, an image of Dennis leaning close, kissing her cheek before he returned to his apartment to work for the afternoon.

''I think that's something we should talk about,'' Pam says. ''I think this is a very important step for you. To let yourself care and be hopeful about something or someone.''

Joan stares out the window at the falling snow, imagining herself walking home through the stinging wind after having her one martini, heavy wet flakes covering the sidewalks, each step carefully chosen lest she slip and fall. Maybe she'll skip the martini downstairs and mix it for herself at home in the warmth of her apartment. She looks at her watch, relieved to find her time is up; this session has exhausted her. She lifts her wrist. ''I'm going to go home now.'' Joan stands, gathering her overcoat off the couch.

Pam stands. ''We'll continue this on Monday. Have a nice weekend.''

Joan walks out into the reception room, quickly eyeing the gentleman in the chair, her doctor's next patient—the man in a business suit her doctor sees after each of Joan's sessions, important-looking, not a housewife—and Joan heads into the hallway.

When she reaches out to push the down button to call the elevator, Joan finds she still has the ashtray in her hand, the crumpled tissue in one hand and the red ceramic ashtray in the other. Joan dabs at her nose with the tissue. The elevator arrives, and she steps into the empty car. She decides not to return the ashtray today. She'll return it on Monday, doesn't want to have to go back up and stand in the hall, ringing her doctor to be let in, Dr. Thompson not know-ing who is there, interrupting the businessman's appointment. She'll return it Monday, not make an issue out of it today, and she slips the ashtray into her pocket, waiting for the elevator door to open.

Pam leans out her office door to Bill Matson, her last appointment of the week. ''Hello, be with you in a minute.'' She closes the door softly, careful not to offend Bill, make him feel shunned, and she sits at the desk, pushing up its rolltop. She pulls the elastic from around the accordion-style manila folder on the top of the pile of today's patients-to-be-seen and opens the most recent of the three small composition notebooks in the folder, Pam's means of keeping track of the therapy's direction. Pam turns several pages, finding the entry from Wednesday's session, skipping a line, then dating today's entry. She jots down the main points, accomplishments, observations, troubles and/or setbacks of the day, less an analysis and more a note taking.

> JD feeling positive. Went out on a date yesterday. Afraid of her hope, fearing it's doomed. Cried when asked about her fantasy with date. Has begun painting and reading. Took red ashtray from end table home with her.

Pam puts down the pen, scans Wednesday's notes.

> Marital breakup. Fifty-minute monologue.

Pam looks over today's entry. An entire paragraph. The first whole paragraph, whole session that's worked between them in a month or more, the first session in months in which Joan displayed more than a depressed affect, thinking about her life, engaged in a discussion and interacting rather than coming into therapy and plowing through the entire session in a nonstop, never-ending monologue.

Pam closes Joan Dwyer's notebook and reads the name on the last folder of the day—William Matson—remembering that today is the day he planned to break up with his girlfriend.

They ride home in a cab from the couple's apartment where they've had dinner this Friday night. A couple that married the same year Pam and Dennis married, eight years ago when all four were in their early thirties. Ed and Madelaine Brownelly with their two children, a girl of seven and boy of four. Before dinner, while the kids were up, the four adults and two children gathered in the living room. Ed,

Madelaine, and Joan sat on the furniture while Dennis sat on the floor with the kids, playing with Legos and Lincoln Logs, going back and forth between the adults' conversation above him and the constructions he was working on with the kids. When dinner was ready, the children were put to bed, and Dennis's attention was undivided.

"The kids seem to like you," commented Ed, a psychiatrist and onetime classmate of Pam's. "Like you better than their regular sitter."

"They're great kids," Dennis responded.

"They can be trouble," Madelaine added. "It's hard raising kids in the city."

Pam gave Dennis a look of acknowledgment. Ed poured his wife a glass of white wine. "We'll leave eventually. Probably in a few years."

"I think I'd feel more isolated in the suburbs with kids," Madelaine commented. "At least here I can go to the park and talk with other mothers."

Pam nodded to Madelaine, acknowledging her friend's position; her eyes then darted to her husband to see his response. When he saw Pam look at him, he looked away.

"I didn't say anything about us having a baby," Dennis says, defending himself, as the cab glides up Park Avenue to the apartment.

"The implication was fairly obvious: sitting around with the kids all evening."

"You're overly sensitive."

"I'm sure."

The cab jolts to a stop. Pam is flung forward into the plastic guard between passenger and driver. "Sorry," the driver calls, and soon enough the taxi jolts forward into traffic again. Pam holds her head, weary from wine and after-dinner brandy. A pain thumps in her temples. Dennis attempts to take her shoulders and lean her back in the seat, but she brushes him off, not wanting to be helped, the pain forcing tears to her eyes, and she tries to continue her speech as if nothing has happened. "Madelaine was a lawyer before the kids. Now she's a lonely housewife. I don't want to become like her.'' She stops, turns, looks out the window as the office buildings of midtown become the large apartment houses of the Upper East Side. The cab jerks to a halt again; Pam's head is flung to the side, against the window.

"Are you okay?" Dennis asks, moving closer, holding her, and Pam waits, waits for the tear of pain to run from her swollen eyes, and she turns to him, the tear on her cheek.

"Forget it. Just forget it." She pushes him back and looks away, ignoring him for the rest of the ride home, for the rest of the evening.

Friday's inch of snow has melted by Saturday afternoon, the weather having turned mild, allowing Joan to sit on the roofless level of the double-decker bus.

The red bus heads through the financial district at the southern tip of Manhattan, having already toured Battery Park City, SoHo, Greenwich Village, Chelsea, Herald Square, and midtown Times Square, where the tour begins and ends.

A nice day for a walk, Joan thought, and she strolled down Broadway, aiming to walk to Macy's department store, trying to put thoughts of Dennis Perry out of her head, to avoid phoning him, waiting for him to phone her. Joan has memorized his number, transferred the number to the notepad by the kitchen phone, the notepad by the bedroom phone, and the notepad by the phone in the family room just in case she does forget the number. He has not contacted her since their date two days ago, has not called to ask her out for a weekend evening of a movie and dinner.

"If you look up, you will see the twin towers of the World Trade Center, the tallest buildings in Manhattan, having left the Empire State Building in their wake upon completion of the towers in 1977. One-point-two million cubic feet of earth were removed to dig the hole for these tall buildings, earth that was used to create part of Battery Park City, which we just passed through to our north. If you look—"

The woman down below keeps talking, the speaker at Joan's knee giving her voice to the upper tier. Joan gazes across to the Statue of Liberty, remembering a school visit taken over thirty years ago. Eating lunch in the park below the statue. Mrs. McCaffer's class. A bologna and cheese sandwich. Eating with Katie and Mary and Amy. Amy ate a cold hot dog her mother had packed for her, and they had all laughed at that, even Amy. When the statue reopened for its centennial, after the cleaning and the new torch, the entire Dwyer family—Al, Joan, Todd, Andrea, and Joan's mother—visited the state park in New Jersey and watched the fireworks show. Joan had bought sparklers for the kids, and they danced and twisted on the lawn, their flickering torches held in the air. "I'm Miss Liberty! I'm Miss Liberty!" Andrea shouted. Two fun memories, and Joan had forgotten she ever had fun in her life, it all feeling so remote, her life with Al and the kids in New Jersey, compared with her single existence in Manhattan. Joan looks to her left and gets a good view of Al's office building, where he worked prior to the divorce and the move to Colorado.

"Dad, you said they'd show us where the bombs exploded!"

Across the aisle from Joan sits a family of three: father, mother, son. The father holds the boy on his lap, one hand around the child's waist, a safety belt, the other clamped firmly on the child's head, cupping his blue knit cap.

"You did see it," the father tells his son. "The two tall buildings. It was down there."

"I didn't see any explosion," the child replies.

"Well, they can't let us go down in there. It's still dangerous," the father explains.

They speak with accents from somewhere Joan can't recognize, hearty, homey accents, and their visit to New York City is as adventurous to them as climbing Mount Everest would be to Joan. What it must be like to view this city as tourists, staring down at the streets from a double-decker bus, looking up in awe at the skyline, no past history impinging on the landscape, giving it a story, context, a meaning. To view this city as a foreign land rather than as a monster that has swallowed her life.

The mother turns her head, giving Joan a kind smile. Blond hair, rabbit fur earmuffs, sparkly blue eyes. The bus rumbles through Chinatown. "I think I've seen more people just sitting here on this bus for a few minutes than live in my entire town," the woman says to Joan.

"Where are you from?" Joan asks. She'd like to invite them to dinner. Like to become a part of their family.

"Wisconsin. You?"

"Right here," Joan boasts. "Manhattan. I grew up here."

"A real New Yorker," the woman says.

And Joan looks away, smiling.

Having dwelled on Dennis Perry's absence from her life for so long, the hope he had initially brought her having dissipated when she received no call Friday night or Saturday morning, thirty blocks into her walk, at Times Square, her feet tired in their heavy boots, Joan gave up on her walk to Macy's; there was nothing she needed to buy, and on a Saturday the store was bound to be mobbed. Joan, spotting the tourist bus, thought it might be interesting to tour the island, not having ventured downtown for quite some time.

In the East Village she thinks of her grandparents' apartment of years ago on the north side of Tompkins Square Park. At midtown she spots her father's old office building. On the Upper East Side the memory is again of her school days, elementary and high school. The bus winds through Central Park at Seventy-second Street, and Joan keeps remembering other happy times in the city: riding a bike in Central Park, sun-bathing in a field, viewing a concert at the band-shell. Alone in the city doesn't feel so bad this Saturday afternoon. This tour of the city, her life, was a good idea, and Joan breathes in the winter air, catching sight of her therapist's building in the distance.

.   .   .

Pam fears having a child because she is sure the baby would become a schizophrenic, psychotic, or depressive, has observed so many mentally ill adults that she finds it miraculous that any people make it into adulthood at all. Even adopting terrifies her: God knows who gave birth to this baby and did some potentially irreversible damage to him. Pam's biggest question is not *How does mental illness happen to people?* but is *Why doesn't it happen to everyone?* With so many things that can go wrong, knowing how extremely sensitive a small child is, knowing that minor, seemingly random incidents can alter a child's sense of self imperceptibly and do emotional harm that may not be displayed in observable symptoms until years later, Pam doesn't understand how she can bring a child into this world knowing she might easily damage him or her without being aware of it.

No message from Dennis, Joan wanders through her apartment, carrying a book in her hand, searching for a spot where she can sit down and read a few chapters.

Joan fears living sixteen stories aboveground for fear of a fire with no chance of escape. Joan fears living on lower floors because of their easy access to criminals. So she remains sequestered high aboveground. "I'd rather die from smoke inhalation than be robbed, murdered, or raped," she's told her children.

Yesterday evening Joan sat in her living room, holding the new book she bought following the date. Henry James's *Portrait of a Lady,* bought because she remembered Emily, her son's girlfriend, discussing how it was a great novel, Joan believing that reading this book will heighten her intellectual awareness, thereby making her more appealing to Dennis. Eventually he is bound to ask her what she's been reading, and instead of answering *TV Guide* or with the name of some best-selling romance novelist, she'll truthfully be able to respond, "*Portrait of a Lady* by Henry James," and Dennis will be impressed.

Joan read for one hour, twenty dense pages, and she was pleased with herself, enjoying the book, the characters' banter, their humor, and the novel's heroine, Isabel Archer, a poetic name for a beautiful young woman of potential. Joan put the book aside only when she could no longer concentrate, thoughts of Dennis and the day's therapy session overwhelming her. She laid the book aside and ordered up a pizza dinner, intending to read more when her thoughts permitted it.

Joan lays the book down on the dining room table and surveys the deep red-brown finish of the wood, then the walls painted with a rich royal blue, the small, simple crystal chandelier. The room hasn't been used since just after New Year's, before Andrea went back to boarding school following her Christmas break. Todd sat at the head of the table as Joan asked, and Andrea and Joan each sat halfway down on either side. Boneless chicken breasts, fresh steamed vegetables, broccoli, baby carrots, and homemade mashed potatoes. Andrea was angry with her mother for not buying her a tight black dress they had seen at a department store earlier that day. Instead Joan bought her daughter a drop-waisted floral print dress with long, full sleeves. "There is nowhere at school where you're going to wear that skimpy black thing."

"I could wear it when I come back here."

"Where do you go at school that you need a little black dress?" Joan asked lightly.

"*Mom,*" Andrea implored. "Just because you don't have a social life in the city doesn't mean other people don't."

"Why don't you shut up already?" Todd told his sister.

Joan shook her head. "I have as much of a social life as I want, and I don't need you criticizing it."

"You're just afraid of going out, that's all," Andrea replied. "Isn't that why you're in therapy?"

Joan smiled. "I suppose that might be a part of it."

"Why can't I have the dress? Give me one good reason."

"You don't need one," Todd helped out.

"I do too," Andrea argued. "I want to look older. You can't look older in flowers."

"One day you'll pray you look younger," Joan informed her daughter, and she took a bite of the mashed potatoes, smooth, creamy, and buttery. "These potatoes are absolutely the best I've ever made," Joan exclaimed.

Todd and Andrea looked away from each other to their mother. Joan wore a bright smile, empty silver-shining fork poised delicately in the air between her slender fingers.

"God, Mom, get a life," Andrea told her. "And get me that dress."

Joan pointed her fork at Andrea. "After I get a life, you'll get that dress. Deal?"

Andrea rolled her eyes. "*Mom,* I want it before I've graduated college."

Get a life, Andrea instructed, implying that her mother had no life, was in need of a life to replace the one lost, the one taken from her in New Jersey. The sorrow of the loss rushes over Joan, angry with Al for taking it away, angry with Andrea for pointing it out, angry with Dr. Thompson for putting her in touch with this pain; this hope for a new life leaving Joan in despair.

Joan walks into the kitchen. Posted on the sheet of paper on the refrigerator is Dr. Thompson's phone number, listed as "Psychiatrist" between "Masseuse" and "Tailor," neither of whom Joan ever calls. The red ashtray sits on the counter by Joan's handbag, Joan keeping it right nearby so she won't forget to bring it to her session on Monday. She wonders if other patients will miss the ashtray— Joan knows she would, and she doesn't even smoke—wonders if they'll ask Dr. Thompson what happened to it, if Dr. Thompson will replace the ashtray with another. Possibly Dr. Thompson didn't notice the ashtray was missing and will be confused when a patient draws her attention to its absence. Or maybe Dr. Thompson thinks Joan's a thief, stealing the ashtray as revenge for making her cry.

Joan picks up the phone, dialing the number posted on the sheet. She has never left a message for her therapist before but now wants to, too ashamed to live with the guilt of this ashtray but also too ashamed to face Dr. Thompson in person and confess, better to make the confession over the phone.

The answering machine clicks on, and Dr. Thompson's soft, compassionate, calm voice speaks. "You have reached the office of Dr. Thompson. Please leave a message, and I'll get back to you as soon as I can."

The machine beeps. "Hello, this is Joan Dwyer. I don't want you to worry, so I'm calling to let you know I have your ashtray. I took it by accident and didn't mean to. If you need it back before Monday morning so no one misses it, let me know; otherwise I'll see you at my session on Monday afternoon. I'm sorry I cried in therapy before. I hope you didn't think I planned that. I don't know what's going on with me that I would do that. Maybe I shouldn't be seeing this man if he's making me so upset. He hasn't called me at all, if you're interested. Doomed, as I'd originally thought. Please don't bother phoning me back unless you want the ashtray. I'll see you Monday. Good-bye."

Joan hangs up. The digital clock on the coffeemaker reads 7:33 P.M. She picks up the phone, not stopping to let herself think. She punches in the numbers. An answering machine answers. His voice sounds clear and stable, and she decides to leave a message, easier than attempting to make her anxious way through a conversation, possibly blundering. The machine beeps, and Joan speaks, "Hello, Dennis. This is Joan Dwyer. How are you? I had a nice time the other day at lunch. I hope we have the chance to get together soon. Hope to hear from you. Bye."

Seven thirty-six P.M. Dennis Perry not home. Not home or screening his calls, not wanting to answer a call from his lunch date of two days ago. Either way she loses.

Joan picks up the phone.

"Hello," Regine says, her voice strong, irritated. Regine Pointer, the elderly woman down the hall, an invalid Joan knew was sure to be home on a Saturday night.

"Hello, Miss Pointer. It's Joan. Would you like to come over for a drink?"

They sit in the living room, the two women. Regine Pointer, the elder, sipping a gin and tonic, sitting in her wheelchair, Joan sipping a vodka and cranberry on the couch.

"You have the better view. I should have bought the Duffys' place when I had the chance. Now that I can't get out without Brooke, a view would be nice, and since I hate being around her, I usually send her out on errands on her own without going along. . . . Sometimes I think she steals from me while I'm napping. I've checked my purse, but since I have such trouble remembering how much money was in there before, I'm never sure." She sips the drink, cupping the glass with both hands, ice rattling.

"Have you thought about writing the amount down so if you don't remember you'll have it on paper?" Joan watches the old woman. Seventy-six years old. Joan's known Regine Pointer since she was a child and Regine moved into the apartment down the hall.

"I should do that." Regine nods solemnly.

Regine Pointer may hate having a live-in nurse, but Joan is jealous, thinks it might be nice having someone around to be there for her whenever she wants. A hired companion. Regine, though, views her solitary life not as the sentence Joan does but as an opportunity to be selfish, giving herself all she ever wanted without taking anyone else into account. Regine Pointer has lived alone her entire adult life. She was thirty-nine when she moved into the building, and she didn't marry, didn't date, as far as Joan ever detected, and has never seemed to miss the companionship. Only recently rendered incapable of walking because of emergency surgery on her spinal cord, Regine Pointer was forced into choosing between moving into a nursing home or taking a live-in nurse.

"Brooke seems nice enough. I don't think she'd steal from you."

Giving the nurse her trust, Joan thinks it might rub off on Miss Pointer, making it easier for her to trust Brooke.

"I can't move my neck to the right," Regine says. "Just turn my chair so I can face north."

Joan walks behind the chair. "Say when." She releases the chair's brake and gently spins it to the right.

"There. *Here,*" Regine cries. *"Oops!"* An ice cube has spilled to her lap.

"I'll go get a towel." Joan moves to the door.

"Never mind, never mind." Regine picks up the dropped cube, puts it back in her glass. "Sit and relax."

Joan sits, studying Miss Pointer's face, wanting to learn how to become like her—content and alone—wanting to detect if Regine's really been lying for her entire life and actually wishes she did have a family, someone more than herself. "You don't find it nice having Brooke there to talk to? Doesn't all that silence drive you nuts?"

Regine smirks. "We do what we have to do together, and that's it. My therapy, getting me dressed. That's it. That's more than enough interaction for me."

"You don't talk to each other? You live together." Joan finds herself beginning to feel sorry for Brooke. A tense situation to be so needed yet unwanted, resented.

"I don't want that from her. I can't get along with other people. Don't really think anyone can really live with anyone else easily. Were you that happy with your husband?" She doesn't look at Joan, only out the window at the view she wishes she had.

Joan doesn't reply, doesn't know how to answer Miss Pointer, this woman so angry and bitter since the operation, since the nurse moved in. "My parents were happy together." Joan tries not to make it sound like a question. She was hoping Miss Pointer's visit would cheer her up, not make her despair for the future: to be alone, angry, and physically weak.

"Maybe they were," Regine concedes. "I can't say. It's possible, but I always thought your father lorded over your mother."

Joan always saw her mother as being happy with her life, not "lorded over." "You think *I'm* better off alone, or should I try to find a new man?" Joan asks this lightly, a game, however seriously she may take it.

Regine finishes her drink, wriggling her shoulders in the chair. "You? I don't know. Me? As long as I have books, my TV shows, radio, that's enough." She smiles, setting her empty glass in the fold of the dress between her thin thighs. "TV is my very best friend," Regine adds, an afterthought.

The phone rings, and Pam stands, "I'll get it," not minding missing any of this TV show. Dennis sips a scotch and soda, watching a TV sitcom from the sixties on a cable channel; he opens the Chinese take-out containers and dishes the food onto the two plates. He sits in the living room on the sofa, eating off the coffee table. A Saturday evening in, having been out last night.

Pam picks up the phone in the kitchen, listens to her machine calling, and presses the sequence for her code. A message not from Tim Boxer but from Joan Dwyer, guilty and confused. Alone on a Saturday night. She hangs up and returns to the living room, looking over what Dennis has ordered, the portion he's served her. "No chicken with cashew nuts?"

Dennis watches the TV. "I ordered the sweet-and-sour chicken."

Pam pokes one of the fried chicken dumplings coated with the bright orange sauce. "I don't understand. This is terrible for you. They call them dumplings because they make you dumpy."

"Call them back and order what you want. Don't leave it up to me to decide for you next time."

"You know what I like. I thought . . . " She lets her voice trail off. Forget it. Eat and be.

"What?" he asks. "Just call them back and order. Here." He hands her the menu.

She lays it down, leans back, plate on her lap, taking a bite of pork fried rice, not in the mood to argue, watching this inane sitcom, hating these shows that depict generic and perfect portraits of family life, making people feel as if their lives were failures if they could not duplicate this sick standard. Joan Dwyer, a case in point, a failure because she's not as savvy and hip as most women on TV, can't keep her husband the way most TV wives can, can't get as many dates as most TV single women can. The laugh track explodes, and Pam grimaces. "If they can have a laugh track, why can't they have a sob track?"

Dennis ignores her.

"Well, why not?" Pam asks, hates it when her husband takes his hurt, little boy stance. "They can laughter; why not tears? Compact the whole of human experience into thirty minutes of simulated living."

"You do it in fifty at work."

Pam ignores him. God forbid she should interrupt *My Three Sons*.

Commercials air, the TV show no longer on to act as a diversion from their own lives. Nothing is said, nothing to say. What he wants, she doesn't, and Dennis finds something selfish in this, their lives without a child, living purely for their own pleasure, to make money and spend it on themselves, redecorating the apartment, and she sucked him into it with the gift of a spectacular new TV. Consumers consuming. Dennis is his own ideal target audience. All disposable income, no dependents. Silence, better to keep quiet, prevent her from infantilizing him, showing him how immature he can be when she's the one so angry about not having chicken with cashew nuts; cashew nuts all fat too, he should point out to her, like the fried dumplings. She stares at him, and he can't stand it. "Is this how you get because you don't like the Chinese food? Is this it?" he asks.

"I'm just having a little fun. Making fun of the TV program. Maybe if you didn't take it so seriously, you'd enjoy it. I'm not upset about the food. You probably feel guilty for not ordering what I asked for.''

And she's turned it back on him. *His* fault she has to talk to him like a child, like one of her patients. The show returns. His eyes remain fixed on the television screen. Minutes pass.

Pam asks, "Are you angry with me?" A wish to clear the air, restore peace.

"Why?" He's surprised she's asked, hates that she knew, that he made it so obvious to her.

"You seem angry and abrupt with me."

"I don't know what you're talking about. I'm fine with you. Nothing's wrong."

"Maybe I'm just a bit paranoid tonight." Pam knows he's lying.

"Maybe." He knows she knows he's lying but wants to deny her the opportunity of analyzing his emotions as if she weren't inherently involved in them—he isn't going to give her that pleasure—Pam using their marriage like therapy as if he were only transferring feelings to *her* and not she to him. Dennis admits he fell in love with his wife for being able to be so comforting and nurturing, giving him so much undivided attention and compassion, but eight years of marriage/therapy later he would like to be able to express himself and have it unconditionally received rather than returned to him as analysis in the form of a question.

Another commercial break. Pam rubs her eyes, and Dennis serves himself a second helping of the sweet-and-sour chicken.

Todd eats eggs Benedict. Joan eats a fresh fruit plate. A table for two in a crowded restaurant, tables pushed up alongside one another with no more than one foot separating the many brunching couples. Joan's embarrassed to say anything to Todd, about Todd himself or about herself or even about the food, and isn't sure she should tell Todd about the date anyway, open up to him and speak about how happy the date made her and how disappointed she is, now as the man hasn't phoned her back and she's once again been cast into the black hole of her depression. Approximately sixteen hours have passed since she phoned Dennis Perry, and still Joan has not received any response. She almost canceled Sunday brunch with Todd, it has upset her so much, but then, thinking the company might do her good, Joan changed her mind.

Trendy young couples flank both sides of their table, speaking in nonstop chatter. "God, I need another Bloody Mary," a woman with spiked red hair complains. "God, do I."

Todd looks up from his plate, sees his mother poking a skinless wedge of pink grapefruit around the rim of her dish. "Isn't it good?" he asks.

Joan places her fork down. "I hate citrus fruits. Why don't you have some?"

"Then why'd you order it?" His mother's always ordering, then never eating, picking but never taking a biteful, mouthful of food. It's always a carefully managed morsel. "Would you like to order something else?" he asks, afraid he sounded too harsh before.

"I'll have something later. I hate sitting so close to people. I hate that about New York restaurants. I might as well be eating on a subway car at rush hour."

"Relax, Mom, no one's listening. No one cares."

"Okay, you're right."

Joan sips her coffee. Not hot, it's tepid. "So, how's the new semester?"

"Good, just getting started."

"Oh, that's right. Of course." Harder talking to her son than to Dennis Perry on her date. Todd always seems to be halfway between consoling and accusing her.

Todd stabs a wedge of the fried potatoes, glistening with oil. "You don't seem as depressed today."

Joan puts the coffee down to explain. "Well, I force myself to do things. That helps. I'm not going to give up like some people and lie in bed all day. If I have to be depressed, at least I can keep myself entertained in my misery.''

''You always seem fairly well when I see you.''

''I'll videotape myself when I'm alone,'' Joan jokes. ''That'll spook you. Then you'll be wanting to send me to the loony bin.'' She picks up her fork, spears a red grape on one tong and a green on another.

''Why?'' Todd asks, hesitant, afraid this will get too serious, afraid he'll learn more than he wants to know. He watches his mother as she pulls the green grape off the fork with her teeth, chewing slowly, and then Joan does the same with the red grape.

''Don't get so worried,'' she tells her son, patting his hand. ''I'm fine. I'm in therapy, and I'm fine.''

Todd catches the waitress's eye and raises his hand, making a ''check'' gesture. Emily's due to meet him in ten minutes.

''Are you in a hurry today?''

''I have to meet Emily. We have things to do for school.''

Joan takes a lipstick from her handbag, rolling out its tip, applying it gently to her lips. ''Tell Emily I'm reading that book she liked last year. That Henry James book.''

''I'll let her know.''

''I should go back to school. I'm sorry I gave that up, investing in your father when I should have invested in myself.'' She puts the lipstick away in time to catch the anger in her son's eyes. She should know better than to bring up her feelings for Al in front of him.

The waitress places the check by Todd's plate and Joan takes out her wallet and puts several bills on the table.

Todd looks up at his mother. ''Where are you off to now?''

''Home.'' Joan puts the lipstick away. ''Oh. I've also picked up painting again. Bought some watercolors the other day.''

He finishes the last of his coffee. ''When did you paint before?''

''In college. B.A.D. Before Al Dwyer.'' Joan couldn't help herself.

"Very funny." Todd stands.

"I thought it was funny." Joan gathers her pocketbook, amused with herself. "I'll have to share that with my therapist tomorrow. B.A.D."

Pam rereads *A Woman with Too Many Wombs,* a recently published novel written by one of her patients. Pam writes notes on a yellow legal pad, questions to ask her patient if they come up in therapy. The book is Rosemary Cutler's second novel, the first having come out three years ago, just after Pam and Rosemary began working together. Rosemary handed Pam the first book a month into their therapy. "This is exactly what happened to me in my family. This is exactly what my parents and siblings were like. Read it so I don't have to go through all of this with you. It will save us time and me money."

Pam read the book but made Rosemary verbalize her family history anyway. "Reading about your family in the book is not the same as your telling it to me in person, both of us experiencing it together."

The first novel, *My Dead Mother,* was dedicated to no one. "I have no one in my life I care enough for. No one in my life who deserves the honor."

Two weeks ago Rosemary reached across the space between patient's and therapist's chairs, handing the second novel to her doctor, the book folded open to the dedication page.

"For Dr. Thompson," it read.

Pam took the book home. That evening she held it open for Dennis to view.

"Isn't this a bit much? A bit scary, isn't it?" He was shocked, couldn't believe one of Pam's patients could be so greatly devoted to his wife, dedicating a book to Pam—Pam, whom this woman *pays* to be her therapist—instead of some—*any*—other person in her life.

Pam took the book back, insulted. "Well, I'm flattered. We've done good work together. I think it shows how important our work is to her, how much her progress means to her.''

"This doesn't strike you as being even somewhat peculiar?''

"No. Why? Should it?''

"Don't you think this might be her way of establishing some kind of bond with you? Her giving you this and then your owing her something in return? What if you have problems with her down the road and she holds this up to you? Isn't this unethical? What did Briden say when you showed it to him?''

"Briden's fucking one of his patients. I'd hardly go to him for ethical reasoning. And anyway,'' Pam went on, reading and rereading her printed name alone on the dedication page of the book, "you act as if this is something *I* did, as if she asked me who the book should be dedicated to and I said me.''

"For Dr. Thompson.'' Pam closed the book. "If this becomes a problem—and I don't see how it will—*we,* Rosemary and I, will deal with it. That's our therapy, not your concern.''

Pam sits in the woven straw rocking chair, legs folded before her on the seat, the book open in the triangle her legs form.

Dennis lies in bed attempting to fall asleep and take a nap. He isn't tired but would rather be alone in the bedroom than with Pam in the living room. He shuts his eyes, then reopens them, rolling over in bed, staring at the four walls of the room. Everything in this room, in the apartment, is Pam's. Chosen by Pam, bought by Dennis and Pam eight years ago, shortly after they married. And now, eight years later, when this apartment is redecorated, it will most likely again turn out the same. He remembers disagreeing with her over the purchase of the black matte halogen lamp in the living room.

"I hate it. I think it's sterile-looking,'' he told her in the store.

"You *hate* this lamp,'' she verified with him.

"Yes, I hate it.''

"This *lamp.*'' Her hand clung around the lamp's long, thin black neck.

"That's what I said,'' Dennis replied.

"How can you *hate* a lamp?" Pam asked. "It's just a *lamp*. It gives off *light*. Is it such a big deal that you have to hate it?"

And he apologized to her, thought perhaps he had overreacted. A lamp is a lamp, as Pam said, and soon the apartment was furnished with lamps, couches, tables, chairs, and carpets all chosen by Pam. When Dennis brought this to his wife's attention, all she had to say was "You never chose anything you wanted us to buy. All you ever did was complain about what I chose, but you didn't bother to present me with any other options." She was right and he was wrong and the apartment was decorated.

Dennis tries to recall a conflict between his parents. How did *they* resolve their conflicts and remain a married couple for forty-six years and counting? Dennis can't imagine his father ever cheated on his mother. Reed Perry, a retired owner of several car dealerships in Maryland, was no adulterer. Dennis can't even remember his father paying attention to *any* woman other than to thank his mother for a plate of food or to scold his sister. "Men are my friends. Women take care of me. First my mother, now your mother. That's the way God wants it," he used to dictate to his two sons, Dennis and Kevin, Dennis's older brother, who now manages the car dealerships. Years ago after Dennis's older sister had put herself through school, Barbara went to her father, asking to be hired as an accountant, but her father refused to hire her, was against her going to school in the first place. "The only women I allow at the dealerships are the receptionists," he lectured. "I'm certain you don't want to be a receptionist. Am I correct?" Barbara got a job working at a toy manufacturing company, where she's been employed for the past twenty years.

The reason there were never any conflicts between his parents, Dennis suspects, is that his mother was never bothered by being left out of her husband's interests. She wanted as little to do with him as possible. They slept in the same bed, ate their dinners together, and barely said a word to each other. But they're still married, Mr. and Mrs. Reed and Bridge Perry, while their son Dennis, one date into an affair, an enticing affair with a woman he finds himself very attracted to, is not sure his marriage will last another two years, let alone forty-six.

"No kids?" his mother asked when they spoke over the phone at Christmas. "Your brother and sister each have kids."

"We don't *want* kids, Mom. We've discussed it, and we don't."

"Your sister has kids, and she has a career. Why can't Pamela?"

"Pam's not Barbara. It's not what we want."

"I'm only sorry I won't get to see your kids. That's all. That makes me sad."

Dennis defended himself. "There's more to a marriage than having kids."

"Merry Christmas" was her reply. "I'll put your father on."

No rings and Pam's refusal to take the Perry family name equals no marriage as far as his family is concerned, and Dennis still finds moments when he is convincing himself that these missing traditions don't bother him. When he once mentioned that he wished Pam could be more like his mother, more committed to their family life than her career, she replied, "You may not see it, but I am a lot like your mother. She is very independent of your father, just as he is of her. She just makes the home and family her career choice as I'm doing with being a psychiatrist. I don't think she hates your father, like you've said. I think they satisfy each other with what the other needs and then each goes their own way to fulfill the needs the other cannot meet. I don't see anything wrong with that."

Dennis disagrees. The romantic notion of two lives becoming one is what he needs: one shared life, not two lives joining for convenience, and what better way to share their lives than by having a child with his wife, the two of them creating one being? But then, Dennis thinks, how can he expect his wife to go along with sharing her body so they can create a life when she is unable to make the redecoration of their apartment a shared experience? "You have no vision of what you want our home to be, that's why I'm taking care of it," Pam has said. "You didn't care when we married, and you don't care now."

A shared home, Dennis thinks, a shared life, if their marriage is to survive. The redecoration is about to begin, and this time they will negotiate and plan together, a shared experience, a joint venture. Dennis stands, pulls on the pair of jeans and sweatshirt piled at the bottom of his closet. He marches into the living room. "Hey, I thought we'd talk about the redecoration plans."

Pam looks up from the book, tapping her pen on the legal pad. "What?"

"The plans for the apartment. I thought we'd go over them together, and we could draw up a plan of when to begin, how to do everything."

Pam folds the book closed, the front cover flap of the jacket keeping her place. "I'm working now."

"The book isn't going to go anywhere, and this is our only real time to do this, when we're both not too tired from work." He seats himself on the couch, at the end closest to Pam, letting her know he is here to work this through and not about to walk off into another room, occupying himself with another project.

She shakes her head. "The apartment isn't going to go anywhere either. I'm reading now."

"You're avoiding me," Dennis states.

Pam remains focused on the book. "How am I doing that?"

"I finally have ideas for the apartment I'd like to go over with you, and because you don't want to hear them, you're avoiding me. You want to make this apartment all your own again." He can't tell who went on the offense first, he or she.

Pam closes the book with a snap, placing it on the arm of the chair, uncrossing her legs and stretching them out before her. "You know, you're making us both sound awfully foolish." She rolls her feet, cracking her ankles.

"Hardly."

She continues, "Suppose then we say that I *am* avoiding you because I want to redecorate the apartment according to what I want. What do you do if that's so?"

He doesn't understand what she's going for. "I come in here like I've done so we can work it out together," Dennis says.

"So in order to work out a mutual agreement between us, you come in here, interrupt what I'm working on, and *demand* we work out this *mutual* agreement, handing me an ultimatum. 'Now or never.'" Pam folds her legs back on the chair, once again placing the book in the hollow they create.

He's caught. She's right and he knows it. What Pam has said makes complete sense to him. That is what he's doing, that is what he's asking of her, and it didn't feel like that—he thought he was coming in here to share, to get closer to her—until Pam tossed it back at him with a spin on the perspective. Dennis is dumbfounded, has no idea how to bow out of this graciously with his pride intact. He's lost to her and he knows it and she knows it, and he wishes she would attack him so he could at least leave in a huff rather than having to admit it openly and leave humiliated and treated like a child. Dennis looks at Pam. "Fine," Dennis concedes, pretending he is letting her off the hook. "We'll discuss it later." He selects a magazine—*any* magazine—off the coffee table and flips it open. To retreat from the conversation in shame is one matter, but if he can remain seated with her in the living room, at least then he's shown her that he won't be scared off or made to feel stupid. At least now she'll have to continue reading with his presence looming over her. Dennis glances at the table of contents, recognizing that the magazine he's selected is *Cosmopolitan,* and he turns the page, feigning interest in a survey concerning women's skirt-length preferences.

The phone Andrea speaks to her mother from is located on the first floor in the front hall, five feet from the first-floor housemother's apartment. Mrs. Montgomery sits in a chair by the open door to her apartment, listening in on the goings-on in the dormitory, eavesdropping on the phone conversations her girls have with parents, siblings, aunts, grandparents, and boyfriends.

Andrea sits on the short wooden stool under the house phone, cupping one hand around the mouthpiece, the other over her ear, attempting to block out the laughter echoing down from the far end of the hall.

She has told her mother how she's doing in school, how all her friends are, when she'll be coming home next (in three months, over Easter vacation) and has nothing more to say, but still her mother keeps her on the line.

"I wish you could come home more often. It would be nice having someone to share this place with. Make it more of my family's instead of my parents'."

Andrea twists the cord around her hand, spiraling it down her forearm. "You're the one who sent me here. I told you I'd rather be going to Dalton or Spence in the city."

Joan sighs into the phone. "You're right. I know. I shouldn't have brought it up. I miss you, that's all it is. You are better off being out of the city, that much I'm sure of."

"What's so much better about me being up here?"

"For starters," Joan says, "it's safer. Much better for you to be raised where there are many good role models about rather than in a single-parent household."

Andrea cannot believe her mother is so dumb. "*Mom*," she moans, "there are fifteen girls living in this house and only two housemothers for all of them. How is that better?"

A pause while Joan thinks, then: "There are security men guarding the campus. There are the housing and kitchen staff to look out for you. The teaching staff that lives on campus. The older girls to help you out."

"The older girls sneak off to the boys' hall and get drunk and laid. We can get into more trouble here than we ever could in the city."

"Then why are you complaining?" Joan rebuts with a laugh.

"Fine, Mom, you're right. It is better here than with you."

"You don't have to be sarcastic."

"By the way, did you get a life yet?"

"I'm working on it, why?"

"I want that new dress, remember our deal?"

"Can't you make one for yourself in sewing class?"

"*Sewing* class? Are you serious?"

"That may be the only way you'll get a black dress for the time being."

"I'm going to hang up now."

"All right. Go. Good-bye. Be good. I love you, honey."

"Yeah, good-bye."

Andrea hangs up quickly before her mother can rescind the good-bye and delay the end of the conversation. She yanks her arm from the tangled cord, and it springs up, bouncing around the phone, hitting the wall. She sits on the stool, alert, listening to the laughs emanating from the end of the hall, identifying those of Kitty March and Rickie Grinaldi, and Andrea stands and runs off in that direction.

The older girls at Andrea's school do not sneak off, get drunk, and get laid. Of *that* Joan is sure. She is sure her daughter was only baiting her, goading her, and Joan walks into the living room, dragging one of the emerald green velvet Queen Anne chairs over to the window, facing it out, and sitting, stockinged feet propped up on the air-conditioning/heating unit attached to the wall.

The bottom opening of her skirt fills with hot air, and Joan parts her legs a bit farther, letting the heat warm the insides of her thighs. Staring out at the cloud-covered city, she flexes the toes on both feet, remembering ballet lessons she was terrible at.

Joan sent Andrea and Todd to a New England boarding school to prevent them from becoming a couple of New York City brats, but apparently many other city parents pursue the same course of action, and ultimately Andrea *is* in school with a slew of displaced spoiled Manhattan girls. Although she may not have become one yet, Joan fears her daughter will be drawn into the Upper East Side social world of martinis, escorts, and little black dresses and pumps. Maturing too young and becoming a party girl, a pretty thing for rich boys to hook on an arm and drag from one event to the next. Joan reconsiders her first thought. Maybe the older girls *do* get drunk and get laid. And if this is so, at what age will Andrea become one of those older girls if she has not become one already? Away from their parents and under the careless scrutiny of adults who resent these girls for coming from wealthy families, the girls are more free than they'd be at home. Maybe these teachers and housemothers and groundskeepers, having to deal with these affected girls day and night, really do allow the girls to run off, drink alcohol, and risk becoming pregnant. After all, what does Mrs. Montgomery have to lose if Andrea Dwyer slips off to a boy's room and beds down, unprotected against fertilization and disease? Must give a woman like Mrs. Montgomery a kick to see these rich girls acting like beer hall tramps, chasing after men for sex.

Andrea Dwyer. Daughter of divorced Al and Joan Dwyer, attending a boarding school in Connecticut. Sixteen years old.

"What most interests you, besides boys?" Joan questioned her daughter over the Christmas break. They watched old reruns from the seventies on the TV in the family room. Reruns to Joan, new to her daughter. "Bob Newhart was a psychiatrist?" Andrea asked. "I thought he ran an inn in Vermont."

"Do you have an answer for my question? In the next year we have to start thinking about colleges."

Andrea stared at the TV. Suzanne Pleshette running off an airplane in a panic. "That's the woman who played Leona Helmsley," Andrea exclaimed. "Bob Newhart was married to Leona Helmsley?"

Joan was losing patience. "What do you want to be so we can start thinking about schools?"

Andrea gawked at the television. "*What do I want to be?* What does Bob Newhart's wife do?"

Joan closed her eyes. "She's a teacher. Now, what do you want to do?"

Andrea shook her head. "Not a teacher, that's for sure. Do I have to be something? What are you?"

Joan didn't know how to answer. "Well, think about it, and we'll discuss it later" was the best she could do.

Attending high school in the late sixties, Joan and her friends went out to Central Park after school, running off into the bushes and discarding school uniforms for tie-dye shirts, halter tops, and miniskirts and hot pants. They spent the afternoon hanging out with boys who went to the public schools and were thus free to let their hair grow long. Joan braided her boyfriend Dana's hair while he smoked marijuana, playing at being a hippie until four-thirty, when she changed back into her school clothes and ran home to help her mother prepare dinner.

"If you were a boy," Walter Robins told his only child, "I'd make you spend your afternoons down at my office, learning about business. When you graduated high school, you'd go on to a good Ivy League school to take courses in economics. You're just lucky you're a pretty girl and can play all afternoon. Just make sure you find a boy with business sense. Don't fall in love with one of those useless kids."

When Joan said she wanted to go to Bennington, her father didn't protest: "A wife with a good arts background is useful to a successful man, makes him look good, fills in the areas of culture he's too busy to attend to."

In college, with so few men on campus in the once all-girls' school, Bennington women often dated Williams men. Al Dwyer, with so much direction, his life so thoroughly planned, attending his father's alma mater with the goal of joining his father's brokerage firm upon graduating, enjoyed spending time with the aimless, fun Joan Robins. Away from her parents, Joan missed the stability of her very secure and defined family life, and Al was a good replacement for her father. "You make the plans. I'm not good at that. That's why I came to Bennington," she told Al when he asked her out on their first date.

Years into married life, Joan found herself with a large suburban house, two kids, four car pools (soccer practice, Brownies, Cub Scouts, and Little League), parent-teacher conferences, bake sales, walk-a-thons, back-to-school shopping sprees, and bimonthly dinner parties for Al's business associates. "I never knew what I wanted to do with my life, so maybe this is good for me," Joan told her mother after the birth of Todd. "Maybe being a good mother and wife is something I can finally stick to and get right."

What am I? Joan has no idea. *No one you should become*, she wanted to warn her daughter, but she was sure Andrea already knew enough than to want to be like her mother without her mother's having to clue her in. Only now, three years and a year of therapy after the divorce, has Joan discovered the consequence of taking no direction in life: Her husband's was thrust upon her, and when he left, so went her direction.

The city is dark, the sun setting early on this midwinter day. Joan sits, resigning herself to the fact that Dennis Perry, like her husband, has dumped her. She focuses on a tall building far across the way, its spire lit green, and then Joan's eyes pull back, focusing in on the glass before her, her feet pressed firmly against the pane. She is struck with the urge to throw herself through the window, throw herself through and pitch her body out into the cold night, to fall sixteen stories, to die on impact with the cement sidewalk.

Not sure where this thought has come from, why she has thought it, Joan stands, backing, then turning, away from the window, heading to the bedroom. Joan isn't sure why she is thinking about killing herself, has no idea, does not like to consider herself suicidal. Since she was a teenager, Joan has often fantasized about her life's being over, about no longer feeling this gnawing, insistent pain deep inside her—a rodent, slowly eating its way from her stomach to her chest, catching in her throat—this is what Joan feels, wants to end, but she has never before had the impulse to act on the feeling, to pursue an action whose objective is to kill this feeling and end her life, but here and now, she has, and Joan is both scared and tantalized. She can easily feel herself falling the sixteen floors, wind rushing around her body, through her hair, under her arms, between her legs. Quickly she strikes the ground, blacking out. No more.

The whole thing doesn't seem so bad, has a certain gross appeal to it, and Joan returns to the living room, looking across to the window, to where she'd been seated. The chair needs to be returned to its appropriate spot, and Joan strolls over, keeping her eyes on the chair's back. Emerald green velvet, soft and cool.

The chair is replaced to its original position, and Joan walks to the far corner of the room by the edge of the row of windows, tugging the drawstring, pulling the heavy green curtains before the offending glass.

4

———

The flowers in the blue ceramic vase on the table in Dr. Thompson's waiting room are changed weekly, appearing fresh and crisp on Monday, then slowly falling into decay as the dry winter air sucks the moisture from the arrangement, leaving the flowers open and wilted, petals hanging back, filaments exposed.

Today is Monday, and the arrangement is new. New and without petals. Without flowers. Weeds and twigs and brush and berries, Joan observes. A delicate bouquet of evergreen branches. The air remains dry, however, and the needles will almost surely die on the branches and drop to the table's surface, falling over the magazines and drifting to the floor. Joan can see this coming, this inevitability, and makes a mental note to observe how much has fallen by Wednesday and again on Friday. She checks her watch. Dr. Thompson is running three minutes behind schedule. Dr. Thompson is allowing the patient before Joan to run over, taking exactly three minutes of Joan's time away from Joan on a day when Joan could fill every second of the session reporting her most recent problems: the phone call to Dr. Thompson, the unreturned message from the man, and the ensuing depression. Joan holds the missing ashtray tightly in the pocket of her coat, anxiously awaiting the moment when she has to return it to her doctor.

Joan spent this morning and afternoon waiting in the apartment for the phone to ring, for Dennis to call, but nothing, no call. This just after she made such a big deal to Dr. Thompson about how important this date had been to her.

Joan grits her teeth, impatient, and reaches a hand toward the floral arrangement, about to pluck a glossy red berry from a branch when the office door opens. A teenage girl rushes out past Joan and into the building's hallway. Dr. Thompson waves Joan into the office. "I'm sorry. I'm a bit behind. We can go over on the other end if that's all right."

Joan stands, gathering her coat, scarf, gloves, and bag, "Whatever," and she walks into the office.

Dennis tosses his jacket, portfolio case, and gloves on the black leather couch in the front room and walks to the kitchenette off the hallway, taking a beer from the near-empty refrigerator, then walking into the back bedroom, where the phone machine sits on an end table by the full-size futon. He pulls out the knot in his tie, yanking it from around his button-down collar, lamely attempting to hurl it into the open closet. The tie drops to the floor in the space between the bed and the wall, and Dennis lets it lie there. He glances at the phone machine—five messages—and he rolls onto his stomach, taking up the large pad of sketch paper and the blue marker beside it.

Complaining clients, Dennis expects, whining account executives and maybe, possibly, a message from his wife informing him of her plans for them for the evening. He reluctantly pushes the play button, and minutes later he holds a list of four names: Joan Dwyer, two business calls, a message from Pam informing him of her plans, one hang-up. "Why don't you hold on there, and after I've finished, I'll stop over? My last appointment of the day canceled so we should be able to catch the seven-thirty of that film at the Lincoln cinemas. I made a dinner reservation for afterward. See you soon." Sometimes Dennis thinks Pam intentionally leaves messages for him at his office when she knows he's not going to be around to disagree with her about any plans she's made. Pam just leaves the message, then becomes unreachable until she's ready to be reached.

Dennis tears off the list of names, throwing it carelessly toward the foot of the bed, watching it float down by his feet before recalling that Joan's name is on the list, and with Pam coming over he shouldn't leave it lying about. Dennis reaches over, awkwardly twisting at the waist, taking up the list, folding and shoving it in a pants pocket.

He walks into the living room, taking his wallet from his jacket pocket, retrieving Joan Dwyer's number. The only reason Dennis can think of not to call Joan is what this might do to his marriage. This should be a major reason, should be the *only* reason or at least enough of a reason for Dennis not to call. It isn't. Loving his wife, being in love with his wife are not enough to sustain a marriage. Love is not enough. Dennis can imagine himself loving Joan as deeply as he loves his wife—not necessarily the same love, but a love equally significant. Loving Joan, whoever she is, or at least who he hopes she is. He sits on the stool by his drafting table, picking up the phone. He keeps the phone by the drafting table and the phone machine in the bedroom, so he will not be disturbed when napping.

"You have reached the Dwyer residence. Please leave a message. Thank you for calling."

The beep, and Dennis speaks. "Hello, Joan. Dennis Perry calling you back. I thought maybe we could chat. Why don't you"—he pauses, thinks things through—"why don't you call me tomorrow midmorning sometime as I'll be going to bed pretty early tonight? Please call me then. So long.''

Joan glances to her left, to the ashtray returned half an hour ago, at the start of this session. She wants to pick it up, something to hold on to and play with while sitting here, but is too self-conscious to, having only just returned it. Joan laughed nervously, handing it back to her doctor, and Dr. Thompson smiled, placing it back on the end table. "It's happened before, believe it or not. Don't worry." Following the return of the ashtray, Joan launched into a monologue detailing the events (the bus tour, brunch with her son, the onset of suicidal thoughts) and *non*events (no call from the man) of the past weekend.

Joan smirks. "It doesn't surprise me. You may not say it, but I'm sure you anticipated this. You probably even like it this way."

"Do you believe that I want you to be unhappy?" Pam watches Joan sitting nervously, Joan's eyes darting to the floor, out the window, to the ashtray, her lap, the bookshelves. Pam hypothesizes that Joan took the ashtray, consciously or unconsciously, so she would have an excuse to call her doctor over the weekend without appearing as if she *needed* to phone her doctor.

Joan looks at her doctor's desk, the glossy dark wood. "You're happier when I'm miserable. You weren't pleased during our last session when I was happy with him, so you asked questions that would upset me and make me cry. You find more satisfaction in seeing me miserable."

Pam watches Joan, giving Joan time to think as well as giving herself time to sort through Joan's thought process: Joan Dwyer believes her doctor wants her to remain depressed, failing to understand, because of her upset, that if Joan is to remain ill and never-changing, her doctor could only think of herself as a failure. The last thing Pam *wants* is for Joan to remain unhappy. "Do you honestly believe seeing you in pain gives me pleasure?"

"Yes."

"Why?"

She should never have accused her doctor of not caring, isn't sure why she did. "I don't know."

"You don't."

"I thought—" Joan stops, actually hasn't thought it through. She picks the ashtray up off the table, rubs her hands over its edges, across its smooth surface. She thinks of Dennis Perry, of his not calling her back, of Al leaving her, of her belittling father, her ambivalent children. Joan looks at Dr. Thompson, and she's looking back at Joan, very attentive. Joan feels her eyes well up, feels the tears waiting to be given a push, and she holds them back, doesn't know why she's taken to crying here in therapy. Joan touches a fingertip to the corner of her eyes, lifting away tears, brushing them on her skirt.

"What are you thinking about now?"

Joan considers not answering but knows she should, knows she has to open up to the doctor. Joan pauses, takes a breath, trying to halt the forthcoming tears. "I don't think people can care for one another. I think people express their vulnerability, and people stomp all over it. That's what happens to people."

"Is that what's happened to you?"

"I don't know."

"Why didn't you ask me to return your call on Saturday?"

"I didn't need you to."

"You sounded upset."

"I made it through the weekend in one piece."

"Is it enough to just make it through in one piece?"

She should have thrown herself out the window, better than being here, forced to confront herself with no escape. Once the words are said and tossed back to her by Dr. Thompson with a fresh perspective, they stick in Joan's mind, echoing there, making her reevaluate how she views herself and others. Dr. Thompson waits. "I can't remember what we were talking about," Joan says.

"I asked if it was enough for you to just be making it through in one piece."

"It's what I can do."

"Does that make it enough?"

Always to be interrogated, always being prodded into expressing herself. "No, it's not enough. It's not enough, but it's what I can do." Joan shakes her head, annoyed, irritated, her teary mood gone. "I don't fool myself. I know what our relationship is. This is your job, to help me. I know you don't really care for me as a person and wouldn't if I weren't paying you. I pay you to listen to me complain about my life. I'm not a real person in your life. You don't care about me like a friend."

"And why do you get to decide that I don't care for you?" Pam's surprised by how irritated she becomes at being accused of not caring; most patients accuse her of this at some point—just part of what doctors and patients go through. Pam becomes deeply affected by it each and every time the accusation is made, always surprised by how much she *does* care for each of her patients, and today she is surprised by how much she does care for Joan, how strong her attachment is to this woman. Pam wonders why. An issue to be examined later. "Yes, we have a working relationship," Pam agrees, dropping her voice, softer than before. "Does that mean that what goes on and is expressed between us is any less real? I wish you *had* asked me to return your call. I felt like speaking to you and seeing if you were all right, and I almost thought I should call. I decided to respect your wishes, so I didn't. To be frank with you, I'm hurt that you don't think I care for you. I know I do, but I think you might not want me to, and I'm not sure you'll let me. I think you're afraid of feeling attached to me."

Joan looks away from her doctor, out the window, annoyed with herself for confronting her doctor, making a scene. The sky is dark, starless. "I don't know what you're talking about."

"Let's look at your behavior. You asked me not to call you when it sounded like you wanted me to. Then you come in here today and tell me I don't care for you and that people stomp all over your feelings. Maybe it's not always about you being vulnerable and people

stomping on your feelings. Sometimes I feel like you make yourself
vulnerable and then run for cover, not giving me or anyone else the
chance to care for you.'' Pam notices the time. Only a few minutes
remaining, and she hopes she can end this at a less precarious
moment.

Joan sits, overwhelmed by all the doctor has said: How true it all
rings to their relationship, her fear of being cared for, her only
wanting to care for others. ''I didn't want to bother you,'' she
answers softly, conceding the point. ''I didn't want to be a burden.''

''It is my job to be there for you when you need my help. I don't
think of it as a burden. It's a privilege that you would trust me enough
to let me help you.''

Joan notes the time. ''I know it's time for me to go, so I'll go.''
She stands and collects her things. Pam stands, watches Joan, and
goes to the door, holding its knob before opening it. ''Please leave a
message if you need to talk. I think it would help both of us here.''

Joan buttons her coat. ''Maybe. See you Wednesday.''

And Pam lets her out.

A message on the phone's built-in answering machine. One red
blinking message, and it's probably, almost surely, from Andrea,
phoning for more money.

A recent conversation between mother and daughter: ''You have
two hundred dollars a month to spend up there. With food, shelter,
and clothing already provided, what in heaven's name do you find to
spend the money on?''

''Drugs,'' Andrea deadpanned.

Joan prays her daughter does not become, has not become a brat.
''I was spoiled,'' Joan plainly admitted to her children shortly after
the divorce, a caution before they moved back to the city. ''Got
whatever I wanted easily. I was never a brat, though. I always
appreciated what I was given.'' Joan hates thinking of herself thinking
of Andrea in negative terms, so she banishes the thought, deciding

that she should be happy her daughter does phone, whatever the reason. Some parents never hear from their children once they're away at boarding school.

Joan plays the message and listens, surprised. The message ends and the tape rewinds and Joan plays the message again, leaning up against the counter. The message ends, the tape rewinds, and Joan reaches over, pushing the play button for a third time.

Pam has been knocking on the steel outside door to Dennis's office for five minutes and has received no response. When she peers through the bars outside the front window, she sees the workroom lit and the hallway extending to the bedroom, but no Dennis in sight. Pam guesses her husband has probably fallen asleep out back on the futon.

The temperature couldn't be above thirty degrees, not even factoring out the windchill, and Pam gives up knocking and climbs the brick steps, reaching the street level, walking the half block to the corner pay phone. If she had a rock, she just might throw it through the front window of his office, lucky for him it's covered with bars, and Pam yanks off a glove, unbuckles her shoulder bag, and digs around searching for phone change. A dime and three nickels later, Pam pounds out the number. The phone rings, the phone machine picks up, and Pam prepares herself to yell into the machine to wake her husband out of his sleep. "Dennis, please pick up! Pick up, please! It is cold out here, and I'm calling from the corner! Are you there?" She pauses, waits to hear her husband's cute, half-awake apology, waiting to lose her anger and be endeared to him. There is no pickup. "Are you there?" she asks again, this time a bit quieter, with less hope. But then she remembers seeing his overcoat on the couch through the window. "I'm going home. I hate you. Remember that when you get home." She hangs up, thrusting her ungloved hand into the air, flagging down a cab.

.   .   .

Dennis awakens. He looks at his watch. Eight forty-three. He notices the message waiting to be heard and spins the volume control up on the machine.

All the message truly amounts to is his wife is angry with him for forgetting about her, and he wonders why he doesn't care more, about how unsorry he feels. A time existed when he would have felt overly guilty, phoning immediately, smothering Pam with apologies. Instead Dennis sits up, picks the two empty beer bottles off the floor, and takes them into the kitchenette, setting them down in the bottom of the cabinet under the sink. Let Pam fume. Let her be out of control and feel the fury of frustration. At this point, crosstown in his office rather than at home facing the woman, he hardly gives a shit.

Pam forces the pizza into her mouth, chewing, swallowing, munching on crust. She has eaten two slices and is now working on her third. Five slices remaining. She'll have to jog additional minutes to-morrow.

Devon Taylor came into therapy with her head shaved, her shoul-der-length blond hair gone, her scalp shining. "I was tired of people telling me how beautiful my hair was so I got it all cut off so they'll leave me alone."

Mitch Breen, a grossly overweight sixteen-year-old, began his ses-sion with "I masturbated thinking about you in the school library bathroom stall this morning. Twice. Once at the beginning of study hall and then again during my break between math and chemistry."

Rosemary Cutler asked Pam how far along she was in the reading of her book, and when Pam replied, "Let's talk about why that's im-portant to you," Rosemary Cutler said she knew she shouldn't have dedicated the book to her shrink.

"I don't think people can care for one another," Joan Dwyer said, and Pam should have agreed, should have agreed but with one qualifi-cation. "People can care," Pam would have liked to have said. "But they can only care when they want something from you that they can't get anywhere else. Or at least at the moment when they want it. That's how people care.''

When her patients accuse her of not caring, Pam would like to turn around and accuse them of not caring for her, of being there only for themselves and forgetting that she too has feelings and needs just as they do. But Pam is the doctor they pay to test their behaviors on, whom they pay to focus upon their needs so they can go back out into the world and pursue their goals of happiness or, at the very least, understand that the goals they may be pursuing are not ones that will actually make them happy. A man is not going to solve all of Joan Dwyer's problems. Becoming a rock star is not going to eliminate Devon Taylor's need to win her stepfather's approval. These are Pam's concerns throughout the day. Her own needs, on the other hand, must remain unmet until she is home with her husband.

She felt disgusted and dirty hearing Mitch Breen's comment, but she replied, a good doctor, ''How do you feel telling me this?'' never mentioning her feelings of revulsion.

How ugly people's needs are, how ugly people become as they take action to fulfill their needs. Joan Dwyer daring to pursue her dream of a man, her desperate need overwhelming her fear of failure and humiliation. Giving birth to two children, left by a husband, pursuing a man. Need and emotion, running—*ruining*—Joan Dwyer's life, whereas Pam maintains a very tight control over her own needs, fulfilling them carefully, as is necessary. To need someone is to be controlled by him. Joan Dwyer would dissolve and reinvent herself if she knew it would secure this man. She becomes more depressed and suicidal as she obsesses about him, making herself vulnerable as she hopes to find happiness and ease pain. Pam wishes she had the daring—or is it the foolishness?—to display her vulnerabilities so prominently, making them attractive, not gruesome. Pam thinks that if she could only give in to what she wants—loving her husband without anger, appreciating his need rather than vilifying it, giving herself the freedom to trust others not to attack her, allowing herself the opportunity of having a child rather than accepting that she would not make a good mother, to be human rather than perfect and impenetrable— then Pam might be able to enjoy other people rather than fear them.

"I do love Dennis and can tell him this in words," Pam told her therapist of years ago, informing him of her engagement. "Only I can't express it. When I tell him I love him, it's all very controlled and planned and intellectual. I know I feel it too, but I can feel it only when I am alone and safe and he's not around. I can't let him see how vulnerable I am. I'm afraid he wouldn't want me if he saw I was that weak."

"He may want you more," her doctor replied.

"He may not," Pam responded. "Who's to know?"

Pam hears a bolt being thrown back in a lock. She sits up, folding the pizza box lid closed, swallowing the last of her third slice. She wishes she had taken a Valium or Xanax, but it's too late now. He's home, and her anger's rekindled.

"You make it sound as if it's the fucking end of the world. Couldn't you at least wait until I got my coat off?" Dennis turns his back to Pam, leaves the kitchen, hangs the coat in the hall closet. Her child again—no wonder she doesn't want kids. She has a husband. She has patients.

Pam remains seated at the kitchen table, decides to reason rather than reprimand. "When you're ready, come in so we can discuss this. I'd like to."

"I'll be in in a second. Once I've changed."

Pam wraps the five leftover pizza slices in aluminum foil, placing them on the middle rack of the refrigerator. She folds the pizza box in half and crams it in the already overstuffed wastebasket. The cardboard box unfolds, pushing out of the basket, and Pam shoves it in again, forcing it into the basket hard, when her hands slip, shoving the basket to the side, and it tips. Chinese food containers, cans, boxes, torn envelopes, plastic wrap scatter around her feet. "Damn it." And she kneels in the trash, reaching to the cabinet under the sink and extracting an additional garbage bag.

Dennis stands in the doorway in a polo shirt and jeans. "Can I help?"

Pam collects the Chinese food containers, dropping them in the now-upright wastebasket. "I've got it. I made the mess, I'll clean it up."

"I don't mind helping."

Pam can't believe how overcome with rage she is, wants to snap at him but checks herself, uses a normal tone of voice. "I'll be all right. It'll be done soon enough." She looks up toward him. "Why don't you go in the other room? I'll be in in a minute."

And Dennis leaves, turning on the television in the living room, tuning into the midpoint of a movie on HBO, a movie Pam and he had seen in a theater together years ago and both enjoyed, an opportunity to connect, to bring them closer together. "Come in here. Come see what's on," he calls.

Pam heads down the hall with the two garbage bags, opening the apartment door. "One minute." She takes the garbage to the compactor chute at the end of the hall and returns to the apartment, standing behind the couch, laying her hands on Dennis's shoulders. "I'm sorry I got so angry with you when you came in. I was just annoyed about—"

"It was my fault. I deserved it." Dennis places a hand over hers. "I shouldn't have fallen asleep there. Sorry. We could see that movie tomorrow night, if you'd like."

Pam walks around, sits beside Dennis, leaning up against him. "I have my group. It's Tuesday."

"Oh, that's right." And out of nowhere the thought occurs to him that tomorrow night he could go out with Joan. Pam has groups on Tuesdays and teaches a seminar on Thursdays; on both those nights he is free to date Joan and go undetected, and Dennis can't believe this thought occurs to him at the one moment in the last week when he and his wife are getting along, sitting side by side, arms around shoulders, watching an old favorite movie. And to make up for this last thought, Dennis leans over, kissing Pam, pulling her toward him. He tastes garlic and tomato, becoming hungry, and thinks about going into the kitchen and reheating a slice when Pam responds, first surprised, then welcoming, her hands going to his chest, gripping his shirt in her fingers, and pulling him close. Dennis eases Pam back. His legs scissor her body, and she feels him stiffening against her thigh. She raises her hip up to him, and he moans, impulsively thrusting. He kisses her neck, and her hands rake over his back, drawing his shirt up around his shoulders. Dennis stands, pulling the polo shirt over his head, and Pam pulls her T-shirt over hers, then leans forward, reaching out, and grabbing his hard-on through his jeans. He takes a step forward, increasing the pressure on his crotch, cupping Pam's firm breasts in his hands, feeling her nipples stiffen, rolls them between his fingers while she unbuttons the fly of his jeans. Dennis's dick is freed, and he releases Pam and kicks off his boxer shorts. Pam takes down her sweatpants, kicking off her slippers, and Dennis is nude, his cock rigid, and he tenses his ass muscles, making his dick throb. Pam's dark bush can be seen through the white sheer panties, and she spreads her legs, folding her knees up to her chest, and Dennis, holding his dick in his hand, wants to put it immediately in her but knows he has to give her head first if she is to enjoy this too. He kneels, his dick head brushing against his wife's calf as he presses his face into her crotch, smelling her through the panties. Pam grabs his head, forcing his face harder against her, and Dennis moves his hands around, under her ass, digging into the flesh of her ass. Pam's panties come down and Pam arches her back and he can feel her heat, her moist heat, and Dennis keeps one hand on her ass and another jerking his dick, his face smothered by her crotch, eating at her pussy. Pam's rocking and moaning, and Dennis hears her cries building, and he pulls himself up, Pam wrapping her legs around him, drawing him close. He stabs his dick in, and Pam squeezes tight, moaning, a rush coming over her, building, and she cries out, Dennis groaning, his thrusts more frantic, his dick sliding in and out, the head of the dick poking up against the sides and back of her. Pam yanks him close, squeezing him with her legs, and Dennis gives one sudden lunge and Pam feels her body contracting, tightening, wanting to let go, and Dennis thrusts again, more desperate, and Pam withdraws, distances herself from this, her body, him, retreating into her mind. She wishes he would just stop trying to please her and allow himself to come and be done with it, but Dennis keeps on grunting and thrusting, his hands holding her breasts, his mouth at her neck, kissing her, spit on her skin. She let him start, so now she has to let him finish. She would rather be watching TV, rather watching TV or sponging the floor where the garbage had spilled—she didn't get a chance to do that yet, and it has to be done—and Dennis finally groans, coming.

Pam holds him tight, letting him know he's pleased her, more than pleased her, and she is thankful that it's over, and after she lets him kiss and cuddle her for three maybe four minutes, Pam excuses herself to the bathroom, opens the medicine cabinet, and takes out the Valium prescription she prescribes for herself, taking two pills.

5

The doorman buzzes. Dennis Perry has arrived, and Joan tells the doorman to send him up. Joan checks her watch, noting his promptness.

At ten-thirty this morning Joan presented Dennis with the plan of coming over for a home-cooked meal, hoping to win the bachelor over with food, a tidy home, a display of artwork, and talk of literature. Immediately after hanging up the phone, Joan set about cleaning the apartment. The morning spent dusting and vacuuming, the early afternoon painting watercolors, midafternoon reading, and late afternoon preparing dinner.

The bell chimes, and Joan opens the wide door. Dennis enters, a smile on his face and flowers, a bouquet of mixed flowers, in his hand. "Hello." He leans forward and kisses Joan's cheek. His eyes drop to Joan's cleavage, her breasts fuller and rounder than Pam's.

"Is something wrong? Do I look funny?" Joan is sure she shouldn't have worn this dress with the low neckline. She reaches into the closet, selecting a wooden hanger.

"No. You look very nice." Dennis places the flowers on one of the tables by the door, sliding out of his overcoat, and handing it to Joan. "Do you hire someone to help keep up the place?"

Joan leads Dennis to the living room. "I couldn't have some strange woman around my apartment, touching all my things."

"What are you afraid she'd do to them?" He walks to the window, taking in the panoramic view of the Hudson River, southern Manhattan.

Joan is at the dry bar. "Would you like a drink? I don't know," answering Dennis's question, trying to come up with an answer. "Do you have a cleaning woman?"

A garbage barge, all aglow, trash on display, floats north, pulled by a tugboat. "I have a woman in for an afternoon every other week. She does the floors, bathroom, and kitchen."

Joan carries a tray over to the coffee table. A pitcher of martinis, a bowl of olives, a bowl of lemon peels, thinly curled twists, a short stack of cocktail napkins, and two martini glasses, foggy from having been chilled. She sits on the sofa, gently stirring the pitcher with a thin glass wand. "I just think it's odd having a stranger in your home, someone you barely know going through all your things, learning all about your most private life when you know nothing of theirs. You have so little privacy in the city, I'm not about to sacrifice that so I don't have to clean and scrub the bathroom floor."

"I guess you've really put a lot of thought into this," Dennis teases.

Joan pours the martinis. "What else would I do if I let someone else clean the place? That would be pretty lazy of me, considering." Joan wishes they would get on to another subject; all this talk about housework and maids feels awkward. She hands Dennis the martini. "A twist or olives?"

Joan takes three olives for herself, dropping them in the glass, through the liquid. "Should have put these in first." She shrugs.

Dennis takes three olives, drops them into his drink. The liquid creeps up to the glass's rim. "So, how long have you been here?" Dennis asks. "This is a beautiful apartment."

Joan nods. "This was my parents' home. I grew up here. My parents bought it decades ago when no one wanted to live anywhere but the Upper East Side. I moved back after the divorce." Joan reaches into her drink, taking out an olive and placing it in her mouth. "I couldn't live in that house after the divorce, so I moved in here." Joan stops, sipping her drink, stopping herself from going on about her ex-husband. "You don't want to hear any of this. I'm sorry."

"Relax. Don't worry." Dennis sips his drink.

Dennis sips, and they're both silent, sipping their drinks. All that can be heard is the slurping of lips against glass. Dennis saying nothing, having nothing to say, staring out the window, sitting beside this wounded divorcée lamenting her past, all she wants to talk about is her ex-husband, and all that's on his mind is his present-day wife. Walking here, anticipating this date, he got an erection at the thought of being alone with this woman who isn't his wife. But now that he finds himself only thinking of his wife, what he is doing to her and their marriage by being in this other woman's apartment, he considers leaving immediately, knowing that if he leaves now, he can return home guilt-free, nothing having transpired between this woman and himself but the sharing of a lunch, a few drinks, and some brief, sad chatter. Dennis puts down his drink, staring out the window at cars driving along the New Jersey coastline across the river, working up the nerve to make his quick exit.

Dennis's martini sits on the table growing warmer and warmer. He stares out the window, bored with his date, and Joan sets her drink down on the table, looking away from her guest and standing, walking across the room to the window, where she gazes out at the city below, her palms pressed flat against the glass. The impulse to jump hits, to open the window and jump and be done with this date, this humiliation, this life, and Joan would rather be dead, cease to exist, than live through this tense silence. All the effort she put into this date: the peeling of potatoes, the dusting of furniture, the painting of pictures, the reading of the book—an entire day spent with hopes of pleasing this man, convincing him to like her when he doesn't care, when all he wants is to sleep with her and be gone. Eyeing the breasts she so obviously displayed.

Joan's shoulders are shaking, Dennis notices from his spot on the couch, and then her hands leave the surface of the window and cover her eyes. He hears a small gasp, a sob and freezes—*to get up and go or to say something?*—and Dennis stands, walking up behind Joan, laying his hands on her slumped shoulders and turning her, leading her to the couch.

Joan's hands cover her face. Her mouth falls open, taking in short gulps of air. Dennis takes his hands from her shoulders and picks up Joan's drink, offering it to her. "Here, take a sip," he says gently, nervously, and Joan takes her hands from her face and lifts the glass, cupping both hands around its cone.

A tear runs over her lip, down the inside of the glass and into the liquid. "Thanks. Thank you." She takes a few more sips, stops crying, and eats an olive. "You can leave if you want," she informs Dennis, her voice low, now composed. "I'm all right. You don't have to stay." She reaches out for the pitcher and pours herself a full glass. "You want another?"

"Please."

Joan tips the pitcher, refilling Dennis's glass, then places the pitcher back on the tray.

"Do you want to be alone?" Dennis asks. "Would you rather I left?"

Joan dabs her eyes with a napkin. "No, I think I'm done crying." He must think she's crazy, a loon, and she smiles at the thought of this second date, at herself crying and falling into despair. "Have you ever had a date cry on you before?"

Dennis laughs. "Ah, no. I don't think so."

"Was it awful?" If he hasn't left by now, he probably isn't going to.

"Not so bad. Do you mind if I ask why you were crying?"

To tell or not to tell, Joan wonders what difference it would make—a lie or the truth—at this point. "I was afraid the date wasn't going well. That and some other things."

"So you cried to liven it up," Dennis suggests.

Joan nods, taking a sip of her drink. "I try to be a good date."

"You really want to hear about my family?" Joan asked at the beginning of the meal, but an hour later, as they're finishing dessert, Joan and Dennis are talking about Al and how he left her for another woman. "She wasn't even as *pretty* as I am," Joan moans drunkenly, laughing, and Dennis laughs, he too a bit drunk.

"Then why would he have left?"

"*I don't know.*" Joan shakes her head, positively dumbfounded. "She wasn't even as *pretty*. I really don't understand it." She turns to face the window, pointing with her chin. "We lived half an hour from here, just over the bridge there. Sometimes I stand at the window and think that if I look hard enough, I'll be able to see the house with all of us in it again as if he hadn't left."

Dennis reaches over, taking Joan's hand in his own, kissing a knuckle. "I'm glad he left you," Dennis says softly, half-sarcastically, and Joan pushes his head away, only partly amused, "This is enough. I don't want to talk about this anymore," and she sees that Dennis is looking at her with a peculiar look. Careful and scrutinizing, and he stares into Joan's wide eyes, moving closer. Joan is tempted to pull back, retreat to the kitchen, but she forces herself to remain still as Dennis leans in, pressing his lips to hers.

.   .   .

Joan takes a breath, looking away to the table. "You should probably go. Don't you have work tomorrow?"

Dennis glances at his watch. Nine-fifty. He'll be lucky to get in before Pam. "I should be going. You're right."

Joan stands. "I'll walk you to the door."

He places a hand flat on the middle of her bare back, touching her soft skin, walking alongside her. "I've had a nice time."

"I'm sure it's been interesting. A regular freak show."

Dennis smiles. "Really, it's been nice."

Joan reaches into the closet, handing Dennis his coat. She's glad she avoided showing him her paintings. Had them prepared but fears he wouldn't like them, isn't sure she likes them herself. The topic of her painting never came up, and she wasn't about to raise it herself, especially when things did get going well. Dennis puts on his coat, and Joan opens the door. He kisses her quickly on the cheek, then again on the lips, longer, more sexual. "I'll call you," he says. He steps into the hall. "Really, I had fun." He pushes the button, calling the elevator.

"I did too. Good night." She gives a short wave.

Dr. Jack Briden lies on Pam's couch, head resting on a throw pillow. He lifts a hand before his face, studying the lines intersecting across his palm. "Why is it so unethical? The more I think about it, the more I can't figure it out. We meet each other's needs. We love each other."

Pam puts the last of the folding chairs in the closet, cleaning up after her group. "You're supposed to be his therapist. He came to you for help." So obvious she shouldn't have to say it.

Jack Briden swings his legs around to the floor. "The therapy's nothing. That's just for fun. Isn't it more honest of me to be his therapist and have a relationship with him than if I was to meet him in a bar, become his boyfriend, and *then* begin analyzing him? I'd analyze him either way, so at least this way I'm doing it with his consent as well as getting paid for it.''

Pam collects her bag and coat from the rack behind the door. ''Do you want me to say it's okay? Is that it?'' Pam circles the room, switching off lamps. ''Are you leaving with me?'' she asks.

''Hold on.'' Jack Briden brushes past Pam, going to his office, grabbing his coat and scarf, and shutting the door. He wants— *needs*—to convince her. *''Yes, it is okay,''* he wants her to say.

Pam locks the door to her office and steps into the hallway. Jack Briden locks the office door behind him. ''I admit it's wrong,'' he confesses. ''I just want to persuade you that it's right, so then I can believe it. Isn't that a natural thing to want?''

Pam pushes the down button at the elevator, fastens her coat. She hopes Dennis won't be home when she gets there, would like time alone, away from her patients, her colleague, her husband, focusing on no one but herself.

''Don't you have any answer for me? Any advice?''

They step on the elevator. Pam hits *L* for lobby, and the door closes. The elevator descends slowly, beeping at every floor it passes. ''I'm not in the situation. It's hard for me to say what I'd do.'' She stares above the door, at the line of numbers. Ten lit for several seconds, the beep, then it's dark. Nine lit for several seconds, the beep, then it's dark.

''You wouldn't do what I'm doing,'' Jack answers for Pam. ''You think what I'm doing is so wrong you're speechless.''

Seven lit, the beep, seven dark.

''Yes, I don't think you should have started. At this point, though, I don't see anything wrong with your continuing to date him so long as you're not treating him in therapy. If he still needs therapy, he should see another doctor.'' She's stated her opinion, she thinks rather kindly *and* honestly, and is relieved, glad it's been said.

Five lit, the beep, five dark.

''Would you treat him? Check him out for me?''

Pam blurts out a laugh. "What? No. Of course not. . . . 'Check him out?' No." Pam laughs again. "I don't think so."

Two dark, the beep, two lit.

"Can't blame me for asking."

A beep, the lobby.

"No, can't do that," Pam replies, and the door opens. Pam steps out, followed by Jack.

"Till tomorrow," he says.

"See you." She hopes she didn't offend him by laughing at his suggestion, and she passes through the lobby onto the street.

Too much need, too much desperate need. She faces it all day long, only to face Jack Briden's pleas for approval. And now on to her emotionally hungry husband, who lives in constant need of knowing he is needed.

"I look at the glass and see myself falling through it, and it doesn't seem so bad. My body falls through the air, with my hair blowing around, and my skirt and blouse are blowing around, and I keep falling. Everything is blurry and I see the streetlights and then I hit the ground and it's over.

"I don't even know where this impulse comes from. I know I should be scared of thinking this way, but I'm not. I'm not even sure why I'm thinking like this now instead of three years ago, when he left."

"Can you guess?"

"I can guess, but I don't think it's right."

"Let me hear what you think."

Joan thinks, wrings her hands, then becomes conscious of wringing her hands and looks down at them and stops. "I was thinking about taking up smoking while I'm here so I'll have something to do with my hands instead of picking things up like the ashtray or playing with my hair."

"Do you feel there's something wrong with picking things up, playing with your hair?"

Joan glances at the ashtray on the table. "I know, but I can become so nervous, and I know I look crazy to be always fidgeting and moving. At least smoking is a socially acceptable nervous habit."

"Do you think you look crazy?"

"Do you think I do?"

"What does a crazy person look like?"

Joan shakes her head, annoyed, embarrassed. "I really don't think I look crazy like a mental patient. Sometimes I don't even know why I'm here. I'm just a little lonely, that's all. Lots of people in the city are lonely. Now that I've had another good date with this man, I feel better about things, am reading more, have done some more paintings, although I still don't like any of them. I'm not nearly as concerned with the divorce. Isn't that an indication I'm doing better?"

Pam nods. "That's true. But at the same time you tell me you've begun thinking about jumping out a window. Why is that, do you think, if things are better?"

Joan clenches her jaw. "I didn't say I was actually going to do it. Jump out a window. This—I can't—" She waves a hand in the air, dismissing her doctor. "I'm not as depressed anymore. I feel good today, so why do we have to ruin that? Why can't I enjoy the one day I feel good?"

Pam watches Joan shifting in the chair, hands gripping the chair's arms tight. Joan Dwyer is falling apart, veering between feeling euphoric and depressed. "I'm not saying you shouldn't enjoy it. I just think we should talk about it realistically in terms of how it fits in with your depressed state." When faced with denial, Pam wishes she could videotape her patients, then later play it back for them, let them witness their own behaviors and come to terms with the seriousness of their problems.

Joan works at remaining calm, not getting angry. "I am doing what I can to make myself better. That's what I came here for, and that's what I'm doing.''

Pam catches her patient's eye, holding her attention. ''I agree with you, you do seem more interested in things than in the past, and I am glad you're feeling better today. There are other things that do concern me still. Would you like to hear what they are? What I think we need to be thinking about?''

Joan turns her head away, breaking the moment. ''No. Not really. Not if you're going to be upsetting me. I'm not going to have you make me cry here again. I don't like what you make me feel when I'm here. All this anger and hate, and I'm always sad. I feel all these things, and it's getting to be I'm afraid to be alone because when these feelings come up when I'm not here, they have nowhere to go, and I can't handle it anymore. When I focus on this man—I have this man—'' Joan stops, takes a breath, feels herself shaking, her hands and arms trembling. ''I shouldn't be in therapy. Maybe I'm too weak to take it.'' Joan stands. ''I think I should go home now.''

Pam remains seated, composed and sure. ''I think you ought to stay. We have several more minutes. If you don't care to talk, we can just sit.''

Joan stands in the center of the room, still and silent, staring out the window at a pigeon resting on the air conditioner's ledge. The pigeon sits, its dark gray head turning left and right and left and right, and the bird spreads its wings and takes off.

''Our time is about up,'' Pam says, taking her prescription pad off the table at her side, writing out Joan's Xanax prescription and then another for Tofranil. Saving Joan Dwyer, focusing Joan Dwyer on understanding herself, being there for Joan Dwyer to lean on when she can't support herself. Pam stands, handing the two slips of paper to her patient. ''I think it might be a good idea for me to call you later tonight at a set time to check in with you. How does that sound?'' The more Joan Dwyer observes her doctor valuing her patient, the more the patient may eventually value herself.

Joan opens her purse, puts the prescriptions away, and snaps the purse shut. "If you think so. It's up to you if you think it's a good idea."

"Is nine good?"

"Nine's fine. I'm going to go now," Joan announces, and she gathers her coat off the couch and is out the door.

Libby Barton laughs shrilly, slapping her thigh. "And so he said he wanted the actress to open the box for this yeast infection medication in front of this luncheon of ladies and sing—guess what song he wanted her to sing?"

Pam hates this woman, Libby Barton, Dennis's former boss from BMA, the agency he worked for before going freelance, and Libby is one of the reasons Pam was so glad when Dennis left BMA's employ: no more dinners with Libby Barton. Late this afternoon, however, Libby Barton phoned Dennis, insisting they meet for dinner, and as Dennis and Pam already had arrangements, he invited Libby along.

Dennis takes a large swallow of the scotch, detects the strain in Pam's smile, and reaches under the table with a hand, giving her leg a light squeeze. Their eyes meet. Pam smiles harder. "What song was it?" she asks, playing along, the good wife. Libby Barton is an ugly, garish woman—makes herself look like a man, dressing in a charcoal gray flannel suit with pants, not a skirt, white oxford shirt, and red and blue striped necktie. Short hair, too. A crew cut. Pam has always wanted to know if she's a lesbian. Dennis doesn't think so.

Libby rolls her head to Dennis, then to Pam, then back to Dennis, leaning into the table. " 'I Will Survive'—you know that disco song Gloria Gaynor sang? The actress is supposed to run around with this box of yeast infection medication singing this song, and soon all the ladies at the luncheon are supposed to be singing the chorus of this song." Libby spins her head. "Where's our waiter"—then to Dennis and Pam—"Sambucas each for all of us and dessert. How's that? Then my news."

"That sounds fine," Dennis replies, and Pam looks at her watch.

Eight-thirty. "Actually, I have to go. I have a patient I'm due to call at nine."

"Can't you call from here?" Libby asks.

"No, I really have to do this from home."

"I had some news to tell Dennis, and I was glad you were along too." Libby looks around the restaurant, can't see the waiter anywhere. "Maybe it's better if I tell Dennis alone anyway. It's business, so it's better we discuss it alone."

"Dessert menus?" the waiter asks.

"Two, please. Him and me," Libby clips, and the waiter places a menu in front of Dennis and hands one to Libby.

Pam remains seated. "What news? I can spare five minutes."

"Well, we're about to pitch this new fast-food seafood account," Libby informs Dennis. "Needing a new senior director on staff to handle this, I thought you might be our fellow. Responsible for all print media. That's why I'm here. I'm in a jam to get someone here I can trust. You could come in slow, part-time, increasing your hours during the next month or so. We don't have to begin showing anything for a few weeks. If we win the account, it'll be full-time by April. Two months till we'd need you on staff permanent. With your background in cartooning, I just thought you'd be ideal to develop this, and if it works out, after a while I'd be able to get you over to the video side, possibly."

Not sure if he's horrified or delighted—an enticing offer but for having to work with Libby again, being under her control—Dennis looks to Pam for her reaction. Her face is blank. She awaits his response.

"What do you think?" Dennis asks her.

Libby studies her. "I think you have to decide that for yourself. I certainly can't," Pam replies. She thought he went freelance to escape working with Libby Barton, to escape working on one sole account. Pam searches their faces, Dennis's and Libby's, trying to read if he had prior knowledge of Libby's offer before dinner. Perhaps Libby told Dennis what she'd be asking earlier, and he then orchestrated this dinner event as a way to break the news to his wife, he too afraid to tell Pam directly that he'd like to go back to agency work so he's having his former and future boss do it for him, fearing his wife will think him a failure for not remaining as independent as she is. Pam stands, gathers her purse from under her seat. "I wish I didn't have to go. Libby's right. You two should talk this out without me here." She leans over and kisses Dennis's cheek. She shakes Libby's hand.

"Say hello to your patient," Libby jests.

"Will do." Pam smiles. "Good-bye."

Dennis watches his wife leave. How angry is she? Does she have a patient to phone, or is she bluffing to get away from Libby? To get away from her husband?

"Is your wife a good psychiatrist?" Libby asks, lighting a cigarette. "I'm trying to find someone to talk to my mother. Someone to convince her she belongs in a home, you know? Without asking too many questions and really doing therapy. Does Pam do stuff like that?"

Eight forty-four P.M. The phone sits on Pam's lap, on her bare thighs where the oversize oxford shirt doesn't cover. The door to the guest bedroom is closed in case Dennis arrives home shortly, drunk from alcohol, celebrating his new opportunity. As far as Pam is concerned, if he wants to go back, he should. The position sounds good, Pam admits, and she will tell Dennis that upon his return; she may even convince him to phone Libby at home tonight and take the offer if that's the vote of confidence he needs from his wife. Pam just hates the thought of him working for such a crass woman. There is Libby Barton and there is Joan Dwyer, and Pam hopes Dr. Pamela Thompson falls closer to Joan Dwyer on this spectrum of femininity than to Libby Barton. She knows she does physically. The emotional side is what Pam wonders about; she knows she may not be a mother like Joan Dwyer, but she does nurture others and help them grow, whereas the only thing Pam can imagine Libby Barton's nurturing is her ego. Libby Barton asking Dennis to return to BMA, making him an offer he can't refuse: a fish account. Pam finds it so sad, she wants to love and protect her husband all the more.

Nine o'clock. The phone is on her lap, and Pam blocks out thoughts of Dennis and Libby Barton, concentrating on Joan Dwyer and her specific needs. Dr. Thompson volunteering to phone Joan Dwyer, showing Joan that her doctor will be there for her when she needs her, that if Joan cannot phone her doctor, her doctor will extend herself to Joan first, and then sometime in the future Joan will be able to phone her doctor of her own will—*there* for Joan, despite all Joan may say or do to make it sound as if she doesn't care whether Pam is there for her or not.

Pam looks up Joan's number in her patient phone book and dials. The phone is answered on one ring, as if Joan had been waiting for it, had planned her entire evening around it.

"Hello?" Joan says.

"Hello, Joan. It's Dr. Thompson. I wanted to call and see how you were doing tonight."

"Well, I'm doing fine."

"You know you can always call and leave a message if you need to."

"Of course. Thank you."

"Good. And we'll meet on Friday as usual."

"Right. Thank you for calling. I'm going to go to bed now. Good night."

"Good night, Joan."

Joan hangs up and is immediately struck with a sinking feeling, a draining, didn't realize before how much she was looking forward to this call, this touch with someone who cares or at least feigns compassion. Joan wasn't aware of how much the phone call meant to her until the phone call passed and she made no use of it, expressed none of all that she's been feeling since therapy, and Joan considers calling Dr. Thompson back but knows she won't. *I'm doing fine,* she said, and now she's stuck with those words. Stuck with "being fine" in Dr. Thompson's mind, giving Dr. Thompson permission to forget about Joan Dwyer until she sees her late in the afternoon on Friday.

Joan sat at the kitchen table for forty minutes, eating a loaf of Entenmann's fat-free pound cake from the rectangular aluminum tray with a salad fork, preparing herself for when the phone rang with Dr. Thompson's call, half fearing, half hoping Dennis might phone before Dr. Thompson called, thereby making her line busy for when her doctor did call. Dennis didn't call, though. The line wasn't busy, and she spoke to Dr. Thompson. A conversation that lasted no longer than one minute, and now that the centerpiece of her evening has passed, the calm eye of the hurricane Joan thinks of as her life has blown by, she ponders her next move. She peers down at the pound cake, three quarters gone, one quarter remaining. Fat-free, so she can eat some more, and Joan picks the fork and tin up. TV time.

The television is turned on in the family room, and the screen is filled with images of murderers, druglords, pimps, prostitutes, parents with smiles, children with smiles, wisecracking parents, wisecracking children, bruised children, burned children, headless corpses, music-video violence, music-video sex, twenty-four hours of live and real true-life news violence and sex and politics, gold necklaces, copper-bottom pots and pans, silver bangles, silk dresses, food storage sealers, VCRs, insect repellents, all of which can be bought from the safety and comfort of her own home, her own family room, public access TV with dimly lit, poorly sounding talk shows and loud leased access sex shows, 970-COCK, 970-BANG, 970-FUCK, 970-LOVE, one dollar a minute, thirty-minute minimum, and Joan scans through the many channels of programming, coming up dry and finally settling on a public access show. A psychic taking calls, answering questions: "I see a summer of love."

TV is my very best friend, Regine Pointer exclaimed. To Joan, TV is

an activity she uses to fill up the empty spaces in her life. The more
TV she finds herself watching, the more depressed she realizes she has
become. The empty spaces filled with Samantha, Sabrina, Gomer,
Jeannie, Lucy, Edith and Archie, Roseanne and Mary and Shirley and
Bob. More equals less. TV equals depression, and Joan turns off the
television, tossing the empty pound cake container in the kitchen
trash, placing the fork in the dishwasher's silverware rack. Dennis, a
real person in her life, hasn't phoned, didn't phone, won't phone,
will never phone, and if she applied her energy to therapy as dili-
gently as she applies it to Dennis, investing in the positive, not
the negative, emotionally, Joan knows, she'd be a much stronger
woman, less susceptible to collapse when a man displays a remote
interest in her.

Joan walks through the living room, down the hall, through her
bedroom and into the bathroom, sliding open the large mirrored
medicine cabinet. She eyes the line of prescriptions and over-the-
counter medications along one shelf. Prescribed by Dr. Thompson.
When the pills failed to deliver results or Joan found the side effects
too upsetting, Dr. Thompson prescribed new drugs, never realizing
her patient was still taking the old prescriptions into several pharma-
cies in the neighborhood and having them refilled as many times as
was allowed, stockpiling, hoarding the pills.

She takes a Halcion—something to make her sleepy, sleep filling
up the other empty spaces in her life.

6

"Who?" Dennis asks the doorman, speaking into the intercom box by the apartment door.

"Sarah Chaplin," the doorman repeats. "Shall I send her up?"

"Can you hold on one second?" Dennis walks into the bedroom, where Pam lies under the covers reading a newsmagazine.

"What was it?" she asks.

"Do you know a Sarah Chaplin? She's downstairs and—"

Pam is up and out of bed, yanking on her bathrobe, rushing past Dennis, straight for the intercom. She pushes "speak." "Can you put Ms. Chaplin on the phone, please?"

Dennis stands watching his wife.

"Sarah?" Pam asks, and then Pam is silent, listening, then: "Come on right up." Pam turns to her husband, stern. "Okay, now, I guess I'll have to use the guest room. This is a patient, and I'd rather you

stayed in the bedroom doing something quiet. Obviously she's having
an emergency, and now I have to go check the guest room, make sure
it's set up all right.'' Pam passes into the guest room, calls out the
door, ''I'll answer when she knocks. You go into the bedroom,
please, now.'' Pam looks over the bed, straightens its cover, and
thinks to get a chair for herself to sit on. It would be rather awkward,
both of them sitting on the bed, and she walks into the kitchen, taking
a chair from the table and dragging it across the hall, placing it by the
nightstand at the head of the bed. Dennis watches Pam's transformation—is it a transformation?—from wife to doctor. There is
some slight shift, but it's not so dramatic that it's altogether
observable. Maybe, after all, she is the same with him as she is with
them, her patients.

   ''The bedroom, please.'' And Pam turns, walking toward the
apartment door.

   Dennis follows after her. ''How did she find out where we live?
You told her? You tell your patients where we live so they can visit us
here?''

   Pam turns on him. ''She lives on the corner. We run into each
other occasionally at the market. She's probably seen me come in and
out of the building dozens of times. Can you go to the bedroom now,
please?''

   Dennis retreats to the bedroom, shutting the door and climbing
into bed as he was instructed. He hears murmurs, the sound of a
woman, Sarah Chaplin, sobbing in the hall. A bit more talking, then
the sound of the guest bedroom door closing.

   Dennis apprizes himself of the situation, thinks about what he's
going to do now that he's been sequestered in the bedroom. The time
is eight thirty-seven, too early for bed. Pam convinced him to take
the job last night; he was glad he had her blessing, was afraid she'd be
the one in need of convincing. He phoned Libby, and they met for a
congratulatory lunch. The background materials Libby gave Dennis
on the seafood chain—Moby—remain on the couch in the living

room, where he'd been lying when the doorman buzzed up. Dennis can't get in there without opening the door and walking down the hall, making his presence known, possibly distracting Pam's patient. If he turns on the television, they'll hear it through the walls.

"The power a therapist holds over a patient is immense," Pam has instructed Dennis on many occasions, when boasting about the success she's had with a patient, when preaching about the sanctity of the doctor-patient relationship. "A therapist can unconsciously will her patient to get better or worse. Very subtly the patient will pick up on these cues just as newborn infants pick up on the very subtle cues their primary caregivers pass along. A patient, vulnerable and trusting in her doctor, often looks to the doctor less for guidance than to have feelings validated and explored. When a patient exposes herself honestly and vulnerably, a doctor must show great care to acknowledge the vulnerability of the patient's position. At these most vulnerable moments, the doctor must be careful not to judge the patient but to ask the patient the correct questions in the correct tone of voice so that the patient can be open yet feel safe and secure. All it can take to lose a patient is a shift of the eyes to make the patient feel you don't care, make her feel dirty or bad for committing some deed. It takes great strength to bare one's soul to another, and a patient who trusts her doctor enough to do this is putting her self-worth— her entire life—in her doctor's hands with the hope that after she has been so open, her doctor and she can work on making her life make more sense by understanding these behaviors. It's scary, but the rewards are immense if the doctor can remain focused upon the needs of the patient rather than fixated on her own desires for how she may or may not wish the therapy to progress."

The lectures Dr. Thompson has inflicted upon her husband sit cold in his mind, lectures dictated over the laugh tracks of sitcoms and gunfire of detective shows, Pam stacking her life up against her husband's, not so subtly letting Dennis know that lives hang in the balance, depending upon the course of action she takes in therapy with patients, whereas the most important thing Dennis may decide during the course of a day is the placement of a tomato in an advertisement for a jar of spaghetti sauce.

A loud sob, a cry from the next room, and Dennis stands, walks to the bathroom, takes up a water glass, wondering if this really helps: to listen through a glass at the wall as he's seen on TV shows. He wants to hear his wife at work, listen to how carefully she conducts herself with a patient, and he walks to the bed, leaning over the headboard, pressing the open end of the glass against the wall. He isn't sure how well the glass will amplify their voices; he could probably hear well enough without it if he listened carefully. Maybe it will work, maybe it won't—an experiment, Dennis is thinking, and he leans into the glass, ear pressed flat against its bottom.

Pam opens the bedroom door, leans her head in. "You can come out. She's gone."

Dennis gets out of bed, walks around it, meeting Pam at the door. "She doing better?"

Pam enters the kitchen, and Dennis follows. Four chairs, Dennis notes, the kitchen chair back around the table, no longer in the guest room.

"No. Won't be for some time, I'd say," Pam says. She opens the refrigerator, takes out a bottle of seltzer water. She's in the process of swinging the door shut when Dennis reaches out, grabbing its handle, drawing a beer off one of the door's shelves.

"How do you feel about her coming here?" Dennis asks. He swings the refrigerator door shut.

Pam takes two octagon-shaped glasses from a cabinet, placing them both on the table and sitting. "Join me."

Dennis sits. "So?"

"How do *you* feel about it?" Pam asks.

"I asked you first." Dennis takes the offered glass, then reconsiders and swigs directly from the beer bottle. Pam pours the seltzer into the glass, bubbles splashing over its side, dotting the table.

"Can't you just answer me?" Pam asks good-naturedly.

"Can't *you* answer *me?*" Dennis counters.

"Does it matter?"

"I asked first."

Pam sips, bubbles coating the roof of her mouth, tickling her tongue. She smiles. "Okay, then. I was fine about it. She did what she had to do to get help. I admire that. Her coming here was warranted."

Dennis, already halfway through the beer, picks up the bottle, downs another quarter.

"And you?" Pam asks.

"It surprised me." Nothing more to add, afraid of letting on that he listened to the whole conversation, heard the entire story of Sarah Chaplin's predicament. Dennis examines the bottle's label, reading its every word. Sarah Chaplin's teenage daughter killed in a car accident and her husband away on business in Taiwan, unable to get home for another day and a half. Sarah Chaplin is going to be alone for the next thirty-six to forty-eight hours. Alone and calling relatives and making funeral arrangements. Sarah Chaplin, afraid to pick up the phone and inform friends and relatives of what has happened, as if through saying it aloud she will have made what has already happened come to happen, somehow making it more true by spreading the bad news. Dennis finishes the beer and goes to the refrigerator, taking out a second while placing the empty on the counter by the sink. He twists off the cap, hoists himself up on the counter, back against the cabinets, side against the fridge, and drinks.

"That's all there is to it, then?" Pam asks, knows Dennis must be irritated with her for interrupting his work, exiling him to the bedroom, making him play second to a patient in their very own home, using the guest room, the room he wants to raise a child in, as an office, a room Pam couldn't have brought Sarah Chaplin into for counseling had she and Dennis had a child. Pam just wants Dennis to admit he's feeling what he's feeling.

"*What?*" Dennis asks innocently. "You did what you had to do. Isn't that all there is to it?"

"You don't have to like it, though." Pam has moved her chair around so she won't have to twist her head to face him.

"Why are you starting to argue with me over this?"

"You're not being honest. I know you're not. First you accuse me of giving patients our address, and now you haven't even asked why she came over. I can't imagine you're not curious." Pam pours herself a second glass of seltzer, feels a dry scratchiness in her throat, immediately thinks they should purchase a large humidifier for the entire apartment instead of just having the small appliance in the bedroom.

Dennis grins, downing more of the beer, waiting for the first wave of alcohol to wash over him. He should be drinking scotch so it will happen sooner and stronger. "I know you can't answer if I do ask, so why bother?"

"In a situation where someone comes here to our own home and interrupts my time with you, intruding upon our life, I think you have a right to know why." She means this sincerely, thinks it to be true although she does not want to share Sarah Chaplin's or any of her other patients' lives with Dennis and hopes he won't ask now that she's set him up to it.

"Why did she come over, then?" Dennis asks, a test.

"Are you asking because I'm letting you or because you're curious or maybe concerned?"

"I'll take all of those." The second beer is gone, and he wants a third but is sure Pam would comment on it. He decides to wait until their talk is over.

"Are you getting drunk?" she asks, not taking to Dennis's amused, light, jokey tone.

"Someone's being a bit evasive."

"I don't want to discuss this if you're getting drunk. I could use some support. This wasn't easy on me either."

Dennis plants the second empty by the first, kicks the refrigerator door open with a foot, leans over, and takes out a third bottle. He hooks his toes around the door's handle, dragging it shut. A monkey, a baboon. Pam watches his display with controlled irritation, knows this show is for her benefit, his way of getting back at her—getting drunk, dumb, and louselike, getting drunk because he knows how much she hates him drunk. Dennis, so totally, passive-aggressively avoiding his feelings.

Dennis holds the bottle between his two hands, palms flat, rolling it back and forth. "You tell me, I'll listen, and *then* I'll get drunk."

"You don't care. It's all just a joke. I support you in your career decision, and you can't handle a little intrusion." Pam stands, takes up the seltzer bottle, and heads to the refrigerator.

Dennis sticks out a leg, blocking her from opening the door. "I do want to know, so tell me."

Pam reaches for the handle, grabs hold of it, and tugs. "Aren't you mature."

Dennis kicks the door shut. "You weren't going to tell me anyway, and you know it."

Pam brings her arms back by her sides. "I would have if you'd been understanding. You can't seem to be the least bit compassionate."

Dennis looks at his wife standing there before him, and he drops his leg back by the counter, allowing Pam access to the refrigerator. He opens the third beer and downs half the bottle in one large swallow. "Keep your secrets," he says.

Pam puts the seltzer bottle away, examining Dennis as he guzzles the beer. He reminds her of some stereotypical blue-collar factory worker coming home and harassing his wife in the kitchen to assure himself that he's a real man with a real dick. "That's my job."

"Not even telling me."

"Not even you. Nope. Sorry." She looks him over, is sure he is testing her, trying to see how loyal she is to her patients and by that same measure how loyal she is to him. "I don't know what you're driving at tonight, but I'm tired, you're being an asshole, and I'm going to bed." Pam turns, walks from the kitchen, enters the bedroom, and shuts the door.

Several minutes and one Halcion later, as she's drifting off to a sound sleep, Pam hears the bolt of a door being thrown open, a door closing, and then the relocking of the bolt.

He sits in the living room of Joan Dwyer's apartment while Joan fetches ice from the kitchen. Dennis phoned Joan from his office while finishing off a second scotch and soda, watching a detective show on TV. Wanting someone to be with, to talk to who could be caring, someone he could be vulnerable with without losing his pride, he thought of Joan.

Joan walks into the living room hugging a brass bucket of ice to her stomach. She wears her velvet bathrobe, Dennis's call interrupting her just before she was to lie down to sleep. She sets the ice bucket on the coffee table and goes to the bar, slippers softly padding across the Oriental carpet. "You like scotch and soda, right?"

He sits, facing the window, staring out at the flurries of snow in the air, blowing and drifting, amounting to nothing. "That's right. You having anything?"

Joan arranges bottles and glasses on the tray. "I'll have some wine." She lifts the tray, tensing her arms and carrying it to the coffee table, placing it by the bucket. She sits alongside Dennis, her man home, placing ice in the short glass, pouring scotch, then soda. She drops one ice cube in the wide, bowllike wineglass and pours white wine from the half-empty bottle kept chilled in the refrigerator.

Dennis stares longingly at the drink, knows he shouldn't drink more, already a bit drunk, but he reaches down, lifts the glass, and drinks. He smiles, eyes widening. "You're a very nice lady." He yawns.

She knows he's drunk and she pulls him toward her, leaning his head gently against her shoulder, brushing his hair back from his face, gently touching fingertips to his forehead, smoothing eyebrows. Dennis shuts his eyes, sets his drink on the table, relaxing into the feel of her hand brushing his skin, grazing his lips.

She knows he's there. There and passive-aggressively angry. "I know you're there," Pam calmly calls into the phone, speaking into the answering machine. "You might as well pick up, so we can talk out whatever it is that's bothering you." She waits, waits for him to pick up. Dennis running off for a night all because Sarah Chaplin paid a visit to their home and his wife accused him of getting drunk, his way of getting back at her. Dennis overdramatizing the situation, running out on his wife and sleeping over at his office. The first time he's taken this route away from a confrontation, and Pam is sure he expects her to rush over to his office before going to her own, begging him for forgiveness. But Pam will have no part of it: talking this out—whatever *this* is—at his office. Following him to his office would only serve to reinforce his running-away behavior, and before Pam knew it, Dennis would be taking off on her every time he felt he needed a little special attention.

"I know you're there," Pam repeats into the machine, and she waits, and then the phone machine beeps, automatically disconnecting her. She hears a dial tone.

Eyes open on a wall of deep green curtains, lit from behind by the sun. Dennis lifts his head, rubbing his eyes, looking about, remembering back through the haze of the previous evening. An argument with his wife, drinks, and comfort from another woman. A down comforter is drawn over him. A pillow rests behind his head. He hears the static whir of an electric coffee grinder in the kitchen.

Dennis pulls his rumpled sweatshirt down over his stomach and straightens the pushed-up leg of his rumpled jeans. He sits, feet touching ground and sinking into the soft carpet. He pulls on his socks, then sneakers, listening to more kitchen sounds. Drawers opening on casters, cabinets closing, a plate clattering against a countertop.

Joan, dressed in a long purple bathrobe, hair up, sits at the kitchen table, and Dennis has a vision of her from last night as if this is how she greeted him then, but he isn't sure, can't pull the memory into focus so lets it slide. "Hello. Good morning," he says, his voice scratchy, contemplates walking over and kissing Joan but thinks not, too intimate and scary.

Joan stands, going to the stove. "There's coffee here. I thought about making something for breakfast but had no idea what you'd like." She shrugs.

"Coffee's good. Black. I don't need anything to eat." Dennis sits at the table, and Joan hands him a mug of coffee.

She sits, takes a bottle of aspirin from her robe's pocket. "You need any?"

He nods. "Sorry about last night." He has no idea what he may or may not have done or tried.

"That's all right," Joan responds. She aligns arrows and pries the cap off, shaking out four regular-strength tablets. "I liked having you over. It made the night go faster." She lays her hand out, palm open, and he takes the pills, his fingertips touching her skin.

"You didn't sleep?" he asks.

She stands, getting him a glass, filling it with water from a bottle on the counter. "I watched you sleep. I wasn't tired. I'll take a nap later." She sits, hands him the water, which he sips, swallowing the aspirin. Sitting alongside Joan, this light talk, the apartment so still, so quiet, feels more intimate, more loving than making love, having sex. Dennis can't remember any weekday morning when Pam and he have sat down together and talked. They both get up at different hours with no words exchanged except over answering machines later in the day, no face-to-face conversations until evening. He wonders what Pam's up to and glances at the kitchen clock. Seven thirty-eight. She's probably on her way crosstown, standing, hanging on to a bar on the crosstown bus. He wonders whether she'll stop by his office, looking for him there, thinking he slept there, and if she does, Dennis can just explain that he was on his way home to their apartment to meet her while she was at his office to meet him.

"Are you feeling okay?" Joan asks.

Dennis reaches out, taking her hand, squeezing it in his own. "I'm fine. But I should leave soon. I have to get ready for work." Then, taking the pressure off his departure: "And you should sleep after taking care of drunk me all night."

Joan rubs her thumb across the back of his hand, can't remember the last time she's held a man's hand in the morning at a kitchen table, can't remember if she ever did with Al but knows she must have in all their years together. "You were good to me when I was upset the other night."

This is what people do for one another, people who are not his wife, not Pamela Thompson, and he leans across the table, drawing Joan close, kissing her. "Thanks for letting me come over. This morning is nice." He kisses her again, feeling her soft cheek against his face. He swallows the last of the coffee in the mug and stands.

Joan resists her urge to take his arm and hold on longer. She reaches a fingertip out, touching one of his knuckles.

"Hello?" he asks.

"Nothing," she says. "I don't know." She stands, taking the mug from the table, going to the sink, her back to him.

"I'm late," Dennis says. "I didn't get everything done last night I should have."

She feels dirty, as if she's been used, a one-night stand. She turns on the water, rinses the inside of the mug. "I'll walk you to the door." She shuts off the water, the mug left in the sink.

They walk, Dennis slightly behind Joan. He takes her elbow. "You didn't sleep at all?"

"How do you feel?"

"Good. I slept fine." They're by the closet, Joan handing Dennis his jacket. "I'll call you later," he says, casual.

"Later when?" Joan asks, scared of scaring him off but desperately needing to know.

Dennis pulls the door ajar. "This afternoon. How's that?" He kisses her on the mouth.

"We'll see each other again soon?"

Dennis thinks. Thursday. The night Pam teaches a seminar at a downtown university. "Is tonight soon enough?" he asks.

Joan blushes. "Tonight's fine," she answers. He's saved her.

March

1

The heels of her feet dig into the back of Dennis's thighs. Dennis wraps his arms around Joan, drawing her up, lifting her to his chest, and she sits on him, hands clinging to his shoulders, kissing his neck.

"Are you okay?" he whispers.

"Mmm-hmmm," biting her lip.

They lie in Dennis's bed this Sunday afternoon, Dennis holding Joan, folding her body into him. He searches her face to see how she is, how she's responding to him.

Sex progressed slowly, Dennis becoming a bit more daring, a bit more infatuated with Joan as weeks progressed. Light kissing to heavy kissing to light, over-the-clothes petting to heavy, half-undressed petting to total disrobement with no intercourse to intercourse. Like teenagers doing it for the first time, Dennis relaxed Joan into sex, getting her to trust him; she had not been with a man in years and was terrified of not knowing what to do, of failing. Making love with Joan is making love to an innocent, an intricate, delicate balancing, a sharing of a sort he isn't accustomed to with Pam.

Joan spreads her legs wider, knees by Dennis's waist. He thrusts deep, slow and deep, and she lifts herself to meet him, hands clasping his arms. He pulls himself out, then pushes in, harder, more desperate.

With Pam, sex (and it is not *making love,* of that Dennis is sure) is an aggressive, selfish act, a *taking from* rather than a *giving to* and *doing for.* To need and be loved by someone whom he loves and needs, to be comforted, supported, and cared for rather than disputed, humiliated, and challenged: the screaming differences between Joan and his wife. Joan needs him to feel complete, as if a half of her were missing when he is not there. He steps off the elevator, and she stands in the doorway, thankful, relieved to be seeing him again. They embrace, and he can feel her shaking, trembling as if she's been dead and his kiss has brought her back to life. Sleeping Beauty and the Prince. In contrast, Pam is more than complete without him, his presence being nothing more than an accessory to her life, his import to her equal to that of a watch, a bracelet, a handbag. An object she wouldn't want to lose but could do without and replace after a short, manageable amount of sentimental suffering. In the past month or so, on any given evening as he's stepped into their apartment after a late night working on the fish presentation with Libby and the BMA staff, he's lucky if she so much as looks up from her journals. She's either reading and won't be interrupted or is in the *guest* room—her name for the room, they haven't had any guests in there for years—on the phone with one or another of her patients, saving the emotionally needy outside their apartment, neglecting and having disdain for her husband, who only wants to love her and be loved.

Dennis grunts. Joan moans, toes curling.

Pam shops for a new kitchen table this afternoon while her

husband grips another woman's thighs, thrusting hard. As Joan comes, he comes.

"You're not going with me? I thought you wanted us to do this together. Don't accuse me of not asking for your opinion if you're not willing to come and offer advice." Pam shook her head at Dennis, amused, not angry, with her husband's increasingly apparent lack of interest in the redecoration scheme.

"I was going to go over and finish up the last of my freelance work. Since it looks like we're going to get it, I just wanted to have that all set so I can begin at BMA full-time at the end of the month."

Pam buttoned up her coat, checking pockets for keys, wallet, and sunglasses. "I thought we'd do this together." She seemed genuinely saddened, and Dennis was touched.

Joan had been waiting for Dennis's call. Waiting for Dennis's calls being her primary occupation other than cleaning the apartment, reading, painting, seeing her therapist, and actually *being with* Dennis. However, *waiting for* his calls takes up the bulk of Joan's time as the hours between their meetings—whether she's cleaning, reading, painting, or seeing her therapist—are spent wondering when or *if* she will hear from Dennis again.

Joan canceled—actually never even bothered to arrange—brunch plans with Todd for this Sunday afternoon. On Saturday morning Dennis phoned, saying, "Can we make tentative plans for tomorrow?" And Joan immediately phoned Todd. "I'm sorry, honey. I can't make it tomorrow. *Plans,*" she stressed happily.

"I'll see you next week, then," Todd answered, trying hard not to sound relieved. "What are you up to?" Couldn't imagine his mother actually having plans, engagements.

"Nothing special. Miss Pointer asked me to help her out with something since Brooke has the day off. Little plans, that's all." Joan played it down, didn't want to let her son know about this man until she was certain it was going to work out.

The Pattern. Dennis phones, explains that he decided not to work

so come on over or *I'll come over there* or *let's go to a movie or an early
dinner* on a Tuesday or Thursday night, never a Sunday, Monday,
Wednesday, Friday, or Saturday night—on those days, only afternoons. And after making love, they lie in bed, holding each other
tight, and Why this awkward schedule? is on Joan's mind. What fills
the other nights, every hour around the time they spend together?
What other people fill out his life? Joan can only guess, can never ask,
and doesn't want to know. Afternoons and early evenings and
midmornings and late evenings and early mornings and late
afternoons, she phones Dennis, listening to his voice on the
answering machine, satisfying herself with listening to his voice, then
hanging up, no message left. Denying her suspicions, enjoying the
satisfaction of hearing his voice, however recorded.

Dennis rolls to the side, pulling Joan to him, feeling her heart
pounding through her chest against his body. Her head is held by his
neck, her jaw resting on his collarbone. She kisses his skin, his sweat
on her lips, her eyes open and staring across the room at the open
closet, the pile of disarranged shoes and sneakers on the floor, the
clothes hung, some with the hanger hooks facing in, some facing out,
Dennis having to twist them around when getting the clothes off the
rack. She tilts her head an inch and bats her eyelashes at his Adam's
apple.

He cups her chin in a palm, stopping her. "Tickles," he whispers.

She can smell herself on his fingers. I love you, she wants to say,
can't say. He knows, must know she feels this, but she wants
to—needs to—say it for herself, an admission. "I love you," she
says, speaking to his chest, a murmur, eyes still on the closet. She
rubs her hand over his body, his body hair bristling against her palm.
Television sounds come from upstairs. The cheers of a sporting
event. "I love you," she says again, more confident.

Dennis lowers his eyes from the ceiling to the top of Joan's head,
the crown of her dark hair. He hears himself say it to her—"I love
you"—feeling he means it, no longer altogether sure what loving
someone should feel like. He does love Pam. He thinks he loves Joan.

.   .   .

"I ought to return home," Joan says. The time is three-thirty, and she would rather volunteer a departure than wait and be asked to leave.

"Do you have to?" Dennis asks politely, playing along, glad he doesn't have to ask her to go, make this situation any more difficult and complicated than it has become.

"I have grocery shopping." She's already out of bed, lifting her blouse from the back of a chair, has altogether stopped wearing bras when she's dressing to meet Dennis.

"Should I get up or can you let yourself out?" The sheet is tangled around his hip, caught between his legs. Dennis watches as Joan pulls up her slip, then skirt.

She sits on the bed, leaning against his leg, picking her shoes off the floor and slipping them on her feet. "I can let myself out. I'm a big girl."

He touches her neck, pulling at her, rolling on his back and dragging her atop him. She laughs, off-balance, a leg in the air. "Oh, my God!" Her shoe flips off, falling between them, the short heel poking her in the side.

Dennis laughs and bites her gently on a calf. Her hands run down his bare sides as his hands go up and under her blouse, rubbing her nipples, feeling them grow firm, before he stops and pulls himself out from beneath her. "No. We shouldn't get started again. I have to catch up on work all evening." He kisses her wrist, her arm. Time to think about getting home to the apartment, to Pam.

Joan sits, finds the shoe that fell off under the bedsheet. "We better not," she agrees. She was ready to leave, but then he embraced her, and now he's done and is sending her off. This isn't the way she likes it to end, but it has.

Dennis sprawls across the pale blue sheets, holding her waist. "Thank you for coming over."

Joan leans over, kissing his cheek, his too-satisfied grin. A whore, his tramp. "Call me. Call me soon."

"I promise I will."

She turns, heading for the door. "Good-bye."

"I'll phone you later tonight. Okay?"

She's halfway down the hall. "If I'm out, leave a message," she says lamely, knows he knows she never goes out at night without him.

"Oh, I will," he says.

And Joan feels a wave of hatred wash over her—a wave of hatred not for him, but for herself—hating herself for so desperately needing and loving this man, this man who needs and loves her too but needs and loves her less.

Dennis stands in the shower stall, washing away sweat, sex, the smells of the afternoon. He steps onto the navy blue terry-cloth bath mat and dries himself with a matching navy blue bath towel. Bath mat and towels to make the office resemble an apartment. Dennis dries between his legs, tosses the towel over the shower door, and opens the large mirrored medicine chest, taking out deodorant. Since the day Joan Dwyer became an affair, the day Dennis pinpoints as the day he slept on her couch, Dennis has been stocking the office with apartmentlike props.

"Why don't you get rid of the office? You can use our spare room since you're barely there and always at BMA," Pam said last month.

Dennis, no longer sure what the state of his marriage was or completely sure BMA would receive the Moby account (the decision being between BMA and one other agency), said he'd decide the fate of the office once the new job was definite.

As Pam purchases new linens, dishes, and appliances for the apartment redecoration, Dennis takes the old goods, installing them in the office. "Just making it more comfortable for myself," he told Pam.

The towels, an extra set of sheets, an old AM-FM clock radio, the old bureau they'd been using to store off-season clothes, the small micro-wave Pam replaced with a larger microwave. To these, Dennis brought his own touches. To the two suits, two shirts, and pair of shoes he always kept in the office bedroom closet, Dennis added five more business shirts, three sports coats, four pairs of pants, three pairs of shoes, and one pair of sneakers. He stocked the storage bu-reau with boxer shorts, dress and tube socks, T-shirts, and an assort-ment of jerseys and sweaters from the Upper East Side apartment. Jerseys and sweaters he seldom wore, would never be missed by Pam, but would be missed by Joan had they not been at the office, letting her know this was also his home. But they, Dennis and Joan, seldom spend time at his office, Dennis preferring to meet at Joan's place for safety's sake lest Pam happen to phone or stop by unexpect-edly. And Joan prefers to have Dennis meet her at her apartment too because it makes her feel more lady- and less tramplike. To be visited and left by a man more comforting than to be a visitor and then leav-ing. With Dennis over, they eat dinner in the dining room, watch TV in the family room, and sleep in the bedroom. "I hope this isn't in-sulting, but I'd rather see you at my place. You're always pre-occupied with your work when you're at home and I'm not that comfortable there," she said after she met him at his place on a Tues-day night, as he walked her home after they'd slept together there for the first time.

"Not settled enough for you?" he teased. "Too much of a bache-lor pad?"

She took his arm, linking elbows. "You don't even have a kitchen table or a kitchen."

"I eat at my desk or in bed."

"And the television's so small and only in black and white. Not even in color or cable."

"I'll buy a new one."

"I'd rather you come over anyway. It doesn't matter."

"I wanted you to see where I live."

"I wanted to see it. I'm just saying I'm more comfortable in my own home."

Dennis laughed, kissed her good-bye in front of her doorman, then walked two blocks north and around a corner, and caught a cab crosstown to the Upper East Side.

Dennis dresses in the clothes he wore over from the apartment on the Upper East Side, enjoying this new life he has created, as proud of himself as he is ashamed. The new job with its long hours makes lying to both Pam and Joan easy; he's always making up meetings and presentations he has to run off to in order to meet one or the other of the women in his life, and for now, until he is forced to come to some decision, it all flows easily.

Dennis makes the bed, smoothing out the sheet and folding its lip over the upper edge of the comforter. He stands back, looking the room over. Everything neat and orderly, no trace of Joan. He strolls into the living room and picks up the phone.

"Hello," Pam says.

"You're back. I wasn't sure you would be."

"I forgot to grab a video yet, so I'm about to go out and do that. You want to watch anything special?"

"Whatever."

"Give me a suggestion."

"I don't care. Whatever you choose is fine." Dennis has to keep reminding himself not to be too helpful, helpful enough to make her happy, annoying enough to let her know he's still himself.

"You have no idea what you'd like?" Pam argues lightly.

"Just pick something out. It doesn't matter to me."

"I'll surprise you with something. You'll be home soon?"

"In half an hour."

"See you then."

"Bye. Love you." The words come out automatically. He's on automatic pilot with her.

"You too. Bye."

.   .   .

When Dennis kisses Pam hello as she sits on the couch, her feet on the coffee table, writing out her notes for Thursday's class lecture, he is struck by the notion of how evil he truly has become. The betrayer and the betrayed. He kisses her a second time.

Her eyes on the papers, her hands filled with a pen and textbook, "Another hour and we can talk about dinner."

She barely acknowledges his existence. "I'll take a nap, then. Call when you're ready." He waits for her to respond. She says nothing, and he is disappointed, still wanting her attention, jealous of her work, needing to know she loves him, that he matters to her. He receives no response, though, and he knows he should be relieved that she has no suspicions concerning his afternoon activities, but her ignoring him flares anxiety. He wants her to love him, need him, and when he turns before walking down the hall to the bedroom, he finds he desires her, wishes he could confide in his wife and explain his unhappiness and confusion so she can tell him that they can work it all out and make it better. He can love Joan only when he's in the mood for her kind of love, and once that is satisfied, he finds himself loving his wife. His love with his wife is more absolute and complex. He'd like to kneel before Pam right now, spread her legs, and press his face into her crotch, eating her out, paying a debt and enjoying it. Dennis enters the bedroom, shuts the door, undresses down to his boxers, and climbs into bed.

For all the reasons he fears, he does at times love Joan—because she is always on edge, unstable and surprising, sincere and vulnerable—he is sure she would be devastated if she found out he was married, blaming herself for not seeing this in her lover, for bringing this upon herself. For all the reasons he is frustrated with his wife—her manipulative, controlling, reserved behavior—Dennis is afraid Pam wouldn't care about the affair, would toss the whole thing off as his male menopause, intellectualizing the event, making him a dog acting on sexual instinct, turning his emotional involvement into a purely physical lust, refusing to acknowledge that the affair had its origins in their marriage.

"If I marry again, I'd have another child," Joan said while they lay in her bed on a Tuesday afternoon. "It's not so unusual as it used to be for a woman over forty." She leaned over his stomach, resting her head by his belly button, a hand held flat to the inside of his thigh.

He stroked her back, the back of her neck just below the hairline. "I can't even imagine being a father." The weight of her breasts pressed into his side.

"If you married someone, how could you not want a child with that person?"

"That's probably true."

Joan slid her hand farther up his body, the V of her thumb and forefinger circling his groin, working to arouse him.

"Don't, please." He shifted. She rolled off him, and Dennis sat up, back against the headboard. "Sorry, I just have a meeting to get to." He reached for the remote, and the TV came on. Dennis scanned the five o'clock news programs, then switched off the TV. "I'm going to take a shower." He was out of bed, in the bathroom, swinging the door shut.

Dennis turns on the bed lamp, taking the *TV Week* from the headboard, flipping through Sunday's lineup of shows. Would he have a child with her, would he marry her if it was a choice between the two, a choice he was forced to make? No, most surely not, but then, Dennis never thinks of it as a one-or-the-other situation but a two-for-one deal, the two women complementing each other, each filling in the spaces her counterpart misses. And although he isn't always pleased with their marriage, he can't imagine life without Pam whereas he can easily imagine leaving Joan, his being needed less important than his needing his wife.

·   ·   ·

Joan stands at the kitchen counter, a large, clear plastic freezer bag stretched taut between her hands, twisting the bag, trying to split it down its seams or poke a hole through it with a fingernail.

The bag doesn't break or split. It *gives*. It stretches a bit, but gives. She cannot tear it to shreds, and for that she is thankful.

Joan has a suicide plan for each room of her home. For each room, excluding the children's bedrooms and bathroom, she has devised a suicide plan. The plan for the dining room is only in its preliminary stages, but in the other rooms the plans have been strategized, perfected.

After shopping on her way back from Dennis's apartment, Joan phoned him, wanting to thank him for the afternoon. Three rings and the machine picked up. "Hello? Are you there working? It's Joan. I guess I'll talk to you later. Bye."

Supposedly in for the evening, and now, only a couple of hours later, he still hasn't returned her call. There exists Dennis and there exists suicide and there is no in between and if Joan fails to win Dennis over and persuade him to love her, never to leave her, Joan has decided that she will kill herself. "Why should I live with no pleasure in my life? This man is my pleasure, and without him, I'm miserable."

"Don't you think there might be another man out there who will give you pleasure? Don't you think one day you might find pleasure from being with yourself instead of looking to someone else to make your life worth living? Isn't that our goal?"

Joan straightened in the chair, fixing her gaze on Dr. Thompson. "We both know that's never going to happen. It took me three years to find this man, and I can't wait another three years like I did before. I can't live with this level of unhappiness for a year or two more until we work things out here and figure out why I am so depressed and then find some solution. I love him. He makes my life worthwhile, and I can't go back to the way it was. When I lose him, when he leaves me, I feel nothing, empty, like I no longer exist, just sitting up there in that apartment, cut off, staring down at the world miles away.''

Losing Dennis—and all that has to happen for Joan to lose Dennis is for him to be absent from her physically for a day or an hour or a minute—sends her spiraling deeper into the depression in which she obsesses about her suicide, preparing a plan for each room so that wherever and whenever the impulse strikes, she will have a plan within an arm's reach.

''In some ways I was better off before,'' Joan proclaimed in therapy. ''This man—this therapy—one minute I'm elated, and the next I'm depressed. One minute I'm excited about life, and the next I want to end it. I was never like this before. Before him and therapy, I was fine. Before, I could manage.''

''Could you?''

''I wasn't as depressed.''

''I don't agree. I think you were numb. Severely depressed and numb for years. Now that you're feeling things—both pleasurable and painful, feeling things you haven't felt for years—as we work through that, life becomes more intense. Depression is an illness you cling to for safety. In giving up some of that safety to feel the good in life, as a consequence, you have to feel the bad as well. With all you've held in for years, from your years as a child to your teens to your marriage with Al to the present, the bad feelings may overwhelm the good for a while until we sort them out. I understand it's hard. That's why I think we need to keep in contact and talk about what is on your mind beyond this man.''

''Maybe it wasn't better before,'' Joan conceded. ''It was easier,'' she clarified. ''He's there and then he's not and I can't say anything to him for fear then he'll really disappear for good. I'm trying to pull myself together. I've tried to take up these new interests, but I'm losing interest in them. Life doesn't interest me. I don't know how to keep myself excited about it. Death excites me. The thought of killing myself excites me. *That* I'm interested in,'' Joan said jovially.

''Why is that, do you think?''

Joan pondered the question. She had never asked herself why she wanted to kill herself, she'd so taken the feeling for granted. "I feel in control of my life when I consider it. Like I'm in charge of what I want to do with it. I have this purposeless life, all my life thrust upon me, and this is my way of seizing control. I have a real sense of power and control."

Joan folds the plastic bag in quarters, inserting it back into the oval opening of the Hefty box, placing the box back in the cupboard above the refrigerator: Joan's "Suicide Shelf" in the kitchen. Joan closes the cabinet, reassured that this plan will succeed, proud of herself for actually creating this plan from scratch like a Betty Crocker recipe. Shopping for items to carry out the procedure, modifying the plan as needed. Joan spent half an hour in the household goods aisle of the supermarket, comparing long, thin rectangular boxes of food storage bags, carefully reading their gallon capacities, width, height, and depth measurements. On all the major-brand labels (Joan was not going to go with the store-name brand, saving a few pennies for a possibly inferior product), the freezer bags were described as being the strongest of the plastic bags, and Joan purchased the largest capacity freezer bags by Glad, Hefty, and Ziploc. Farther down the aisle, hanging on a Peg-Board next to the toilet brushes, was a selection of ropes. Joan passed over the darker, coarser rope, fearing it might tear at the bag and form a hole that would allow in air. Instead she chose a soft white cotton rope clothesline, twelve feet in length.

Joan tested one bag each from the three sets of bags she'd bought. The Glad bag was too small and tight, only coming down to her chin, pressing her nose flat against the plastic. The Ziploc product, although large, was easily pierced by her fingernails. Joan knew she was bound to panic once her lungs began to hurt for lack of air, knew some inherent survival instinct was bound to take over and try to keep her living, and she wanted to beat that out with indestructible bags. The Hefty bags were large, dropping smoothly over her head, down to her collarbone with plenty of extra bag hanging below her chin to make for easy rope tying. The bags were thick, their inner

borders melted together and forming a one-half-inch-wide strip framing the bag's side, preventing its seams from splitting because there
really wasn't any seam but just one solid piece unto itself, not two
pieces stuck together. Joan could stretch and distort the bag's shape,
but she could not tear it, and so the other bags were relegated to the
cabinet with aluminum foil and plastic wrap while the Heftys were
placed with the rope and black nylon shopping bag on the Suicide
Shelf.

The kitchen plan: Insert four indestructible gallon-size freezer bags
inside one another, slip them over her head, cover with a large black
nylon shopping bag, take a two-yard-long piece of cotton rope and
wrap it around her neck several times before tying it in a knot at the
back. Wrap the rope around the neck several more times, tie a second knot, and wait to suffocate. Feel the panic set in as pain grips the
lungs, hands clasped tightly together, nails digging into palms, resisting grabbing at the rope and attempting to untie its complicated
knots, unable to see them because of the nylon bag over the freezer
bags, unable to see the knots in a mirror, and suffocation doesn't take
nearly so long as to allow herself blindly to pick out the complicated
knots and free herself. A foolproof plan for a kitchen suicide.

In the other rooms the plans are far less complex. In the bedroom
there are the pills, hidden in a shoe box in the closet rather than kept
in the medicine cabinet. With Dennis often over, the last thing Joan
wanted was for him to peek in the medicine chest and discover a slew
of vials of pills for psychiatric disorders, Dennis discovering how mis-
erably—not comically—unstable the woman he's loving truly is, discovering the woman he sleeps with is not only seeing a therapist but
also hoarding pills. She imagines the questions: Why are you seeing a
shrink? Why do you need so much medicine? Are you on it when
you're with me? Do you need it when you're with me?—and if he has
to keep portions of his life safe from her, she will keep portions of her
life safe from him.

In the bathroom Joan's plan is to fill the tub, immerse herself in the
water, and then drop in the hot electric curling iron. In the family

room she keeps a small revolver inside the hollowed-out pages of a book, the hardcover of Sidney Sheldon's *The Other Side of Midnight*. A gun Al sent Joan from Colorado once he'd learned she was sending the kids to boarding schools and would be living alone in the city. "For your peace of mind," the accompanying note read, written on Mr. and Mrs. Al and Linda Dwyer stationery. He neglected to send her bullets, and although Joan has no idea where to purchase them in the city, never having seen a gun shop on her walks down Fifth Avenue or Broadway, she figures she could get some if the need arises and she does decide to pursue this course of action. No plan has as yet been worked out for the dining room. Joan suspects that the chandelier is simply too weak for a hanging. She is sure the fixture would fall from the ceiling under the stress of her weight and doesn't want to explain to the building's maintenance man or her children how the chandelier was torn from the ceiling. She imagines herself pinned under the crystal and brass chandelier, a limp rope around her neck, wire stretching from the ceiling to the chandelier fixture atop her body, hollering for help and then rescued by Martino, the maintenance man. An embarrassment to fail at suicide, a humiliation. "If you can't do it correctly, don't bother at all," her father lectured Joan, furious that she'd tried cooking the family dinner herself, ruining a casserole dish, forcing Walter Robins into taking the family out to dinner for the evening.

Don't bother at all, Joan agrees, and so she hasn't, hasn't at all for years, and if she is going to bother with killing herself, she will do it correctly and not from the chandelier.

In the living room the window is Joan's escape. Simple, clean, and efficient, no props necessary, only the strength of will to open a window and pitch her body into space.

Joan stands in the dining room, considering the afternoon: Dennis sleeping with her, then asking her to leave, using her as if she were a Dumpster for garbage. Joan grips the edge of the table, staring across its gleaming, polished surface. Waxed before the last dinner she prepared for Dennis and herself. Solid and large and flat, a plane of solid wood, and Joan hoists herself up on the table, legs dangling, kicking off her slippers. Joan places her hands by her sides and pushes back, sending her body into the center of the table, sitting with her bare legs straight out before her, the skirt of the robe fanned around her body.

The table feels good, firm, beneath her, and Joan tilts her head toward the chandelier. Brass and crystal only a foot above her head she cannot hang herself from, and she lies down flat on the table, drawing the skirt of the robe above her hips, exposing calves, thighs, and abdomen, forming a pillow of velvet on which to rest her head. She stares at the ceiling, picturing herself as if she were sitting in the chandelier looking down. A middle-aged woman sprawled across a dining room table, legs bared, silk lace-edged panties available for all to see, arms flung dramatically out to the sides, palms held flat against the wood like suction cups, fingers wide. Crazy Joan Dwyer in 16B, perched atop a table, floundering between suicide plans, a boyfriend, and a therapist.

"He's only using me. We both know it, only you won't say it."

"Why do you believe he's using you?"

"Because that's the way people are with me. He uses me. My husband used me and wants nothing to do with me. My son is only thankful I no longer obligate him to Sunday brunch. My daughter's nothing but a siphon for money. I mean nothing to anyone. Not to myself, and you're so sick of my complaining you wish I *would* kill myself so you could get a better patient. I know. I may fool myself for moments and give myself a treat of hope once in a while, but I know the truth when I'm alone and there are no distractions. People exist only for their own needs. No one can help me and no one really wants to."

"Then what do you think we're doing here?" Dr. Thompson asked gently.

"*Exactly.* What *are* we doing here?" Joan returned. "*What?*"

Joan shuts her eyes, pressing the small of her back into the table, feeling its support. She supposes she shouldn't force people to care any longer, supposes she should make everyone's life a whole lot simpler and kill herself. Andrea would have her father to dole out her allowance, Al probably giving her all she wants, no questions asked. Todd could move into the apartment and be free to roam the city without fear of running into Pathetic Mom. Dennis would phone, leave a message, not have the message returned, and forget all about her, easily finding another martini-swilling woman to occupy his afternoons. And Dr. Thompson would find a new patient to occupy three fifty-minute slots each week. Lives would proceed nicely, without Joan Dwyer's nonexistence causing much, if any, disturbance. Gliding along so swiftly her suicide would hardly be felt, nothing more than a tiny bump in the road for all involved. Joan wishes she had switched the chandelier light on before lying down on this table because the sun has now set and the room would have been lit instead of dark.

Awkward polygons of light drop in through the dining room's two windows. Odd angles of harsh yellow light from the city outside, falling across an arm, her chest, her face, intruding on her thoughts, bringing in the world beyond her apartment walls. An entire world of department stores, phone machines, fruit stands, boxy apartments, icy sidewalks, sliver-thin skyscrapers, rude doormen, movie marquees, diet sodas, ignorant cabbies, perfume boutiques, turkey club sandwiches, cash machines, waiters with attitude, car alarms, half-hour pizza delivery, liquor delivery, windchill factors, deli counter clerks, angry beggars, three-lettuce salads and tricolor pastas crushing, pressing Joan from all sides, every angle, stranding and immobilizing her atop the island of her dining room table.

Far down the avenue a stream of taillights all unrelated and flashing in different directions, red, yellow, white, green, and Joan cannot look, looking away to the chandelier instead, dark with occasional flashes of pale light, refracting off the crystals, curling around the brass arms. Taillights blink and brake, and the thought occurs that now is the time, the best time, to kill herself.

Joan swings herself up, sitting prone, bringing the robe in close around her as she eases herself to the table's edge and then down upon the carpet. The apartment is dark, black, and Joan walks into the living room, the velvet of the robe touching lightly at her arms, soft and comforting, and Joan goes to the corner with the drawstring, grabbing hold, yanking three sharp tugs until the windows are clear. She approaches the middle window, seating herself on the radiator beneath it, the medium-hot air burning the robe against her thighs, and Joan pushes the window wide; a chilling blast of air blows into the apartment, raising goose bumps on her flesh.

This is how far Joan has come in her life, how far she has traveled, and she braces her hands against the window frame, leaning her head out, taking a deep breath of the cold air. Lean a bit farther out, lean her upper body a bit farther out, release the window frame, and let herself drop is how close she is, and Joan peers out, a rush of wind enveloping her head, all sound blocked out but the wind. She could do this, she tells herself, she has the courage to follow through, but a doubt lingers over whether this is her only option, her only choice. Dr. Thompson phones her patient once, sometimes twice a week for reality checks: "I do care. You're a very loving person, you have a lot of good in you to share, and when you meet someone who recognizes that and doesn't take advantage of it—" and the longer Joan waits and considers this doubt, the faster her will dissolves. Joan knows she's supposed to call Dr. Thompson when she becomes like this, actually should have called Dr. Thompson *before* becoming like this, before climbing on the dining room table. Somewhere inside Joan she has some shred of a belief that Dr. Thompson may be right, that this life of Joan's may be worth a phone call to her doctor on a Sunday night. She pulls herself inside the window, leaving it wide, plodding into the kitchen, switching on the fluorescents hanging under the cabinets, and dialing Dr. Thompson's number within their blue glow. She could be dead by now if she weren't such a coward, could be dead, and now she has to figure out how to get through another night or day or year until she works herself up to killing herself again.

The phone rings. The machine answers. "I'm at home," Joan

says. "This is Joan Dwyer. Call me when you can." She hangs up and sits at the kitchen table, hands folded gently in her lap.

Her phone rings twenty-four minutes later. Joan moves quickly to the counter: Dennis or Dr. Thompson, Dennis or Dr. Thompson? "Hello?"

"Hello, Joan," Dr. Thompson answers, as calm and compassionate as ever.

"Sorry for calling you." She is almost not disappointed it's her doctor, not Dennis. Almost.

"Having a difficult time?"

"I can't do this much longer."

"What's happening with you now?"

"I don't know what I'm doing anymore. I was just lying on my dining room table and—" Joan stops, sees herself lying on the dining room table, an obscene, monstrous figure.

"Joan?"

"I don't know anymore."

"It's all right. I know you're upset, and I want you to call me whenever you are having a hard time. What are your plans for the rest of the night?"

"I don't know."

"Have you had any dinner?"

"No."

"Why don't you order in dinner, then? How does that sound?"

"I don't know what I want. I can't decide that. I can't decide anything. I just don't know anymore."

"How about Chinese food? Would that be good?"

"I think so."

"Do you have a place you usually order from?"

"It's down on the corner."

"Why don't you call and have them deliver? How does that sound for a start?"

"I guess."

"I think it might help to eat and do some reading. Get yourself involved in some activity outside your own thoughts."

"I'm alone too much. I think too much."

"I know. I can hear that. Do you think you can order in food, then?"

"I'll do it after we're done."

"Good. Would you like to speak later or will you be okay until we see each other tomorrow?"

"I'll be okay. Mornings are usually better than nights."

"Leave a message later if you need to."

"I will."

"I'll see you tomorrow."

"Thank you."

"You're welcome. Take care, Joan."

"I'll see you tomorrow."

"Yes, I'll see you then."

"Good. Good-bye until tomorrow. I'm all right for now. Thanks for talking to me."

Pam returns to the kitchen, where Dennis has set the table, laying out the spread of Chinese take-out in white cardboard boxes. Pam sits, and Dennis places a seltzer bottle by her place and a bottle of beer by his own.

"A problem solved?" Dennis is not sure whether he's asking or accusing. He sits, taking up the carton of chicken lo mein, spilling a pile of noodles across his plate.

Pam stares at the food, pours herself a glass of seltzer, and sips. "As much as can be done in a two-minute phone conversation." Pam can't believe she told Joan to order in Chinese food, as if a pan of steamed vegetables could solve her problems.

She stares at her plate, looks up at Dennis, who's serving himself a chicken dish. An inventory of miserable lives: Joan Dwyer, Tim

Boxer, Devon Taylor, Mitch Breen, Bill Matson, Rosemary Cutler, Arthur Greene, Sarah Chaplin, and the sixteen others who are her patients. Although not all are overwhelmingly miserable, and most are feeling significantly more positive about their lives since starting therapy, Pam becomes more and more convinced that the Tim Boxers and Joan Dwyers of this world should kill themselves if they wish. Pam isn't sure she has any right to say it's wrong. She does, though, and isn't sure she says so because it *is* wrong or for selfish reasons: because she'd feel like a failure if one of her patients did kill him- or herself, because if she cannot convince her patients life is worth living, she may not be as able to convince herself that it is.

At the age of eleven, it occurred to Pam that she was born only six months after her parents' wedding. Studying a photo album, the wedding invitation stuck in the book, she noted the date, the significance of this never having occurred to her before. Pam never brought it to her parents' attention. She just watched them to see if they were happy together, searching her mother's and father's eyes as they looked at her across the dinner table, eating their pot roast, carrots, and oven potatoes. Resentment? Anger? The want of sex and its aftermath—a pregnancy—signaled the inevitability of Cheryl Atkins and Eric Thompson's wedding day, and Pam can't help but wonder whom they blame. Does her father blame his wife, his daughter, or himself? Whom does her mother blame? When Pam's sister, Jennifer, raised the issue of Pam's birthday and the wedding date, Cheryl slapped her daughter's face. "Pamela was born prematurely. That's how it happened, now, don't think you're so smart." Checking her weight on her birth certificate, Pam knew this could not have been true. Whereas before she had figured this out, her parents could scold her and it would be attributed to something she had done, from this point on, Pam saw all their anger toward her as directly linked to their being forced to get married. If they were good to her, it was because they felt guilty. If they punished her, it was because they felt shame.

Hating herself but too afraid to take her life, Pam ate herself fat, making herself as ugly as she felt. When her parents forced her to diet, she starved herself, sometimes fasting for days in a row, of which her parents did not disapprove: Fasting was a display of discipline. As a thin adult financially independent of her parents, Pam cut herself off from her family, only sending them the photo postcard once a year. "I've given them what they wanted all along," she told her therapist while in medical school. "A life without me, and I didn't have to kill myself to do it."

"Why do you send them the postcard if you want nothing to do with them?"

"Guilt. Just to let them know I exist. Just to keep reminding them of how much they hurt me."

"What about how much you hurt yourself during those years? Hurting yourself first by eating too much, then by eating nothing at all. Do you still feel a need to punish yourself or are those feelings gone?"

"Those feelings are gone," Pam replied, believing it at the time. "They're completely gone."

But each time Pam has a patient with suicidal fantasies, a part of her wants to cheer him or her on, let him or her succeed where she has failed. She's taught herself not to act on these suicidal feelings, has taught herself to understand why she may have these thoughts every once in a while and search for the real answers to the problems, not avoid them by indulging in suicidal thoughts, but when she encounters a Tim Boxer and a Joan Dwyer, Pam finds herself drawn to these patients, almost wanting to live her fantasies vicariously through their actions. Tim Boxer and Joan Dwyer believe that suicide can solve all their problems, that suicide is their only option toward ending their pain, and Pam, Dr. Thompson, attempts to help them understand that this suicidal fantasy is *not* the only option, that their lives are valuable, that they are valuable people with lives worth investing in.

The problem, Pam has discovered, is that she is no longer sure this is true. She helps Tim Boxer, who is eventually, inevitably to die of AIDS, appreciate the time he does have left to live so he can then suf-

fer the pain of losing it. Joan Dwyer, slowly, painfully awakens from
a depression, only to become highly unstable and suicidal. Pam wonders if perhaps living in a depressed state, shutting down one's emotions and recognizing no pleasure or pain, is better than feeling bits of
both and facing how truly empty life can be.

Her husband eats Chinese food.

"What's that there?" Pam points to a dish. "Is it good?"

"Chicken with black bean sauce." Dennis hands Pam the tray, and
she takes it, spooning herself a portion, then adding white rice to the
plate.

"You seem a bit out of it." Dennis attempts to connect with Pam,
make her his wife.

"Tired." She forces a smile for his benefit.

"You don't have to be happy for my sake," Dennis replies.

Pam lays her fork across her plate, her smile becoming a smirk.
"My world doesn't necessarily revolve around you, all right? I was
trying to lighten my mood, make *myself* feel better. That was a difficult call." She picks her fork up.

"Sorry." Dennis hears her perfectly, her world not revolving
around him. And Dennis knows that had he ever said the same about
Pam, she'd pounce, make him define and analyze the thought from
every angle and perspective, explore any possible underlying thoughts.

Pam wants to change the subject, forget work, and she glances
over her shoulder to the large microwave sitting on the kitchen
counter. "I was thinking we should extend the counter along the
back wall. With the larger microwave, we've lost counter space. If
we add more counter, we could put in a couple cabinets underneath." Joan Dwyer and microwaves. She comes back into Pam's
mind again, is unavoidable.

"What are you going to obsess about once the apartment is all redone?" Dennis asks, joking. "What hobby will you pick up then?"

Pam smiles. "I haven't thought that far ahead. . . . What about the
cabinets, though? I like having lots of storage space."

Through a mouthful of pork fried rice: "If it makes you happy, why not?"

"I know you're sick of this," Pam goes on, "and I promise that once the apartment is all done, I'll calm down, but today I saw some tile—I know we hadn't planned on doing the bathroom—it's a black and white and pink pattern."

Dennis laughs. "Do we really need it?"

"Of course not."

"But you want it?"

"Yes. It really is beautiful, and the bathrooms are so dull now."

Dennis nods. "You know best." He takes a chicken finger, dipping it in duck sauce.

"We'd have to have men in here working, tearing things up." She can't believe how agreeable he's being.

"They have to come to do the kitchen anyway. It's no big difference."

"True. You're right." She picks up a pea pod and a water chestnut, eating. So complacent, too complacent, not argumentative, and Pam doesn't get it, how *congenial* Dennis has been recently. Busy trying to finish up the freelance work while taking on the new position, he should be more tense, less patient with her as he was when he initially went freelance. In the last month Dennis has only become easier to live with. The issue of the baby went to where she doesn't know. All she knows is that he hasn't even hinted at it in the last four to five weeks. His interest in the redecoration is completely gone. He is not even irritated by the fact of it anymore. "You know best," he said, and Pam wonders if he is so agreeable because he's happy with his life, with their marriage, or if something else is going on. His long work hours, many working dinners. Logic dictates that he is just swamped with work and excited about this new opportunity, that she's overanalyzing the situation, looking for bad whenever there is only good to be found. She's not used to seeing her husband so relaxed and content. "We could put off doing all of this until after you're more settled at BMA," Pam suggests.

"Let's just do it now. You've already started."

"You seem so much happier recently. Is it because of the job? Were you that unhappy before?"

"I think it's because of the job." He lays down his fork and takes Pam's hand, worries about her suspecting anything. "I'm just preoccupied with the Moby thing. I am very happy with us, more happy than ever." And he means it, feels it—can love his wife more freely now that he has Joan to love, too. "Does something seem wrong?"

"We just haven't spent a lot of time together recently. I wondered if you were avoiding me for some reason."

Dennis stands, coming around the table to his wife, holding her, leaning over, and kissing her. "I love you. I do." His eyes water at the thought of what he's doing to Joan, to his wife, to himself. He tilts Pam's chin up, looking into her eyes.

"We're together?" she asks. "You're happy with this job change?"

"I am," Dennis replies, and from the look on his wife's face, he can tell she believes him, and for now, that's all that matters. He returns to his seat, takes a sip of beer.

Dennis in place, life at home serene, Pam's thoughts return to Joan Dwyer. Pam decides she'll phone later and make sure Joan has calmed down and not thrown herself out a window, knowing Joan is all right so her doctor will be able to sleep better tonight.

"What video did you end up renting?" Dennis asks, making the effort to connect with his wife.

Pam looks up at her husband. "I got—" She thinks, remembering the box. "It has Sally Field and Kevin Kline in it."

"A comedy or drama? It's not *Norma Rae*, is it?"

"No, it's a comedy. Whoopi Goldberg's in it too."

"Good," Dennis says. "A comedy's good."

One of everything that begins with the letter *D*, Joan decided, and she sits at the kitchen table with eight dishes of Chinese food. An hour ago she took the take-out menu from the drawer by the phone, scanned the three columns of listings, and circled the numbers of those items that began with the letter D. Dragon and Phoenix Lobster and Chicken platter. Duck King special. Diced chicken with hot pepper sauce. Diced chicken with bean sauce. Diced chicken with cashew nuts. Delightful chicken and shrimp combination. Double sautéed sliced pork. Dried sautéed string beans. Eight D dishes—$55.25— and Joan stares at the eight rectangular pans of food, all full and steaming.

2

Joan sits silent, staring at Dr. Thompson's attentive gaze, her doctor's rapt look, thinking through all she's just said. She shakes her head, a smile appearing, then disappearing across her face. When she speaks, her voice is soft, calm. "I've begun talking about this as if I'm really going to do it. I know I eventually am. It's too much pain going on like this, and it's not as if anything's going to change." Joan tugs at the sleeves of her sweater, straightening the seams at the back of her forearms. "When I'm home, it's like entering this dark cave, and I just get so lost in there, like I'm in the middle of nowhere and no one else exists, I'm so unconnected with reality. The sick part is *that is my reality*." Joan is dry-eyed, not upset, only reporting the facts of her life as she sees them. She looks away from her doctor to her lap, arranging the pleats in her skirt. "I look at how my life has changed since meeting him, and it's not all bad. I spoke to Todd last night and asked him to bring Emily along next time we had brunch. I thought we could discuss the books I've been reading. I told Todd I'd read the James, *The Great Gatsby,* and *The Sun Also Rises,* and I asked him if he thought Emily would like to come and then we could all go to the Met together, and he agreed. I took the old lady down the hall to the park yesterday. I've realized I don't like her. She told me she's seen a man coming and going from my apartment. She said it with such disdain as if it were a weakness not to be alone. I notice I usually do these things with other people immediately after being with him. Like after our lunch together, I went home and took Miss Pointer out. Or if he leaves me some evening, I'll end up reading for a couple hours instead of only watching TV. After seeing him, I feel good for a couple hours, but it doesn't take long before my perspective on the world comes back to the fact that he's treating me so terribly. Only seeing me during the afternoon or on specific nights he decides, never on a weekend evening. I'm with him, and I feel my age or younger, and when he goes, it's like I'm shriveling up and becoming an old invalid like Miss Pointer.'' Joan leans across to the couch, reaching into the side pocket of her coat. ''Look at this. See? Look what I bought him this morning. He probably won't like it, but it gives me an excuse to visit him. Just to drop this off as a surprise. I almost hope he doesn't like it so then I can kill myself without any lingering hope that he does care. I'm just tired of giving myself hope that this relationship will become more than a series of one-night stands.'' Joan reaches back to her coat, returning the gift to the pocket. She looks at her watch and stands, lifting her coat, putting it on, picking up the book she's currently reading, *Mrs. Bridge.* ''I'm not painting anymore. Threw all the paintings I've done and all the paints down the compactor chute last night. I wasn't enjoying it and am glad I never showed them to him. Too embarrassing. I have come up with an idea for a children's book I want to write. It's about a giraffe named Figgy who doesn't have any friends in Africa so he takes a boat to Antarctica and tries to become a penguin.'' Joan buttons her coat.

"I have to stop punishing myself like this, trying so hard, keeping this hope. *Figgy the Giraffe?* I must be nuts. I swear, I have to kill whatever this thing is inside me that's making me so crazy and unhappy, and if I have to kill myself to do it, so be it. Hurrah."

Joan, having composed herself in the elevator on the way down, having drunk a martini in the bar in Donnelman's, peers through the grilled windows of Dennis's basement apartment, spying. He works at his drafting table. Joan pushes the door buzzer, watching his head look up and around to the window, smiling when he sees her. Joan smiles in return, and moments later they are sitting on the couch, Joan's head on his shoulder.

"I have to get back to work."

"I know. I just wanted to stop in and say hello."

He kisses the top of her head. "I'm glad you did."

She sits up, better to leave before being forced out, and she stands, reaching into her pocket, taking out the small navy blue velvet box. "I got you something."

"Oh. Thanks." He leans over, giving Joan a kiss, opening the box, staring down at a small jade camel. He picks up the piece, standing it in his palm. "It's cute. What's this for?"

"Do you like it? I don't know. I saw it and liked it and wanted to give it to you." It means nothing to him. She shouldn't have stopped by, given him a gift, taken this chance.

"I like it. It's very nice." He curls his fingers around the camel, wrapping an arm around Joan, escorting her to the door.

He bolts the door behind Joan, then walks to the drafting table, opening his fist and releasing the jade figurine. He selects a light blue pencil from the carousel on the shelf, using the tip's side to shade the whale illustration on the layout board. He draws the pencil gently underneath the length of the whale, the thin line of blue slowly fanning out as it approaches the treasure chest overflowing with fish sandwiches.

A dog, his wife would call him, as Pam calls men who cannot control themselves and must have a lot of women. Dennis would argue with this label. Not a dog because he does not want *a lot* of women, only one more than one, and he wants this one more for all the qualities his wife lacks. Not so much cheating on Pam as attempting to fulfill his own life, letting himself be needed and loved, letting himself need and love with the possibility of someday having a family.

The blue pencil is put away, and Dennis selects the pale green, shading the blue shadow with a green tint. He lays down the pencil. A pile of illustration boards are stacked on the floor. An entire aquarium of original characters: a set of porpoises, girl and boy, a school of fish, crabs, a family of whales, sea horses, sharks, turtles. Dennis bought a reference book on marine animals, using the illustrations as rough models for his cartoon illustrations, which will be included in the final presentation to the clients.

This combination of work and play space is distracting, Joan showing up unexpected so soon before Pam is to arrive; Dennis finds it hard to concentrate when he has to be afraid that Joan may show up on a whim, meaning well but creating tension. In a week and a half the presentation will be over, he reminds himself, the position at BMA may be definite, and if it is, he'll have a viable excuse to Pam for why he may need to be away on an overnight business trip every now and then, thereby allowing himself to spend an uninterrupted evening and morning with Joan, allaying her unspoken, yet obvious, concerns and solidifying their relationship.

Pam stands in Dennis's office, looking over the drafting board at a set of eight starfish, all with bright, smiling faces, wearing pink high-heeled shoes on each of their points. A clear Plexiglas T square bisects

the large sheet of paper, and a small jade camel, one-half inch high,
stands off the border of the paper at the table's edge. They meet at his
office before heading off to dinner, a reservation having been made at
a new Italian restaurant on the Upper East Side.

Look at this. See?

"What do you think of it?" Dennis stands behind his wife, not the
least bit interested in hearing her criticism, knowing she's likely to
analyze it for sexual content, but he asks anyway, making her think
her opinion matters.

The green camel screams at Pam, and she breaks her fix on the
figure and turns to her husband, not altogether sure what he's asking,
what she's been asked. "I like it. It's cute. The colors are nice. What
do you think? Does he or she have a name?"

"Copy's doing the names. We're meeting tomorrow to finalize
everything."

Pam turns back to the sketch, blocking out the camel. "I do like
it." She kisses his cheek. "It's really, really cute." He does have
talent for this, Pam notes, and she finds this man attractive, this man
drawing all these cute illustrations, so childlike and witty, much more
interesting than the man designing ads for shampoo bottles and liquid
detergent. This is the man she loves, she married, and she reaches for
the camel at the edge of the table, pinching it between thumb and
forefinger. "What's this? This is nice." And her voice does not
waver.

Dennis steps to her side, taking the camel from her hand,
"Something Libby at BMA gave me today. A good-luck token." The
lies come easily. To Joan. To Pam. *Slick*, and for the first time since
this has begun, he feels sleazy, like an operator, connecting and
reshaping lives; lies are his padding, his bumpers to protect against
collision.

Pam sits on the couch. "That's nice of her. Is she happy with the
work?"

Dennis places the camel on the drawing board, dancing among the starfish. ''She seems thrilled. She's convinced we're going to get this. She thinks all my characters will be merchandised. Not that I'll own any of the rights to them.''

Pam nods, crosses her legs, studies him. ''Oh, well. We'll get rich some other way.''

''I think this is going to be exciting if it works. I really do.''

The jade camel on the table across the room. ''I'm glad it's working out. I like seeing you so happy.'' Pam stands, suddenly feeling overwhelmingly claustrophobic, her mind stuck on the camel in her husband's office, *Joan Dwyer's* camel in her husband's office, not from Libby at BMA, a woman who would offer her husband a job but never give him a cute gift—Libby is not a cute-gift woman—and Pam's suffocating, needs to get out to the restaurant. She cannot look at him. She looks to the floor, her shoes, black leather flats. ''Are you almost ready to go? We should try to make the reservation.''

Dennis walks to the bedroom. ''In a minute.''

Joan Dwyer has never uttered, never stated, her lover's name in therapy, so maybe, Pam considers, she's just forcing pieces together that do not fit, a psychiatrist's imagination, searching for disaster. Dennis walks to her side, his arm too naturally slipping around her waist. Is he drifting away, has he been drifting away, slowly, carefully becoming more vacant, less *there* in their life? He escorts his wife to the door. Everything feels the same as it always has.

Pam is obsessing, wants to blurt out her newborn suspicion but cannot, will not. Her presumption is too premature, too irrational to be true, and all she'd be doing, whether the accusation be true or false, is humiliating herself and placing Dennis in a position of superior power. Placing Dennis in a position where he knows she knows he has another woman, thereby forcing Pam to be a *good wife*—the kind of wife he wants, a wife like Joan Dwyer—otherwise he may leave her for the other woman. A threat he can lord over her, making her his subordinate, his ''lesser half.'' At this point, Pam is sure, it is best to keep quiet, to gather information supporting or refuting her suspicion, to eat her linguine in clam sauce before it becomes too cold.

Pam takes up a strand of the wide noodle, twirling it against the corner of the square plate, lifting it to her waiting, open mouth. The linguine is warm and good.

"How is it?" Dennis asks.

Pam looks at him. "It's very good. Would you like a bite?" She lifts a biteful across the table, and Dennis leans over to eat off her fork. He sleeps with a mistress, her patient, and eats off his wife's fork. Pam's stomach tightens; she feels the urge to gag, to vomit, but remains steadfast, composed, remains *herself*, denying Dennis the trophy of her tears.

"Would you like a bite of the lasagna?" he asks.

"Please," Pam says, and then she eats off his fork. He's sleeping with another woman, her patient, and she's eating off his fork. Pam swallows, smiles. "It's very good." She stands, "Excuse me for a minute," and walks off to the rest room.

In the toilet stall, door locked, skirt around her ankles, panty hose around her hips, Pam shuts her eyes.

One jade camel.

Miniature jade camels can be picked up in any of a hundred primitive art or jewelry shops in this city. Maybe even sold by a street vendor or at a weekend flea market in a schoolyard, and from this Pam has concocted the unlikely story that her patient is having an affair with her husband. Pam is certain Dennis would never use one of her patients to get at her in this way. Pam is certain that Joan Dwyer would never manipulate her husband to embark on an affair with one of his wife's patients. One jade camel, a coincidence—*only seeing me during the afternoon or on specific nights he decides, never on a weekend evening*—and Pam stands, blotting out the memory of Joan's words, pulling up her skirt and the skirt's side zipper, turning and flushing the toilet, a reflex. A coincidence and nothing more, and Pam returns to the table, seating herself across from her husband, finishing off the remains of the now-cold pasta.

Joan Dwyer on the answering machine, the woman her husband is not having an affair with: "Hello, this is Joan Dwyer calling. It's eight-thirty on Monday night. If you have the time, I'd like to schedule an additional session for tomorrow. Thank you."

Pam thinks through Tuesday's lineup of patients, if she can fit Joan in. Eleven to eleven-fifty, and Pam decides to give it to Joan. An extra session. Having observed Joan Dwyer's behavior and listened to her fifty-minute monologue today, Pam senses that Joan could use additional therapy time, additional time to reinforce the hope that coming to therapy gives her, that being with her doctor gives her. Pam lifts the phone receiver, dials out Joan's number from memory, no need to look it up in the book.

"Hello," Joan answers.

This woman is not sleeping with her husband. "Hello, Joan. This is Dr. Thompson. I got your message."

"I thought you might not want to speak with me tonight. I was so depressed today."

"If that's how you were feeling, I'm glad you could express it." This is not a therapy session; Pam doesn't want to get into anything over the phone she can't wrap up quickly. "You seemed very depressed. I'm glad you called me tonight." Pam validates Joan's feelings without dismissing them. Joan and her husband. Joan kissing her husband, her husband's hands on Joan. "I have time to see you at eleven tomorrow morning if that suits your schedule."

"That would be fine. Thank you."

"Then I'll see you then."

3

Pam can hardly pay attention to a word Joan says as Joan spews forth her depressing lament of dreariness: self-hatred over feeling Pam is tired of being her doctor, self-hatred over getting herself involved with this loving-yet-distant man—"He says he's going to call me and then he doesn't, and when I call him, he's not even home"—self-hatred over sending her children off to boarding schools, self-hatred over losing her husband, self-hatred over having been a spoiled child and now being a spoiled adult. Pam listens, but all she wants, needs to hear is the man's name. Hear the man's name is not Dennis Perry, get Joan Dwyer to say the name that is not her husband's, allay her suspicions, and then return to being a therapist instead of the jilted wife confronting her husband's mistress, and the sooner Pam accomplishes this task, the better therapy will be for herself, Joan, and every other of her patients.

"—so I could be more secure in this relationship, but I can't."
Joan tosses up her hands in frustration, then quickly folds them in her
lap. A finger reaching to the circular brass buckle on her wide leather
belt and toying with its clasp. She looks away from the doctor to two
pigeons sitting on the air conditioner outside the office window.
"Pigeons are such filthy birds. My mother used to drag me away
whenever we saw them on the street. She said they carried diseases
and was afraid she or I would catch cancer or the flu or something."

Pam ignores Joan's pigeon tangent, it probably having everything
to do with how Joan is feeling. Pam knows she should ask Joan about
this memory and her mother and try to link it to the speech Joan
made prior to the pigeon comment, but as clearly as Pam has heard
the pain expressed so desperately before her, she asks, "Why is it you
avoid mentioning the name of your boyfriend here with me?"

Surprised, the question catching her off guard, Joan looks at her
doctor, then down to her hands. Joan examines her chipped nails,
noting that she needs a manicure and can either go to her regular
manicurist or do it herself at home, providing herself with an activity
while TV watching.

A mistake to have asked, Pam notes. A mistake to have asked how
and when she did, and Pam is at once ashamed for making this very
unprofessional, manipulative move, letting her personal concerns
override her professional obligation; but having asked and wanting a
response, she waits. She had planned on asking this question, had
prepared herself to, needing to know, and now she must live with the
results of this transgression.

Joan looks up from her hands, nail polish colors running through
the back of her mind. "I didn't think it mattered," she answers,
trying to keep it light, not get defensive.

"Maybe I should have asked you his name a long time ago, but I
thought you would tell me when you were ready. You never did,
though, and I just wonder why you avoid saying his name. It's
important that we discuss these things that you feel you have to
conceal. To discuss why you want to conceal them as well as the

issues concealed themselves.'' Pam hopes she's making sense, that her argument is substantial.

''I don't understand why it matters,'' Joan persists. ''I don't understand.''

''Is there a reason why you feel you can't tell me his name? Maybe we can start with that.'' She is being as delicate and professional as she can be in this unprofessional matter.

Joan runs a hand through her hair, to the back of her head, twisting a strand between fingers, not wanting to say his name, as if by saying it aloud and sharing his existence, the force of all the pain and love will become that much more overwhelming and unbearable. ''I would really rather not discuss him, that's all. There's no other reason.''

''Why is that?'' And this discussion *is* therapeutic, Pam thinks, maybe not what Joan wanted to discuss, but still therapeutic and beneficial—*no harm done*—and Pam gives Joan time to think through how she's feeling.

Joan speaks slowly. ''I feel I need to protect him and that if I say his name, he'll go away and I'll lose him.'' Joan pauses. ''When I talk about him here now, he's very distant and unreal, and it's easier that way. I'm afraid of him being too real and letting my feelings out and making him more real because if I do say it, I don't know what would happen. This is my way of controlling this, and I'm afraid I couldn't if I let him become too much a part of my therapy and overwhelm everything here.''

Pam responds, ''Don't you think that by so actively attempting to keep him from overwhelming our work, you've already let him overwhelm it? Maybe by letting out these feelings, you'll discover that we can achieve a balance where all things can be discussed, no secret holding any power that can obliterate our work together or your life outside therapy.''

Joan nods, agrees, takes a tissue from the dispenser on the table by her side, rolls it into a ball, then smooths it across her lap. ''That makes sense,'' she says, looking over the patterns in the wrinkles of the tissue, many awkward stars, triangles, boxes. "I know it's true in my head, but still . . . I've never said his name to anyone before. My kids don't even know I'm seeing someone. You're the only one who knows besides Miss Pointer."

Pam, feeling her pulse quicken, keeps herself from growing impatient. Remain pleasant and talky, not confrontational. She smiles, making it a game. "Are you going to tell me his name?"

Joan breaks into a grin. "I don't want to." She laughs. "I want him all to myself."

"All to *yourself*?" Pam queries.

"Yes," Joan says. "He's mine. Not to be shared or threatened."

She does not want to say, is not going to say unless Pam pressures her to, and Pam is not prepared for this, to manipulate therapy in such a manner, to make it an interrogation, but the longer Joan holds out, the more likely it seems she must. One jade camel has prompted this outrageous behavior from her, and if her suspicion is right, she is doomed, and if it is wrong, she may have done harm, possibly irreparable, to their therapeutic relationship. Pam needs to know. Her smile is gone, the game over. "I'd like you to explain why you feel you can't tell me." More a parent, a disciplinarian than a therapist.

Joan immediately drops her eyes from her doctor. She stares at the tissue in her lap, torn with her play, and she lifts it, tossing it in the wastebasket at the chair's side. She notices an empty bottle of seltzer in the basket, an open paper bag with a half-eaten strawberry icing doughnut.

"I'd like to know, Joan."

Like her father scolding her for not helping her mother in the kitchen. "Your mother tells me you got home too late this afternoon to do the errands she had planned. Why is that? That's your responsibility to our family. We expect so little and you can't even do that? Is your family so meaningless to you that you can't help out at all?" Joan looks at Dr. Thompson. "I suppose that by keeping his name a secret, I make him seem less important than he is. If you knew his name, all you would have to do is say it and hurt me whereas if you don't know his name, you can't, and so he almost doesn't exist but is only something I've made up when I'm here.''

Pam leans forward in her chair, looking across at her patient. ''I surely don't want to see you in any more pain than you already are, but don't you think that by sharing your feelings, you'll be more likely to understand what you're going through instead of keeping it a secret and living with your pain alone? I'm not going to hurt you. I think you know that. That you can trust me.'' Pam pushes further, wants this over and done. ''I've made an extra effort with you. I shouldn't have to convince you to trust me. I've been your therapist for over a year already.''

Joan's eyes begin to tear. The pressure building, Dr. Thompson so stern and distressed over her patient's inability to trust her. ''Why do you think it's so important for me to tell you?'' She takes a tissue, touches it to her eyes.

A pure bullying session, and Pam tells herself to act, not think; she will repair the damage done later, in future sessions. ''What you can't express here in therapy is usually very important toward making advances in our work together. It says a lot about where we are in our relationship. Are you going to tell me or not? Our time's almost up.''

Joan cannot get his name out of her mind; to say it or not to say it, and will saying it be a release of pressure, the letting of air out of an overinflated balloon or the opening of Pandora's box? Dennis Perry, Dennis Perry, Dennis Perry, Dennis Perry, and Joan looks at her therapist, Dr. Thompson, waiting for an answer, so generous in her help of Joan, this woman who has made herself available at all hours of the day and night for this patient's depressive, suicidal emergencies, this woman who took the time to fit Joan in for an additional session this very day. This woman who is her doctor, who knows more about what is best for her than Joan does herself, who cares more about improving Joan's life than Joan does herself. Whom is Joan helping by not telling her doctor his name? Whom is Joan hurting? Dennis Perry, Dennis Perry, Dennis Perry echoes through

Joan's mind, Dennis Perry, Dennis Perry, Dennis Perry, she can't stop herself from thinking; she opens her mouth. "Dennis Perry," Joan says. "His name is Dennis Perry. There. I've said it. Are you happy?" And Joan sighs, exhausted, relieved, annoyed. She wipes more tears from her eyes and breathes deeply.

Pam ignores what Joan says, absorbs the name of the man Joan is dating, but closes it away, to be considered later, at a more opportune moment than when she is with a patient. "We'll have to stop for now. I'm glad you came in today. I think this has been very useful." Pam stands.

Joan stands. "Thank you for fitting me in."

"How do you feel about what we discussed?" Focus on Joan's need. The information received, she can focus on Joan.

Joan shakes her head, bewildered. "I don't know."

Pam walks to the door. "You know you can call me if you need to. And we will be meeting tomorrow at our regular hour." She opens the door. "I'll phone you this evening at ten. We'll talk then."

"Thank you. Good-bye," and Joan leaves, Pam shutting the door after her, walking to her desk, sitting, and covering her eyes with her hands: *I should refer her to another doctor immediately. I should immediately terminate therapy with Joan Dwyer.* Pam reaches into the top desk drawer and takes out a vial of Xanax tablets, placing two pink tablets on her tongue, and swallowing with a swig of cold coffee that's been sitting in her mug since nine this morning. Two Xanax should get Pam through this day. Two Xanax and Pam glances at her calendar, quickly reminding herself who is due in at Tuesday's noon hour.

By 1:00 P.M. Pam's efforts to focus on Tim Boxer falter. By 2:00 she is in and out of Pearl Strada's session, barely picking up half of what her patient says, responding only with the briefest and most general of comments. By 4:00 Ethan Blount is a blur before Pam's eyes, and

Pam can't bear to listen to his whining and moaning. The touch of Pam's fingertips to the smooth leather of her chair fills her with revulsion.

Following each patient's exit, Pam rushes to her notebooks, scrawling down as much as she can remember from the session, information the patient dispensed that his or her doctor failed to analyze, information for Pam to examine at a later date when her mind is once again functioning in a therapeutic mode.

Pam sits at the desk. Dennis Perry and Joan Dwyer. It's 7:15 P.M. In fifteen minutes the Tuesday night group arrives, and Pam thinks she should cancel, post a sign on the outer office door informing her patients that she was called away on an emergency or is ill. All so she can go home and face her husband that much sooner.

The thought then occurs to Pam that her husband may not yet be home, that he may be out on a date with Joan Dwyer, and if Pam could choose a moment when she didn't exist, could choose a moment when she could cease to exist, this would be it, so Pam decides to go on with her schedule as if nothing had happened. Once she greets and commences the discussion, the group's participants can keep themselves going, only needing Pam to direct and monitor when they are at a loss as to how to help one another out. Pam is positive she can conduct group far more successfully than she conducted herself during the afternoon's therapy sessions, and she walks to the office closet to take out three folding chairs.

The last of the plates is placed in the dishwasher, and Dennis observes Joan scrubbing the last of the pots used for cooking the night's dinner. He went shopping after work, buying fish, fresh vegetables, and an apple pie. He came over to Joan's and prepared the entire meal while Joan watched from the kitchen table, amazed, having never had anyone cook a home meal for her since she was a teenager. ''Al never cooked for me, never even sat down at the dinner table with me after a while, and the kids never had any interest in cooking, never even cooked me an awful breakfast-in-bed on Mother's Day like they do in all those TV shows." Dennis cooked Joan a meal while Joan watched, half delighted, half frustrated over not being the one doing all the work.

Dennis closes the dishwasher, securing the latch, then pushing the regular wash button. Joan hangs a saucepan on the rack on the wall, then goes to Dennis, hugging him from behind, hands folded across his chest. "Thank you for dinner." He takes her hands, twisting out, turning and facing her before reeling her back into his body.

Pam doesn't ask herself what her husband sees in Joan Dwyer; it's all very obvious, and it's more than just the possibility of a child: It's an entire lifestyle of homespun goodness, and Joan Dwyer is queen of the hearth.

Pam, sitting at home on the couch watching the thirty-minute *Headline News* for the second straight time through, contemplates how she could emotionally torture her husband, cripple him so as to leave him weak, wounded, and committed to her, begging for forgiveness. That is what Pam must do, Pam thinks before reconsidering, realizing that if she did attempt to humiliate and leave him in despair, now that he has Joan Dwyer, her act of revenge would backfire, most likely serving to propel Dennis more tightly into Joan Dwyer's comforting and consoling arms. If Pam is to engage in vengeful acts, Dennis will be able to exit guilt-free, justified in leaving his heartless, unforgiving wife, and knowing that this is precisely what her husband would want to happen, Pam will deny him the pleasure; the knowledge of the affair will be kept private to herself.

Just the other week she had conceived of the possibility that Dennis's brighter demeanor was due to happiness from outside their marriage, but Dennis kissed and hugged his wife, and Pam let herself be convinced that all was fine, that she was being paranoid. Only days later Pam finds she's been lied to: Dennis not only does want more than their marriage offers but will actively pursue it with another woman if he is denied it from his wife. Pam never believed he would cheat on her, thought she had him completely under her control. Presently finding she does not, Pam pauses, reevaluating who she is in this marriage. How much is she prepared to change if she wants to keep this husband she is in the process of losing? She *can* let herself learn from this experience and become more of the wife he wants. She *can* be more open, understanding, and vulnerable than she has been in the past, Pam knows, and if she does show Dennis that he is not only loved and needed but *wanted,* maybe she will have given him all he is missing so he has no reason to stray.

A report on a hazardous waste dump site. A school's water system contaminated. Two hundred and fifty children exposed to the chemicals . . . the dismembered limbs of several women's bodies have been found in an apartment in Brooklyn . . . an escaped convict holds his elderly mother and father hostage in their mobile home.

And what of Joan Dwyer? Depressed Joan Dwyer loves a man who has brought pleasure into her life for the first time in years; if he does end their relationship, isn't it likely she'll try to kill herself, moving beyond fantasizing about suicide to actually attempting the act? Most likely, Pam guesses, and she wonders if it would be considered murder for her to prevent her husband from seeing his mistress when she knows for him to do so—not to see Joan—could send Joan through the window of her apartment. Which is more valuable, Pam asks herself, her marriage or Joan Dwyer's life? Knowing she could not live with the burden of being responsible for Joan's death, the answer is obvious. To be even partially responsible for Joan Dwyer's suicide would make her unworthy of being a doctor *and* a wife— unworthy of living at all, as far as Pam is concerned, and how much better would she be if she were to work slowly toward severing Joan's relationship with her husband and *then* abandon Joan to another therapist, leaving another doctor to pick up the pieces of Joan's shattered self-image, provided Joan doesn't kill herself first after having just lost her lover and then the therapist she entrusted to see her through her depression?

A key in a lock. Pam stands, clicking off the television, picking up the day's paper, opening to the second page of the metropolitan section. Bronx couple arraigned for selling their three children. She will do what is best. Best for Joan, best for Dennis, best for herself.

Dennis hangs his overcoat in the closet. "Did you eat? I hope you didn't wait. We all ate in at the office." He turns to Pam, and she drops the paper on the couch, looking him over, searching for clues that he's either just had sex or showered, but he only looks tired and as honest as he has every night she's ever known him.

Dennis catches her bemused expression. "You waited for me?"

Pam feels her eyes begin to water, to glaze over, and she turns away, shocked at the tears, walking down the hall. "I'll just call down to the coffee shop and order up a sandwich or something."

Dennis follows. "You want me to make you something?"

"You've worked late. Sit down and relax. Change out of your suit." The suit is rumpled, wrinkled as if it had been lying on the floor at the foot of a bed.

"Where are you ordering from?"

"Just downstairs. Nothing special." Pam files through a stack of take-out menus, her hands shaking as she folds them open and closed. "Do you want something?"

"Order me some onion rings." He walks into the bedroom.

"Anything else?"

"No, that's enough."

Dennis showers. Pam phones the restaurant, orders herself a grilled tomato and cheese, a garden salad, and half a grapefruit. "And one side order of onion rings." Joan Dwyer three years ago before her husband up and left her. Joan Dwyer three years ago when her depression became more pronounced, more debilitating. Pam reminds herself that she's due to phone Joan Dwyer in half an hour, at ten o'clock. A supportive call from a good doctor. Pam stands at the counter, waiting for the food to arrive.

May

1

F our pale blue rectangles of paper, PHONE MESSAGE printed across the top in block letters. "Pam" written in cursive letters with red pen along the line next to FROM and a check by the box PLEASE CALL. "Joan" with WILL CALL AGAIN checked. Two messages from "Sid." The first checked PHONED. The second PLEASE CALL and a note written in the message space, "Please don't have Annie the angelfish kissing Sam the octopus on the new cup design."

Dennis places Joan's and Pam's messages aside, picking up his desk phone, pushing the pound sign, then the number three, speed-dialing Sid at his office in Louisville, Kentucky. Sid Victor is the director of marketing and media for Moby. BMA was given the account, and Dennis began working full-time early last month. Dennis and his team are currently at work designing print advertisements and in-store materials, Dennis coordinating his team's efforts with those of the copy and creative staffs, who are busy developing Moby's broadcast radio and video advertising. Dennis is in the midst of receiving information from Sid Victor concerning a Christmas movie tie-in Moby plans for the upcoming holiday season. A change that's dismissed the presentation work BMA had planned for the Christmas campaign, forcing all those who work on Moby to create a new campaign that coordinates the characters of the movie with those of Moby's, which Dennis created.

The phone rings, then a click and "This is Sid Victor speaking on a recorded message. I am not at my desk at the moment. Leave your name and number, and I will get back to you ASAP." A beep, and Dennis speaks. "Sid. Dennis. We'll redo the cup without the angelfish kiss. Not a problem. Call if you need anything else. Thanks. Bye." Dennis hangs up, glad not to have had to speak to the man; speaking to a client only brings bad news, more changes of plans, more hours of work. Dennis looks up to see Olivia, one of the designers, leaning against the office doorway, a layout board tucked under an arm.

"Olivia."

Olivia pulls herself straight, places the large board down on Dennis's drafting table, folding over the sheet of tracing paper protecting the work. "The Christmas Porpoise Pack," Olivia commences, weary and cynical. "This is just the layout of the pictures. Copy's assured me the puzzles can fit in here and here and here. They're a crossword, maze, and connect the dot, all with copy tied into the movie concept. I've taken the characters from the movie and have them playing around with our characters. Can I pass this on to production? It needs to go in today."

"Let me take a look at it. I'll leave it on your desk after lunch."

"It has to go in today, remember."

"I'll remember. Go to lunch."

Olivia grins. "Too wonderful," she says, and leaves the office.

Dennis looks over the work. Sam, the octopus, and a reindeer building a snowman. The Flying Fish School pulling Santa in his sleigh. Hobart, the crab, skating figure eights alongside an elf.

The intercom buzzes, and Dennis picks up the phone. "Joan Dwyer on two, Dennis."

"Thanks." Dennis spins his chair so he's facing his desk.

"Dennis?" Joan asks.

"Hello. How are you?"

"Nervous about tonight. Are you still coming?"

"Yes, of course," Dennis responds.

"You can be here by seven-thirty? That's not a problem, is it?"

"No, seven-thirty's good."

"Okay, I'll let you get back to work. See you later. I love you."

"You too. Good-bye."

"Good-bye."

Looking over the Dwyer family photo albums several weeks back, Dennis offhandedly mentioned he'd like to be introduced to Joan's children, and when Joan protested, resisting the idea of his making their acquaintance, Dennis pressed her, wanting to see why she was trying to keep him from her kids, wanting to observe Joan as a mother, finding it hard to imagine this nervous, mannered woman raising kids. "I find it hard thinking of you as a mother when it always seems to me that it's you who needs to be cared for."

Joan was offended: "I take care of myself. I've raised good children. Do you want to meet them? I can arrange a dinner."

Since joining BMA full-time, Dennis has lied to Pam about two business trips. One for two days, one for one. Both were spent in Joan's apartment, the couple playing house, cooking, ordering in, and renting videos. Joan waited on Dennis; Dennis waited on Joan. They woke up together in the morning, Joan saw him off to work, and he returned home to her apartment in the evening, dinner ready and wine chilled. He was surprised by how easily he forgot about Pam and settled into this new life with Joan, not even bothering to phone his wife once during the two days away.

"You could have called to check in with me. At least to let me know where you were in case of an emergency,'' Pam reprimanded him upon his return that Thursday evening.

Dennis gave her a guilty kiss, enjoying the fact that she was concerned and apparently missed him.

Working at BMA gives Dennis the freedom to lie to Pam about his schedule but also restricts his schedule, preventing him from seeing Joan as freely as before. No longer taking weekday afternoons off as he wishes and visiting Joan during day hours, he is forced to lie to Pam about working late in order to see Joan during the week. On Friday nights lies are told, explaining that he must work Saturday or Sunday, so he can meet Joan for an afternoon date. And although Joan never asks why she never sees him on a weekend night or why he can so very rarely spend the entire night on a weekday evening, Dennis is sure she is smart enough to detect that this awkward schedule he keeps is in order to prevent her from discovering a truth of some sort. But since Joan doesn't confront him and force him to lie to her, and so long as she's willing to accept this situation blindly, there's no reason to broach the subject; they can continue on as is.

Dennis looks at Olivia's layout for the lunch box design. The two leaping porpoises that make up either side of the box's handle resemble penises, and Dennis isn't sure whether to let this pass and sign off on it or to bring it to Olivia's attention and have her work out a new design or redraft the porpoises completely. Dennis decides on the latter, writes out a Post-It note, and fixes the yellow square to the protective sheet covering the board. He turns back to his desk—to call Pam now or to take lunch and call her after—and he decides, here, on this matter, on the former—call her now—preferring to get the lie over with rather than contemplate it over a sandwich and soda.

Two twenty-five. Pam is most likely with a patient, and Dennis can call with the safety of knowing he'll only have to lie to the machine. He pushes speed dial number one.

"Hello," Pam answers, not a recording.

"Oh. Hello," Dennis responds, trying hard not to sound surprised, disappointed.

"Is something wrong?"

"I just expected to get your machine. You're usually in session."

"Well, I'm not."

"No, I know," Dennis says.

"Well?"

Dennis is shaken alert. "Sorry, was interrupted by someone. I just wanted to tell you that I have a business—"

"I have to go," Pam interrupts. "My two-thirty's arrived. I'll try to reach you later."

"I have a business dinner," Dennis interjects.

"Then I'll see you at home tonight. Bye. Love you." And she's gone.

Dennis listens to the dead line, his wife having hung up on him for one of her patients. *He* can wait, but her patients cannot. Maybe if she put her personal life before her professional, Dennis wouldn't be carrying on this affair, lying to her and dining with the children of his mistress, getting deeper into Joan Dwyer's life while easing out of his wife's for a few hours.

Asparagus for Todd, salmon for Dennis, and a white chocolate mousse for Andrea. One each of their favorites to ensure that all will be happy on the occasion of her children meeting the man with whom she has become serious. She serious with him and he with her, Joan assumes. Assumes while he is with her but then thinks otherwise when he disappears for a day or two, not even a phone call, leaving her apartment at eleven-thirty at night, never sleeping over except on three occasions. The best Joan can do to keep herself from killing herself is either to drink until she's passed out or to phone Dr. Thompson for a late-night emergency conversation. Even then, talking to Dr. Thompson doesn't help as much as the alcohol.

"I understand alcohol is a depressant, but when I'm sober and suicidal, the best I can do to calm down from actually killing myself is to drink. Rather than the alcohol being something that depresses me, it acts as something that saves me just as you do. It's my medicine just like any of the drugs you've prescribed.''

Joan rinses the asparagus, then lays the stalks atop three sheets of paper towel, wrapping and rolling them to absorb the water drops. Tonight Dennis meets her children, becoming a part of her family, not appearing, then quickly disappearing, and Joan looks over her recipe for the salmon before going to the spice cabinet to select the ingredients to prepare the fish's dressing.

The apartment door opens, and Joan hears the voices of Andrea and Kitty March, her daughter's best friend from school.

''Hello, girls,'' Joan calls. ''I'm in the kitchen.''

Andrea and Kitty appear in the kitchen entrance. ''Yes, you are,'' Andrea remarks, and she walks to the refrigerator, taking out two diet sodas, handing one to Kitty. The crackle of plastic caps turning, the hiss of pressure being released from the bottles.

''Nice to see you, Mrs. Dwyer,'' Kitty says politely.

Andrea laughs. ''When's dinner?''

''Thank you, Kitty.'' Joan turns her back to the girls, opening the spice cabinet. ''Dinner will be at seven-thirty. Todd and Mr. Perry will be here too.'' She selects the sesame seeds and the celery seeds.

Andrea nudges Kitty's side. ''My mother has a boyfriend.''

Joan's back stiffens. ''He's a man friend of mine,'' she corrects her daughter. ''Not a *boy*friend.''

''You're dating him, aren't you?'' Andrea teases her.

''We have dinners together.'' Joan never thought she'd have to have a conversation like this with her daughter, but then again, she never thought she'd be single and dating at the age of forty-two.

''Is he handsome? How old is he?''

''You'll see tonight,'' Joan replies. ''I think he is.'' She takes down the jar with the bay leaves, then picks up the index card, reading the recipe. She hasn't made this in years.

''Let's go into your bedroom already,'' Kitty interrupts.

''I think that's a wise decision,'' Joan says, taking her measuring spoons out of the silverware drawer. "And don't you ask him his age tonight."

"How old is he, then?" Andrea asks. She opens the snack cabinet, looks in, then closes the cabinet. No potato chips.

"He's a bit younger than me," Joan states, hoping to end the discussion.

Andrea swigs from her soda bottle, opens the snack cabinet again, and takes out the bag of pretzel sticks. "A younger man. Is he closer to my age or your age?"

"My age." Joan laughs. "Only a year or two younger."

"It's nice to see you're finally doing something with your life."

Joan takes two glass measuring cups and a mixing bowl from a cabinet. "Raising you was doing nothing with my life?"

"I raised myself." Andrea leaves the kitchen, trailed by Kitty. "My mother wants to marry him. That's why he has to meet us," and Joan has to restrain herself from slamming the cabinet door.

Lying in bed the night before Andrea arrived home from school, Dennis, drunk on a bottle of red wine, said that he considered Joan his lover, that he wanted to call her his lover, that he felt close to her, needed by her, needing of her. An entire waterfall of emotion Dennis lavished upon Joan, and only five minutes later, after having clung to Joan, one hand on her breast and another on the glass of wine, he was reaching for the remote control. "I think a rerun of *Green Acres* is on now." He propped the pillows up against the headboard, bent his knees up, and sat watching the television. Dennis laughed aloud at the show, his eyes never leaving the screen, and as he dressed over the closing credits, Joan realized, feared, that this was all the love she could ever expect to get from him—half a night's worth, approximately four hours. After he left, Joan sat on her bed with the shoe box full of pills, counting out the numbers of Valium, Tofranil, Xanax, Asendin, Norpramin, and the sleep medications she'd saved.

"We could try the Prozac again to see if that will help you. Of course, it can't help if you drink. Alcohol will defeat the effects it might have.''

''Would I be able to drink at all?'' Joan asked her doctor.

''Four ounces a week. The equivalent of four drinks.''

Joan laughed to her doctor's face. ''You expect me to restrict my drinking to four drinks a week and pray that this drug is going to erase my depression when none of the others you've prescribed has? The alcohol's the only thing keeping me alive at this point. None of the medication helps at all and you want me to stop *drinking*?''

''Then we might as well stick with the Tofranil, but I have to tell you, no antidepressant is going to be of any help when you're drinking. Alcohol is a depressant.''

Joan takes one Tofranil capsule each morning. Joan drinks at least six ounces of alcohol each evening. She hasn't noticed any change in her depression since beginning on the medication six months ago.

One hour and forty-five minutes before Dennis is due to arrive, a great deal of preparation remains to be done, enough so that Joan is tempted to ask Andrea for help setting the table. But Joan knows better than to ask. Andrea would only perform the task lazily, causing Joan to have to redo it herself. She reaches into her skirt's pocket, taking out a Xanax tablet, placing it on her tongue. She swallows it dry, hoping the pill will calm her until she has her first drink of the evening sometime before dinner.

Wednesday, and Bill Matson has left Pam's office, leaving Pam alone. She writes notes in Bill Matson's book, then places the cap on the black rolling-ball pen. Pam draws the rolltop cover over the desk and opens a drawer, taking out the vial of Valium, spilling out one of the yellow pills with the *V* cut from its center. She places the flat tablet on her tongue, swallowing it with a lukewarm glass of water. She walks to the window and shuts off the air conditioner.

The reflection of a worn woman stares back at her from the glass. The silk cream blouse, bow untied and dangling over her chest. The cotton skirt, wrinkled, belt buckle askew, a few inches off center. Strands of hair escape the clip at the back of her head, dangle over her forehead, and curl around an ear. The skirt feels tight, and Pam hopes it's not because she hasn't been exercising as much as she used to. Only running three mornings a week at most, not trying for four, sometimes only making it for two, Pam remains in bed most mornings, resting next to her husband. Now that he likes to be at work by eight-thirty, he's leaving only shortly after her, so they rise together, the morning news playing in the background as they take turns in the bathroom. Last week Pam slipped into the shower with Dennis, went to her knees, sucked him hard, then had him put it in her. They stood, water and soap running over their bodies; Pam tried to picture him doing it with Joan in the shower, and she couldn't and was pleased. She didn't want to do it for her husband in a way that would remind him of Joan.

"I have a business dinner," he wedged into their short conversation as if it were essential that he say this to his wife at that very moment, as if it couldn't wait another hour, another second, as if she had asked him for an excuse as to why he wouldn't be home on time tonight.

The more of an effort she makes to work things out, to make herself a better person and make up for her erroneous ways of the past, the more Pam perceives Dennis to be slipping further into Joan's life. A business trip to Louisville, he told her one morning, on the morning he was leaving, as if it had come up only the night before and he'd forgotten about it, and Pam placed a short note in his luggage: "I love you. Thinking of you. Call me." The following afternoon Joan came into therapy jubilant that Dennis had spent all of the previous night with her. "It's changing. He seems more committed now than he used to be. He does."

Pam just stared at Joan, concealing her shock. That night, returning home, Dennis embraced his wife with affection. "Thank you for the note. I liked it very much." He hadn't phoned her, as she had asked in the note, and when she looked in his eyes, she saw love there, sincere love, and wondered who was being taken for a fool, Joan or herself. Since she knows this affair is going on yet does nothing to stop it, Pam guesses she's the fool. She's the one resting her head in her husband's lap while they watch TV, asking him to rub her back; she's the one sending him flowers at work; she's the one giving him relaxing massages before bed, hoping to work Joan Dwyer out of his system and draw him back to their married life. Despite all her efforts and how much happier her husband does seem at home, he still invests more time with Joan Dwyer than with his wife. He is not awakening to the fact that Pam is working at being a *better wife*. He has not discovered he no longer wants his fling to continue. He wakes up in the morning and finds his wife by his side, holding him, and that is still not enough to keep him from Joan Dwyer.

Pam props a pillow at the head of the couch and lies on her back, waiting for the Valium to kick in and relax her so she doesn't care or at least cares less and can regain her appetite and go out to dinner. She is failing, has realized her errors and corrected her ways too late for her husband either to notice or to care. Days pass, and Dennis and Joan accumulate more and more experiences between them, creating a foundation upon which to build a relationship, while Pam watches her marriage erode.

With increasing frequency, Pam finds herself using Joan's therapy as a means to learn about and understand her husband, discover how to make herself more of what her husband wants, learn the truth about how her husband feels for Joan Dwyer, what he will do for Joan that he will not or cannot do for his wife. Pam feels herself becoming two people. There is the woman who is slowly disappearing—the good, caring, kind doctor, analyzing her patients—and there is the woman she is becoming—a desperate, needy woman running scared, terrified of losing the pillars that support her life: her husband and her pride in her work. And by attempting to save both, she jeopardizes each as well.

"What do you like to do in bed with him?" Pam asked Joan after a prolonged silence one session. Pam heard herself ask the question,

but it didn't feel like her asking it, so unfamiliar was she with the
fear driving the query. Another boundary crossed, Pam recognized,
Joan's sessions less directed by the patient's needs than by her
doctor's.

Joan looked up with a start, flushed. "What do you mean?"

So angry at Dennis and Joan for putting her in this situation, Pam
could not help wanting to hurt them. "When you and Dennis engage
in sexual activities, what do you prefer? What does he prefer? What a
person enjoys or does not enjoy during sex reveals a lot about you
and the relationship. I think we should examine that."

Joan toyed with the sunglasses she held in her hands, flipping their
arms open, then closed, bringing them up to her lips and gnawing on
their already well-chewed tortoiseshell tips. "We kiss. Nothing
unusual. He's very gentle with me. Very caring."

"Does he bring you to orgasm?" A question intended to shock.

Joan folded the sunglasses in her lap. "Sometimes. Yes."

"What are you thinking?" She'd gone too far, Pam recognized.

Joan looked up. "I'm not comfortable discussing this, that's all,"
she replied firmly.

"Why is that, do you think?"

"This is private. Between Dennis and myself."

"It certainly affects how you feel on a daily basis, and if it can help
our work, we should discuss it, but I can't know that unless you tell
me, and if you fail to do that yourself, as your doctor I have an
obligation to ask, don't I?"

Joan put on her sunglasses. "I don't want to discuss this."

"Then we won't." And Pam let it go, already having heard
enough and recognizing that Dennis's sex with Joan was a far cry
from the quick, frantic bouts of sex she engaged in with her husband.

A rock rolling down a hill, gathering speed and power, losing
control—the unexpected comes at her constantly from her husband,
from Joan. Pam barely has time to sort it out and digest her feelings
from one episode before another occurs, inciting stronger emotions.
What has she said to Joan, told many of her patients? "When you

deny your feelings, they'll come back at you in unexpected ways, surfacing at inappropriate times when you aren't prepared to deal with them." Pam sees herself as evidence of this maxim. Anger at Dennis from last week surfacing with Joan in therapy. Despair felt with Joan on a phone call rising during the dinner she prepared for Dennis celebrating the new job. With either direction she turns for a sense of accomplishment and confidence—work or home—she feels defeated and overwhelmed and she sees no relief in sight from this triangle. It only gets worse, more depressing, not less as she struggles to find a solution.

A business dinner, Dennis lied. Business dinners. Business trips. Business deadlines. Late-night work at the office. Unreachable at the client's office. Unreachable in meetings, at dinners, at banquets, giving presentations. Upon taking the new position, Dennis still refused to abandon the office space on West Seventy-third Street.

"I got the lease cheap, fixed it up myself, and I like having my own space with my own stuff so it's not cluttering up our home. And don't tell me you never just hang around your office when you want to clear your head before coming home."

Pam smiled and nodded. "You're right. I can't argue with that." No point in forcing the issue; Dennis would only insist on keeping the office—or *apartment,* as Pam is sure he has represented it to Joan. No point in demanding he give up the space so he'll be forced to refuse his wife, a confrontation driving him to stay in his office-apartment for an evening or two, making him that much more available to his mistress.

"Have you thought about how much your life has changed since meeting this man over these past few months?" Pam asked Joan during a mid-April session, hoping Joan would arrive at the conclusion that Dennis is the wrong man for her, not wanting to have to tell this to her patient directly.

"There have been many changes," Joan replied, not sure what her doctor was aiming toward. "I don't blame how I've been on him. I think he helps me out of my bad moods just like you do."

"What does he do for you?"

"He makes me feel loved and needed and good about myself. There's nothing wrong with that, is there?"

"No, not in the least. But don't you think you should feel good about yourself without having to rely on Dennis to give that to you? I just think you need to think about the emotional changes you go through from when you're with him to when he leaves you and you're suddenly alone with yourself again." All very plain and clear, not out of bounds.

A long pause. Joan held her purse in her lap, wrapped its long black leather strap around her fingers. "I can't do that for myself. That's why I need him."

"You certainly won't do that for yourself if you have him to do it for you." A cutting remark, making Joan aware of her behavior before Joan was ready to face it, and Pam felt herself crossing another line.

Joan looked up at her doctor. "Do you want me to leave him? Is that your suggestion? To be alone and miserable with no love or to be with him and at least have it some of the time? I'd kill myself without him. He's the only thing I have anymore."

"I don't believe he's all you do have, for one," Pam argued. "And doesn't your reaction to his presence indicate that there's something inherently wrong in your relationship if he makes you feel suicidal every time he leaves? Is that how love should make you feel?"

"I can't leave him," Joan stated, standing abruptly, and the session was over, leaving Pam to address the topic at the following session and the session following that and at every following session to this day in May, when Pam lies stranded on her patient couch in her office while her husband meets the children of his mistress.

Confrontational instead of supportive, she's taken the wrong approach with Joan Dwyer. By coming down hard on her, all Pam has done is alienate herself from her patient and force Joan to seek additional comfort from Dennis, needing him more. Pam might as well have confronted Dennis himself and been a better doctor to Joan this past month and a half, giving Joan the strength to be on her own once Pam got Dennis to leave her, if she could get Dennis to leave her.

During the weeks since hearing her husband's name from Joan Dwyer, Pam took to overhauling the apartment with more expediency than she'd taken prior to the discovery. Immersing herself in the redecoration, hiring craftsmen and carpenters, choosing tile, carpeting, a hand-braided rug, a handwoven rug, bathroom fixtures, and charging it all on their shared credit card accounts, her store charge accounts, writing out checks from their joint accounts and her personal account, leveling, then rebuilding each room, room by room, Dennis passively observing his wife reshelve books from the living room in the guest room. The leather sofa he saw in the living room when he went off to work in the morning was gone by the time he returned home that evening. An entire room was transformed from leather and chrome and glass to pastels and fabric and wood. Where an old movie poster hung in a thin silver frame, a row of blue, green, yellow, and white plates were arranged horizontally, each painted with identical twin ducks facing each other, beaks kissing.

Pam observed Dennis observing the transformation, listening as he complimented her on the choices made, how light and fresh and airy the apartment now felt. He said he loved the new tiled kitchen, each white tile on the table painted with a different vegetable. "I never would have thought of it," he said too gleefully. The new bathroom with the modern fixtures. "Very elegant," he commented, never once mentioning the inconvenience of having to go without a toilet for two full days. Pam accomplished the apartment's renovation swiftly and easily, her husband applauding every change as if he had been consulted and taken into account long before the choice had been made and implemented. Returning late from the office one night, Dennis walked into the living room, sat down on the new sofa alongside his wife, put his feet up on the new coffee table, switched on the TV, which stood on a new antique oak chest, and said, "Every night I look forward to coming home and seeing how you've redone the place." He leaned over to give Pam a kiss, a hug, an embrace, looking into her eyes, smiling brightly. "It's like it's my birthday and Christmas every day." All said with utter sincerity, not even a hint of a sarcastic overtone. And what bothered Pam the most was that she couldn't ever remember him sounding so loving toward her in all the years they'd been together. She only wondered if he sounded as good to Joan.

While having sex this past Saturday evening in their as yet unrenovated—but soon to be renovated—bedroom, Pam attempted to be like Joan. She tried to move with and not against him. Dennis didn't notice and fucked her as mechanically and manically as he always did, his dick driving between her legs more from a sense of anger, obligation, and habit than from one of love. Pam grew increasingly tense as she worked harder and harder to please him, and only when Dennis finally came could she relax enough to open her eyes and witness his sweaty, bored, pained expression: a grimace of exhaustion, of relief. A performance for him too. "I love you," he said remotely, rolling onto his side, his face in a pillow.

"I love you too," Pam promptly replied, sliding out of bed, heading into the bathroom for a Halcion tablet.

Pam sits on the couch in her office, no longer anxious, only depressed, the Valium having kicked in and taken over her mood. She stands, taking her light khaki jacket and shoulder bag off the coat rack behind the door. Her options for the evening: go to a movie alone, a dinner out alone, or a dinner in alone with a videocassette.

"I'm going to have to cancel on Wednesday," Joan informed Pam last week. "My daughter will be home, and I'm having him meet my kids. I hope my informing you now is okay, but if it's not, you can charge me for the session. I think this is a really important step for us. Me and him, I mean."

Pam wouldn't let Joan go that easily. "I think it is also an important step for you and me. Canceling a session in order to be with your boyfriend. You could have chosen another night at another time. But you didn't. Why do you think that's so?"

A discussion ensued in which Joan defended herself, claiming Wednesday was the only night Dennis could get off from work when both her kids would be available. Pam hypothesized that Joan was sending a signal to her doctor that her boyfriend was more of a help to her than her therapist was.

"I think we're going through a difficult period here, things being so intense, and you may feel you want to avoid the conflicts I present you with. It's easier to seek comfort from this man who doesn't challenge you to examine your feelings," all said by Pam with perfect confidence that the words were not affected by the fact that the man Joan was involved with was her husband.

"I cancel one session with you five days in advance, and you act as if I'm ignoring all the work we've done here."

"I'm just telling you what I observe from your behavior," Pam explained.

Joan played with the cuff of her blouse, unbuttoning and buttoning the sleeve. "I'm just being practical," Joan said. "It's the only night we can all make it."

"Except for you," Pam replied.

"This is something good," Joan declared. "He's really beginning to make an effort and become a part of my life, and you're making it all seem bad, like this is only about me canceling an appointment. I'm having my kids meet him, making him a part of my whole life instead of separating him away, and all you do is criticize me for having it on a day when we have a session. This is hard for me, and you're not even helping."

Pam observed her patient, Joan's face so red, red the way it becomes just before the tears fall, and Pam decided to drop the issue; therapy with Joan was tough enough without inventing new conflicts to complicate matters. "Why don't we try to reschedule Wednesday's appointment, then?" Pam suggested. She checked her schedule book on the desk. "How is next Thursday at noon?" The soonest Pam could fit Joan in following the dinner, Pam caught herself thinking. There *is* no way to separate her life from Joan Dwyer's;

they live the same life—both in fear of losing the same man. They're partners.

"That's fine," Joan said.

Pam wrote Joan's name in the book, filling in the blank hour and turning back to her patient, catching the time. They'd run a couple of minutes over. "Our time is up," Pam informed her, and Joan stood, buttoning her cuff for the last time this session, picking up her pocketbook. As she passed, Pam took Joan's arm, stopping her. "I'm sorry if I came across a bit harsh. I didn't mean to upset you, I just think it's my obligation to let you know how seriously I take our work together."

As Pam stands in the elevator going down, she cannot decide what to do with herself. She walks down the street past closed shops, bright restaurants, multiplex cinemas, and construction sites, a homeless man begging for change, a young couple embracing on a corner, a street vendor selling used paperbacks laid out across a dirty blue blanket, and soon, surprisingly, Pam finds herself standing opposite Joan Dwyer's building. Knows this is Joan Dwyer's building because this is the street and street number on the check she receives from Joan each month. Pam counts up sixteen floors to a row of windows that could be Joan Dwyer's apartment: 16B. No figures stand in the bright, curtain-framed windows of the apartment that might belong to Joan Dwyer, the windows Joan thinks about throwing herself out of, and had people been standing in the windows, from this distance they'd hardly be recognizable.

"My mother said you're not her boyfriend. She said you're her *man* friend," Andrea says to Dennis across the dining room table.

They are seated with Todd at the table's head, Joan at its end by the kitchen entrance, Dennis to Joan's right, and Andrea and Kitty March to Joan's left.

"You know I'll be better behaved if Kitty stays," Andrea informed her mother, and Joan, too anxious to take any chances, invited Kitty for dinner, but considering Andrea's last remark, Joan isn't sure Kitty's presence has any effect on her daughter.

"Well, I probably am a bit too old to be called a boy," Dennis replies, playing along. He breaks the salmon fillet with the side of his fork, bringing the pink meat to his mouth. "What about you?" he asks Andrea. "Do you have a boyfriend or a *man* friend?"

"Why do you care?" Andrea lifts a stalk of asparagus with her fingers. She shakes it at Kitty. "And don't you say anything." She bites off the asparagus tip, punctuating her statement.

"Just curious," Dennis answers innocently. He turns to Kitty. "Does she have a boyfriend at school?"

Joan watches Dennis toy with Andrea and Kitty, not sure if this is going in a good or bad direction.

Kitty looks to Andrea. "Why won't you tell?"

"She must." Todd joins in. "She always had one while I was there."

"Why *must* I?" Andrea sneers at her brother.

"Because you're desperate." He sips his glass of wine, Todd allowed to have the wine, Kitty and Andrea denied any alcoholic beverage.

"I am not desperate," Andrea blurts out. "*Mom* is."

The table falls silent, everyone's eyes on Joan. Dennis takes her hand, a gesture for the kids to see. "Do you mean she'd have to be desperate to be with me?" he asks, taking the heat off Joan.

Andrea looks down at her plate. "I didn't mean anything. I was just pissed at Todd."

"She does have a boyfriend, though," Kitty suddenly volunteers, feeling guilty for Andrea's insult. "Randy Hoffsteader."

"Randy Hoffsteader's the boy who was almost kicked out for setting fire to the gym," Joan states, horrified that this is whom her daughter has chosen to be her boyfriend. "Isn't he the boy you told me about at Christmas?"

"Kitty's wrong," Andrea moans. "I am not going steady with that loser. Don't worry." She gives Kitty a sharp look. "Now shut up or I'll tell about you with Brian and the snorkel. How would you like that?"

Kitty's face instantly turns red. "There was *never* any snorkel. Brian made that up."

"Doubt it," Andrea mutters, and the conversation is dropped. Both girls eat their dinners, ignoring each other and the rest of the table.

"Is the food good?" Joan asks, an easy subject.

"Everything's great," Todd says.

"Delicious," Dennis says.

"As good as Moby's?" Joan inquires.

"Almost," Dennis says, "except it's not oily enough."

"How did you two meet?" Kitty asks, her plate clear.

Joan looks to Dennis and Dennis to Joan—who's to answer? "We met in a restaurant," Joan says.

"I bought your mother a drink," Dennis adds.

Andrea laughs. "Trying to get her drunk?"

"Trying to be a gentleman," Joan says, defending him. She has no idea how this dinner is progressing. The determining factor is Dennis, and he's been unreadable since he arrived. Gracious and social, but completely unreadable.

"How many years do you have until college?" Dennis asks Andrea, forcing her to talk about herself, not bad-mouth others. "Will you be a senior?"

"I'll be a junior," Andrea replies. "So will Kitty."

"Have to start thinking about college," Joan reminds her.

"Not yet," Andrea says. "We have time."

"Not too much," Joan warns. "You have to begin taking tests this coming year. Have you taken any test courses, Kitty?"

"I'm taking one starting next month," Kitty says.

Andrea shoots her friend a dirty look. Then, to her mother in a voice tinged with victory: "Hey, I can't take a course anyway. I'll be with Dad in Colorado all August."

"That's fine," Joan replies, wishing Al hadn't been brought into the conversation, doesn't need the reminder. "We could talk to a counselor, though, in the next couple weeks. That might be a help."

Andrea shakes her head, adamant. "I'm not seeing a shrink just because you do. I don't need one."

"Mom meant a *college counselor*, not a psychiatrist," Todd points out. "They help you select colleges you might be interested in attending. I met with one when I was a junior."

"Is that what you meant?" Andrea asks more softly, no longer defensive.

"That is what I meant," Joan says, her face gone ashen, afraid to meet Dennis's look, her secret of the psychiatrist out. "Maybe we can arrange that early in September, before you're back in school." She will pretend that all is well. She will not panic, she tells herself.

"That's fine," Andrea says. "I don't mind that." Andrea looks at her watch, then pushes her plate into the table's center. "Nice to meet you, Mr. Perry." She stands, taps Kitty on the shoulder. "Let's go to your house. Come on."

Kitty stands, "Nice to meet you," she says to Dennis, then, "Thanks for dinner, Mrs. Dwyer. Bye, Todd."

"Nice having you, Kitty," Joan says, and the two girls leave the room, giggling their way through the living room to Andrea's bedroom, back to the living room, and finally out the apartment door.

"When will you be home?" Joan calls too late, the girls already gone, the door already shut, and she looks down to her plate at the half-eaten salmon fillet. "God, has she grown up since December. I wasn't like that when I was sixteen. At least I don't think so."

Joan rises to clear the dinner plates, still can't face Dennis, but then Todd stands. "I'll do it."

And Joan is forced to retake her seat. "Thank you," she says.

Todd collects Andrea's, Kitty's, and his own plates and walks past his mother and into the kitchen.

"Those are my kids. What do you think?" Joan asks, avoiding the obvious subject between them.

Todd reenters the room, picks up Joan's plate, then turns to Dennis. "Are you all finished?"

"Yes, please. Thanks," Dennis replies.

Joan touches Todd's elbow. "Thanks for your help. I'm sorry Emily couldn't come." She smiles at him, and Todd walks off into the kitchen again. Joan looks at Dennis. "Andrea has a hard time adjusting to being back home again. Not used to having a parent watching over her."

Dennis shrugs his eyebrows, waiting for Joan to bring it up. Joan smiles and stands. "I'll go see about dessert." She takes Dennis's hand, her smile quickly fading. "I'd have told you about the therapy, only I didn't think it mattered. Does it?"

"That's fine. Don't worry about it." He gives Joan's hand a light squeeze, and Joan lifts his hand to her lips, kissing a knuckle before exiting to the kitchen.

The Dwyers. Todd silent and brooding but manageable, and Andrea, typical of her age, spoiled and nasty. And if Andrea is indeed typical, Dennis thinks, that's reason enough never to have a child. Maybe Pam's refusal to have kids *is* the correct move, and she has always known something he never knew: that having kids is ideal in concept but hell in reality. Maybe it is to Dennis's benefit that his wife has denied him children.

Dennis swallows the last of his wine and the bottle on the table is empty and he wishes he had more. Todd comes in, extending his hand to be shaken. "See you later. Nice meeting you."

Dennis stands, taking Todd's hand. "Thanks, you too." They say their good-byes and Todd leaves and they are alone, Dennis and Joan, and Dennis thinks about Joan in therapy, isn't sure if it bothers him or not. If he's more than a bit annoyed that other people confide their innermost secrets to his wife, giving her secrets to keep from him, taking her time away from him, how does he feel now knowing that his girlfriend can't talk to him but must confide in someone else?

Joan returns with the white chocolate mousse cake and two forks. She places the cake and utensils by Dennis, then pulls her chair up by his and sits. "Todd's gone home to study with Emily. God, I hope Andrea's not going steady with that teenage arsonist. She's already sixteen, and I have no idea how to deal with her." Joan sighs, altogether worn out from this family gathering. Dennis says nothing.

"Are you upset that I'm in therapy?" Joan asks to be polite; now that it's been said, she might as well acknowledge its existence. "I'm not crazy or anything. I'm not like Sybil with fifty personalities or anything like that," Joan soothes.

"If it helps, I think it's great." He completely dismisses it; the dinner was tense enough for him, knowing Joan's kids were evaluating him, lining him up next to their father. A discussion of her therapy can wait.

The freshly sliced strawberries around the cake's top border have an orange glow under the light of the chandelier, and Joan selects a fork, picking at the cake's edges, digging into the top, taking a bite of mousse and strawberry. "Go ahead," she says. "It's only the two of us, so you might as well." She hands Dennis the second fork. "This is Andrea's favorite. Serves her right for being such a nuisance that she's missing out."

"Why not?" He takes a bite, taking the opportunity to glance at his watch, discovering the time to leave has arrived. "Guess what?" he asks Joan casually.

"What?" A mouthful of mousse on her tongue, sugarcoating her teeth.

"I have to go. I'm sorry."

Joan shakes her head vehemently. "No. No. Not yet."

He lays down the fork. "Joan, I have to. I have a breakfast meeting tomorrow."

She lays down her fork. "You could still stay over tonight. We'll get up early."

"With Andrea here?"

"Yes."

"Really?"

"Serves her right," Joan repeats, joking.

Dennis stands, doesn't want to, argue a point when there's no chance of his relinquishing. "Walk me to the door and give me a kiss." He extends his hand and is pleased that she stands and takes it. She has accepted his inevitable departure.

Pam sits in the all-night coffee shop by the window, a once-hot but now-cold slice of apple pie before her, french vanilla ice cream melting over and around its crust.

The blue-suited doorman pulls the heavy glass door open for her husband, and he leaves Joan Dwyer's building, walking to the corner, raising an arm, instantly hailing a cab. Dennis's forefinger arcs a curve to the right, indicating he wants the cab to turn crosstown rather than continue farther up the avenue. Dennis enters the taxi, and the car speeds off and out of sight, red taillight blinking.

She slashes at her left shoulder with a quick flick of the wrist. Her skin splits like a seam, opening, pulling cleanly back from the cut. For a moment no blood seeps from the opening between the parted skin, and Joan can see the pale pink flesh of her muscle. Pink and white, glistening with moisture. The elliptical space begins filling with blood, slowly drawing into a puddle, bulging, then rolling out in a stream, down her shoulder and around to under her armpit.

She sits on the toilet in the bathroom off her bedroom, the left-hand strap of her sleeveless nightgown hanging down by her elbow, her bathrobe hanging on the hook on the back of the closed door.

The single-edged razor is clasped between thumb and forefinger, and Joan flicks it again, a larger arc, cutting a neat line an inch and a half long. Again the skin pulls back to expose the inner, soft flesh. Not a gash or a messy scrape, as one might experience when falling on one's knees or elbows as in childhood, but a precise, clear snap of a cut. The skin less broken than sliced like paper with shears.

Painless cuts. Swift and painless. Joan goes at her shoulder a third time, razor pinched tight between fingers, crosscutting a line through the other two.

The blood is red, and the red is pretty, Joan thinks. Pretty and red, as red as her glossy fingernail polish, and Joan cuts at her arm again as if to prove that she exists and is alive and living on this planet.

Home late but, remarkably, before his wife, Dennis undresses and steps into the shower, half fearing, half hoping that Pam is cheating on him. An affair on her part would be an indication that she too is unhappy in this marriage whereas Dennis remains undecided over what he wants. Possibly Pam, in the midst of her own affair, knows precisely what she wants, and that want doesn't include Dennis. Her decision to reject Dennis will be his to embrace Joan fully, and all will be decided for him, and everybody will be happy with the results.

Mr. and Mrs. Dennis and Joan Perry's life. The married couple lives in Joan's apartment. Dennis goes off to work every day and returns home to his loving wife, tending to their newborn child. Stepson Todd lives with his girlfriend in their apartment and stepdaughter Andrea lives in boarding school until she graduates to attend a college such as Vassar, Smith, Holyoke, or Bard. The older children return home for holidays and vacations, pleased to see their mother happy with her new husband, pleased to have a young baby sibling to coddle, pleased to have their mother occupied with a man instead of hounding them. The Dennis, Joan, and baby family spends weekdays in the city and retreats to a country house for extended weekends and summers. Pleasant, loving, low-key living. Dennis steps out of the shower and into the bathroom, drying himself with a plush towel, pulling on a pair of gray sweatpants and a white T-shirt.

Joan in therapy. Surprised at first, a bit threatened that he can't be all things to her, Dennis has come to think it's not a bad thing. Letting his pride go, looking over Joan's anxious behavior, thinking back to their second date of months ago, Joan crying at the window, he recognizes she has an obvious need for stability, and as he can't always be there for her, *may not* always be there for her, Dennis is somewhat relieved that Joan sees a therapist, is working to understand herself better. Maybe if he knew himself better, he wouldn't have stumbled into this affair and he'd be talking his problems out with his wife.

Back in the bedroom, Dennis finds Pam half undressed, arranging a skirt carefully over a wooden hanger. She unbuttons her silk blouse.

"You're home late," Dennis comments, brushing his wet hair back from his eyes with a palm.

Pam hangs the blouse on a hook along with other blouses that must be dry-cleaned. She pulls a red tank top over her bra. She pulls a pair of faded jeans up over her hips, buttoning the fly. "Got caught up in things. Scheduled a late last-minute appointment."

Dennis approaches her, kisses her cheek. "Hero to all."

Pam walks off into the kitchen, leaving Dennis behind. "Yeah. Hero to all."

He follows: Is he overdoing the affectionate bit? "Something wrong?" he asks.

"No, why?" she asks in return, wondering why he's carrying on this conversation, why he's bothering if he doesn't care. Pam opens cabinets, randomly scanning items. "What is there for dinner?" She scans the shelves. The phone rings. Frozen Tater Tots she could heat up in the microwave.

Dennis answers the phone, "Hello." A pause, and he holds the phone out to Pam. "Your phone machine."

Blueberry Pop Tarts for the toaster oven. "I'll phone back after I have something to eat."

Dennis hangs up. Pam stares into the new cabinets, so clean and new, no dents in the white wood. Pasta soup with lentils, Pam thinks, and she knows the message recorded is most likely from Joan Dwyer. A desperate plea for help in the midst of her suicidal agony. Canned chili with no beans. One of Dennis's favorites. Either to be micro-waved or heated in a pot on the stove. How would he feel if Joan killed herself? How would he hide his grief from her?

"I'm going to go read in bed." Dennis speaks to Pam's back, turns, and leaves the room. His wife is too narcissistic to recognize his existence. He could have stayed at Joan's all evening and Pam would never have noticed. Dennis turns the air-conditioning unit on high, reads the latest Scott Turow novel.

Pam pulls open the Tater Tot cover, folding it around back and under as the directions on the box indicate. She arranges the small potato chunks in a single layer along the box's silver bottom. Having failed to win her husband back by becoming the wife she thought he wanted, failing with Dennis as Joan did with her husband, Pam must take action to make things right and save her marriage and Joan Dwyer. Pam is not the one hurting Joan, Dennis is, and the sooner he leaves Joan, the sooner Pam will be able to help Joan help herself in therapy. Pam inserts the box into the microwave, shutting the oven door, and setting the appropriate time and heat settings before pushing the start button.

The box of Tots spins on the glass turntable, under the white overhead light, the light illuminating the microwave's interior. She's the one letting him get away with it. By keeping quiet, she is letting him get away with it, cheating on her, ruining Joan Dwyer, destroying their married life. She could be putting a stop to it, it is within her control, and Pam counts how many times the carousel spins before the Tater Tots are done, hot and golden brown. Fourteen rotations.

． ． ．

"Who cares about me?" Joan asks into her doctor's answering machine. "Not my kids. Not the man. I've had enough. The whole dinner was a mistake. Everyone aggravating each other. Andrea announced that I was in therapy, and then she left. Todd left, and then my date barely gave me a chance to explain before he was gone. I tried. I can do all I can to be there for people and let them care for me, but if they leave me, it's hard to think they do care, isn't it? Isn't that some indication that people don't care? I'm seeing you tomorrow anyway. We'll talk then. Good-bye."

Pam hangs up, letting the office machine rewind to tape over Joan Dwyer's message. One listen is enough. She switches off the lights in the guest room, kitchen, and hallway and heads into the bedroom, which is lit by the small reading lamp on Dennis's night table. She'll see Joan tomorrow, has had enough of her life for today, for tonight. Time to arrange her own life. Dennis lies in bed shirtless, propped against two pillows, one hand holding a paperback book, thumb wedging the binding open close to his face, his other hand hidden under the covers, palming his crotch. Pam undresses for the night, taking off the jeans and bra, wearing only a pair of sheer panties and the red tank top. Like Joan, she's had enough, and she eyes the dirty T-shirt she wore while jogging this morning as it hangs on a hook on the back of the closet door. Pale blue with a faded picture of a trolley car, "San Francisco" silk-screened across the chest in decaying yellow, red, and green print. An August vacation taken how many years back? Two? Three? *Five*, Pam suddenly remembers. *I have not been a bad wife. Not perfect, but not bad,* and if Dennis can't face her to solve their problems and continue on with their marriage, if he can only take a mistress in order to satisfy himself for what he's afraid of asking his own wife for, then Pam will be the mature one, the one who must cut through all the crap and broach the subject that has as yet remained unspoken.

She leaves the bathroom door open as she takes a Dixie cup, filling it with cool water, downing two Halcion, all the better to give her a full night of sleep, needing a good sleep, deserving a good sleep, considering she has a full day's worth of patients due in tomorrow. Her final adult ed lesson of the semester having been taught last week, she has the night free. Some comfort, if not much.

"I can be done whenever you want," Dennis says, covering his mouth as he yawns.

Pam steps from the bathroom, shutting off the light, again noting Dennis's hand between his thighs, a common resting place for most men's hands as they relax while sitting or reclining or sleeping. Always covering and protecting their most vulnerable parts as if the only thing on everyone else's minds is to castrate and mutilate a man's fragile genitalia. Dennis looks away from the book to Pam. "Are you ready for bed?" he asks.

Pam takes an elastic band from her top bureau drawer, twists it in two, and pulls through a loose ponytail, low at the back of her neck. Pam draws the end of the ponytail over her shoulder, staring down at the thick hairs, examining for split ends. "You are cheating on me. I know that." She says this not cruelly, but softly, gently. "You are cheating on me." Does it sound as severe as she intends or only as if he's cheating in a game, like poker, Monopoly, Chutes and Ladders?

Dennis closes the paperback, forgetting to mark his place, looking up, staring at the line the loose tank top cuts just below the curve of his wife's ass. "*Cheating?*" he asks.

Pam stares into the mirror opposite the bed, gripping her ponytail in both hands, twisting ends of individual hairs. "You are saying you're not, then." Her voice becomes hard, deliberate.

"I'm saying—"

"I *know* you are. Don't lie. Just admit it. Admit it, and we can go on from there. *Here.* Please. For both of us." Pam feels she's in control and has trapped him. She turns to find Dennis with a sheepish look, his knees bent up, shoulders bunched together, both arms extended under the covers between his folded knees: a seated fetal position. "I don't know why I love you, but I do even after knowing this." Pam stands at the edge of the bed, looking down at him. "What do you think of that?"

Suddenly conscious of his body posture, that he's being observed, analyzed, Dennis straightens, then swings his legs out so he's sitting on the bed, arms loose at his sides. He notices the few hairs on his feet, wants to ask how she found out, thought he had been careful, *very careful*, but knows this is an inappropriate question to ask. "I don't know what to say," he says. "I love you. I just don't know what's happening to us right now."

"How do you think we can find out?" Pam sits on the bed by Dennis's side, forming an alliance, reestablishing a frank closeness. She lays a gentle hand on his bare shoulder, and he leans into her, a pulse of desire rushing between them.

He still cannot look at her face, stares into the dark of the bathroom at the blue wastebasket overflowing with white tissue. "I want us to be together, just not like this anymore. We have to be different somehow. I was very unhappy." And it's already in the past. *Was* very unhappy.

"That can't just happen overnight."

"I know but—"

"It can't happen if you continue with this woman. Whatever it is you're missing here, you're getting from her, and if you continue having her satisfy these needs, you won't bring them to me. I know we're both at fault. I know I'm to blame too. I know what I've done. We both created this situation, and it will take both of us to correct it. I'm upset, not unforgiving. I'm still here."

"I'm here too," Dennis replies feebly, knowingly feebly. A pause while he considers what he's supposed to say, what he wants, what he will do, decide. Too long a pause, and he reaches a hand out, covering Pam's hand on his shoulder with his own. "I really do love you," he says, the only response he can think to give. "This was never about not loving you."

An image of Joan Dwyer crying during therapy tomorrow, crying, threatening suicide. Pam stands, shutting out the thought. "So it will end? You won't see her anymore? You'll rent out your old office? I'm sure that's where this took place. I've been wondering for months but was hoping . . . I've been trying to be more open with you so you would stop and it would end, but it never did, you never noticed me trying, and so I thought . . . I guess I didn't want to believe that you would do this to me."

At this moment, sitting on the bed, Pam standing sadly before him laying herself bare, he can only think to keep Pam and lose Joan. *Cheating. Losing.* The next choice is easy; there is no choice. "I will phone her and tell her tomorrow. I promise." He takes Pam's hand, pressing her palm to his cheek. "I love you. I do. I'm sorry . . . it was just an escape. You and I are all that matters. I want it to be better. Really I do."

"I think we can be better together," Pam says. "I want to try to be better with you."

"I do too," Dennis says. "I do too."

She wipes his hair back from his face. "We can work this through," she says. "We'll go over what's wrong, make it right and go on." Pam yawns, withdrawing her hand from Dennis to cover her mouth.

"You're tired," he says.

"You really want to be with me?" Pam asks. "You don't love her?" She watches him closely, examining for the lie, and Dennis takes her hand, holding it tight, giving it a kiss.

"I'm glad you're back," Pam says. She climbs onto the bed, sliding under the covers. "I'm glad you're back with me."

Dennis wraps his arms around his wife, shutting off the lamp, his lips to the back of her neck. "I am back," he whispers. "I am back, I am." And he kisses the back of Pam's neck, feeling her body relax into him.

2

There is no good time or way to do this, and if he faces her in person, he knows he won't be able to go through with it, so the only way is quickly, concisely, impersonally. An operation, cutting Joan out of his life. *Over the phone.*

Dennis considered actually not phoning, considered exorcising her from his life without a word, moving out of the basement apartment and leaving no forwarding address, the phone disconnected. If she phoned him at the office, the calls would be screened by his assistant, Roberta, and go unreturned. If she happened to call and he picked up the phone himself, he'd just tell her he was on another line and would have to phone her back later. Blowing Joan off in order to save his marriage, he'd simply disappear from her life, no trace left that he'd ever existed, only a memory in her head, no final confrontation indicating that whatever had happened between them *had happened between them* and now must end.

Dennis, as reluctantly as he admits it, knows he owes Joan the decency of some truth, and he picks up the office phone at eleven-fifteen on this late Thursday morning, getting it over with so he can continue on with his work.

"Hello?" Joan says.

"Hi, it's Dennis."

"How are you? Sorry about last night. I should have told you I was in therapy. I'm just a bit defensive about it. You shouldn't have found out like that."

"It's okay, don't worry. I know lots of people in therapy."

"I'm glad. When Andrea said that, I didn't know what to say." Joan forces a laugh. "She's very outspoken."

"She certainly is." Dennis lapses into silence.

"Dennis?" Joan asks.

He imagines her sitting in the family room in her bathrobe, drinking coffee, eating a toasted bagel, a talk show playing before her on the television. "You see," Dennis begins, stacking papers on his desk, clearing colored pencils to the side and putting them in their carousel stand, "the problem I have is not you. It's me and who I am and where I am in my life right now. This has nothing to do with you or your kids or you being in therapy." He collects a handful of paper clips, tosses them in the empty Moby coffee mug on his windowsill, a large blue whale, the company logo, staring back at him. "I'm married," Dennis confesses. "I'm sure you suspected. I'm sure you knew this," he says, rejecting Joan but giving her the benefit of his thinking her intelligent. "My wife sensed something was wrong and confronted me, and we talked this out last night. We've been married for eight years, and I made a huge mistake involving you. I'm sorry. I don't know what else to say, but I'm sorry. I think you're wonderful, and I meant everything I said to you. I honestly never meant to hurt you or my wife. I know I did, though, and I feel awful, and so it has to stop." He takes a pile of office memos from his staff, notices about meetings scheduled, new office procedures, recent hirings and firings, and tosses them away.

He hears Joan clear her throat. "Al and I were married for nineteen years before he left me," Joan says, quietly, plainly. "The affair had been going on for two years before he left, and I never even knew about it. You're a good man to stay with your wife. I wish my husband had stayed with me."

"I'm really sorry, Joan. I am."

"You don't have to worry about me. I won't bother you anymore. I'm fine. I always suspected something so . . . I'll be all right."

A click, and Joan is gone, has hung up, cleanly, neatly, ladylike, disconnecting him as he has her—as polite as always, even through betrayal and deceit.

Rolling up the sleeve of her white silk blouse, Joan speaks to her doctor. "All the while I was doing it, I knew I wasn't trying to kill myself but only seeing what it was like. And it wasn't painful. It really wasn't, that's what surprised me, and I wondered, if I had actually slit my wrists, whether that would hurt or not." Joan stares at the cuts on her arm. Dennis phoned and ended their relationship. It is over, and she can go on. She can go on as if it never happened; he never existed.

Pam examines Joan Dwyer's show-and-tell from across the width of the room. The cuff of Joan's blouse is unbuttoned and rolled up to Joan's left shoulder. Seven thin slashes up against Joan's pale, bone white skin. Three along Joan's upper biceps, three along her shoulder and shoulder blade, and one lower, just above her elbow. "Why do you think you wanted to do this?" Pam asks.

"I wasn't trying to kill myself." Joan defends herself, rolling down her sleeve, refastening the cuff. "I was only experimenting to see what it was like." She hadn't planned on displaying the cuts to

her doctor, but if she hadn't, she knew they'd have to discuss the
dinner, her call to her doctor of last night, and her feelings about
Dennis.

"What were you hoping to discover?" Dr. Thompson asks.

Joan stares blankly at her doctor. "I don't know."

The time is 12:10 P.M., and Dennis has as yet not informed Joan of
his intentions to leave her and remain with his wife, at least as far as
Joan's behavior indicates. "Did you phone me before or after you'd
cut yourself?"

"A few before. Three before. Four after," Joan answers remotely.

"Was this your way of punishing yourself for the dinner with the
kids and Dennis? Because it didn't work out as you'd hoped?"

There's no avoiding him. "Partially, maybe," Joan admits. "I
wanted to hurt myself, to see myself hurt, and when you didn't
phone me back, I just did some more."

"You were angry at me, you were angry at your children, and you
were angry at Dennis."

"I wasn't angry at anyone, only myself," Joan clarifies. "Angry at
myself for trying so hard, wanting too much."

"You were also disappointed with Andrea, Todd, and Dennis."

"Why should I care about myself if nobody cares about me?" Joan
asks, thinking more about Dennis's call of this morning than the
events of last night.

Pam looks over at Joan, hoping Joan will continue speaking, not
knowing what to say herself. If this is Joan's state of mind now, *before*
Dennis has told her, Pam can only guess at how she will react once
she learns he's ending their affair. Joan cups her right hand over her
shoulder, rubbing the cuts through the silk. She looks out the
window.

"You seem very distant today," Pam comments, hoping to arouse
some feeling from Joan.

Joan shrugs, doesn't even look at her doctor. "I've just come to realize and accept this life I have." No point going into the call from Dennis. It's a done thing.

"Can you explain that to me?"

Joan fixes her gaze at the skyline, the line of apartment buildings across the street. "I think I'm just seeing things exactly as they are, and I've finally learned to accept and not fight it. I've made my effort and tried, even you can't deny that, and I've seen it can't work out. You've been keeping me going, and this man has kept me occupied, but I still am who I am and that's not enough. If you want to kid yourself into believing my life is worth saving, go ahead, but you're only fooling yourself, not me."

Joan has spoken, deadpan and sure, and now Pam has to respond but is not sure what sort of comfort to give; if she looks at life from Joan's perspective, it does appear bleak and hopeless. Pam has no answer for her patient; all she can come up with is quoted directly from a textbook: "Your depression is affecting the way you view things, and once we've explored and worked through this depression, you'll feel different."

"Nothing has ever been clearer to me than it is now," Joan says, peaceful, secure in her despair, and she looks at her doctor. "This all really does make sense for me. I know you can't admit it, being my doctor, but I know you think it too. I see it in your expression that you have given up on me too."

"I have not given up," Pam says emphatically. "You may feel that way, but that's the illness of the depression affecting you, and you can't give in to it. If you can't trust yourself, trust my judgment to know that things can change for the better. With or without this man in your life, you have your children, you have me—"

Joan shakes her head. "You keep talking about this as if the depression is altering my thoughts to make them untrustworthy and I should only trust what you say. My thoughts are supposed to be wrong because I am depressed and yours are right because you're not. It's like you don't understand that mine are just as real to me as yours are to you. Why is that?''

''You're suffering from a severe depression, Joan, and that's an illness that attacks your thought processes as well as affects your physical health.''

Joan glances at her watch. Ten more minutes. She looks back to Dr. Thompson, altogether weary from explaining herself, making herself understood. ''I've been depressed all my life, and now I'm just coming to terms with that.''

Pam tries to meet Joan's eyes, tries to connect emotionally with her patient. When their eyes do meet, no connection is made. Joan stares at her doctor impassively. Pam could be a log for all Joan cares, and Pam stands, walking across the room, sitting on the couch next to Joan's chair.

Joan wishes Dr. Thompson would let her be, not try to wear her down. ''I don't want to feel anything anymore. I've had enough.''

Pam touches Joan's shoulder lightly, aware of the cuts hidden by the shirt, a movement to get a reaction, and she can feel Joan shiver under her hand. Joan pulls away quickly, standing. She collects her purse from the end table. ''I'll be going now.'' She walks to the door. This is over. Life is over.

Pam follows. ''I am going to call you early tonight at seven and then again later this evening. I think we should keep in touch and see this thing through. And of course, we have our session tomorrow afternoon.''

Joan smiles wanly. ''Of course.'' She thumps her pocketbook against her thigh. ''May I go now?''

Pam opens the door. ''I'll speak to you at seven.'' A permanent point in time for Joan to focus upon, and so long as Pam keeps giving Joan these points to anticipate, one after another after another, Joan's life will move along in a series of connect-the-dots between their interactions until Joan is feeling good enough to carry herself through her own life of her own accord and will.

Joan steps through the door, not another word said. Pam watches as her patient leaves the office, feeling emptiness envelop her, the gloom and despair of life thrust upon her by Joan Dwyer. But Pam has her husband back now, that is what is most important, and the affair will be officially over by sunset. Tomorrow, therapy with Joan Dwyer and all her other patients will resume as usual, a marriage salvaged, an upset world reconstructed.

Pam closes the office door, collecting herself for Sarah Chaplin, daughter dead and buried eight weeks ago and her husband arranging to be away on business trips for six of the last eight weeks, leaving Sarah Chaplin alone to grieve for a daughter and family lost.

The buzzer mounted on the wall by the desk buzzes harshly. A theory in which Dr. Pamela Thompson must believe, always believes, always has believed: *I can right the wrongs of the world and soothe tortured minds.* That is who Dr. Pamela Thompson is—soother of afflicted minds—and she presses the button on the wall, releasing the lock to the outer office door.

Pam swallows a Xanax, then walks into the reception area, going to the kitchen, straightening up before phoning Joan Dwyer.

Jack is placing a plate and mug in the dishwasher. "Let me," he says, taking Pam's mug from her hand and putting it in the top rack. "How has your day been?" He comes into the reception area, seating himself in one of the wingback chairs. "Sit with me for a second."

Pam sits, thankful to have someone to talk to. "I'm fine. Tired. Problems with a patient. That sort of thing."

Jack leans over to the coffee table, shuffling through the pile of magazines, scanning covers. "What patient? Fill me in."

Pam sits back. "She depresses me, scares me. I'm afraid for her . . . I'm not sure. How are you and Mr. Flanting doing?"

Jack crosses his legs, begins flipping through an issue of *National Geographic,* the terrain of Sri Lanka. "We have our problems like any couple."

"Which are?"

"You really want to hear this?"

"I can handle it."

Jack Briden puts the magazine aside, leaning forward, eyes wide. "He'll have sex with me only if we're in the office. Absolutely refuses in our apartments or anywhere else. Only in the office. If I say no to it here, we don't have it at all. I've asked him to go to a relationship therapist with me, and he got turned on thinking I wanted to have a ménage à trois. When I explained that it was for us to work out our problems, he refused to go. Said he didn't have any problems, said he didn't need to be in therapy with anyone, even me." Jack laughs. "Of course, when I asked if he didn't want to see me as a therapist anymore, only to date me, he said no, so he still does come in to see me."

Pam stands. "Sounds like fun."

Jack stands, going to the kitchen. "So what are you going to do about your patient?"

She steps into her office. "We'll work it through. What are you going to do about Flanting?"

"Up his fee," Jack responds with a grin, and Pam smiles, shutting her office door.

The time. The time: Five four-eight, the digital clock on the coffeemaker reads. Five four-nine. Five five-O. Five five-one. She sits at the kitchen table, eyes fixed on the three bright blue digits, the bright blue colon separating the hour digit from the minute digits. Six two-three. The bright blue lowercase letters P.M. perched down in the lower right corner, half the size of the digits themselves. P.M. lit in the lower right corner while A.M. remains unlit in the upper right corner until twelve midnight, when P.M. goes dark and A.M. lights. Six three-nine. Andrea sleeps over at Kitty March's this evening. Six five-O, the evening is still light, the days long, nights short, sunsets late, sunrises early. *May.* May twenty-fourth. Memorial Day weekend coming up this weekend. Seven O-two. A phone rings. The phone is ringing. Joan lifts the receiver from the phone hanging on the wall by the refrigerator, the phone on the wall by the refrigerator beside the list of numbers she most frequently calls. Dennis's phone number not on this list, never on this list. She never posted Dennis's number on the bulletin board so she will now not have to take it off since she will never be phoning him again. ''Hello,'' Joan says. Seven O-three.

''Joan, it's Dr. Thompson. How are you feeling?''

''Better. I think things are going to be okay tonight.''

''Has anything happened to make you feel better?''

''I don't know. I just feel okay. A bit more relaxed than when we met.''

''You don't sound as depressed.''

''Maybe by talking it through in your office and leaving it there, I could relax more out of there. I had a nice walk home, and that made me feel a bit better.''

''I'm glad to hear that. Do you have any plans for tonight?''

''There's a movie I was thinking of seeing on my own. Try to get out on my own more.''

''Good. What time do you think you'll be back in?''

''Nine forty-five it starts, so probably a bit after midnight. I was going to go to the coffee shop downstairs before.''

''Would you like me to call you when you get in, then?''

''No, that's okay. I'll be seeing you tomorrow.''

''You know you can always leave a message if you need me later.''

''I will, but I think I'm okay for tonight. Really I do.''

''Please call if you feel you'd like to.''

''I will. Good-bye.''

Pam stands at the bus stop, anticipating the luxury of the upcoming three-day Memorial Day weekend. Saturday, Sunday, and Monday to make reparations with Dennis.

Has he told her? She gets on the bus and is surprised to find an empty

seat next to a clean-cut businessman reading a tabloid newspaper, a
seat *not* next to a crazy, dirty, smelly beggarwoman, but a normal,
clean-cut person like herself, and Pam sits, placing her pocketbook in
the lap of her skirt, glancing at the man's face, detecting a shift in
his eyes, quickly from the paper to her thighs back to the paper. Her
eyes steal over the man's pin-striped arm, scanning the headlines of
the metropolitan pages: Dachshund run over by subway train: DOG
TAKES THE A TRAIN TO HEAVEN! All the world's sick horrors become
amusement for the masses, twisted into catchy one-liners.

Pam was glad to hear Jack Briden's illicit romance had not yet
ended, his conflict making hers feel less unethical. And whereas Jack
chose to mix his personal and professional lives, Pam's dilemma was
thrust upon her, an accident beyond her control, which she has now
managed to work out and correct after a brief period of adjustment
and lapsed judgment. An experience she can learn from.

At Third Avenue Pam steps off the bus onto the street, the sky a
hazy orange as the sun sets. Pam strolls the four blocks to her
building, listening to her heels click on the pavement, passing
sidewalk cafés where the diners observe her walking by as she
observes them eating pasta, burritos, roasted quail, and tekka maki
rolls. One more day until the three-day weekend. Two more months
until August and a four-week vacation from patients. Pam rides the
elevator up to the twenty-seventh floor.

Tablets, capsules, caplets. Hexagons, ovals, rounded cylinders,
flattened spheres. White, yellow, orange, pink, blue, forest green.
One liter of peach-flavored seltzer in a bottle standing on Joan's
nightstand alongside a tall glass, no ice but the glass cooled in the
freezer. Even in Joan's heavily air-conditioned apartment, vapor
clings to the side of the clean glass, making its sides opaque.

There is no reason to leave a note. Joan has said all she has to say,
and if she had something more to explain to someone about why she's

about to do what she's doing, if she had someone she cared to write a note to in the first place, if she had someone she believed cared about her enough even to read the note, maybe if she thought some-one—*anyone*—could be affected by anything she had to say in a note, maybe if she thought someone—*anyone*—would be affected by what she is about to do, maybe then she wouldn't be doing it.

Joan lounges on her unmade bed, pillows, comforter, a white silk floor-length sleeveless nightgown under her purple velvet robe, pills lined up along the down comforter's quilted lines. Pills align-ed according to their specific type and categories: antidepressants, antianxiety medications, tranquilizers, and a row of extra-strength Tylenol caplets. "Pain relievers," Joan murmurs aloud. Because that is what this is: pain relief and resignation. Resigning herself to life, to who she is.

A failure at saving her marriage and keeping a husband from going astray, Joan today once again finds herself a loser in the game of love, this time not as the abandoned wife but as the rejected mistress. Unlike Al's mistress, Joan is—*was*—a mistress not worth leaving a wife for. And beyond all the failures of mother, wife, and mistress, Joan finds herself in the position of doing to another woman what was done to her. *A home wrecker, the Other Woman,* Joan has become, and she can feel Dennis's wife's pain and grief and humiliation as her own, as the pain and grief and humiliation she still holds for the loss of Al. This woman trying to save her marriage from the likes of Joan. A woman, possibly with children, a family in need of a father's presence and not one absent from their lives as he affords himself the pleasure of weekend afternoon encounters with a mistress. Family comes first, and Joan failed at preserving her own family, failed at attuning herself to her husband's needs and thus lost him, not for a month or two, as Dennis's wife has, only to recognize he'd gone astray and then to bring him back, but *forever*, never recognizing the affair existed until her husband told her about it in order to get her off his back.

Joan pours herself a full glass of peach-flavored seltzer and scans the eight rows of pills, deciding to start at the row farthest to her right and work her way left to the center of the bed.

Antidepressants: three large Tofranil capsules, Joan's current antidepressant, eleven Asendin left over after Joan experienced side effects of diarrhea and asked to be switched to another medication, fourteen Norpramin left over after Joan experienced the side effects of dry mouth and nausea, and five Prozac capsules, which Joan went off because she said it did absolutely nothing for her.

Thirty-three antidepressants downed with two thirds of a glass of seltzer, and Joan refills the glass to within a half inch of its rim. First she swallows the twenty-eight remaining Valium left over from the prescription Dr. Thompson made out to her approximately one year ago. The Valium, although beneficial in reducing Joan's anxiety level, increased her depression. Dr. Thompson quickly took Joan off the Valium once the increasing depressive side effects had become evident, replacing it with Xanax.

The stockpile of Xanax is swallowed ten, ten, ten, ten, ten, ten, and four, and Joan is glad there remain only the tranquilizers: four Halcion, three Restoril, four Vistaril (all prescribed to Joan over the course of the last year during bouts of insomnia), for her stomach is close to bursting with peach seltzer and she badly needs to urinate.

After two sips the prescribed pills are gone, and Joan decides to skip taking the odd number of Tylenol caplets left on the down comforter. Better to settle for what she's swallowed and succeed than to overfill her stomach, vomit everything up, and fail. Joan stands, her legs weak, takes off her robe, and hangs it on the brass hook set on the back of the bathroom door. She draws the silk nightgown above her hips and sits on the toilet seat, urinating the liquid she's just drunk. "I've always had an extremely speedy metabolism," she often boasted to Al when they first dated. "Can eat whatever I want and never gain an ounce." She thought Al would be pleased to know that if he ever did decide to make Joan his wife, he needn't worry about her blowing up into a fat balloon after having a child or two; she would always remain precisely as she was when they initially met.

Joan flushes the toilet. The silk gown drops smoothly and swiftly to her ankles, and Joan turns, catching the reflection of her shoulder in the mirror. Joan momentarily focuses on the healing cuts, the pattern of *x*'s she cut into her arm, the once-red cuts now dark and brown. She gently scratches at the markings, the skin itching, and then reaches down, closing the toilet lid, leaving her robe hanging on the door. Joan knows she is killing herself, but it just feels ordinary. Swallowing pills, drinking seltzer, going to the bathroom—Joan can't think much of it, it all feels so undramatic, this ending as natural and correct as her birth, as the sun rising in the morning and setting in the evening. She shuts off the lamps on either side of the bed and slides under the comforter. Her head rests on a soft pillow.

Sitting across the dining room table from his wife, enjoying this steak dinner they prepared together, Dennis can't imagine why he ever cheated on his wife, at this moment those feelings so absent and alien. Pam's face glows in the candlelight, and Joan Dwyer means— meant—nothing to him. Joan Dwyer amounts to nothing more than a way through which he could make his wife understand how hurt and neglected he felt, nothing more than a prop to be employed and discarded, her use done. Dennis has reconciled with his wife, and they can work out their differences and remain a married couple.

Upon returning home, Pam encountered Dennis in the kitchen as he unpacked several bags of groceries. He told her he had called the woman and broken it off, that the woman accepted it and it was over. "All the while it was going on, I wanted you to find out so I could stop being with her. I think I was afraid you'd laugh at me if I told you how unhappy I was. I guess I felt I had to prove it to you another way. I'm not justifying what I did. I just guess that's why I did it," Dennis told Pam as he examined the fillets under the oven's broiler.

"I suppose," Pam replied, making sure she didn't sound too understanding, as if she had not known all this and had it figured out months ago. How did she *really* take it? Pam wanted to ask, but instead she walked off to the bedroom and changed out of her work clothes.

Catching his wife's face in the yellow-orange flicker of a candle flame, "I do love you," Dennis says. "I do, and I'm glad I'm here with you."

Pam looks up from her dinner plate, a leaf of lettuce speared at the tip of her fork. Her husband of eight years. "I love you," she says. "I need you." And she does love and need him. Deep inside herself she actually does feel love and need for her husband. The thought almost makes her cry.

3

Joan Dwyer is late. Usually fifteen minutes early, Joan Dwyer usually arriving at four forty-five for her five o'clock appointment, today, Friday, Joan Dwyer has not arrived, and the time is five-ten, Pam's previous patient having left her office twenty minutes ago.

Pam stands in the open doorway to the office, contemplating the empty reception area, the three empty chairs. She glances at the outer door to the office, anticipating Joan's finger on the buzzer, the sound of the buzzer.

At a quarter past five, when the buzzer has still not sounded, Pam returns to her office, shutting the door and sitting at her desk. She picks up the phone and dials Joan's number. Joan Dwyer is late, has been delayed by some unforeseeable circumstance—caught in traffic in a taxi after an afternoon shopping, waiting in a café for an over-harried, overly inattentive waitress to hand her the check, her watch broken and time miscalculated while strolling through the park on her way to her doctor's office—these are possible causes of Joan Dwyer's tardiness.

I think things are going to be okay tonight . . . a bit less depressed . . . I'm okay for tonight. . . .

The phone has rung six, seven times, and Joan Dwyer said she was going to a late movie last night and was feeling okay about things even after the man she was having an affair with, the man she was desperately in love with broke off with her. The phone rings for an eleventh time and no phone machine picks up and Joan's daughter does not pick up and it is very unlike Joan Dwyer not to be early—forget late—for an appointment. Unlike Joan Dwyer not to phone if she thought she might be a minute—never mind several minutes—late, and the phone rings a fifteenth time, and it is unlike Joan Dwyer not to remember to put on the answering machine if she was to be going out, whether to therapy or the store. On the eighteenth ring Joan Dwyer has not arrived and buzzed to be let into her therapist's office. The time is five twenty-two. Twenty-two minutes past the hour of her appointment. Thirty-seven minutes past the quarter of an hour early, when Joan usually arrives. Thirty-seven minutes past on the day after her lover left her, the man she swore she couldn't live without, the man she introduced to her family only two days ago rejecting her the following day. Twenty-four rings.

Pam will let it ring until (1) Joan or Andrea answers and she learns why Joan is late, (2) Joan Dwyer buzzes and walks in through the office door, or (3) Joan Dwyer's fifty-minute session is over and Bill Matson has arrived for his six o'clock appointment.

Five twenty-seven. Pam has lost count of how many rings it's been.

The ringing does not, will not, stop, and Joan Dwyer rolls about on her bed, disturbed, her eyes opening upon a blast of early evening, bright, hazy sunshine. She shuts her eyes, recognizing the ringing as the phone by her bed, the phone at her bedside ringing and waking her, and it keeps ringing, and the only way to stop it is to answer. Joan keeps her eyes shut, a hand grappling for the phone, finding it, lifting it with a jerk and pulling it to her face, hitting the side of her face with the phone. The ringing stops. Joan lies back in bed, phone clutched to her face.

"Hello?" a voice says into Joan's ear. "Hello." The voice is familiar, registers. Dr. Thompson. "Is that you, Joan?" Dr. Thompson asks.

Joan says nothing, just breathes, her eyes shut.

"Joan, this is Dr. Thompson."

"This is Joan," Joan replies, her words slurred.

"What's going on, Joan?"

"I'm fine," Joan says. "I'm fine." She drops back off to sleep, the phone off the hook, cord twisted around her elbow.

"Joan? Joan?" Dr. Thompson says into the abandoned phone. "Joan, I'm coming right over."

Joan reflexively, impulsively, shoves the receiver away, off the bed and onto the floor, ridding herself of the annoyance.

The elevator stops four times on its way down to the lobby, and Pam wants to scream at each of the three people who take their time getting into the elevator, wants to scream at the elderly woman who mistakenly presses "Door Open" instead of "Door Close," causing the elevator to pause, delaying it from moving on for an additional thirty seconds, scream that her patient is dying, may be unconscious, near death, comatose, and Pam wishes she had taken a Xanax before leaving her office, but in her panic to get over to Joan's as soon as possible, she forgot.

The time is five forty-five. Too late to reach Bill Matson at his office, and not wanting to interrupt Jack Briden's therapy with a patient or involve him in her patient's problems, Pam left a note in an envelope taped to the outer office door, "Bill Matson" hurriedly scrawled across the envelope in Pam's illegible doctor's hand: "Bill, an emergency has come up. So sorry. Will phone you at home later this evening. Dr. Thompson." Bill Matson is, fortunately, stable enough to endure the mishap of an unexpected, canceled appointment by his doctor.

The elevator door opens, revealing, finally, the lobby of the building.

Awakened a second time by the loud, persistent buzz from the doorman in the lobby of the building, Joan rolls over in bed, the silk gown feeling wet, clinging to her stomach and thighs. The buzzer sounds again, loud and shrieking, and Joan's head spins, the walls folding in, eyes spinning from ceiling to bedsheets to windows to rug, a blur, and the buzzer keeps sounding, the loud buzzing driving and consuming her thoughts. Joan braces her hands on the bed and stands, knees quickly buckling beneath her weight. She makes a second attempt to balance herself, and she pushes off the corner post of the bed, propelling her body toward the bedroom entrance. Her doctor. Dr. Thompson. Her hip hits the doorframe, her legs falling out beneath her, and she slides down the doorframe's length. The buzzer sounds again, long and harsh, unforgiving, and Joan draws herself onto all fours, knees and elbows, crawling through the hallway, the wet nightgown dropping away from her stomach and legs. Joan keeps her eyes looking above the floorboards, making her way from the hall's soft pile carpet to the living room's Oriental to the foyer's cold marble, which strikes her joints hard. She leans on one of the half tables for support, her upper torso thrown forward to get at the intercom box. Her side hits something—something in the way—and Joan shoves a hand back, sending a vase spinning onto the floor, where it shatters around her feet. Joan slouches across the table, resting her head on an arm. She reaches up to the intercom box,

taking the receiver from the wallhook, shutting her eyes. "Mm-hmm
. . . Yes . . . Fine, that's fine."

Joan drops the receiver, letting it hit the wall, then swing pen-
dulumlike, scratching at the flowered wallpaper. Minutes pass, Joan
rests, and then there's a knock at the door. "Joan, it's Dr.
Thompson."

Joan lifts her head, extends an arm for the doorknob, but cannot
reach it from where she stands, half on, half off the table. She lurches
forward, securing a grip on the brass handle, turning it, and yanking
the door with a quick jerking movement. The door swings open,
slamming into the wall, and Joan reels back, into the table, her feet
stepping among the shards of porcelain, causing Joan to fall to her
knees, crawling away from the broken vase, toward the center of the
foyer, swaying, staring at her doctor with a fixed, blank expression.
Dr. Thompson visiting her here in her home. Joan can't figure it and turns,
stumbling to the living room.

Pam walks up alongside Joan, putting an arm around her patient's
waist, leading her to the room and seating her patient on the couch.
Joan's eyes remain open but void of emotion, knowledge, only blank
and hazy, her entire face as expressionless, lifeless as that of a corpse.
A pale yellow stain spreads over the nightgown from Joan's legs to
her stomach. Pam can smell the urine. The medication Joan so
obviously has taken has relaxed her system enough to cause her to
urinate on herself. Pam sits and takes Joan's hand, checking her pulse:
weak and slow. "Joan, do you know who I am?" She clasps Joan's
hand between both her own.

Joan looks to the doctor, focuses upon her for a moment, then
loses the thought. Her eyes drift off to the right, out the living room
window to the large, orange, setting sun.

"Joan?"

Her head swivels back to Dr. Thompson. "What?" Joan asks with
annoyance. "Yes." She takes her hand from between those of her
doctor's. Joan stands and turns in a circle, scanning the room for a

clock. She makes her way to a table, reading the brass hands, the black onyx numbers on the clock, and she lifts it close to her face to get a better look, thinking through the time before dropping the heavy clock down on the wood, scratching its grain. She feels dizzy, tired, her doctor here—this is all Joan has on her mind. The time is seven o'clock and her doctor is here and her limbs feel heavy, as heavy as the clock, and Joan walks past her doctor and out of the room, into the family room.

Whatever her state, she *is* alive, drugged on an overdose of pills— The blaring sound of a television interrupts Pam's thoughts, volume loud, Alex Trebek hollering *Jeopardy* first-round categories. Joan is alive and must be brought to a hospital, voluntarily admit herself. Voluntarily for her own benefit, so that she will appear to be seeking help of her own will, recognizing that she needs help, this being a sign to the admitting psychiatric doctor that Joan knows what she did is wrong. Admitting Joan against her will not only takes more time and presents more trouble for Pam legally—involving at least one other psychiatrist as well as the police—but will also place Joan at the disposal of the hospital staff to whom she is admitted. The last thing Pam wants is for Joan to get caught up in the bureaucracy of mental hospitalization. The first thing Pam wants is to discover what Joan has taken and when Joan took them. Then she must get Joan to agree to accompany her to the emergency room of Lenox Hill Hospital.

Pam looks in on Joan. She sits on the sofa, speaking in questions to the television, safe for now, giving Pam the opportunity to search for what Joan has swallowed. She glances in the kitchen and dining room, then back through the living room to explore the rest of the impressive apartment. Off the hallway are the two children's rooms. Andrea's, identifiable by its half-unpacked suitcase, a pink T-shirt reading ''Private Schools Are for Bitches'' tossed across her unmade bed. Todd's bedroom is empty but for its furniture. The kids' bathroom and then the master bedroom, identifiable by its large size and king-size bed. This is where they made love, enters Pam's mind, a picture unfolding before her. This is where they made love, slept, ate, and watched the old sitcoms I dislike watching with him, Pam thinks, and she walks around the bed to a nightstand, blotting out an image of Dennis and Joan lying naked in bed, relaxing after making love, eating take-out sushi, watching *Mary Tyler Moore* reruns. She picks up the assorted empty vials of pills, reading their labels: the medication, the prescribed dosage, and there down at the bottom her own name—Dr. Thompson.

Eight empty orange vials, one empty Tylenol bottle, a third of a liter left of warm peach seltzer, the phone off the hook, lying by her feet, busy tone pulsing from its earpiece. Pam lifts the receiver, places it in its cradle, and restores it to the bedside table. She gathers the nine pill containers up and drops them in her handbag, looking over the room for signs of alcohol. The bed is a tumble of sheets, several dozen white Tylenol caplets strewn in their folds, flung all over. The large drinking glass lying next to one of several pillows smells only of peach seltzer, no alcohol, and no bottle of alcohol in sight. A semidry urine stain forms a wide oval on the bottom sheet, its scent lingering in the air. Scanning the bed one last time to make sure she hasn't overlooked anything, a pill catches her eyes: not a Tylenol, but a Xanax Joan must have missed while taking her overdose, and Pam picks it up, placing it on her tongue, and swallowing. No sense leaving it for Joan when it could do Pam more good now, help her remain calm and clearheaded.

Pam enters the family room, taking a seat on the ottoman before a large leather chair. Joan's attention remains entirely devoted to the Double Jeopardy round of play; she doesn't even acknowledge the presence of her doctor.

"Joan, may I turn this off so we can talk?"

"What is *Hopalong Cassidy*?" a contestant answers, and Joan keeps staring, her eyes fixed on the blue glow of the game show set, registering but ignoring her doctor's presence.

"What is *Bewitched*?" an elderly female contestant echoes.

"Joan, I'm going to turn off the television." Pam stands, walks to the television, pushes the on/off button on the cable box. By the time Pam has turned to face her patient, the television is back on.

"I'm watching this." Joan stares, rapt as an announcer details the prizes for second- and third-place contestants, remote control enfolded delicately in a hand. Pam retakes her seat on the hassock. Joan looks to her doctor. "I am fine."

"It looks like you took a lot of pills." Pam holds open her handbag, displaying the empties. "How long ago did you take all this?"

"And our Final Jeopardy category today is," a pause, then Alex Trebek announces, "the United Nations."

A commercial for sliced luncheon meat. Pam proceeds. "When did you take these, Joan?"

"Why are you here?"

"I phoned when you missed your appointment today. I was worried and came over. I think we need to get you to a hospital."

Joan looks to the television, feeling fine, never having felt more calm and relaxed, her muscles never less tense. "I feel fine," Joan reiterates, and when she looks to the Final Jeopardy answer, she cannot comprehend, let alone answer it. An answer concerning an event that occurred in 1956. Joan closes her eyes, settling back on the couch.

"Joan?"

Joan opens her eyes, taking in her doctor. Dr. Thompson sits close by, in front of her to the right. Joan drops her eyes to her doctor's legs, notes her doctor has moved the ottoman from before the chair where it belongs to before the couch by Joan's side. "That doesn't belong there," Joan informs her. She holds her head up straight, consciously making an effort to keep her chin from sagging to her chest, her eyes from rolling back in their sockets, her body from falling to the side. She grips the armrest with as tight a grip as she can.

"*WHEEL!*"

"OF!"

"FORTUNE!"

Joan turns her head to face the television, but Pam takes Joan's chin, bringing her back to her attention. "No, Joan, you are not fine, and I will not leave you alone. I think we have to get you to a hospital." Pam releases Joan's chin. "You can barely move without falling over. You can barely speak. You've urinated on yourself. Your feet are cut and bleeding. You've obviously tried to kill yourself, and I cannot leave you here alone. We have to go to the hospital."

Joan looks down at the soles of her feet, twisting a leg to the side, noting several small cuts. She lifts her gown at the lap, bending her face close to the fabric, smelling the stain. "He left me," Joan says, arranging her gown over her knees. "He's married with a wife." She looks back to the television. "Person" is the Wheel category.

Pam watches Joan. Joan gazes at the television.

How much of this is her own fault? Pam wonders. How much of the blame lies with her for confronting her husband? How much with Dennis for using Joan as a means to get his wife's attention? *Dennis could have left me, Joan could have been happy with him, and I could be the woman on her own, working all day helping others, then returning home to an empty apartment—a divorced woman, near forty with no kids—an empty life.* Pam can easily understand why Joan has done what she has done, why Joan wants her life to end, because Pam knows that for all the independence Pam hides behind for safety, to be alone in this world is hellish, to have no one to protect you, no one to confide in, no one to share your life with is lonely and scary, and having almost lost her husband, Pam can appreciate how Joan must feel having lost not only a husband but an entire life she had built around herself. It should be no surprise that Joan dwelled on the divorce for an entire year of therapy; with nothing to fill the void where her marriage and family once were, what else could Joan think about but that loss?

The first puzzle has been solved: Eleanor Roosevelt.

Joan has completely passed out. Her mouth hangs open, but no drool spills over her lips. No drool because one side effect of the medications is dry mouth. Pam checks Joan's wrist, her pulse still faint, not solid and steady. Less a pulse than a ripple, steady but precarious, unbalanced. *Arrhythmic,* Pam's—Dr. Thompson's—training tells her. The pulse of a woman fading out of life, into death, slow and irregular, and Pam has been in Joan's apartment for over an hour, watching her patient die, doing nothing or—at the very best—*near* nothing, and Pam wonders if this is what she wanted for Joan all along: not only Joan out of her and Dennis's life but Joan out of life altogether, making Joan happy, making both Joan and her doctor happy.

Pam shakes Joan's shoulders, rousing her patient, and Joan sits up, eyes open.

"Joan," Pam calls.

Joan stares widely at her doctor, and Pam grips Joan's face, pinching her cheeks together in the grip of one hand. "If you don't come with me to the hospital voluntarily, I am going to have to call the police, and they will come up here and escort you against your will. Do you understand that?" She releases Joan's face.

Joan says nothing, only stares, uncomprehending.

Pam takes Joan's shoulders. "You have to go to the hospital. You have no choice. Now, would you rather it be me or the police? If the police take you, it will be a lot more trouble for both of us. Do you understand that?"

Joan nods. "No police." She looks past Pam, pushing herself up and across the room.

"Joan?"

"I know."

Pam stands. "Let's pack a few things you might need, and we'll go." Pam takes Joan's arm, guiding Joan through the living room to the bedroom. Joan's ankles twist every other step, and Pam supports her weight until they reach the master bedroom, where Joan suddenly pulls herself upright, coming to, going to the closet and dragging a brown leather overnight bag from its top shelf. The urine stain on Joan's gown is still wet, still smells, but Pam isn't going to chance trying to change Joan's clothes—what a horror show that could prove to be, Joan selecting an outfit, insisting it be put on—best to get Joan to the hospital while she's willing.

Joan rummages about at her bureau, jerkily shoving things aside while collecting others in her hands. She stuffs the overnight bag with an assortment of clothes and objects before heading into the bathroom. Pam follows quickly, fearing Joan may lock herself in, but Joan leaves the door ajar as she drops two lipsticks, a compact, a can of hair spray, tweezers, toenail clippers, a Lady Gillette, and facial moisturizer in the bag, more like Joan's preparing herself for a beauty makeover than a trip to the emergency room.

Joan lies on a cot, her bathrobe open, the straps of her nightgown down at her elbows, the upper two thirds of each breast exposed just above the nipple. A tube runs in one forearm. Electrodes, sensors, wires attached to small adhesive-coated circular pads, are taped over Joan's exposed chest. Four over the left, two over the right. Two taped to her forehead, one on her neck, one on her wrist.

Joan, oblivious of the rush of the activity going on around her in the emergency room, remains a center of calm. A nurse stands idly by, watching a cardiograph machine, a respirator machine, a machine measuring brain activity. Green lines of irregular blips measure Joan's heartbeat.

To Joan's left, hidden behind a shower curtain–thin screen of blue, is a stabbing victim. He screams, blood pouring onto the white tile floor from a gash in his thigh. Curtained off to Joan's right is an elderly woman, stricken with heat exhaustion. Across from the nurse and the machines sits Pam in a red plastic chair with steel legs, waiting for the examining physician to declare Joan stabilized so she may be moved up to the psychiatric unit. Pam and Joan arrived at Lenox Hill Hospital at ten before nine. Only at a quarter past eleven was a cot available so that Joan could be tended to. During the two-hour wait Pam phoned Bill Matson, apologizing for the inconvenience. Pam phoned Dennis, explaining that she had an emergency and might not be home until later this evening, early the next morning. Pam phoned Todd and told him to stay where he was, that his mother was at the hospital and that she would phone once Joan had been seen by a physician. Pam asked Todd to pass the information on to his younger sibling. Realizing Joan's stomach must be empty, Pam bought an apple, a Coca-Cola, and a Butterfinger bar from the cafeteria on the floor above. Joan refused everything but the candy bar, stating that she drank only diet sodas and hated apples. Joan ate the candy bar, then fell back to sleep. Pam ate the apple and gave the cola to the mother of the stabbing victim.

Joan said she would do this if Dennis left her, and true to her word, she has. However, the fact that Joan has survived creates a whole unknown future she hadn't anticipated. Life after Dennis, life after a suicide attempt. What comes next? If Joan had handled the breakup well, Pam could have foreseen referring her patient to another doctor, but after this suicide attempt Joan will likely need someone who understands all she has been through, not a new therapist she doesn't yet trust. Pam recognizes that she is the only doctor for Joan.

"Seventy-five to eighty percent dead" is how the doctor diagnosed Joan's condition. Joan's heart, brain, body slowing down to a point where she was barely alive. Seventy-five percent dead, 25 percent alive, and nothing to be done but monitor her heart rate to make sure it picked up and did not falter. "You might have just saved this woman's life," the doctor informed Pam. "Just rousing her and getting her up and around might be what's kept her from slipping into a comatose condition."

Saved from death by her psychiatrist, Joan slowly recovers from the shock of the overdose. "Physically speaking, by morning she should be well enough to be moved upstairs. But as you know, it will probably be several days before the drugs have worked their way through her system. By Monday or Tuesday most likely. Emotionally, well, you know her better than I do." Pam listened, the doctor sounding so positive that Joan Dwyer would pull through this incident. Joan Dwyer alive to live a life she doesn't want.

"Your mother's going to be all right," Pam tells Todd over the pay phone. "You'll be able to visit her tomorrow. She's being moved to the eighth floor. You can phone the desk there to get the visiting hours."

"What kind of ward is it?"

"It's a locked unit where—"

"Locked?"

"Well, until the medication has passed through her and she's had time to grapple with all the issues and implications of what she's done, she'll need to be watched and observed for—"

"She's in the mental ward."

"It's not as scary as it sounds. It's a good unit, not like what you might imagine."

Silence.

"I understand it's difficult, but I think she'd appreciate a visit from you and your sister. She is going to be here for several days, so you may want to bring her some of the necessities she might need. A toothbrush, shampoo. You know what I mean."

"Sure. No problem. Thanks. I'll take care of it."

Four fifty-two A.M. Joan sits up, her gown dropping swiftly to her waist, her chest exposed. "Are you okay, dear?" the nurse asks, touching Joan's shoulder, picking up the chart hanging by Joan's bedside.

Pam leans forward, takes Joan's hand. "How are you doing?"

Joan looks down to her chest, her eyes following the yellow, blue, and red wires to the monitors at her side. The green blips bouncing steady, if not strong, and Joan watches their parade across the black screen, no sooner disappearing off to the right then reappearing again at the left, bouncing a bit higher, a tad more sure.

Late May—
Early June

1

Dennis awakens to find his wife still not home, not in bed sleeping beside him so he can reach over and slide a hand up along the inside of her smooth thigh. He eyes the clock by the side of the bed. And at 8:18 A.M., where is his wife this late—*this early*—on a Saturday morning, what emergency could have prompted such a delay? are on his mind.

Three days since he last saw Joan with her family, two days since he phoned explaining that their relationship must end, Dennis, lying alone in bed with an erection and no woman to put it in—neither wife nor mistress—wonders what his wife is up to, having spent all of the past Friday evening out on the town. Joan Dwyer would never leave him alone to be out all night, whatever the circumstances. Joan Dwyer would always be at home for her husband, loving him and no one else, not caring for a couple of dozen strangers who pay to confide intimacies in her. Joan Dwyer makes her husband number one whereas only two days after he's ended his affair to be back with his wife, his wife has taken to staying out all night to care for a patient, not the husband who's at home waiting for her, keeping the bed warm and the air conditioner on high cool on this hot first day of the three-day Memorial Day weekend. What is Joan Dwyer doing now that he is not a part of her life? Thinking about dating other men or mourning the end of their relationship? If he ran into her on the street, would she acknowledge him or walk past like a stranger?

The apartment door opens.

Dennis feigns sleep, wanting Pam to discover him asleep and unworried as if he had never missed her at all.

Pam opens the bedroom door, observes her husband, sleeping like a little boy, his back curled, knees bent. She hangs her pocketbook over the closet doorknob, then sits on the bed by his feet, running a hand over the down comforter, feeling through its soft feathers to the sole of his foot, wiggling his toes. Pam wants him awake to hold and support her, comfort her after all she's been through in the past fifteen hours, he being partly responsible. She tickles his foot, and Dennis reflexively kicks out, his foot against her hip. His eyes open.

"Hi," Pam says sadly, tired.

Dennis looks her over, his erection subsiding. The bags under Pam's eyes, her posture, shoulders slumped forward, her blouse wrinkled, coffee-stained and untucked, creases in her skin around her mouth, at the corners of her eyes, across her forehead, a dirty, sweaty glaze over her entire face: She has obviously been up all night with a patient. Dennis leans forward and pulls Pam against his bare chest, her head to his chest, and Pam leans into him, glad to have his arms around her, her weight supported by him instead of Joan's by her.

"It's been a really crappy night," Pam says to his chest, her hand on his stomach, playing with the dark hairs just above the waistband of his shorts. "A really crappy night."

Dennis strokes Pam's head, her dirty hair, and holds her against him, glad to have her relying on him, glad he can be there for her as he rubs the back of her neck—*this marriage can work, is working,* things *have* changed—and Dennis kisses the crown of his wife's head as he kissed Joan's so many times. "Are you all right?" he asks softly.

Pam looks to the shaded windows, the light touch of her husband's fingers on her neck and shoulders, soft and caring, and she shakes her head, tears coming, cannot keep herself from crying after all she's been through in the past fifteen hours. Hustling Joan into the cab, Joan passing out during the ride, dragging Joan through the emergency room, the two-hour wait, watching Joan's vital signs, 75 percent dead, close to death, sitting by Joan's side all night long as she lay close to death after overdosing on a multitude of pills she—Pam, Dr. Pamela Thompson—prescribed for her patient, Joan's scared, abandoned, otherworldly stare as Pam left her, Pam hailing a cab on the deserted Upper East Side street and the driver's annoyed, hostile look when he discovered she was only going five blocks from the hospital, five blocks she was too tired to walk. Keeping herself strong and sane for fifteen hours, fifty-four thousand seconds, she calculated, as she waited for the elevator downstairs in the lobby of the building and fifty-four thousand seconds later, her patient locked on a psychiatric ward—her patient and her husband's ex-mistress—*"Five blocks!"* The driver sneered.

"Please," Pam replied wearily, and the man drove the five blocks, angry and hostile.

Dennis holds Pam against his chest, massaging her back, feeling her warmth. "It's all right," he says. "I'm here. I'm here." He rocks Pam gently, holding her strongly. "It's okay, I'm here, I'm here," he keeps saying, and Pam cries into his chest, clinging to his back.

Joan sits in the dining room—ten square, bone white Formica tables surrounded by steel-framed chairs with blue plastic backs and seats—facing Todd and Andrea. Her first visitors, her first day in the hospital.

Todd hands his mother a paper shopping bag filled with some of the necessities Pam mentioned as well as several gossip, news, and fashion magazines. Andrea gives her mother a small suitcase and her mother's pocketbook, filled with her wallet, a travel brush, and several tampons. Joan places the bag in her lap, rummages through its assortment of goods, then looks across at her son. She has spent the day lying in bed, and only when a nurse entered informing Joan that she had visitors did she rise, pulling on her robe, slipping on a pair of pale blue hospital slippers, and proceeding down the hall and around the corner to the dining area.

Rolled onto the ward in a wheelchair this morning, her overnight bag in her lap, Joan wasn't sure where she was, the psychiatric unit looked so unhospitallike. The emergency room nurse wheeled Joan off an elevator and down a long corridor to a steel door with a large vertical window, steel mesh running through the glass. The nurse pressed the black button by the door's side and a bell rang and there was a click. The nurse turned the doorknob counterclockwise, pushing Joan forward, onto the ward.

A long, carpeted hallway extended to a large reception desk at the far end, and the nurse took Joan's arm, helping her stand. A woman seated behind the reception desk rose and approached, and then the nurse who wheeled Joan onto the ward turned the chair around, giving a wave to the man and woman still behind the reception desk. A click of the lock, and she opened the door and was gone. No one—no Dr. Thompson or emergency room nurse—familiar to Joan any longer.

"I'm Caroline, one of the nurses on the unit. I'll be showing you to your room and getting you oriented to the ward." The woman did not wear a starched white uniform as the nurse from the emergency room did. She wore a turquoise T-shirt and black jeans; a red bandanna covered her head, pulling back her long blond hair.

The man behind the desk wore a plaid button-down shirt, the woman a flowered dress with white lace collar. Joan looked away, taking in her surroundings: mauve, pink, purple, and gray. Pale gray wall-to-wall carpet underfoot, pink plaster ceiling, and purple-and-mauve-striped glossy wallpaper. The overhead fluorescent lighting was the giveaway that this was not a hallway in a hotel but an institutional setting, that the desk at the end of the hall, slick pale wood top and mauve fiberglass stand, was not a reservations desk.

"You lucked out," Caroline said with a smile. "The only room available is a private room."

Joan stared, blank-faced, running her fingertips over the grain of the leather bag.

Caroline took Joan's elbow, easing her forward, and they walked down the length of the hall, past several closed pale wood doors, past one open door leading to a large room resembling a cafeteria where many people sat, some dressed in street clothes, some in night-clothes, eating off plastic trays, off plastic plates, from plastic cups, with plastic spoons and forks. Not a hotel, a hospital cafeteria. They moved past the dining hall, past the nurses' station, where they took a right turn, passing the lounge with its deep burgundy cushioned chairs and sofas, a television mounted on a shelf overlooking the room, just within the reach of any hand attempting to change a channel.

Six open doors along the right and left sides of the twenty-yard hall, Degas and Monet prints, glass-covered and chrome-framed, spaced between every other door on either side of the hall. Almost a hotel, almost like being in a hotel, fine prints on the walls.

Joan is not yet able to register completely where she is, why she is here. A sleepwalker.

"Is there anything else you want or need?" Todd asks. His mother is a wreck: hair stringy, face pale, weak and jerky movements. His mother stares at her children, her lips slightly parted, expressionless, as if her entire personality had slipped out and abandoned her and all that's left is the flesh it once inhabited. Todd's reminded of the pod people from the film *Invasion of the Body Snatchers*. Empty shells. Andrea begins to cry. Joan looks off across the room to other patients meeting other visitors.

"I want to get out of here," she says, her voice low and affectless. "I want to go home."

"I think you have to stay here until you're better, Mom," Todd explains, wishing Andrea would keep in control; it's hard enough for him to be here, hard enough to keep himself from breaking down without worrying about her too. "The nurse said—I think her name was Carol—that it would take some time until you felt better."

She doesn't hear him. "I want to go home. There's no one I know here. There's no doctor here for me." Not pleading, just stating her wishes, the facts as she interprets them.

"*Mom*, you can't come home," Andrea cries. "Why did you—why are you—"

"You have to stay here for a little while," Todd cuts in. "Dr. Thompson said she would be in to see you after the weekend and that she'd be calling you after dinner tonight."

"I need to go home," Joan persists in a monotone.

Andrea turns to Todd. "Maybe we *can* help her at home better."

Todd gives her a sharp look and turns to his mother. "You will get to go home. You know that."

Joan stares at him, then down into the shopping bag. She spots an unopened bar of Dove soap, reaches in, taking it out, placing it on the table, and then she searches through the bag and extracts a bottle of shampoo, placing it alongside the soap and then placing the bag at the side of the chair. "I'm tired. They took my hair spray away."

Andrea looks away from her mother to her left, where she sees a patient playing himself in checkers, chewing on a black checker as he thinks through his next move for red: Jump or don't jump? Todd can't even picture his mother as the young suburban housewife of Ridgewood, New Jersey, she once was, icing cupcakes, cheering him on at soccer practice in a navy blue wool sweater and jeans. He can't figure out where she went, what happened to that woman, and as he looks at his mother's face, trying to figure it out, Joan rises and begins walking away.

"Mom?" Todd calls, but Joan doesn't look back.

She keeps walking, the soap in one hand and the shampoo in the other. "I'm going to take a shower," she says, not loud enough for her kids to hear.

"What happened last night? Can you tell me?"

They sit on the sofa in the living room, a sports show on the television. Just having woken after sleeping through the day, Pam rests her head on his shoulder, Dennis's arm sliding around her back, squeezing her shoulder with his hand.

A very tan man in a red bikini suit jumps off the flat black rock. He performs a twist, a pike, a turn, and a somersault before straightening and diving into the wavy waters below. Pam thinks of Joan leaping from her penthouse down to the Upper West Side pavement.

"Can't you tell me?" Dennis re-forms his question from positive to negative.

A former pro athlete appears on the screen advertising deodorant.

"Wasn't he a baseball player?" Pam queries.

Dennis looks from his wife to the screen, but the athlete is gone, replaced by a speeding Mercedes sedan. "What's going on?" he asks, pushing.

Pam sits forward, taking the remote, flicking off the television. She's expected he would ask, considering it first during the long stretch of hours she sat at Joan's bedside, then while standing in the hall waiting for Joan to be admitted. And at this point in their newly revived relationship her husband does deserve an answer—a quasi-truthful answer—allowing Dennis into the emotional truth of the previous evening without leaking any of Joan Dwyer's life into the story.

Pam leans back on the arm of the couch, chin on knee, examining her chipped fingernails. She sighs, reaching down and curling her fingers around her toes. "Remember Sarah Chaplin, who stopped by a few months ago? The one who buzzed up?" She pauses, allowing Dennis a moment to recollect the visit.

Dennis watches Pam pick at her toenails, keeps himself from telling her to stop, and thinks back to the night he eavesdropped, glass against wall, hearing the woman's hysterical crying, the car accident, her daughter's death, her husband's being far away. "Yeah, I remember. It was her?"

"She's been very depressed recently, and last night she tried to kill herself. Her daughter phoned and told me she came home from school and found her in bed with empty prescription vials all around. And so I went over there and met the ambulance before—"

The nurse who identifies herself as Shelley hands Joan a tray of food from a large metal cart stacked with shelves of trays, and Joan scans the dining room full of people, searching for an empty table. She sights one over in the far corner, proceeds there, and sits.

A menu card alongside the pale green plastic plate has her name written on a line across its bottom, and a series of *x*'s marked off beneath each category heading. Joan reads what has been marked off for her: Green Salad. Turkey and Mashed Potatoes. Chocolate Brownie. Milk. She surveys the tray of food. Three pale, thin slices of turkey loaf and a scooped–like–ice-cream pile of mashed potatoes, turkey and potatoes covered with a veil of brown juice. A small rectangular dark brown block with three walnuts adorning its top. A pale green bowl holds scraps of iceberg lettuce, two thin slices of cucumber, and one cherry tomato. A thimbleful of oily residue sits in a paper cup by the salad's side.

Joan scans the room to see what others are eating—*if* others are eating—and as she glances at the twenty to thirty people in the room, taking in their worn, dazed faces, their tired, apathetic looks and movements, where she is, who all these people are finally begin to dawn on her.

An old fat woman licks clean a plastic bowl of cherry gelatin dessert. A pretty young woman sits alone at a table, wrapping a brownie in a napkin, then stuffing it in the side pocket of her flimsy blue-and-white-striped bathrobe. The young woman then proceeds to eat her salad with her fingers, piece by piece, dunking each scrap of lettuce in the dressing before inserting it into her mouth. To Joan's immediate left sits a table of three. A middle-aged man, eyes closed, sleeps at the table, snoring, his tray of hospital food apparently untouched. A middle-aged woman wearing a bathrobe identical to that of the pretty young woman speaks nonstop to a young man with long black hair. The young man's eyes never leave her face as he lifts forkfuls of ravioli to his mouth.

"—kids. Samuel! Samuel! Samuel!" the woman exclaims, "Never—will never—no matter—never will he no matter—" The woman reaches out to the young man, reaching toward the man's head, and the man flinches back, turning away, and the woman withdraws her hand, insulted, and she reaches for the sleeping man's tray, taking the brownie, and inserting an end of the dessert in the sleeping man's open mouth. The brownie hangs half in, half out, a precipice extending from his face. The man does not wake up. The young man swaps his empty plate for the sleeping man's full plate of ravioli and begins eating a second meal. "My son would never do that," the woman criticizes. The young man pays her no mind.

I am on the mental ward in a hospital. My son and daughter came and visited me on a mental ward in a hospital. Joan lifts her tray, weaving between the tables, handing the untouched food to the nurse.

The nurse surveys the tray. "You should eat something after all you've put yourself through. You need some food in your stomach."

"This isn't what I like," Joan replies. *A mental patient on a mental ward.* "I don't want any of this."

"You can pick up a menu at the nurses' station and choose what you'd like for tomorrow's meals. We had to decide today's for you since you only arrived this morning."

"I'm going to my room now."

"I hope to see you out later."

Joan walks to her room and shuts the door. She goes to the desk and opens the bottom drawer, examining the two packages of candy her son has brought her, selecting the red licorice, furiously tearing open the package and devouring three strands of the candy. A knock on the door, and Joan tosses the package into the desk. She stands and opens the door.

A mustached man stands at the entrance. "Hi, I'm Richard, one of the nurses. I wanted to let you know that you can't close the door all the way. You have to leave it a bit open. Sorry." He sounds kind, just letting Joan know the way it is.

"How much *not closed* does it have to be?" Joan replies, blocking the doorway to the room.

Richard smiles slightly, taking the door from Joan, closing it to within an inch or two of the doorframe until he can no longer be seen from Joan's side. "This is fine," he says.

"Thank you," Joan says, and she returns to the desk, opening the drawer, this time leaving the package of candy in the drawer but taking the red licorice from the package one strand at a time lest she be interrupted again.

After all you've put yourself through.

Joan tries to think back to yesterday, the day before this one. Her memory is hazy; she can barely remember anything from the past twenty-four hours, distinctly remembers taking the pills, laying them all out before her, sorting and swallowing them with the seltzer water. Remembers Dr. Thompson being in her apartment, watching television with Dr. Thompson. The lobby of her building, the face of the doorman, Antoine, looking at her from under his navy blue cap with the gold band at its crown, a confused expression on his face as he held open a taxi door. Tubes running in and out of one arm, wires attached to her chest, to her head, screens of black with lines of bright green. Standing from a wheelchair, the urine stain on the gown, the can of hair spray being taken away, lying down to sleep under the blue bedspread, over the yellow blanket and white sheets. Her children visiting, unpacking what they brought her, taking a shower, peeling the sticky circular tabs from the emergency room off her chest and dropping them to the shower stall's tile floor. This is what she can now remember.

The package of licorice has been consumed, all sixteen ounces gone. Joan feels full and stands, going to the mirror above the bathroom sink, gripping the sink's edge, feeling the smoothness of its scrubbed clean porcelain.

The reflection in the mirror is of Joan Dwyer alive. Joan Dwyer not dead or even asleep, but alive. Alive and living on a mental ward in a hospital wearing the Laura Ashley dress she packed in her overnight bag, the black leather shoes Andrea brought over this afternoon, and the pair of gold seashell earrings she had in her pocketbook. Portrait of a mental patient.

"Do I have information?" Dennis asks. He stands in the kitchen, running his hands across the smooth new tile, fingers tracing the outlines of the hand-painted vegetables on each tile. Broccoli, parsnips, celery, radishes, lettuce, carrots, etc. Pam has been out for an early-evening jog in the park for the past fifteen minutes. Dennis keeps an ear listening for her knock on the door, the weather so hot and humid he is sure she won't be jogging for much longer. "Are you sure you want to?" Dennis asked. "Why don't you wait till tomorrow morning when it's cooler?" Pam wanted to, thought it might relieve some of the stress left over from last night.

"This is Mount Sinai patient information. How can I help you?"

Ever since Pam told him her story of last night, the lie about Sarah Chaplin's daughter finding her mother, Dennis has speculated on what Pam was really up to Friday evening. Over and over Pam kept repeating she was with Sarah Chaplin's daughter in the emergency room of Mount Sinai Hospital, and Dennis sat there stone-faced, unable to accuse his wife of lying for fear he may have heard wrong when he listened at the wall two months ago. Maybe he'd misunderstood what Sarah Chaplin had been saying and Sarah Chaplin's daughter had not died in a car accident. The only solution he could come up with outside of confronting his wife and admitting he'd eavesdropped on her session with Sarah Chaplin was to phone the hospital and have her story confirmed or proved to be a lie. "Do you have a patient named Sarah Chaplin listed?"

A pause, then, "No, I do not have a Sarah Chaplin," the woman responds. "No one by that name."

"She's a new patient," Dennis goes on. "Would you have someone who came in late last night?"

"If she was admitted, yes, I would."

Dennis picks at the edge of a tile. Cauliflower. Each four-by-four-inch tile cost $5.25. The counter and the wall space between the counter and cabinets are covered with hundreds of tiles, more than 720, Dennis calculates. Including tax, more than $4,000 spent on the tile alone, not adding in the cost of labor, and he let it happen, he was so involved with Joan Dwyer. "Thank you," Dennis says, and hangs up. He surveys the kitchen. The room does look great, he admits. The counter, the cabinets, the floor, the new table and chairs, the clock and hanging lamp: Pam knew what she was doing, and if she invested that much of her time and energy into making their home as comfortable and beautiful as it now is, why is he suspecting her of something—of *what* he doesn't know—all because she lied to him about Sarah Chaplin?

A knocking at the door, his wife back from jogging and needing to be let in— What does it mean that she lied to him? A lie to hide something that would affect him or a lie to protect a patient's privacy? Dennis walks down the hall, feet padding across the teal blue Persian runner. "In a second," he calls through the door to his wife.

"Joan Dwyer!" a deep male voice hollers. "Phone's for Joan Dwyer!"

Joan wipes the tears from her cheeks with the heels of her palms and walks into the hall. At the far end stands a young black man holding a large black book, "Holy Bible" embossed across its cover in gold lettering.

"I'm Joan Dwyer."

"Phone for you." He gestures to one of the two pay phones

hanging on the wall by the nurses' station; the receiver of the phone hangs straight down off the hook, pointing to the floor. The man walks off, entering the dining room, from which other voices can be heard in discussion. Joan picks up the dangling phone, sitting beneath it in a wooden chair much like the desk chair from her room. She presses the receiver tightly against an ear and, looking up, finds herself squarely facing the lounge ten feet away. Six or seven patients—or are they nurses? Or patients and nurses? Everyone here dresses alike, in street clothes, and the only people Joan is sure are the patients are those wearing bathrobes and slippers, and the only ones she's sure are nurses are those behind the desk at the nurses' station, and Where are the doctors? crosses Joan's mind. Where is *her* doctor?

"This is Joan Dwyer." A man of forty or so stares at Joan from a couch in the lounge, his face turned away from the television. His mouth hangs open, and Joan can see that the man is missing his upper and lower front teeth. Joan cannot see the television from her vantage point but hears *The Golden Girls* theme song play.

"Joan?"

"Hello?" Joan says.

"Joan, it's Dr. Thompson."

"I want to go home," Joan says, panicked. "I want to get out of here." The man with no front teeth purses his lips, attempts whistling along with the television show's theme song.

"You need to be there for a little while."

"No. No, I don't. There are no doctors here. Where are the doctors?" An Asian woman lying on a sofa by the back wall of the lounge rolls onto the floor and stays there, unmoving, eyes wide. No one bothers to help. No one but Joan even looks in her direction.

"Your body's in shock. It could take days for the medication to work its way through your system. I'm sure a doctor will see you tomorrow, and I'll be in to see you on Tuesday."

"When is that?" Joan has no idea what day this is.

"That's in three days," Pam explains. "We'll speak on the phone before then."

"I won't stay here for three days. I can't," Joan argues.

"You need to give yourself time to work this through, Joan. There's no other way."

"No, not three days. I have to leave." Joan's eyes begin tearing. The woman on the floor staring with her vacant eyes. The toothless man smiling wildly at the television. "Why did you bring me here?"

"I think you're in the best place for you right now. It's a very good hospital."

The toothless man laughs, a bleat like a goat. "I'm going to leave," Joan repeats. "Todd will take me home. They can't keep me here." Tears run down her face, and she wipes them away on the arm of her robe.

"They can keep you there as long as they think they need to, until they think you've recovered from what you've done."

The middle-aged man who'd been sleeping at the dining room table walks by, dressed in a three-piece pin-striped suit, carrying a brown leather attaché case. Joan watches the man approach the nurses' station. "I don't want to be here," Joan cries.

"I'll phone you tomorrow afternoon. I promise."

"Don't leave me here."

The suit man opens the briefcase, flipping its top.

"I'll phone you tomorrow."

"Please—" Joan pleads.

"It's the best place for you."

The man smooths his hands over the attaché's burgundy silk lining.

"Don't leave me here!" Joan screams into the phone, her voice catching, becoming a sob.

"I'm not leaving you there. I promise."

"When can I leave? When?"

An elderly woman wrapped in a blanket passes by. "I am not a Golden Girl . . . I am not a Golden Girl," she repeats.

"Soon," Pam soothes. "Pretty soon. Why don't you go to bed? You must be tired. I'll phone you tomorrow."

"Shut up!" the toothless man yells at the old woman. "Shut the fuck up!"

"*No*—" Joan cries, *"please."*

"You need to rest, Joan."

"I hate you! I hate you for leaving me here! I hate you!" Joan slams the phone down, hanging up, and she instantly regrets it, cutting herself off from the only person who can help, and she breaks down in tears.

She hangs up the phone, sliding down in the upholstered chair. Forest green fabric with tiny white fleur-de-lis stitched into its weave. Joan Dwyer is safe. Joan Dwyer is being watched over and tended to, and I possibly saved her from death after leading her to it, Pam concludes. But then, if she hadn't brutalized her patient in their last few weeks of sessions together, perhaps Joan would have phoned and talked to her doctor about how she was feeling rather than opted for suicide. Quite possibly she scared Joan off just enough so that her patient felt she had no choice but to attempt suicide, and sitting in the den, the former guest room, her husband waiting for her on the other side of the door, cleaning up after the dinner they cooked together, side by side, she making mashed potatoes according to his instructions as he prepared the chicken and salad, Pam knows she would not—could not—have done it any differently. Although her behavior was far from perfect, she did her best and survived, as have both Dennis and Joan, and for that Pam must give herself some credit.

"I hate you! I hate you for leaving me here!"

Those weekend afternoons spent shopping for the apartment knowing her husband was with Joan Dwyer during those hours. Examining samples of cabinet doors, feeling the textures of upholstery for curtains in the living room, Pam thought the redecoration would serve one of two purposes: Either it would help lure her husband back to her or it would be a start to her new life, creating a new home because Dennis was leaving her for Joan Dwyer. Pam worked quickly, making decisions and paying on the spot, taking whatever was in stock so it could be delivered immediately. The kitchen, the hallway, the living room, guest room, and bathrooms have all been redone. All that remains is the bedroom with its unfinished furniture and futon mattress. However, since reviving her marriage and hospitalizing a patient, Pam has lost interest in the final chores of the redecoration. A self-evaluation of how keen an observer of human nature she must be when she couldn't recognize her husband was carrying on an affair with one of her patients, when she couldn't detect Joan Dwyer was going to attempt suicide, is of greater concern to her. The type of blinds she wants for the bedroom windows—vertical or horizontal?—can wait.

"I can sit here now. I can sit here, as depressed as I am," Tim Boxer told his doctor, Dr. Thompson, several months back, "and I can promise you I will not try to kill myself and will call if I feel I've reached a point where I will. But if I ever truly do reach that point, I will have already accepted the illusion that you are of no help to me and that suicide is the only way to help myself stop the pain. If I care about myself enough to phone you, obviously I have not crossed the line over where I will definitely do it. If I cross that line and only care about stopping the pain of living no matter what the cost, you are no longer an option. I have no problem making you a promise that I won't do it, but if I ever cross that line, my promise becomes meaningless. Understand?"

Pam may not be able to save patients from killing themselves if they really want to, but she can help them find alternative ways through which to solve their problems beyond suicide. "You have other options, and if you can't see them for yourself, I possibly can guide you to them." And so Tim Boxer's problem of being alone and living shamefully with HIV was not solved but was helped by Pam's guidance two months ago, when she coaxed him into joining an HIV-positive therapy group.

"This doesn't mean I won't kill myself," Tim stated defiantly. "It only means I won't for the time being. I have not abandoned suicide as an option."

She may have almost lost Joan Dwyer, but she's almost saved Tim Boxer, and if Tim's reprieve cannot cancel out Joan's near demise, at least she shouldn't consider herself a total waste of her patients' time and money, especially the majority of her patients with their less-than-life-threatening crises.

Pam stands, her morale boosted—she's not a worthless doctor—and opens the door of the den. Dennis stands in the kitchen, cleaning up after dinner. He scrubs a pan's copper bottom. Pam walks up behind him, arms going around his waist, one hand edging under his shirt at his stomach, then sliding to his chest. A splash of soapy water hits her forearm as he continues scrubbing. "I thought I told you I'd do this," Pam says, kissing his earlobe.

"I'm almost done. How did it go with your patient?" Not Sarah Chaplin but possibly another patient or something else altogether, some other secret. A life of secrets. Dennis rinses the pan, places it on the counter, bottom side up, angling its handle against that of a drying pot. He turns. Pam's hand slides from his front to his side to his back, pushing up the shirt at his back as it falls over his stomach in the front. He locks his arms around her waist. Hard not to love her when she's being so loving. "You don't want to talk about it?" he asks.

"She's scared, doesn't know what's going on. She's still so gone on drugs. At this stage there's little I can do. I just comfort her. After the weekend—then I'll be able to help once the effects of the drugs have worn off."

"She has her family too," Dennis says, playing along with her lie. "It's not as if she's alone without you."

Pam smiles, almost believing that Sarah Chaplin is in the hospital and not Joan Dwyer. "She does have her family," Pam agrees.

.   .   .

"Mom"—Todd implores her—"I will bring you food at lunchtime tomorrow. I will bring you a bagel, cream cheese, and lox from Zabar's. How's that? But it's not visiting hours anymore today. It's already past nine o'clock."

"I need to be out of here," Joan insists. "Don't you understand that?"

"I'll stop by tomorrow at one o'clock," Todd says. "Good-bye, Mom."

"I can't eat the food here. I'll starve."

"I'll bring you food, Mom."

"Help me out of here. You have to help me out."

"I'm doing all I can. Good-bye, Mom. I love you."

Joan listens as Todd hangs up the phone. She sits in the chair by the hall phone, calling card in hand, and dials out the Marches' phone number, then, after the tone, her calling card number.

"Hello?"

"Lana, hello. Is my daughter there?"

"I'm sorry, Joan, but she and Kitty went to the movies."

"Oh. Of course." Her daughter out of reach, out of touch, at a movie.

"How are you feeling?" Lana asks.

"I'm fine," Joan replies. "I'm okay. Andrea's not there, so I'll call back later."

"Of course. I'll let her know you phoned."

"Thank you so much."

"I will. Take care."

Joan hangs up. Lana March living with her fourth husband in fifteen years. Two husbands since Joan has been divorced. Four for Lana versus one for Joan, and Joan grips the phone receiver tightly in a fist. No son, no son or daughter available to rescue her from this locked ward.

The young man with long hair stands at the second pay phone, a finger repeatedly flicking the change return opening. Joan dials Dr. Thompson's number, dials in her calling card number, and waits. The machine picks up, and Joan slams down the receiver, scaring the long-haired man into taking a step back from the other phone.

The man pulls on the ends of his hair. "I'm going to tell Richard you're abusing the phone. They'll take away your phone privileges." The man walks off, away from Joan.

Joan dials Dennis's office number at BMA, then her calling card number. His voice answering system answers. "Hello, Dennis," Joan begins nervously. "This is Joan. I'm sorry for bothering you, but I wanted to hear from you. I'm not at home right now. Please phone me. I miss you. I'm at—" Joan looks up to the number inserted beneath the pay phone's clear plastic plate and reads it off. "I hope all is well. Good-bye." Joan hangs up the phone, stands, and walks down the hall. She enters her room and sits at the desk, eating handful after handful of sugar-coated jelly rings.

He enters the den. This room, like all the others, is meticulously decorated, Pam planning and organizing it all so well. The sofa bed, the matching chair, an antique end table, antique lampstand, antique coffee table, and two matching sets of bookshelves filled with books formerly kept in the living room. Best-selling spy and horror novels, graphic arts collections, and comic book anthologies bought by Dennis, and psychology texts, novels of dysfunctional family drama, and travel books bought by Pam. A perfect and cozy room.

Pam sleeps, exhausted from the previous evening, asleep and will definitely not awaken, having taken two tranquilizers. After watching a *Saturday Night Live* rerun from last fall, Michael Keaton the host, Dennis sits on the couch, pulling out the drawer in the end table and taking out the hardbound, black leather-covered phone book listing Pam's patients. He glances at the small travel clock on the bookshelf: 1:10 A.M., and most people will be in for the night if they were out earlier. If she is not in the hospital, she will most likely be home.

Never having had any interest in the exact names and phone numbers of Pam's patients, he's always respected her privacy and never looked in the book. With the lie about Sarah Chaplin, Dennis makes an exception, curious to learn whether Pam was with her patient at a hospital last night or up to something else. Sarah Chaplin may have been transferred to another hospital and thus would not be listed as a patient at Mount Sinai. Maybe Pam only lied about the daughter's finding Sarah Chaplin to cover for herself. Maybe she was the one who found her patient, and Dennis would like to give his wife the benefit of the doubt before declaring her a liar.

He flips the book open to C, holding the page out in the patch of light falling in from the hall. Three names are listed, the second being Sarah Chaplin's. Dennis memorizes the phone number and puts the book away, picking up the phone on the table, and dialing.

"Hello," a man answers, half asleep.

Dennis can feel his heart racing. "Hello, is a Ms. Sarah Chaplin there?"

"May I ask who's calling? Do you know what time it is?"

"I'm conducting a survey for—"

"*Who is it?*" Dennis hears a woman in the background. He can picture them, Mr. and Mrs. Chaplin lying in bed, him sitting up and on the phone, her rolling over, gently touching his arm.

"*It's no one, go back to sleep.*" Then to Dennis: "We're sleeping. She's asleep. Good night."

Sarah Chaplin's husband hanging up on him because Sarah Chaplin is asleep, not in the hospital after attempting suicide but well and asleep and fine.

Dennis returns to the bedroom, shutting off the hall light along the way. What is he to do with this information now that he has it? And who is *he* to begrudge her one lie after all the lies he's told over the last few months? For all he knows, she just needed to be alone and spent the evening at her office on the couch, pondering recent events and putting them in perspective. Who is *he* to make her account for her time? What purpose does it serve if he loves Pam and wants to remain with her? Dennis has no idea. He climbs in bed next to his wife, putting an arm around her, trying to love without doubt.

.   .   .

The gathering of eight patients watches *60 Minutes*. Morley Safer deftly inquires why some young businessman, now a convict on death row, did something to some woman with a crowbar. The man describes what he did to the woman, and as horrifying and grotesque as the act is, the eight patients watch on, undaunted, as if a sunny weather report were being broadcast. To the patients locked on this ward, the outside world coming in to them via television is meaningless beyond its value as a diversion from their own lives. The emotional pain radiating through the two corridors of the ward is so immense that the violence of the outside world feels mundane in comparison. Murder . . . torture . . . war . . . what one person can do to another being far less harrowing than what one person can do to him- or herself.

Joan sits in the corner of the room, her eyes leaving the television screen and scanning the backs of the heads angled up to the TV. She has remained out of her room since this morning, when she met with her doctor, Dr. Hepp informing Joan that her recovery and readiness for discharge would be measured by the quality and quantity of time she spends out of her room interacting with the patients and staff: ''I consider the reports the nurses make on your chart and make my decision based on that.''

Before lunch Joan met with Todd and Andrea, eating the cream cheese and lox bagel her son brought while Todd told his mother about the summer courses he was taking at school. Todd handed his mother two paperbacks from Emily: *The Bonfire of the Vanities* by Tom Wolfe and *The Fountainhead* by Ayn Rand. ''She's read them both and says they're very good.''

Andrea, speechless, only gawked at her mother.

Once they'd departed, Joan examined the books, impressed by Emily's thoughtful gift. She looked over the covers, reading critics' quotes before folding the books open, scrutinizing a page in each, and comparing the size of the print. Joan found *The Fountainhead*'s print

too small, so she opted to read the Wolfe book—an activity to pursue while outside her room so as to receive favorable comments on
her chart.

Thirty-six pages and one hour later, Joan was asked to attend the
group meeting in the dining room. The tables had been pushed aside,
and the chairs were arranged in a large oval. The nursing staff and one
half to two thirds of the patient community attended the meeting.
"How has the weekend gone so far?" a tall, thin woman named Francine asked the group, and for the next fifty minutes Joan listened as a
trio of patients quarreled over what station should be listened to on
the community radio. The young man with the Bible demanded that
religious programming be played at all hours. A frail old woman
shrieked that she wanted to hear jazz music. The man with no front
teeth argued that the nurses must destroy the radio because whenever
it was on, he could feel his brain boiling like beans in a can over an
open fire. "And they don't smell good," he warned. Toward the end
of the discussion, Francine introduced Joan to the other patients,
asked Joan how things were going. "I feel good," Joan replied somberly. "My daughter and son visited and brought me two books. I did
some reading this afternoon. I forgot how much I enjoyed reading."

"Sounds nice," Francine replied to Joan, and Joan could tell she
would obtain a favorable comment from Francine for attending the
meeting and speaking confidently and calmly in front of the group.

At dinner Joan ate the hospital food like the others, showing the
nurses she was not a difficult patient. A woman with dirty blond hair
sat across from Joan. The woman wore one of the hospital-issue bathrobes over a red-and-black-checked flannel shirt and a pair of neon
orange sweatpants. Mindy told Joan that she had admitted herself to
the ward, that she had phoned the police and told them she would kill
herself unless she was locked in a hospital. Mindy said she lives on
Fifth Avenue across from the Metropolitan Museum of Art. She said
she lives there with her lawyer husband and their two children.
"They were out at the Museum of Natural History when I phoned
the police," Mindy explained. "I *told* them not to leave me alone that

afternoon, but did they listen to me? Now look what they've made me do.''

Joan stares at the back of Mindy's head as Mindy stares up at the television, attentively watching a commercial for a Nissan Sentra. The face of the stopwatch reappears, ticking loudly, forty minutes of the sixty minutes having passed.

2

Pam and Joan sit facing each other in the room where Joan and Dr. Hepp met two days earlier. A small nine-foot-by-six-foot room with only a small table in one corner and two folding chairs. Joan wears one of the thin, lightweight blue-and-white-striped hospital-issue robes over her cotton nightgown, the bottom third of the nightgown, from the knee down, exposed below the hem of the bathrobe.

Yesterday, Memorial Day, Joan participated in an art class in which patients placed tiny square and circular white, yellow, and pale pink tiles into an aluminum frame with a thin layer of putty on its bottom. The seven participating patients filled their frames with the colored tiles, settling each tile into the white putty and lining another tile up alongside it with a thin space in between. "Not too close," Bethany, the art therapist, warned. Joan quickly finished the project to Bethany's cheers of approval: "Have you done this before? You've got a knack for this."

Joan sat at the breakfast table this morning and ate the spongy pancakes covered with the sugar-sweet syrup, talking with the man with the missing upper and lower front teeth. "I pulled my teeth out with my bare hands," he told Joan. "I tore them out of my gums because that's what the man in the TV told me all about to do." Joan listened, nodding as if she understood and it all made perfect sense, and then she excused herself to the nurses' station, making her selections for lunch that day: club sandwich, milk, chocolate pudding. If eating bad food and conversing with social misfits would prove she was stable and able to be sent home, then Joan decided she would play along.

Following breakfast, Joan returned to her room, planning to change into the navy blue dress Andrea packed for her and then go watch morning TV talk shows in the lounge with the other patients. As Joan took off her robe, she spied the urine-stained nightgown crumpled on the closet floor, the healing scabs on her shoulder and arm itching where she'd cut herself. Joan sat on the edge of the bed, stifled a cry, and gripped the collar of the robe tight in her hands. She clawed it and tore down, splitting the robe's back seam and shredding the velvet with her hands. Joan began sobbing, and when Caroline entered to check on Joan, Joan told her that she wanted to go home, that she was sorry she tried to kill herself, that she was sorry for what she had put her son, daughter, and doctor through, that she never meant to hurt anyone but only thought no one cared.

Caroline comforted Joan, held Joan's shoulders, handed Joan tissues, brought Joan one of the hospital-issue robes, and Joan, after half an hour of alternately sobbing and talking, calmed down until Caroline left the room to check on other patients, whereupon Joan immediately began crying again. Tears shed for the robe, the horrible meals, the suicide attempt. Because the attempt had failed, because the attempt had almost succeeded, because she had acted on her suicidal thoughts and put her doctor through so much.

Pam observes Joan, takes in Joan's tired appearance. Nothing like the well-dressed, well-made-up, perfectly accessorized patient she so often saw in her office three times each week for the past year and a half. No matter what raged on in her mind during the previous eighteen months, Joan Dwyer never let her depression affect her physical appearance. Joan always maintained a polished, well-groomed exterior, and now, Pam observes, only this—the breakup with Dennis, the suicide attempt, the move to the emergency room, then up to the locked ward—has broken Joan into exposing all that she feels inside in her appearance, on her face, and in her body and voice. Joan Dwyer the mental patient: the scraggly hair, the puffy red face, the mismatched clothes (long gown, short robe), all of which demonstrate that maybe Joan has finally come to acknowledge how sick she truly is and has ceased to pretend she only needs a man, a husband, to make her better. If a stay in the ward helps Joan to recognize *that,* helps Joan to take therapy more seriously, as someplace more than a place to go to when she feels lonely, then maybe this is all worth it. Pam looks at Joan, whose mouth is half open, about to speak.

"I'm sorry," Joan says, her hands folded in the lap of the thin robe, fingers fiddling with the belt's ends, eyes staring down at her hands. "I'm sorry you have to come visit me here. I'm sorry for what I did. I'm sorry I didn't call you."

The remorse seems genuine, sincere, not faked to get her out sooner. "I'm just glad we got you here. How are you feeling?" Pam asks.

Joan unties, then reties the belt, knotting it around her waist, its tightness giving her a feeling of security. "I think I'm better. I think so." She looks up at her doctor, beginning to cry for the eighth or ninth time today. "I don't know how this happened. I was doing it and watching myself doing it and I just—" Joan gasps, choking, then coughing.

Pam reaches out, taking Joan's hands in her own. "It's all right. It's all right. I'm here. I'm still here."

"I don't know why . . . I do know why . . . I just—" Tears run down Joan's face, and Pam looks to the table for a tissue box, but none is there. She opens the one drawer under the tabletop, but it is empty. Joan wipes her face along the sleeve of the robe. She shuts her eyes, takes three deep breaths, then looks back at Dr. Thompson. "How—*when* can I get out of here?"

"We have to make sure you're emotionally stable and will be safe at home again. Can you tell me what coping behaviors you've learned since Friday so we know you'll be okay if you're released?"

Joan catches her breath. "I know people care for me. I know people really care for me that I could have called and didn't. You, either of my kids, even Todd's girlfriend sent me some books. Dennis leaving doesn't matter anymore. It doesn't. I know the most important people care for me. I understand what's important now."

Pam believes Joan believes what she's saying while she's saying it; she only hopes Joan can believe it when she's not in the hospital and the urge to kill herself returns, as it inevitably will. "I'll speak to Dr. Hepp and see what he says."

Joan leans forward. "He never even sees me, has only seen me once for ten minutes in all the time I've been here. He doesn't know anything about me, and he's deciding when I can go." Joan begins chewing on the skin at the corner of her thumbnail.

"I will speak with him before I leave today. That's the best I can do to start."

"But you do think I'm ready to leave, that it would be better for me to leave?" Joan stares at her doctor, leaning forward in the chair, dry tear lines connecting eyes to nose to mouth to chin.

"I think you need more time here," Pam answers honestly: Joan is plainly too unbalanced to leave, her nervousness, her emotionality, her fidgetiness, all reactions to the enormous amount of medication she took. Pam watches as her patient's face goes slack, hopeless, eyes spilling over with tears. "It's only for a short time more," Pam comforts her.

"No," Joan says quietly, defeated. "Please get me out of here."

Pam stands, places a hand on Joan's shoulder, giving a hard squeeze, and then she reaches out with her other hand, embracing Joan, a hug of support. Joan cries. "It's okay. Everything will be okay." And Pam releases Joan, feeling her own tears on her face. She wipes them away with a hand. "I'll go talk to Dr. Hepp." She opens the door and walks into the hall.

Joan follows. "When will you be by again?"

Pam watches a line of patients, some young, some old, some fat, some thin, some pretty, some ugly, some dressed in robes and others in jeans and T-shirts, all shuffling into the dining room across the hall: a parade of lost lives. Maybe Joan would be better off dead. Maybe she should have given Joan more pills to swallow instead of hauling her to the emergency room. "I'll stop by at seven-thirty tomorrow evening. How's that?"

"Can I call you if I need to?"

"Of course."

"I should have let her die. That's what I should have done. Look at what I've done to her. She's a wreck. She's given up."

"You put your patient—Ms. Dwyer—in a place where she'll be safe from herself, where she can begin to put herself together for the hard work she'll have to undertake in therapy once she's out. None of that is bad." Jack Briden watches his colleague from across the room, a solemn expression on his face. He sits in a large gray upholstered chair, Pam opposite him in an identical chair.

Standing in the kitchen at midday, Pam, just in from seeing Joan, feeling depressed and guilty for using Joan's therapy against her, for being a manipulator of lives, almost costing Joan her own in the process, turned to Jack Briden as he poured himself a cup of coffee. "Do you have any time after work tonight? A few minutes to talk?"

Pam places a hand on each arm of the chair. She squeezes her hands tightly to the arms, careful to avoid gesturing in the air. "I saved her when she wanted to die, and I'm not sure if I did it because if she died, it would mean I'm a failure as a doctor, or if I did it for her own sake to help her, or if I saved her so she would have to live in her miserable life as a punishment for sleeping with my husband.''

"Do you wish ill on her?"

"Not consciously, but I don't want her involved with Dennis."

"Do you fear she will be?"

"He ended it with her. It wasn't her choice."

"Do you think she'll contact him?"

"She might. I don't know. She wouldn't have tried to kill herself if she thought she could get him back."

"You have no fear of her seeking out your husband?"

"Even if she wanted it, Dennis wouldn't let it happen now."

"It doesn't sound like you wish ill on her. To me it sounds like you wish ill on yourself for what you've done. That's why you're here." Jack gestures at Pam sitting in his office. "To confess and be absolved by another doctor, your equal."

Pam stands; she is not his patient. The office door is open, so she has no reason to make herself feel like a patient by sitting under Jack's cool gaze. She walks to his desk, a large, highly glossed and polished oak table. Papers are piled neatly around its sides. Pam looks over the desk calendar. "Flanting" marked in at nine-thirty tonight, an hour and a half from now.

"What would you have done?" Pam asks. "I wanted to save my marriage. How else could I do it but to have the relationship end?"

Jack goes after Pam at his desk and shuts the calendar, leaving Pam staring at the gold ink printed on the book's burgundy leather cover: "Dr. John P. Briden." "Please, don't poke over my things," Jack asks.

Pam walks to the leather couch with its inclined side in the classical therapeutic mode. She sits at its foot. Jack sits behind his desk.

"Do you think I did anything wrong? Coercing her into giving me the name, using her therapy to learn about my husband? Do you see anything else I could have done to make myself sane again?"

"No . . ." Jack answers slowly. "Of course, as you know, you don't think me the most moral of men. What's my opinion worth to you? You're seeking absolution from a man who sleeps with a patient.'' He shrugs and smiles a sly smile. He flips his desk calendar open, looks over tomorrow's lineup of patients.

''That doesn't matter to me. You've made mistakes, I've made mistakes.'' She means what she says, is aware of what it must have been like for Jack to go home alone every night: He is in his late forties with no one to love, no one loving him, and then a handsome young man expresses interest. To break a rule and find love or to suffer alone? Pam knows the answer.

Jack nods lightly. ''How kind of you to presently understand. However, from what you've told me, *you* have not cared about *this* patient from the start. You were only beginning to make progress with her earlier this year but then ended up twisting her therapy to suit your own purposes. And only *now,* after she's attempted suicide, are you questioning your conduct. I may be no saint for my recent indiscretions, but Michael Flanting and I are two consenting adults. We discuss the implications of what we're doing and what boundaries we've crossed. Your behavior, in contrast, is *much* more extreme. I can't tell you what you should do. You should have referred her to another doctor months ago. Why didn't you?''

''I wanted to know. I thought I could make things right.''

''If I confessed something as heinous to you as you've confessed to me, what would you do? Give advice to the doctor or work to save the patient?''

Pam tries to read the doctor, what he is getting at, what conclusions he is drawing. ''I think I would want to help both.''

Jack looks away from Pam, opening his desk, taking out a legal pad. ''Pamela, you shouldn't be allowed to see Ms. Dwyer anymore. I shouldn't have to tell you that. Personally I feel I should turn you in to the APA after what you've told me.''

Pam is shaking with fear of Jack Briden and of the contemptible doctor he has described her as being: Jack Briden confirming her guilt, not pardoning her crimes. Pam stands, wants to get her bag from her office and take a cab home, no patience for a bus. ''You said you'd keep this in confidence,'' Pam reminds him, backing toward the door. ''I'm trying to work this out. I questioned myself. I tried to do what's best.''

Jack spins his chair to the file cabinet behind his desk, pulling out a drawer, taking out an overstuffed legal-size manila folder. ''I didn't say I *would* turn you in; I just don't know what to tell you. This is your responsibility. However, a patient's at risk, and I can't forget that. I don't know this patient, I don't know how much she needs you, but it is something I must consider.''

''I came to you for help.''

Jack Briden opens the folder across his desk. The pile of papers shifts to the side, spilling across his leather blotter. ''Shit.'' He shoves papers around and begins flipping through the stack, page by page.

Pam holds a hand to the doorjamb. ''Please. You won't tell anyone for now?''

Jack sighs. ''Let me know if I can help you out in any way.''

Pam backs out of his office, her eyes fixed on his hands, turning and arranging papers, from upside down to right side up.

3

The door to the office is shut. Dennis skims a page of ad copy, examines the layout he's designed, and observes that the copy's too long to fit into the prescribed space in the ad. Either the design or copy must be altered, one rewritten and shortened or the other redesigned, and Dennis is not in the mood to deal with this problem. He just wants to lie down and sleep. He slept so poorly last night because he knew today he would betray Pam, phoning Joan in response to the message she left on his voice mail over the long weekend. He dials the number scrawled in blue pen on the scrap of paper.

The phone rings twice. "Hello," a gruff male voice answers.

"Hello. I'm trying to reach Joan Dwyer."

Silence. Dennis thinks perhaps the man has hung up when he hears, "Joan Dwyer! Joan Dwyer!" The voice of the man who answered the phone.

Receiving the message on Tuesday, he gave himself a day to consider not calling, a day to convince himself he didn't owe Joan even one more call if she needed to speak to him, but Dennis couldn't, not with Pam's lie fresh in his mind—a marriage possibly founded on lies: his to her of these past months, hers to him concerning a child, Sarah Chaplin, and who knows what else during the course of their eight-year marriage.

"How's Sarah Chaplin?" Dennis asked Pam last night upon her return home. "Did you visit her today?"

"She'll be better. She's doing okay." Pam tossed her pocketbook on the couch and walked to the bedroom, her eyes never even glancing at her husband.

"How's her daughter doing?" Dennis followed.

Pam undressed, kicking off shoes, unbuckling the belt on her skirt. "Why are you so interested all of a sudden?"

"I've always been interested in your work," Dennis informed her.

Pam dropped her skirt in the pile of clothes to be taken to the dry cleaner's. "I have some books you might like to read, then." She never answered her husband's question.

"Hello?"

Joan's voice sounds normal, the way it always has; he misses hearing it. "Joan. Hi. This is Dennis. I only got your message yesterday, so I'm sorry I didn't call sooner. How are you? Where are you staying?" Polite and formal yet not too distant, warm and friendly but not too caring: these are the things—the *emotions, feelings*—he hopes to convey and keep a check on.

"I'm doing fine. How did—I left a message—I'm sorry."

"It's all right. Where are you?"

"I'm at Lenox Hill Hospital. I'm okay. They just want to make sure, so they're observing me. That's why I'm here, but I'm okay. I just can't wait to return home."

She sounds cheerful, upbeat, better than most people at work he's spoken to today. "I don't understand. Were you ill?"

"I'm sorry. I don't even remember phoning you. I'm sure I just wanted to hear a friendly voice when I first arrived."

"What happened?"

"I had some problems with the medication I'm taking, but everything's fine now. I'm much better. Really."

Dennis is suddenly aware of how dry his mouth is, how sweaty his palms are. The phone receiver almost slips in his hand. "What happened? You're doing better?" Joan seriously ill in the hospital. "Tell me what happened."

"I'm all right. I shouldn't have phoned."

"I'm glad you did. I only wish . . ." His voice trails off; he doesn't know what he wishes.

"You don't have to worry."

She keeps evading him. "Please, Joan, tell me what happened."

A pause. "I wasn't feeling well, and I overreacted and took too much medication."

"You took an overdose?"

"I was trying to make myself better. I was in such pain, and I wanted to stop it. . . . It was all a big mistake. That's what it was."

Joan Dwyer took a serious enough overdose of medicine to land her in the hospital—a suicide attempt—yet makes it sound as if she'd taken three aspirin instead of two.

"I'm all right. Really, I am," Joan repeats, breaking the silence. "I think I'm ready to go home now, but they still want to observe me. I don't know why."

"Can you receive visitors? I'd like to see you."

"Are you sure?"

"I can come by tonight after work. At around eight o'clock if that's good? Would you like me to?"

"That would be fine. I'd like to see you. I need visitors."

"I'll stop by then. Is there anything you need?"

"Todd and Andrea brought me some things from home, but thanks."

"Good. I'm glad you have them. Where are you staying?"

"I'm on the psychiatric ward at Lenox Hill. I don't know what floor."

"I'll see you tonight. Take care. I care about you. Remember that."

Joan Dwyer attempted suicide thanks to him, Dennis reflects. He strung her along, used her at his convenience, and dismissed her from his life cruelly and callously. Joan, left alone and deserted once more, humiliated, then attempted suicide.

The lights are dark in the office. Dennis sits, arms folded atop his desk, head resting over a forearm. How responsible he is for Joan Dwyer's condition plagues him. Is he wholly or partially responsible? He fully comprehends the fact that he doesn't know enough about Joan Dwyer's past to understand why she is the woman she is today: a woman recovering from a suicide attempt. However, not knowing anything more but that she is also seeing a therapist, as Andrea let slip during dinner, does not soothe Dennis or free him from guilt. It only gives him knowledge enough to blame himself and no one else.

Dennis sits up, spinning his chair from the desk, holding his watch under the thin arc of orange sunlight falling in through the window. Seven-twelve. He is to meet Joan at eight, and this afternoon he phoned Pam at her office and left a message stating that he would most likely be home late tonight; their marriage was unraveling as quickly as it had been patched back together.

He cannot go empty-handed to the hospital but is unsure of what is appropriate to bring to a patient on a mental ward. Flowers? Candy? Not a get-well card, he knows that. Dennis has no idea what a mental ward even looks like, never mind what it allows its patients, so what Joan may or may not be able to receive as a present is impossible to discern.

Dennis hails a taxi outside the office building, figures he can shop at any of the stores uptown in the neighborhood of the hospital for a gift. "Seventy-seventh and Lexington, please," he tells the driver.

He wonders if this is a good idea to meet with Joan when she is in a state of recuperation. Will he be helping or hindering her recovery?

Dennis feels he owes her this much, feeling more than partly responsible for her being in the hospital. This much and this little, this visit, riding uptown, the cab starting and stopping amid midtown eastbound traffic. Tires screech as they make the turn onto Third Avenue. Horns blare from trucks, cars, taxis, limos, vans, bells ring on bicycles, dogs bark, people scream, sing, and preach on the sidewalks and in the streets, skyscrapers tower magnificently above his head, subways rumble through the ground beneath his feet, and Dennis feels a sudden, tremendously guilty, tremendously satisfying, ego-enhancing narcissistic rush of pleasure to be riding uptown to a hospital on the Upper East Side of Manhattan—city at the center of the universe, world stage—to be visiting his ex-mistress, who has attempted suicide on his behalf. A grand gesture befitting the drama and romance of the city: his mistress attempting suicide in her apartment on the Upper West Side. How thrilling for a woman to want to end her life because she couldn't live her life without him, and then, just before Dennis scolds himself for turning Joan's personal tragedy into his own private monument, the thought occurs: *Would Pam kill herself if I left her? Does she love me enough to kill herself if I left?* The answer takes all of a second to be arrived at. No. Definitely not, and Dennis knows this is a good thing, that killing oneself is no way to prove that one loves someone and cannot live without him, that killing oneself is a selfish act of anger against oneself and not a gesture of selfless affection toward another, but he cannot help feeling a bit flattered that Joan chose him to leave her mark on: the man she couldn't live without.

The cab stops at a red light at Sixtieth Street. Dennis looks to his left, spotting Bloomingdale's, people entering and exiting through the revolving doors. He reaches into his pocket. "I'll be getting out here," he says, and pushes a five and three singles through the slot in the Plexiglas divider. He steps out of the cab, taking long strides in the direction of the department store.

.   .   .

Wearing a simple deep plum silk dress with sleeves that fall to just above her elbows, the better to cover the thin scab lines on her shoulder, having showered and blown-dry and brushed her hair and applied light makeup, Joan is prepared for Dennis's visit. Although she previously looked forward to the visit from Dr. Thompson, now, sitting across from her doctor in the small office room, Joan can hardly wait for her doctor to end the session so she can inspect herself in the mirror once more before Dennis arrives. Joan phoned her daughter this afternoon, insisting she bring around the dress, a pair of shoes, and her makeup case.

"Mom, where are you going that you need all this stuff?"

"I want to look nice for myself. Is that so bad? My doctor thinks it's a positive sign that I'm beginning to care about my appearance."

Her patient is taking care of herself again, and Pam is as pleased as she is fearful of this radical change from Joan's ragged appearance yesterday. Joan's whole attitude seems to have shifted. Today, so far in this session, Joan has all but forgotten why she was brought to the hospital. She displays extreme anxiety about leaving the ward, complains about having to be kept in the hospital, but has not once spoken of the conditions that propelled her to take the overdose.

"I'm pleased to hear you're feeling better today. It shows. What do you think accounts for this change?"

Joan is not going to inform her doctor about tonight's visitor. Not going to tell Dr. Thompson because Dr. Thompson would not like it, would disapprove of her continuing this affair with the man who has toyed with Joan's emotions, and Joan does not want this evening ruined.

Joan folds her arms, a hand over each forearm, fingers rubbing her soft skin. "I looked at myself this morning, looked at what I'd done, where I am, and decided that if I am going to help myself get better, I should take better care of myself. I understand a dress and makeup won't change me, but considering what the last few days have been like, having a clean dress and looking pretty, reading a book, watching a funny show on TV—things I took for granted only a week ago—being here for five days has forced me to realize how much I do enjoy these little things in my life. Wearing this dress won't keep me happy forever, but having it with me here helps me realize how much more I have that does make me happy. Todd and Andrea. My home.'' Joan stops herself from speaking, wipes tears from her eyes, fooling her doctor but now seeming to have fooled herself as well. ''A week ago I was preparing to kill myself. I honestly don't understand it, what's happening to me in my head, but I do feel better.''

Their time together is up, and Pam stands. ''It will take some time to figure it all out. I'm glad you now feel you care enough to try. I know being here is difficult, but I think it's been helpful.''

Joan stands. ''How much longer will it be, do you think?''

Pam opens the office door. ''I'll phone Dr. Hepp tomorrow morning. Hopefully he'll meet with you and review your case so it won't be more than a couple days.''

Joan, as she is today, newly rediscovering her life, is someone Pam finds she'd be able to work with in therapy, someone more open and ready to face her problems than she was a month or week ago. If Joan is not ''better,'' she is at least coming to terms with what she does have in her life, and Pam is impressed, wishes she could appreciate something as simple as wearing a nice dress or reading a good book. How can Jack Briden find fault with his colleague's continued relationship with Joan when Joan is progressing so well?

The two women step into the hall, Joan facing the locked door of the ward and Pam facing Joan. Joan smooths out the hem of her dress, checking for wrinkles. ''When do you think you can come next?'' Joan examines one sleeve, plucks away a strand of hair, then looks over the bodice of the dress for others.

''Tomorrow isn't going to be possible. I will phone, though, after I speak to Dr. Hepp. You're also welcome to phone me at the office early tomorrow evening. I'll be in until seven or so; otherwise I can be by at this same time on Friday.''

Joan looks up from her dress, her examination complete. "Hopefully I'll be out by then, but otherwise that's fine." Past her doctor's right shoulder Joan sees the door to the ward open. A man in a tan suit carrying a small Bloomingdale's bag enters. Dennis stops just inside the entrance, the door swinging shut and locking behind him. Joan looks at her doctor, who has just said good-bye and is now writing a reminder in her schedule book.

"Okay, then, good-bye, see you Friday." If only her doctor will turn and walk past Dennis before Dennis calls out to her, all will be fine, but Dennis is walking down the hallway toward them and Joan watches him, notes he has not yet spotted her, Joan being hidden behind her doctor. Dennis's head turns to the right as he peers into the dining hall for a moment, and not seeing Joan in there, he pulls his head out of the room's doorway and looks to his left, immediately sighting Joan, a wide, nervous smile breaking out on his face. "Joan," Dennis says, low and soft.

Pam zips her handbag and turns her head, seeing a man approaching, Dennis approaching.

"You look so nice," he says, coming at Joan, his eyes locked on her, and suddenly Dennis is standing beside Pam as they both stand facing Joan.

Joan looks at her doctor, embarrassed, found out. "Dr. Thompson, this is Dennis Perry. Dennis, this is Dr. Thompson, my psychiatrist." Her secret is out: Dennis, her lover, is paying a visit—that is why she is hopeful today—and she is sure Dr. Thompson will bring this issue up with Joan over the phone tomorrow and then again on Friday, when they meet.

Pam looks to Dennis, and Dennis looks to his wife.

Pam extends a hand. "Nice to meet you."

Dennis shakes his wife's hand, avoiding any look to her face. "Nice to meet you," he answers, and before he can say more, his wife has shaken and withdrawn her hand and turned back to her patient.

"I'll phone you tomorrow after I speak to Dr. Hepp," Pam says.

"Take care." She turns away, walking the length of the hall and off the ward.

Joan smiles anxiously. "I didn't tell her you were visiting," she confides. "I think she's annoyed that I kept it from her." Joan shrugs and gestures to the dining hall. "They won't let us take visitors to our rooms so we'll have to sit in here if that's all right."

Dennis had many questions to ask Joan regarding her condition: the effect he has on her, whether that be good or bad, how Joan is feeling now, how Joan was feeling while they had been seeing each other, how much had she concealed herself from him. Questions he arrived at the hospital with, with the hope of finding answers to, questions he is now not asking Joan.

Joan speaks to Dennis from across the square table, casually volunteering information about her condition and how her doctor found and brought her to the hospital, the events spilling off Joan's tongue as easily as if she were sharing gossip read in a magazine. Dennis stares at Joan, dressed prettily in her plum dress, her words a jumble to his ears, as nonsensical as any foreign language, his mind so focused upon the confusion precipitated by discovering his wife with Joan Dwyer. *"This is Dr. Thompson, my psychiatrist,"* Joan said by way of introducing Dennis to Pam, and Dennis reaches across the table, grasping Joan's hands in his own, a pile of four hands at the table's center.

Joan stops speaking, has been telling Dennis about Dr. Hepp and their ten-minute session. "Is something wrong? Do you not want to hear this?"

Any words he says to her, any words he may have already said to her, could eventually—if they have not already—be offered to his wife under the confidentiality of therapy. Dennis takes his hands from Joan's, leaving hers alone and stranded at the table's center.

"I'm worried about you." He feels the table shaking under his elbows, realizes he has been lightly kicking the table's post with a foot, and he stops. "I don't know what to say to you. I wish I could be of some help, but I don't know what's right or wrong for you."

"Seeing you is a help," Joan responds. "Helps take my mind off being here."

As pleasant as always, Dennis observes, and he can only wonder why such a loving, warm woman leading such a charmed life is now on a mental ward. Can only wonder, considering all he knows of Joan is what she has chosen to let him know, whereas his wife must know precisely what has brought Joan to this point in her life. "I'm glad seeing me helps but what—" He has absolutely no idea what he is to say or ask. Joan has spoken about her suicide attempt in the same tone of voice she uses when speaking about dinner recipes or selecting videocassettes to rent for an evening in. Joan Dwyer speaks about her suicide attempt with all the cheer of a morning news show hostess, her suicide attempt being just another incident in which she somehow got herself involved. Dennis would love to delve into the truth of Joan's life, her life beyond their affair together, but realizes he's supposed to be extracting himself *from* her life rather than becoming more involved in it. *He is only here to pay a friendly visit,* Dennis reminds himself, and the visit paid, Dennis glances at his watch. "I should be going. I'm expected—" He arrests his speech, does not want to say "home" or "by my wife for dinner." Dennis stands, buttoning his suit jacket, not lending Joan the opportunity to talk on and keep him seated.

On the street corner, masking-taped to a Walk/Don't Walk post, hangs a notice for a lost two-year-old Yorkshire terrier. A grainy photocopy of a picture of the dog's face appears at the bottom center of the leaflet, "Newton" written above the dog's ears in a scrawling child's hand. Beneath the dog's missing notice hangs a sheet of yellow paper with thick, green marker writing. "Calico cat missing since 4/25. Marissa. If found, please call . . ." The bottom edge of the yellow sheet is fringed, a row of ten slips cut into the paper, each written with the cat owner's phone number; none of the ten slips has been torn from the sheet. Pasted up next to this is a red and white poster: "Stop Violence Against Women—Ban Men!"

In the Korean deli, selecting a can of soda, Dennis notices the picture of a child, brown hair, blue eyes, six years old, missing from his Brooklyn home for seventeen months. Beside this milk carton stand three other milk cartons, each displaying the photo of another missing child from the New York City metropolitan area, and when Dennis tilts one carton forward, he is greeted by the face of Patina Walbach, another missing child.

Children, pets, wallets, briefcases, gloves, key rings—all vanishing, disappearing and swallowed up by the city. Haphazard and scary and chaotic, people falling in and out of one another's lives, stealing, killing, victimizing. Collisions: random encounters between individuals producing disastrous results. Cats and dogs disappearing, women afraid of men, children vanishing off the face of the earth, a chance meeting in a bar leading to an attempted suicide. Dennis only wishes he could disappear now and become as mysterious and lost as a missing child on a milk carton.

Stepping to the corner of his block, Dennis accidentally kicks a bottle lying on the sidewalk, and the half-full soda bottle spins out into the street, a spray of yellow-green splashing across the street in an arc before the bottle hits the opposite curb, shattering across the pavement. The dark green canopy awning of his building is ten yards distant, and Dennis considers how he is to approach this moment he has been carefully blocking from his mind, how to proceed without stopping in a bar or hailing a cab to take him crosstown to his old office.

Never one angry word said upon confronting him about the affair, Pam remained in total control, so readily forgiving her husband under such very trying circumstances. Any other woman would have been furious, lashing out to hurt and shame her spouse, but not Pam, who just sat down alongside her husband and tenderly instructed him in what they had to do to rebuild their marriage. At the time Dennis was so relieved his wife would accept him back that he didn't bother to question it. Today, considering her many speeches concerning the power a therapist has over a patient, considering her past manipulative behaviors and her unnaturally cold and clinical way of confronting him about the affair, Dennis cannot get himself to ignore the possibility that perhaps his wife was not only orchestrating the end of an affair but also, quite possibly, an end to a patient's life.

He finds himself standing in the hallway of apartment 27C, his briefcase on the floor by the closet door as he drapes his suit jacket over a hanger. The walk past the doorman, the ride up in the elevator—*did I ride up alone or with others?*—he cannot remember, and he unknots his tie while kicking black loafers off and onto the living room's Oriental carpet. *Where is my wife,* is his first thought, *where is my wife and Joan Dwyer's therapist?* and Dennis heads down the hall in search of Pam.

Two Xanax taken, Pam sits in the den, in the chair facing the door. She hears Dennis enter, at the closet, then walking down the hall. She doesn't move. "I'm in here," she calls.

Dennis stops, looking in at his wife in the dark room. He can't bear to face her, and he looks out the window at the building across the way. A man sitting peacefully at a computer. A woman on a Stair-Master and a man on a couch behind her, reading the newspaper. A family at a dinner table, passing plates, sharing food. Glimpses of other lives that are not his.

Facing the window, his face lit to her, she sees him avoiding her. "Did you tell her?" Her first and greatest concern.

The thought never occurred to him, Dennis now realizes, and he finds that odd. Possibly the shock was too great, is too great. "No, I didn't tell her." He turns from the window and walks into the bedroom. He hangs up his tie and unbuttons his shirt. His wife offers him no explanation.

Pam comes into the room and sits on the bed cross-legged. Her strategy is to give off a sense of confidence and control, and hope the mood will transfer to Dennis and prevent a blowup, a scene. "There's no point in telling her," Pam rationalizes. "She cannot possibly benefit by knowing. Not when she's in need of such help, and I'm the one she trusts to help her."

With every prepared and tailored word she utters his anger intensifies. She has this situation mapped out, everyone's actions planned and calculated for a best possible solution to this crisis, this crisis he's not sure she hasn't created. He walks to the bureau and opens the bottom drawer. A Baltimore Orioles T-shirt is on top, so he puts on a Baltimore Orioles T-shirt. A gift from his parents, a reminder of where he came from.

"What are you thinking?" She thought his silence was what she wanted, but now she only finds it menacing.

"I don't know." He takes off his pants and tosses them on the bed, averting his eyes from his wife. He picks up the sweatpants left on the bed from this morning and puts those on.

"You must be thinking something." He is about to blow; she can feel it, his tension growing, his confusion, his frustration, and she is the only one he has to direct it toward. "I need to know what you're thinking," she says.

Always the therapist, never the wife. "I was thinking that I had thought you lied to me about Friday night with Sarah Chaplin, but I guess you didn't except for changing the name of the patient, not saying it was Joan." First time he's said her name aloud to anyone other than Joan, and it makes their relationship more real, the whole affair suddenly feeling more substantial and significant than when he shut it away to a corner of his life, contained by his lies. "Poor Joan," he mutters, and he ties the drawstring to the sweatpants, then stands at the window, looking down twenty-seven stories to the street. A dark clear night, bright moon, the streets lit with bright, exciting signs— so much prettier, more embraceable than on his walk home, this bright city shining in the night, lighting up the sky. His romantic vision of a drama playing out against the backdrop of the city is gone, and all that remains is his wife sitting on a bed asking him, over and over asking him what he is thinking and feeling. Joan Dwyer almost dead, in no small part thanks to his behavior. And God only knows what role his wife played in this escapade, which she will never admit to, not even to herself. Dennis thinks of Joan not alive, almost dead, and feels his body shake with the anxiety and fear of what could have been. His heart pounds, and his eyes tear up, the street below replaced by a blur of black. "I want to help her," he says, forcing the words out.

Pam looks at his back, a list of all the last names of the ballplayers from a few years ago. "We will help her. She'll be out of the hospital soon and back in therapy, and we'll sort this out. She's going to be okay."

"No." Dennis turns from the window. "*I* want to help her. I want to give her the support she needs."

"You've ended your relationship with her. She and I have to work this through."

"I am going to do this," Dennis insists, his face so grim and severe Pam isn't sure what, if any, logic he's employing so that he actually believes *he's* the best person to come to Joan Dwyer's aid.

"You cannot help her. Joan needs to be free of you. She needs a doctor who can understand her problems. You can't help her with that. With you around, she'd never solve her problems for herself but would always use you as an excuse not to have to bother. Joan needs therapy," Pam dictates. "She's a very depressed woman."

"You're just afraid I'll tell her."

"How can I help Joan if you're going to be her friend?"

"How can you help Joan anyway, knowing I was seeing her? What good could you be to her?"

"I know Joan, and she trusts me," Pam says, facing her husband down. "We have a therapeutic relationship, and without you involved, that can continue successfully as it had before you were involved with her." A lie, Pam knows, but one Dennis will never be able to uncover.

"How long did you know I was seeing her?"

"A couple months."

"How long have you been treating Joan?"

"A year and a half."

"Why didn't you stop the affair earlier once you knew? Why did you wait?"

Pam looks into his eyes, wants him to understand how hard this was. "I was afraid of Joan's reaction. I was trying to find a time when Joan was less at risk. I thought she might——" Pam stops. What she thought might happen did happen, her waiting two months having been proved pointless.

Dennis imagines how difficult the past weeks must have been for his wife, the sacrifice she made in order to help her patient, but a question lingers. "She never mentioned my name until two months ago? I've been seeing her since January." He wants to rub this in her face. "How can she have such a great working relationship with you if she can't even tell you what's going on with her?"

Pam sits, annoyed. "She never mentioned your name before then. I knew she was seeing someone, and when she gave you that camel thing, she showed it to me, and then I saw it on your drafting table that night. I began suspecting something, and then she eventually told me your name."

"Wait," Dennis says, thinking back, remembering to the time in March—only a bit over two months ago—when Joan gave him the jade camel. "So she told you my name just after you suspected it? After months in therapy when she didn't say it? Months of seeing each other and she coincidentally tells you after it occurs to you yourself?"

Pam stands, goes to her dresser, has to get away from under his glare. She opens a drawer. A pile of jewelry she never wears: enamel necklaces, strings of wooden beads, turquoise pieces, everything tangled in a mess.

"What is your explanation?" Dennis pressures her.

Pam realizes it was a mistake. She thought she could be truthful but realizes he won't possibly be able to understand all she was going through at the time. She picks up the clump of necklaces and sits at the foot of the bed. "I had to know," Pam says simply. "I had to know so I could continue working with Joan. I couldn't do that if I thought—"

"You forced her to tell you. You made her do it."

"I did what I had to do to help us both." The turquoise necklace freed, Pam tosses it over her neck. She can't remember who gave it to her.

Dennis comes around, faces her. "Help *who*? You and her? You and me? What? I don't get this." His voice rises, loud and hard.

Pam drops the necklaces. "I love you, and I needed to help her. I couldn't do both without knowing."

He tosses his arms up. "For all I know, you're the reason she's in the hospital. You've known for two months. You've had two months to convince her to do this. You prescribe the medication she took to do this. How do I know—"

"I *saved* her." Pam defends herself, standing. "I saved her life. She would be dead if it wasn't for me."

"She was almost dead *because of* you," Dennis accuses her. "God knows what shit you filled her head with. You're telling me all that crap about the control a therapist has over her patients. How you can will a patient to get better or worse and pass that on to her. And you're telling me *I* can't help her, that I'm not right to help Joan? Do you plan to go on treating her as if this never happened?"

Her own words thrown back at her, Pam is dumbfounded; there is no convincing him she did what was right at the time. "She trusts me." All that's left to be said.

"*But she shouldn't,*" Dennis yells at his wife, fascinated with how infallible she finds herself. "Look at you. Look how you've treated her. You treat everyone like this. Manipulating and controlling, so it's ordered the way you want it. It's all yours or no way at all." She's a thief, and he's finally caught her. Her face is red, eyes are swollen, and he wants to make her cry, see her tears. He smiles, repulsed. "You aren't capable of loving anyone, caring about anyone unconditionally. I fucking walk around here trying so hard to be as independent and uncaring as you, but I can't, and I shouldn't have to. You're the fucked-up one. You're the one that can't express anything. Half the time I'm with you I wonder if you even want me around at all, you seem to need so little. Your emotions are so controlled, everything you feel so carefully thought out and planned that I don't get anything from you anymore." He's made her cry, has finally made her cry.

"I was doing this for her own good," Pam answers lamely. "I was trying to—"

Dennis laughs. "For her own good you did this? She tried to kill herself. To save *this* marriage?"

Pam sighs, catching her breath, giving up, wiping her tears away. She's let him hurt her, but it's enough, and she doesn't have to listen anymore. Let him be outraged for now. She'll speak to him later once he's settled down and absorbed the situation. She stands and goes to the bathroom, splashing cold water on her face. If she hadn't taken the Xanax, she would have been better able to talk with him. Under the illusory peace of the drug, she didn't have the will to argue very persuasively. She dries her face on a towel. "I hope you're all done, because I am."

Dennis is pulling a garment bag and suitcase from the top shelf of his closet. He tosses both on the bed and opens a bureau drawer, grabbing at clothes and piling them in the suitcase. He takes several suits and all his shirts from the closet, inserting them into the hanging bag. He's glad he hasn't yet moved his clothes back from the old office. Makes his getaway that much easier.

Pam takes the aspirin from the medicine cabinet, anticipating a headache. She expected he might leave, wasn't sure he would come back at all after the hospital, knowing he would need time to digest this newest information and reconfigure the past several months he thought he was in control of. Time apart will help him consider what she was going through, making him judge her less harshly than he is tonight, only having just heard of her connection to Joan Dwyer.

Dennis places three pairs of shoes in the suitcase and zips it shut. He looks around for his wallet and keys and remembers he left them in the living room as he came in earlier. The whole world changes in a night. He picks up his bags and walks off down the hall.

"I'll phone you tomorrow at work. I love you," she says. She hears the apartment door open and close. *He is gone, but this is not hopeless,* Pam tells herself, *I am not unforgivable and unworthy of being loved.* She closes the medicine cabinet and stares at the woman facing her in the bathroom mirror. She *does* look like the cold, thoughtless woman Dennis told her she was. She is *that* controlling and manipulative, Pam finds, and maybe she has been wrong. Maybe Joan's, Dennis's—even her own—life is beyond her control; she does not know what is best for everyone and never has.

June

1

Joan is at once shocked upon stepping away from the hospital's revolving door and onto the sidewalk. Following ten days of life confined to two climate-controlled, air-conditioned corridors, the heavy, stifling heat of early June smothers. Dennis walks out after her. "You doing okay?" he asks.

Joan smiles, opening her purse, taking out her sunglasses. "I'm good." Dennis steps past her to the curb, hailing a taxi. The car pulls over, and Joan slides in with her handbag and the overnight bag. Dennis climbs in next to her, Joan's small suitcase at his feet. "We're going to Seventy-fourth and West End Avenue," Joan tells the driver, and the cab starts off and out into the street full of midday crosstown traffic. She takes Dennis's hand. "Thanks for picking me up. I'm glad you could get the morning off."

He leans over and kisses her cheek. "I wanted to."

During Joan Dwyer's remaining four and a half days spent in the hospital since Dennis's initial visit, Joan displayed an increasingly cheerful outlook, an outlook she took great pains to display for all nurses, doctors, and patients. Showering and dressing in a fresh, clean outfit before breakfast each morning, speaking up in group therapy meetings—"There are other ways of solving problems than doing what I did. I think I thought it was more important for me to remain independent than call on the people who could help me. It's hard to believe I couldn't recognize how much people were willing to do for me when it's now so clear how much they care"—ordering and eating all the hospital meals, taking part in the clay sculpture activity—"I'm making a tree," she gleefully told Bethany, the art therapist—chatting with the staff and displaying equal parts remorse and hope. All calculated to get her out of the hospital as soon as possible.

"Does your therapist know I'm picking you up today?" Ever since knowing it took two months for Joan to use his name in therapy, and *that* only after being prodded by Pam, he isn't sure what she may or may not tell his wife, isn't sure he can trust Joan to tell him about therapy, anyway, considering she kept it a secret until Andrea mentioned it at dinner.

She looks out her side window at a two-ton sculpture of a walrus sitting on the meridian dividing the uptown and downtown lanes of Park Avenue. "She said she could arrange her schedule to meet me, but I told her I had someone else coming. She asked if the person was you, and I told her it was." Joan doesn't like speaking to Dennis about her doctor or to her doctor about Dennis. Dr. Thompson hasn't said outright that she thinks Joan shouldn't be dating; she only attempts to persuade Joan that since Dennis is still married, he is liable not to be as dependable a source of support as Joan needs him to be, and given Joan's condition, perhaps she should be careful how involved she becomes with him.

"He wants to help me get better," Joan told her doctor on Friday.

"Since his visit I've really been working more on myself, so I do know why I did this. He's a positive influence. Now that he knows I'm in therapy and knows my problems, he can support me better. We talked about me having to allow people to care for me, and I am. I'm letting him care for me, and he wants to."

Dennis can only imagine Pam's reaction, her fury. He hasn't spoken to her since Wednesday evening, has heard her many desperate phone messages urging him to contact her, but thus far he has resisted, not yet ready to forgive her. "Did she say that was all right?"

The cab glides through the park, and Joan can't see any buildings, only trees, green with leaves, like a drive through the country, this winding park road, until they reach Central Park West at Seventy-second Street, her doctor's building fifty yards away, Dennis's home one block north. "It doesn't matter what she said. She never tells me what I should or shouldn't do. We only discuss things. I decide for myself."

"Do you think she might be jealous of me?" He likes this idea, wants to plant it in Joan's head, a fortification against an offensive by Pam.

Joan points as they pass Donnelman's. "That's where her office is, that's why I was down there; I'd just had therapy."

Dennis looks away from the building to Joan. Her face is bright, so thrilled to be out of the hospital, so thrilled with every visit he paid her on the ward. He may be partly responsible for making Joan as unhappy as she was, pushing her toward taking the many pills, but he can also be the one that brings her back to a life worth living. "I love you," he says.

Joan turns her head from the window, facing Dennis with a smile. "I love you too," she says, and the cab pulls up to her building.

He has brought Joan home.

.   .   .

"You didn't phone me back."

Tim sits stiffly in the leather chair, staring at his doctor, feet planted firmly on the floor, hands gripping the arms of the chair. He locks eyes with Pam.

Pam returns his gaze, looking back with less intensity. She didn't phone Tim back last night not because she couldn't, but because she didn't want to, didn't feel like hearing any more of his whining and complaining about how terrible his life is. "No, I didn't," Pam says. "I'm sorry, but I got in too late to phone you back and we were meeting this morning anyway so I didn't think it was necessary to call before the appointment today. I apologize if I made a mistake. I am sorry that you are upset."

Tim shrugs. "It just seems, I mean, now it seems like I can't count on you to be there for me either. That even you won't be there for me when I need you."

"I can't be there for you every moment you may want me to be, no, you are correct," Pam replies with a nod. "That's why I think it's important for you to rely on other people as well. What about your friend from the support group—Rachel? Did you think about calling her?"

Tim Boxer laughs, clapping his hands, crossing his legs, grinning wide. "I told you she died weeks ago. Weren't you paying attention even *then*?"

Three years of therapy later Jessica Poulin smiles nervously at her doctor. The final minutes of their final session. "I don't know what to say." Jessica wipes tears from her eyes and glances at her watch. "Four more minutes."

"I'll miss you," Pam says, wiping a tear from her own eye. "I think you know you'll be all right now."

Jessica keeps smiling. "I know. I know I don't need to be here anymore. It's just I can't believe how much different I am now from when we started." She reaches over, taking another tissue, wiping her eyes again. She looks at her watch. "Only another couple minutes."

"I know."

"I'll miss you."

"I'll miss you. Thank you for being my patient. You've done a lot of work on yourself here, and you have that whether you're in therapy with me or not. I'm very proud of you. It's been hard at times, but you stayed and we worked it through; that's not easy and I know you know that."

"My time's up," Jessica Poulin says, and Pam nods, agreeing, saying good-bye to a healthier, happier patient.

Mitch Breen has a hand down his pants as he talks to his doctor. "I didn't jerk off this morning before school, and since I had to come here after, this is the first place I can do it."

Pam keeps a composed face, neither amused nor disgusted. "You've masturbated in school previously. Why didn't you today?"

"Didn't feel like it." Mitch spreads his legs in a V, working his other hand down his loose-fitting jeans. Through the material, Pam can see him cupping one hand over his testicles while the other jerks the shaft of his penis.

She stands, walks across the room, hand on the office doorknob. "I'm going to sit in the waiting room and drink a cup of coffee. Call me when you're ready to work." Not willing to give Mitch Breen the satisfaction of her attention, not caring to question him and remain composed through his point of orgasm.

Mitch pumps his hand faster. "I'm about to come. I'm almost there, just hold on, wait." He cranes his neck to the door to watch Pam.

"I'll be in the waiting room." Pam leaves the office, Mitch Breen moaning as she shuts the door.

. . .

Sitting across from Pam, Joan Dwyer wears a fresh, clean, silky yellow sleeveless dress. A large silk scarf of varying shades of green is draped across her shoulders, over her arms, and loosely knotted over her chest, the gift from Dennis at the hospital.

Five o'clock and two minutes. Two minutes spent in silence. Has he told her? Pam asks herself. But then if he had, Joan would most likely not have shown up for therapy, and if he hasn't said anything yet in the last five days he's known, he possibly never will. Pam waits for Joan to begin. Joan sits, rearranging the scarf around her shoulders, the dress's pleated skirt around her legs. Joan rubs her bare forearms, "Goose bumps. It's so chilly in here with the air-conditioning compared to outside."

"Should I turn it down?" Pam asks. Dennis bringing Joan home from the hospital this morning, making Joan his mission.

Joan lets each arm go, clasping the chair's arms. "I'll adjust. It's so hot outside, it's nice in here."

"Okay," Pam says, and she waits, waiting for Joan to begin, make some comment or observation, speak some feeling concerning her first day out in the world and back home since the suicide attempt, back home in the apartment where she'd attempted suicide.

Over the past five days Pam has had away from Dennis and three since her most recent session with Joan, she has worked on compartmentalizing her life, separating Joan the mistress from Joan her patient, Dennis her husband from Dennis Joan's boyfriend. Pam has been keeping these conflicting perspectives on Joan and Dennis separate—yolks from whites—and has believed she arrived at an ability to conduct her personal and professional lives independent of each other. When in therapy with Joan on Friday at the hospital, the Dennis Joan spoke of visiting her was not the Dennis who is Pam's husband, who left her and won't return her phone calls. When Joan spoke of him, Pam told herself to focus on Joan's feelings and thoughts, not to cross-reference Joan's comments about Dennis with how Dennis fits into her own life. When leaving messages for Dennis, Pam focused on the fact that Joan is her husband's mistress and not on the fact that she is also her patient. This is the method by which Pam has conducted her life these past five days—the only way she knew she could without destroying herself or those around her. But this strategy was all devised while Joan was in the hospital, Dennis and Joan's time and behavior restricted by the hospital's visiting hours and rules of conduct. Sitting with Joan in her office today, Joan out of the hospital and Dennis free to see her whenever his schedule permits—he can become much more a part of Joan's life than her doctor will ever be capable of—Pam finds she must reconsider her approach to Joan's therapy. If she is to help Joan, she must have a complete knowledge of Joan's relationship with Dennis and how it is affecting her depression. Since Pam fears Joan will no longer tell her all she is feeling because Joan has correctly ascertained that her doctor doesn't want her in a relationship at the present time, Pam's only method of helping her patient is to ask Joan directly how Dennis makes her feel, how he is treating her now that is different from before the suicide attempt. Until Joan is free of Dennis and more stable in her depression, Pam allows herself this liberty of direct inquiry. What the patient does not address, she must, and she only hopes Joan does so she does not have to.

"I went home this morning," Joan finally says. She raises her eyebrows, lightly touching her dress, caressing a fold of the skirt.

"How does it feel?"

"Like I've been set free from prison," Joan answers. "Just being able to put on this dress was so nice. I mean, I've worn this dress many times, but being able to put it on today . . . I was overwhelmed by how good I felt to be home again. Andrea was home, and she'd cleaned the apartment of the mess I'd left it in. I feel like this is a new start. For me here with you. With my kids. With this man. I can understand how the hospital helped. It's like I've been given this chance to see it all fresh but to do more with it and make it what I want if I'm unhappy."

"I think the hospital stay did help," Pam confirms. "Let's hope we can keep all of what you've learned in mind. These thoughts will be important; they're what will keep you going if things become more difficult again, as they're likely to.''

"I can't imagine not feeling so good," Joan states. "Everything is as I want it to be. I have my kids. I have this man.''

"Dennis."

"Yes," Joan says, trying hard not to let Dr. Thompson's saying the name arrest her thoughts—"Yes, I have Dennis"—but it has.

"What does it mean that you 'have' him?'' She isn't sure if she's asking as therapist or wife. Isn't sure there's a distinction any longer, the boundaries are so broken down, so many unintentional and intentional errors with Joan Dwyer, asking an inappropriate question, putting her own interests before Joan's, using Joan to get at her husband, her husband to get at Joan. How could she ever have thought she could remain objective and clearheaded?

Joan sits up, more alert, less casual. "I meant he's decided he wants to continue seeing me as he has been. I've told you that.''

"How does it make you feel that he's married?''

Joan worried this might come up again and is prepared to steel herself against any doubt her doctor introduces. "He's told me he's left her. That he's not going back to her. He's committed to being with me. He's told me that.''

"He's left his wife, then?''

"He has.''

"How does that make you feel? Al did leave you for another woman.'' A reminder. A blow to Joan to take her back to reality, out of her dumb, lovestruck pose.

Joan darts her eyes away and down to her lap. She reaches up to her scarf, both hands arranging its drape across her shoulders. She reknots the scarf loosely at her neck. "I have to think about myself. What's best for me, what's best for Dennis. I have to work on my life.''

Joan can't even bear to hear mentioned the existence of the other woman. The thought that she is doing to another what was done to her racks her with guilt. "Survival of the fittest?" Pam asks, forcing the sarcasm out of her voice.

"He came back to me," Joan instructs her, looking up. "If he wants to be with me, should I tell him he has to go back to his un-happy life? He's making himself happy and me happy by leaving her, is anything wrong with that? If he stayed with her, all three of us un-happy, would that be better?"

All spoken so rationally, so confidently. Pam finds herself smiling at her patient, proud of the strength Joan's displaying. Joan *is* impres-sive today. Thinking of herself first, dismissing the wife are not easy, but possible. Dennis's return has given her a greater value in her own eyes. "That makes perfect sense," Pam responds. "You're right." And for today Pam gives Joan—and Dennis—this victory.

"Keep her on hold, and I'll pick up in a minute." Dennis speaks to the speaker in his phone and his assistant says okay and Dennis watches as line four stops blinking red, holds a still red, then begins blinking red again. Pam on hold. Phoning several times a day at work, leaving numerous messages with Roberta, his assistant, and on his voice mail, leaving messages on the answering machine at his base-ment apartment, begging for an opportunity to talk this through.

The messages left from Thursday and Friday, the days after the en-counter at the hospital and confrontation at home, were apolo-getic, self-effacing.

"I'm sorry for last night. I'm sorry for how you found out about this. Let's try to work it out. I've really been trying to make our mar-riage better. I think the last few weeks have improved for us. I know you know that. I've made mistakes in handling this. I admit that. I hope you're not planning on seeing Joan tonight. Please don't. She's so vulnerable. I love you . . ."

". . . If we don't communicate, we can't make things better. At least give me the opportunity of explaining myself. Your seeing Joan only confuses matters and helps no one. Please, come home. You're imagining I've done things far worse than anything I have . . ."

"If you won't consent to seeing me, then please call. Please. I know you're listening to me now. You're not at your office, so if you are listening, know I love you and always did. I never wanted to hurt anyone. Not you or Joan. Please pick up . . . or phone. When you get home tonight, please."

By Saturday the messages had taken on a more aggressive tone.

". . . I hope you don't really believe I had any part in putting Joan in the hospital. I hope you can't think that. And I know Joan would tell you the same. If you won't let me explain to your face, I don't have any choice but to explain to your machine. I saved Joan's life. She's told you that, I'm sure. Joan needs me. I understand her. Please stop seeing her or at least talk to me about it. Do you think I really tried to have her kill herself? Do you think I would sacrifice a patient's life in order to save our marriage?"

"If this is your way of punishing me and making me feel terrible, your goal has been achieved, and I'm miserable. I'm not going to talk about Joan because I shouldn't have to discuss my patients with you. Have you even once considered how difficult this has been for me? For all I knew, you never ended your affair with her when you said you had. For all I know, you're with her tonight. I get caught in an impossible situation, do my best to right things and you make it worse. Makes a lot of sense. Think about it."

Pam left only one message for Dennis on Sunday.

"It's two-thirty P.M. Hello. I really hope you are not picking Joan up at the hospital. Have you even considered your role in Joan's life and what you've done? You may blame me, but I wasn't the one who put Joan Dwyer on an emotional roller coaster, loving her at one moment, then abandoning her the next. The last thing she needs is you reappearing to make her more unstable. For you to be involved with her at this point is a huge mistake. Not only because I want us to work things out but because I'm not sure what Joan might do if you were to hurt her again. And as I'm trying to help her, it would make it that much more difficult for me to remain objective in our therapy. She's depending on me to help her; this is hardly a good time for her to be starting with a new therapist whom she doesn't know and trust. I hope you'll just have the good sense to keep our marriage and my name out of any conversations you may have with her. I still love and miss you. I'm waiting to hear from you.''

Dennis looks away from his desk, blotting out the ad of a cartoon crab holding hands with a photo of a six-year-old boy: ''No Crabby Kids at Moby's!'' He picks up the phone. ''Hello,'' the first contact he's had with his wife in five days, the longest period they haven't spoken to each other in years, probably since before they were married.

''Hello.''

''So what do you have to say?'' He looks out the window of his office, which faces an office building with dark tinted windows. Dennis can't see inside the building and can't see even a patch of sky, the building across the street is so high and wide. He might as well be facing a brick wall.

''I was hoping we could set a time to get together.''

He can sense how scared she must be, is not used to his wife's being so tentative with him. ''I'm not sure what we have to discuss.''

''How do you feel about me?''

''I don't know.''

''I miss you.''

Her voice sounds so sad and hollow he's tempted to believe her, to go along with her suggestion. A reconciliation could be nice.

''What do you think?''

Dennis looks back at his desk. A boy holding hands with a crab. A girl on the back of a sea horse. An entire family having a picnic spread atop a whale's back. Pam doesn't even mention Joan, pretending Joan doesn't exist. ''What about Joan? I don't think I should be seeing you if I'm with her. I don't think it's right.''

''We need to work this out,'' Pam stresses.

"I have," Dennis responds. "It's worked out. You're just not satisfied with my decision. Aren't ever satisfied with a decision unless it concurs with your own." He reviews an ad with an outline of America, Moby characters frolicking all across the land and in the Atlantic and Pacific oceans. "Moby and You. From Sea to Shining Sea!"

"Then I guess we do have nothing to talk about for now."

"You've caught on."

"Please call when you're willing to talk. Please. I love you." He thinks he hears her gasp on these last words, but it could just be a sigh of annoyance. He fights the reflex to tell her he loves her too, reminding himself of why he is not with her, what she has done to deserve this.

"Good-bye." He hangs up before reconsidering.

The notebooks detailing the history of Joan's sessions with her doctor provide Pam with no new insights into her patient's behaviors, no ideas about how to persuade Joan that being on her own is more beneficial to her than being with Dennis. Pam puts the notebooks away and closes the file cabinet drawer.

"Dennis and Todd and Andrea and I are all having dinner tonight," Joan said, ending her session today on a happy note. "Todd's bringing Emily too. A little welcome-home dinner for me."

"If you need to, leave a message" was all Pam had to say. "I'll be in the office late tonight."

Hoping to receive a call of distress and wanting to be at her office when the call came in, not wanting to chance Joan's not leaving a message, Pam ordered dinner up to the office, sat in the reception area, and ate a tuna melt sandwich and side of cottage cheese while reading a magazine article about custody battles raging throughout the nation: a surrogate mother fighting to keep her baby from the contractual parents; a divorced woman fighting for the frozen embryos fertilized by her ex-husband; a foster child divorcing his biological parents so he can be adopted by his foster family—a never-ending list of struggles to determine who can best raise the next generation of this country. "I want what is best for the child," each parent pleads so desperately, but Pam knows this is not true. Bottom line, everyone, whether he or she knows it consciously or not, wants what is best for him- or herself. The child, the patient, the world all can go to hell. *That* is the nature of people. Trying their best to help Joan, Dennis and Pam are two parents battling for custody of a child. Joan Dwyer, a prize to be won, a trophy determining who is the better mate, the better therapist, the better all-around person.

As of ten-fifty, no message yet received from Joan, the evening almost past, Pam guesses the dinner went well and was not a repeat of the experience prior to the suicide attempt. Dennis, Andrea, Todd, and Emily celebrating Joan on her recovery, a welcome back to the land of the living, Joan basking in the happiness of her freedom from the hospital.

Pam shuts off the office lights and picks up her handbag, locking the office door on her way out. She might as well go home. She is not needed tonight.

2

Andrea is out with friends, won't be home until after eleven. Dennis called this afternoon and told her he'd be working very late tonight and wouldn't be able to stop by. This is Joan's first night alone on her second night home in the apartment.

A rented videocassette plays on the television. Andrea still cannot look her mother in the eyes, avoids Joan as much as possible, speaking into a fashion magazine at breakfast, when Joan asked her about her plans for the day, staring at the TV when Joan asked her what she'd like for lunch.

"I'm going out tonight with friends." Andrea stood at the kitchen counter, facing the cabinets as she poured a can of diet soda into a glass, intently watching as the foam rose to the glass's rim as if a spill would bring about the end of humanity.

"I'm over here," Joan said from the kitchen table. "Can't you look at me when you're talking?"

"I already know what you look like," Andrea remarked. The foam subsided, Andrea poured a bit more. "I'll try to be home by eleven or twelve."

"Okay," Joan replied to the back of her daughter's head. "Do you need any money?"

Andrea did face her mother to be handed two twenty-dollar bills.

Rising early this morning, thinking there was so much to do this first full day back at home, Joan anticipated a hectic, busy schedule of accomplishing many tasks, but by 11:30 A.M. all her errands were tended to. The grocery shopping was taken care of, the house restocked with food, the dry cleaning dropped off, a video rented for an evening in with Dennis. Everything accomplished, nothing left undone, and Joan sat on her living room sofa with her stocking feet resting on the Matisse art book on the coffee table, gazing out across the hazy gray-sunlit city, the skyline steely and dull in the harsh noonday light. After lunch Joan phoned Regine Pointer, inviting her over for a visit. Regine agreed but insisted she be wheeled into the family room so she could watch a soap opera. Only when the show ended did Regine consent to having the TV turned off. "I'm missing *Guiding Light* for you," she announced, examining Joan with her eyes, the first time she'd seen Joan since the hospitalization. "You look the same to me. No better or worse."

"How would I be different?" Joan wished they'd left the TV on; the conversation was already making her tense.

Regine took her *TV Guide* from the pocket of her robe, flipped through the day's listing. Yellow marker highlighted those shows Regine planned on watching. "You had a near-death experience. Everyone on the shows says it changes them."

"Did what I did surprise you?" Easier to ask when Regine wasn't looking directly at her.

Regine read the topics of the talk shows for the four o'clock hour: man sleeps with wife's brother, the cast of *Full House,* nurses who kill their patients, highlighted in yellow. "Look here." Regine handed the magazine to Joan. "We'll watch this at my place. I want to see Brooke's face when it comes on."

Joan passed the magazine back to her neighbor. "Do you care about what happened to me? Does it affect you at all?"

The magazine was slipped back into the robe's pocket, and Regine stared Joan down. "It didn't *happen* to you. You did it to yourself, and if that's what you want to do, that's for you to decide, not me."

"Do you think it's wrong?"

"If you don't care about your life, why should I?" Regine Pointer asked. "Wheel me home," she dictated. "I'm not comfortable with this conversation."

Joan watches the video she rented. *The Boys in the Band.* Joan had thought it was a musical, a cheerful movie to lift her spirits, to replay and sing along with, but *The Boys in the Band* is no musical but is the story of a group of whiny, unhappy gay men. And no one in this entire city—entire country, entire *world*—is most likely watching this videocassette movie but Joan Dwyer herself, alone in her apartment on West End Avenue, and the thought at once strikes her cold. Joan switches off the tape and then the VCR, watching as the television readjusts, switching back to the cable station Joan had been watching an hour ago. A *Thirtysomething* rerun plays, and Joan feels at once depressed and satisfied, depressed at her plight of being alone, but satisfied that thousands, if not millions, of other depressed, divorced single women are also lounging, stranded in their apartments and homes, manless and silently comparing their lives with those of Nancy, Hope, Ellen, and Melissa.

Thirty-six hours ago the thrill of returning home and wearing a fresh yellow dress was enough to lift her spirits; thirty-six hours later, as she wears the same dress she so happily changed into yesterday afternoon, the thought occurs to Joan that she is still living the life she so desperately wanted to end. Nothing has changed since her stay in the hospital. Not her apartment. Not Dennis. Not her children. Not herself and not her life. She spent the afternoon cleaning the apartment and the early evening doing the laundry before settling into watching the video and ordering up dinner, expecting an uplifting musical and Chinese food would please her this second evening back, but Joan finds she was wrong; the joy hasn't lasted. A yellow dress, Chinese food, and a video cannot make her as happy as they may have a day and a half ago. The thrill of leaving the hospital and being home is gone.

The show ends, eleven o'clock, Andrea not home. Everyone around for all of one day, going through the motions of the nice dinner party her first night back, and tonight Joan might as well have succeeded, might as well try again. Regine Pointer is the only one who dares be honest—*If you don't care about your life, why should I?*—and she's right: Joan doesn't care, and the only reason she did was so she could get out of the hospital. Life is no better now than it was eleven days ago. *Worse*, actually, for today she has one less method to kill herself, the pills gone, wasted because of her doctor's heroics. Joan reaches for the phone, forcing herself to call someone before she gets any more carried away with her thoughts.

Dennis's machine answers; still not home at eleven-ten. "Dennis, this is Joan. Are you in? Are you at work?" She disconnects the line, then dials his office number. The voice mail answers. "You're not there . . . Where are you? . . . I need you. . . ." She hangs up, Dennis not at home or work, at least not at his desk at work, and for all Joan knows he's reconciled with his wife again, treating Joan as he did before, a tool to be picked up, used, and discarded as needed. Joan picks up the phone, trying Dennis at home again. The machine. Joan speaks. "If you're with your wife—" She stops, has no idea what she's saying, what she's doing, and she hangs up, feeling herself beginning to break down, her mind a confusion of anger, depression, sadness, and remorse.

She phones Dr. Thompson's office. "Hello," Joan says to the machine. "Please call me when you can. I'm at home." She hangs up, keeps her hand on the receiver, expecting the phone to ring momentarily.

. . .

"Hello?"

"Hello, Joan. It's Dr. Thompson. How are you doing?"

"I thought everything would be better when I got out. It's all the same, nothing's changed."

"It's still difficult."

"I thought it would be different."

"It takes time. Your entire life can't change in a day."

"Will it ever?"

"I believe so."

"I'm sorry for having to call."

"That's all right, Joan."

"Thank you. It does help."

"I'm here for you, Joan."

"I'll see you tomorrow at five."

"That's right."

"Thank you so much for calling. Good-bye."

"Take care, Joan. You're very important to me."

Her best course of action, the moral course of action, would be to refer Joan Dwyer to another psychiatrist, informing Joan Dwyer that she is afraid she can no longer help her. "Through attempting suicide, you showed me that you are no longer able to work in therapy with me, that you wish to terminate therapy with me. For your own sake, I think it best that you work with someone you can better connect with. Possibly someone who you'll be more willing to work with." Pam can turn Joan Dwyer over to an objective therapist, who can better help work out Joan's problems, Joan Dwyer establishing an honest, respectful, trusting relationship with a new therapist, Joan Dwyer free to act in her life without her doctor imposing any personal agenda upon her. The best thing to do, what Jack Briden has advised her to do.

Pam imagines herself alone. Dennis has left her, and she has referred Joan to another doctor, Joan Dwyer no longer Pam's patient.
In this fantasy Pam spends morning after night after day after morning
after night after day alone. She's lying in bed in her redecorated,
empty apartment or sitting in her office during the ten-minute breaks
between sessions, always wondering if Dennis and Joan are together,
making love in her apartment on her large beautiful bed or in his
apartment in the shadowy back bedroom furnished with the original
pieces from Pam's and his married-life apartment, wondering if they
are together and, if not, if Joan Dwyer has killed herself because, rejected by both Dennis and her doctor, she had no one to turn to in
her most desperate, darkest hours.

Why is Joan Dwyer depressed? Why is she suicidal? Because Joan
Dwyer, at bottom, is no one. Her sense of self is so low that to Joan,
without other people defining her life and who she is in her life, she
ceases to exist. From her parents to her teenage hippie friends to Al
and the kids, Joan has become what others make her to be, and thus,
without others around telling her who she is in relation to them, Joan
Dwyer's void of self overwhelms her, a bottomless well, a phone call
from her doctor being a crevice she can momentarily cling to on her
way down.

Why is Dr. Pamela Thompson depressed? What void does she feel
growing in her life, an emptiness expanding, threatening to engulf
her? With every line crossed, with every betrayal of a trust and ma-
nipulation of a life, Pam feels the person she knows of as herself being
slowly eroded. Her college and medical school years, her adulthood,
the last twenty years of her life have been spent becoming a doctor,
establishing her private practice, building a marriage and a home she
could be proud of. For two decades she has worked to make herself
Dr. Pamela Thompson, confident and noble and devoted to her patients and husband, but presently Pam finds the values she once believed in and religiously adhered to have vanished. Risked and lost for
the sake of holding on to the life she so carefully constructed. Jack
Briden, her immoral friend and colleague, warned her that he should

call the APA, reporting Pam for review by the board, and despite Jack's recent indiscretions, having published numerous articles in professional journals, he is well respected among his peers. Any attempt by Jack to have her relationship with Joan Dwyer investigated could result in the loss of her license to practice. Her entire life gone because Jack Briden fears for Joan Dwyer's safety. Pam has successfully avoided her colleague since their last encounter, when he criticized her behavior, doesn't want to speak to him about Joan until she has worked this conflict out and shown him there is no longer anything to report, that she alone has made it all right and she has always been and remains an upstanding doctor.

She leans on the kitchen counter, thoughts rolling around in her head, pushing up against one another, refusing to rest: a way out of this situation, how to please everyone, how to please herself, how to save the life she worked so hard to create. She doesn't know how to help, whom to help first, where to turn for advice, speaking with Jack Briden being her final option, a last resort. Dennis with Joan Dwyer . . . Joan Dwyer with Dennis. There is only one way to go, and that is to improvise, make it all up as she goes along, a blind woman stumbling through a maze. Pam grips the edge of the kitchen counter, immobilized by her thoughts, rooted to her spot on the tile floor. Analyze to paralyze.

3

"At—" Joan checks her watch. "Exactly in one hour. Downstairs at the place here where we met. I thought it might make it romantic for us to get together where we met."

"It could be."

"He keeps telling me he loves me, and I'm trying to believe it, but I don't always. I find it hard to. You heard me last night. I keep waiting for him to change his mind and leave me again."

"Do you believe he's going to?"

"No . . . I really don't know. It's just that I feel so unworthy of others and gave my potential over to Al for so long that now that I've got a good man—I don't know . . . I can't trust it."

Pam takes in all that Joan's said in the last few minutes: Joan's meeting Dennis at the restaurant where they first met, finding it hard to believe Dennis could love her, her hope of today versus her despair of last night, feeling so unworthy of others—so many means through which to get Joan to analyze her behaviors in therapeutic terms but "Don't you think you're just giving yourself over to Dennis the way you did with Al?" is the first question off Pam's tongue.

Bill Matson reaches into his pocket, takes out a packet of cigarettes. "So then after I said that, she asked me for twenty-five dollars. Am I wrong to be—"

"I think we need to stop now." Pam cuts Bill Matson off mid-thought, cutting their session short by a minute or two and hoping he doesn't notice or, worse yet, notice and bring it to her attention.

Bill Matson stands, giving a tug at each of the cuffs of his white business shirt, making sure the sleeves extend beyond those of the suit jacket. He looks down at his chest, straightens his tie, and aligns it so it falls neatly over the shirt's buttons. "Friday, then?" He lifts his head, looking into Pam's eyes. "I'm so damn anal. Fixing my tie for my walk home three blocks." He walks to the office door. "Anal, anal, anal." He turns to Pam. "Good-bye. See you Friday."

Pam looks at the answering machine, the unblinking red light. No messages waiting, and she skips making any notes on Bill Matson's session in the notebook, going for the cream-colored cotton jacket hanging over the back of her desk chair. The air conditioner is shut off, and she grabs her leather bag off the coat rack by the door.

In the reception area Michael Flanting sits reading a magazine, one loafer off and dangling from his bare toes. He looks up at Pam with a pleasant, relaxed smile. "You look like you've just got the shit kicked out of you."

Pam locks her office door. "Remind Dr. Briden to lock up, will you?"

"Sure." Michael nods. "See you around."

She opens the office door. ''Good-bye, Michael.'' She's out of the office and waiting for the elevator.

The brass door opens, and Pam steps in, thankful that the elevator is empty. She reaches into her purse, finding her sunglasses, polishing the lenses, and slipping them on as the door opens on the ground floor.

Pam passes out of the lobby and steps immediately to the side, leaning against the building's pink marble facade, caught between the building's entrance on her right and the Donnelman's large street window. Pam knows that if she turns and faces the window, the bar will be immediately before her at the left, with the restaurant section off to the right and extending back to the swinging kitchen doors.

One hour since Joan left therapy, Pam wonders if they'll be drinking at the bar, will have moved on to eating dinner at the restaurant, or will have left for another restaurant or to Joan's apartment or his now that he is free of his wife. Or perhaps none of the above as the doubts Pam placed in her patient's mind took hold and caused Joan to stand up her date.

Pam turns her head within the window frame.

She scans the bar, the room, each table and booth, and they sit in a booth, dark wood and red leather, Dennis's back to the window, Joan facing the street, but her eyes fixed on Dennis. *There they sit,* and Pam's and Joan's eyes meet. Joan sees her doctor watching her—her doctor's looming presence, an influence, a reminder to Joan that she is always there for her when he is not—and Pam quickly turns away as if this were an accident, as if she hasn't seen Joan watching her, and she walks off in the direction of her bus.

A pause as the waiter clears the entrée plates. Joan places a hand at the edge of the plate of the home-style fries, piled high and golden brown. Dr. Thompson is gone, has walked off. The waiter leaves, his arms full with plates. Joan selects a fry, dips its tip in the pool of ketchup on her bread plate. Dr. Thompson thinks Dennis and Al are one and the same to Joan, that Dennis is merely a substitute for Al. Joan denied this when confronted, but sitting with Dennis, feeling herself wanting so much to be a part of *his* life, she can't be sure.

"Is something wrong?" Dennis asks. "You look upset."

"It's nothing. I just saw my doctor walk by." She could use his support when faced with the rebukes of her doctor. "I think she's angry with me."

An opening into the conversation he wants to have. "I think she's jealous of me."

Joan shakes her head, doesn't want to believe it. "She thinks you're interfering with therapy, preventing me from working on myself."

"Am I?" He's genuinely interested in hearing Joan's opinion, already knows Pam's.

Joan bites the tip of a fry and dips its white, open end into the ketchup. She doesn't know the answer and refuses to consider it, afraid the answer might be yes. "No more than she affects our relationship."

"She does help you, though? Right?"

"She helps a lot. She's very helpful."

"Is she?" Dennis prods.

"I think so."

The waiter brings dessert menus, and Joan lets him take the plate of fries. Hearing Joan's messages of last night in reverse order, first the one at the office and then the two when he arrived home, Dennis began to fear that Pam is correct in asserting that Joan Dwyer should not be involved with a man at this time; a man is the last complication Joan needs in her life. *If you're with your wife* . . . But when he called Joan and spoke to her live, not recorded, she sounded so happy that Dennis thought his wife was wrong: Maybe he is not the problem in Joan's life; maybe his wife is. He places the menu down. "You always seem a bit upset after talking to her," Dennis comments.

Joan reads over the list of six-dollar desserts. White chocolate mousse in a milk chocolate shell. "Therapy can be upsetting." Defending her doctor to Dennis and Dennis to her doctor. "Does it bother you that I'm in therapy?"

"No, not at all." He takes Joan's hand, rubs her palm. "I think it's good for you. I do." He reaches into his jacket pocket and takes out the business card he had loose in the back of his Rolodex. He places it on top of the menu before Joan, between caramel nut sundae and chocolate hazelnut cake. "Dr. Edward Brownelly, Psychiatrist." He watches her eyes read the card. She takes her hand from Dennis's and places it in her lap. Her face is stern, all serious. She won't even touch the card.

"What's this for?"

"I thought you might want to try a new doctor if this one isn't helping you," Dennis explains. "I thought you might be better off with a male therapist. How much of a help could she be if she couldn't help you enough to keep you out of the hospital?"

Dr. Edward Brownelly. The address is downtown on West Twelfth Street. "Do you know him?"

"He's an old friend." Dennis asked around his office for names but, in the end, decided to refer Joan to Ed Brownelly, Pam's old friend. A man with a wife and kids, someone to understand Joan's needs better.

The waiter returns. Joan orders the white chocolate mousse and a cup of coffee; Dennis, only coffee.

He picks up the card, taps its edge on the table. "I'm sorry. It was only an idea. A bad one."

Joan shakes her head, her hair falling forward and brushing her cheek. "I don't want to have to start over again with someone. I'm used to Dr. Thompson."

"Are you sure she's the right doctor for you?"

She pushes the hair back from her face. "I think so. I don't want a new doctor." Even as she's saying this, Dennis has placed doubt in her mind. "Why do you think a man would be better?"

He isn't sure if he's doing this to help Joan or hurt Pam. Isn't sure he's done anything since leaving Pam for Joan's benefit and not as revenge against Pam. Revenge for knowing about the affair when he thought he'd gotten away with it. Maybe this is all about his being angry because she caught him, outsmarted him. If he didn't still love her, would he be trying so hard to hurt her? He places the card flat on the table, facing him. "I don't know if he'll be better," Dennis says. "I just thought it might be different, and considering how things have been with Dr. Thompson, I thought it couldn't hurt at least to try him." He offers her the card, edging it toward her, and Joan picks it up, twists it between two fingers.

"I don't know," she says, reading the name and address again. "I'm not sure."

"It's entirely up to you."

The waiter places the coffee on the table, cup and saucer before Joan, cup and saucer before Dennis, small plate with selection of sweeteners. Two spoons. Who is right for her? Who is wrong for her? Dennis? Dr. Thompson? Dr. Edward Brownelly? Who makes her feel better? Who makes her feel worse? Too many questions, and Joan places the business card in her purse and reaches for a Sweet'n Low packet.

After leaving a message on Joan's answering machine, Pam hangs up the phone and reaches into a drawer to take out a menu for the gourmet pizza delivery restaurant up the block. Pam calls and orders a medium-size cheeseless pizza with spinach and mushrooms. She glances at the clock on the microwave, adding forty minutes to arrive at the time when the pizza is due to be delivered.

Sitting before the television, a twenty-dollar bill standing stiffly in a fold of the pale purple T-shirt she wears, Pam waits for dinner to arrive, watching the TV but unable to focus on the show's plot. Characters move, and people speak, but their actions lack meaning and motivation. The good and evil ensuing on prime-time television shows come too easily, no moral judgments made, everything being

either right or wrong, black or white in their Technicolor Surround
Sound cable-equipped TV frame, everything looking and sounding
and feeling better than how things look and sound and feel in life. An
ad for a soap bar comes on with a woman taking a deliriously sensual
shower, a shower more peaceful and beautiful than any shower Pam
has ever taken in her life, soap foaming, skin glistening. A celebration
of cleanliness, this pink rose bar of soap is, an overwhelming and
sensual experience in this black-and-white-tiled bathroom with a
bright pink towel. The woman has sparkling blue eyes and pink lips.
She is in ecstasy, and Pam can feel none of it, can take no part in this
alien woman's colorful experience. Life is not colorful. It is gray, and
every action she takes is both right and wrong, black and white—
gray—leaving Pam emotionally, indeterminately lost.

Dennis is left reclining on the couch in the living room as Joan makes
her way to the kitchen for the white wine she planted in the
refrigerator before leaving for therapy this late afternoon. Joan is
pleased to have the apartment to herself until eleven, when Andrea
will return from a school get-together of kids from the region. Her
not wanting to be around her mother comes in handy when Joan
would like to be alone with her boyfriend.

The machine blinks two messages, and Joan isn't sure she wants to
know who's phoned when the only one she wants to be with is with
her in this apartment. One or perhaps both messages might upset and
ruin this perfect evening, one or maybe both throwing her into a
worried, anxious state, taking her mind away from Dennis and
sending her thoughts elsewhere. Joan is about to take two wineglasses
from the cabinet when the thought nags her as to who has called, and
she realizes that if she doesn't find out, she'll be fretting over it all
through the rest of the evening. Joan places two wineglasses on a
wood tray and reaches over, pushing the play button on the
answering machine, turning away, and opening the refrigerator, the
bright white light burning her eyes. She bends to the lowest shelf for

the bottle of wine as a familiar, distant voice plays, causing Joan to stop, holding on to the refrigerator door's handle for support.

"Joan. It's Al, Joan. Hello. Heard from Todd earlier about last week. Glad to hear you're out of the woods and home. Glad to hear you've made it through this. If you need anything, anything at all, you know you can call. It can wait another week, but we should talk about Andrea coming out here in August. Thinking of you. So long."

Joan stands, shutting the refrigerator. The phone machine speeds on to the next message. Joan goes for the utensil drawer, for the corkscrew. The machine beeps. Joan nestles the corkscrew's steel rim around that of the bottle, aligning its spiral tip with the cork's center.

"Joan. Hello. This is Dr. Thompson phoning to see how you're doing tonight. I'll be at home for the remainder of the evening, so if you'd like to connect with me, please call. If you don't feel like phoning tonight, I'll be at the office tomorrow. Maybe we can schedule an additional session if you find it might be helpful. Good-bye."

Therapy and Dennis—giving her life over to Dennis as she did to Al . . . Considering how things have been with Dr. Thompson, another doctor might be better—therapy and Dennis. Joan carries the tray to the living room, the left side light with the weight of the two glasses, the right heavy with the full bottle of wine, cork set tight in its opening, corkscrew standing straight from the center.

The living room is empty of all signs of Dennis save his burgundy tassel loafers. Joan stares at the pair of shoes, one lying flat on its sole by the sofa, the other three feet away, tipped on its side, worn leather lining facing her.

The sound of familiar music makes its way into Joan's thoughts, and she walks toward the family room. Dennis kneels on the floor in stocking feet, sorting through a library of records several hundred thick, one by one by one in alphabetical order. Simon and Garfunkel sing "Bridge over Troubled Water," and Joan sets the tray on the coffee table. "I thought you'd abandoned me."

"Not at all." Dennis reaches to the tray, grasping the bottle and releasing the cork. "I like this room better than the living room. It's more relaxing."

Joan takes the open bottle from Dennis, half filling each glass with the wine. She sits on the couch, across the table from Dennis's spot on the floor. He takes a glass, lifting it toward Joan, catching her sullen expression. "Should I make a toast? What do you think?"

She sips the wine, cradling the glass's bowl in a hand. "No. I mean, yes, of course." Joan raises the glass, meeting Dennis's, then taking a sip. She slides her legs out along the couch, reclining. She sips the wine, looking over the stack of *People* magazines on the table, the two issues delivered while she was in the hospital and the four before them she never got around to reading. She can't get Dr. Thompson out of her head, and every time she looks at Dennis, she feels guilty for being with him, feels it's a betrayal of her work with Dr. Thompson to be seeing Dennis when he makes her so emotionally unstable. She picks up the most recent issue of *People*. A familiar actress stands on the cover holding her newborn twins, a boy and a girl. EMMY AND OSCAR! the headline shouts in large white letters.

"I always put my magazines down the compactor even though I know I should recycle," Joan says, lifting the top issue, flipping through to its table of contents. "I know I should, but after seeing all those homeless men selling magazines with other people's subscription information printed on the covers, I'm just afraid of walking down the street one day and coming across one selling my old magazines, my name and address there for everyone to read and know what magazines I subscribe to." Joan closes the magazine, returning it to the stack on the table.

Dennis glances at the cover, then looks to Joan. "Is everything okay? You've seemed a bit out of it all evening. Would you like me to leave?"

Joan looks away from Dennis, wonders what Todd told Al when they spoke, if he made fun of his mother to him: "God, Dad, Mom is so loony. Crazier than even when you divorced her. I can barely stand being around her anymore, and Andrea hates staying at home with her. We both want to move out to Colorado with you and Linda."

Dennis watches Joan finish off the last of her wine, and he lifts the bottle, pouring a large spill into the empty glass. Joan's wrist jerks toward him with the surprise weight of the wine, and she quickly rights her glass, catching the alcohol before it spills over the rim.

"You want me to leave?" Dennis asks again. Who knows what's going on in her head? They've still never discussed her suicide attempt, if he was a factor in it. He tilts the bottle, waiting for her reply before refilling his own glass.

"I got two phone messages." Joan sits up on the couch, feet on the floor. "I wasn't going to listen to them, but I did, and now I'm distracted. I'm sorry. They were from my ex-husband and Dr. Thompson."

"Your doctor?" Dennis less concerned with, less threatened by Joan's ex-husband than his wife.

"She's worried about me. She calls to make sure I'm okay."

"Isn't that a bit excessive?"

"What's excessive?"

"Her calling you at home."

"She's being supportive. I appreciate it. Do you think it's a problem?"

"It doesn't feel intrusive?" Referring her to another doctor, trying to drive a wedge between Joan and her doctor could be a mistake; he's possibly underestimated Joan's attachment to Pam.

"Not at all." Joan drinks the wine, shrugs, the glass trembling between her fingers. "I think she's just concerned after what happened."

"Of course."

Joan looks at his face. She laughs. "Are *you* jealous of *her*? Is that why you want me to see another doctor? A doctor that's a friend of yours?''

Dennis smiles. ''I am *not* jealous of your doctor. *Really*. Go ahead, phone her right now, see if I care. I'm only trying to understand, that's all.''

Joan leans forward, runs a hand across Dennis's scalp, his hair falling around her fingers. ''She said to call if I felt I needed to.''

''Will she worry if you don't?'' Dennis slides over to the couch, his back against the armrest, his head by Joan's knee.

Joan's fingernails graze the rim of his ear. ''She might. I don't know.''

''Then maybe you ought to call if it makes you feel better.''

Joan places her glass on the table. ''I'll call and tell her I'm all right so I don't think about it anymore, okay?''

''Go ahead,'' Dennis says, and Joan stands and goes to the phone. She dials the number of Dr. Thompson's office.

''You have the number memorized?''

Joan looks away from him to the line of Ian Fleming books on the bookshelves, her father's. ''Dr. Thompson. This is Joan Dwyer. Thanks for calling. I'm okay tonight. Thanks again. Good-bye.'' Joan hangs up and turns to Dennis. ''All done,'' she says, and Dennis leans back, reaching over and grabbing Joan's bare ankle, ''Got you.''

Dennis slips two fingers inside Joan, massaging the walls of her vagina as she spreads her legs farther apart. The phone rings, and Joan arches her back, pressing her body down into his fingers.

''Do you want to answer?'' he asks. Pam calling back. Pam, home alone and calling back. ''Answer,'' Dennis commands. ''Answer and carry on a conversation.''

The phone rings a second time. ''No,'' Joan gasps with a laugh, her face breaking out in a smile. ''Uh-uh.''

Dennis grabs for the phone with his free hand and passes the

receiver to Joan. He works three fingers inside her. Let Pam hear
this. Joan clamps her legs shut on his hand.

"Hello." Joan catches her breath.

Dennis attempts to pull his hand from between her legs, but she
keeps him there, thighs locked together.

"What time tomorrow?" Her eyes meet Dennis's and he shakes
his head. "Hold on a minute, please." Joan presses the phone to her
breast, covering the mouthpiece. "What's wrong? It's my doctor
setting up an extra session."

"I want to see you tomorrow for lunch and all afternoon," he
says, speaking in a normal tone of voice, hoping Pam hears.

"You can meet me for lunch? You're sure?" She parts her legs,
and he rubs her clitoris.

"You meet me at my office." He makes this up on the spot, not
even remembering if he already has a lunch scheduled for tomorrow.

Joan pulls the phone from her breast, the sound of a suction cup as
the mouthpiece leaves the skin. Dennis presses his face between
Joan's legs.

"I can't," Joan manages to say. "I have plans with And-Andrea
then." She kicks Dennis away with a heel, and he falls back off the
bed—"Ouch!"—and Joan laughs aloud. "No, I'm fine, everything's
fine." She speaks into the phone, trying to control her laughter.
"Good-bye." And she hangs up the phone.

Dennis's laugh tapers off. He crouches on the floor, thinking about
Pam, wounded and furious, and he stands, gazing at Joan from his
spot at the foot of the bed. His dick is only semierect with the
distractions of the call, more interested in the woman on the other
end of the phone—What did she say? Was she angry? He resists
asking—than the woman before him.

"Well, I can meet you tomorrow." Dennis is so obviously staring
at her she becomes self-conscious. Joan slides under the covers, afraid
he'll notice the pale scars on her shoulder, only barely concealed by
makeup. "Come to bed. Andrea won't be home for another hour."

He didn't even want to meet Joan for lunch. "What if she comes home early?" He bends and picks up his boxers.

"Andrea never comes home early." Joan folds back the comforter. "Come on. What's wrong?"

Dennis begins dressing, his prank through: having sex with Joan while Pam's on the other end of the line. That's what he arranged to happen, and he's succeeded, besting Pam, making her his loser, not he hers, and thinking it through, imagining how angry Pam must have been initially when she hung up and how depressed she must now feel, her husband rubbing salt in the wound of his affair, he begins feeling sorry for his wife. Pam, alone at home as her husband uses one of her very sick patients as a means to get back at her for not loving him enough, bruising her both professionally and personally; what an asshole he's become. "I should get home."

"Why?"

He can see Joan's face tense up, struggling to hold back tears. Initially, keeping Joan a secret from Pam and now making sure Pam knows when he is with her . . . Joan *is* only fun with Pam involved, Dennis realizes. This *is* only his revenge for her manipulating his life, treating him like a child, refusing to have a child. And so he became one for her, pursuing his pleasures with no regard for others, with only his own needs in mind. He draws up his pants, pulls on his shirt.

"What's wrong?" Joan asks. "What happened? Why can't you stay?"

And all at once he hates Joan for being so needy, so desperately needy of him each and every night. It's her need that keeps him here as much as it's his desire to be needed. Joan's as much to blame for putting herself in this vulnerable position as he is for exploiting it. Allowing herself to be persuaded to call her doctor and then to speak to her during sex—no will of her own, anything to please a man, as his wife had said. Dennis searches the carpet for his socks and finds he has them on, never took them off. "I have work to prepare for tomorrow morning I haven't done yet." He looks for his shoes, remembers he took them off in the living room earlier. Joan sits in bed, the comforter drawn up around her shoulders. He knows she will cry the minute he leaves. She may even phone Pam and leave a message, apologizing for the previous call, begging her doctor to phone her again, setting an appointment for tomorrow.

"Why do you have to go?" Joan asks, an attempt to salvage the evening. "Why?"

Dennis walks around the bed, sitting by her side. "I'll see you tomorrow," he promises. He kisses her cheek and stands. "I'll call you in the morning." He walks and opens the door.

"I love you," Joan calls, and Dennis leaves the room, walking down the hall to the living room, going for his shoes. He doesn't know how he's ever going to end this affair if he wants to. He doesn't control it. Joan does—Joan and her need. He slips on his loafers and leaves the apartment, as much Joan's captive as she is his.

4

Heidi Sklar, Pam's bulimic patient, leaves the office, and Pam walks to the answering machine to play back the three messages received within the span of Heidi Sklar's session. The first message came in at 9:10 A.M., while Heidi detailed vomiting up a Caesar salad in a ladies' room before returning to the restaurant table and sharing a deep-dish pan pizza with her date. "The croutons were still intact." Heidi laughed. The second message came in at 9:23, while Heidi told Pam how disappointed she was in the size of the man's penis. "No bigger or thicker than this." She held up her bare ring finger. "I could just have easily fiddled myself." She jerked her finger up and down in the air, laughing with a hoot. The third message came in fifteen minutes later, while Heidi sobbed into a facial tissue, lamenting the fact that no man would ever truly, unconditionally love her, that she was incapable of loving or being loved by another person. "I'm not good enough for anyone, and no one is good enough for me," she declared through tears, and Pam held out the tissue box and escorted her patient to the door as the session reached its dismal end.

The tape rewinds.

Message One: "Hello, Pam. It's Dennis. Please give me a call when you can. We need to talk about Joan."

Message Two: "If you haven't given away my time, I would like to come in today. The interview—fuck it—canceled. I can make it after all. Ross Bimmellman calling. From home."

Message Three: "Dr. Thompson. Hello, it's Joan Dwyer. Thanks for calling me last night. I'll see you later today at noon."

Two weeks since her last contact with Dennis, when he hung up on her, three weeks since he moved out of their apartment; Pam, thinking through the recent history of Joan's sessions, has a good idea why Dennis is initiating contact at this point.

"He thinks I should be seeing another doctor," Joan told Pam a week and a half ago. "I don't want to, though. He gave me the name and number of a doctor to call."

"He's coming over all the time; only all we do is watch television, eat dinner. We drink too much and then he leaves and he isn't interested in sex anymore. It's like I don't make him happy anymore," Joan told Pam last week. "I'm afraid he's getting ready to leave me."

Pam thought Joan was being her usual paranoid and depressed self. "Sit down and talk to him about it, ask him if anything is wrong. Maybe he's just happy to be spending quiet time with you at home."

Last night Joan left this message for Pam: "He said if I won't see another doctor, he'll leave me. He said that if I wanted him to see me, I'd have to see another doctor who could help me more than you do."

Pam phoned Joan at home. She was drunk and crying, and Pam

told her to go to bed, told her she'd see her at noon tomorrow, today, and they could talk it out when Joan felt better.

The machine resets itself, and Pam goes to her desk, checking her address book for Ross Bimmellman's number.

"Hello, Ross," Pam speaks. "This is Dr. Thompson returning your message. Your session hour is still available, so I'll see you then. Good-bye." A short, professional message, and Pam looks to the clock, no time left to answer Dennis's call without taking Claire Maerer late. She will phone him during the ten-minute break between sessions, between Claire Maerer's departure and Susan Rosche's arrival.

His secretary answers. "Hello, Mr. Perry's office." Pam gives the girl her name, and a moment later she is connected to Dennis.

"Hello. You called. It sounds like you're putting Joan through the wringer." Pam's caught off guard by her hostility, hadn't been aware of how much anger she's been stifling.

"I want to see you," he says, his voice shaky.

"Why?"

"To talk this out. I'm ready to."

"I don't know if I want to anymore. I'm just starting to get used to being alone. I kind of like it."

"Can't we talk?"

He gets what he wants when he wants, first substituting Joan for Pam and now wanting his wife again. "You want to reconcile? What happens to Joan then?"

"I don't think I'm good for her. I think she's becoming more unstable."

The buzzer sounds, and Pam leans over, pushing the button that releases the office door's lock. She hears Susan Rosche open the door, and she releases the button. "So?"

"I can't help her anymore."

"What do you want to happen to her now that you're done with your ego trip? What happens to her now that you're tired of her?"

"I don't know. I just don't think I'm right for her anymore."

"Who are you trying to persuade her to see instead of me? Anyone I know?"

"Ed."

"She told me you'll break up with her if she doesn't."

A long pause. Dennis speaks. "Why can't she see Ed and then we might be able to put this in the past? Can't that happen? This isn't doing you any good either."

"You want to refer Joan to a friend of ours so she can possibly tell him she's been dating a man named Dennis Perry?" Pam looks at her watch; she's going to have to take Susan Rosche late and run over on the other end a few minutes. "Joan still loves you. She *needs* you," Pam emphasizes.

"She could see someone else, then. Why not?"

"Joan's my patient. I have a commitment to her." Pam watches the second hand move around her watch.

"What about us?"

"I don't know if I want to be with you," Pam asserts. "I want to help Joan. I haven't given up on her, and I'm not sure our marriage is worth saving anymore. You're the one who threw it away in the first place. You decided that, not me."

"Can't we meet and talk at least? A dinner together or something?"

"I have to go. I have a patient waiting."

"Of course." An edge to his voice, the anger back.

Joan tugs at the sleeves of her peach cotton jersey. "It's so hot and humid. I don't know how many days it's been like this, but I hope it ends soon." She settles back in the chair, arranging the white linen skirt to make it easier to cross her legs. She smiles at Dr. Thompson, "Anyway, here I am."

Dr. Thompson gives Joan a sober stare. "Here you are," she feeds back. "What are you thinking about concerning Dennis's demand?"

"I don't know," Joan says, her smile quickly disappearing. She looks over at her doctor, who is staring—*glaring?*—at her.

"Have you thought much about it?" Better to lead Joan to her own conclusions than to put the thoughts in her head.

"I don't know what the answer is."

"Do you want to be in therapy?"

"Yes."

"Do you want a new doctor?" Taking a gamble.

"No, not at all." Joan shakes her head. "I want to keep seeing you."

"It sounded like he gave you an ultimatum."

Joan looks to her lap. Her stomach tightens; she hasn't eaten anything yet today. "I'm not sure what to do. He thinks you don't help, and you think he's bad for me."

"Have I said that?"

"I—" Joan grips the arms of the chair, can't recollect Dr. Thompson's ever saying it but somehow thinks it has been said. Joan sits, thinking, feeling foolish for trying to remember if her doctor has said something both her doctor and she know her doctor never said. "No," Joan admits, "I guess you never did say it. I guess I just thought you did."

"Why is that, do you suppose?"

"Because he was so bad for me before. Because he's forcing me to choose between you and him." Joan shifts in the chair, recrossing her legs, hands automatically going to the skirt and adjusting to make sure it's arranged nicely over her knees. "I thought everything could be okay with him and me now that he's left his wife . . . I don't understand why it's not. He's with me so much, only it feels as if he doesn't want to be. I'm beginning to feel like I did when Al left. He's with me but treats me like I've done something wrong, and I can't figure out what it is. When I ask, he says it's work or he's tired. I'm never sure if each date with him is going to be the last. It's like

reliving the divorce over and over and over on a daily basis, and now
he says if I won't get better help for my problems, he can't be with
me."

"It sounds like you're very angry with him."

"I just want to know why he's pressuring me like this."

"Do you think he's bad for you?"

"I think you do."

"Can you explain that?"

Joan takes her hands from the chair, suddenly aware of the pain in
her finger joints caused by gripping the arms so tightly. She flexes
both hands, stretching the fingers stiff and wide, then curling them
into fists before draping each hand back over the chair's arms. She
drops her eyes from her doctor's face, staring across the room at the
bookshelves, reading the titles she's read time and time over:
*DSM-III; Homosexuality: A Comprehensive Study; Case Histories: Abuse and
the Family; The Interpretation of Dreams.* Joan looks back to her doctor.
"I was only thinking about it because I suspected you were."

Pam says nothing, giving her patient the silence needed to arrive at
her own doubts.

Joan leans forward, running a hand down, then up the back of a
calf. She leans back in the chair, one hand feeling the bumps of the
other's knuckles. "He isn't bad for me. Even if he will leave me all
over again and I do kill myself, I don't think he's bad for me, and I
don't want him to go away. I was depressed and suicidal before I met
him, so he hasn't changed that. At least being with him delays it
more. It's inevitable that I eventually do try again. I'm not getting
better, only worse, and I can't see my life going on and on like this
for much longer. It's just a part of who I am. One day when I was
fifteen, it just occurred to me that I hated my life and wanted it to
end. I was lying in bed in the room that's now Andrea's, and I just
thought that I had to do something so I wouldn't have to feel so much
pain anymore. Nothing bad happened that day to make me think of it.
I hadn't fought with my parents or anything. It was just a day like all
the others. Since then I've just been distracting myself in the hope of

finding some reason so as why not to do it. With the kids grown and the divorce and having no interests, I've found fewer and fewer reasons not to anymore. Dennis is just my last way of delaying it. That's all he is, and I'm so afraid of him leaving that I don't think I actually enjoy my time with him.'' Joan takes a deep breath, reaching over to the tissue box and taking a tissue, touching it to her eyes. ''I'm trying hard to hold on however I can,'' she explains.

Pam observes her patient, a woman turned inside out trying to salvage some happiness from life, some true reason why life is worth living. ''Don't you think Dennis's actions contribute to your feelings of despair and push you deeper into your depression? Doesn't he make those sad feelings a bit more unbearable?'' Pam begins gently. ''I don't believe you when you say he's just something for you to focus on until you decide to commit suicide, and I don't believe you believe that either. I think his actions affect you profoundly and play upon some of your greatest vulnerabilities and leave you *a lot* more depressed than you were previously. You tell me he makes you feel better, but all I see is how little self-worth you have left after spending time with him.''

Joan looks at her watch, wishes the session were over, altogether tired of defending herself, defending Dennis to her doctor. ''Do we have to discuss this anymore? It's not going to change anything. If I were never to have met him, I'd be feeling suicidal, so what difference does it make if I feel like doing it after he's left me? When he leaves me, we can work it out then.''

''So Dennis is your temporary cure for your depression. A delay from the inevitable?''

Joan lifts her head: Her doctor has finally understood the situation. ''That's it exactly.''

Pam nods and leans forward slightly, meeting her patient's eyes. ''I believe you. I believe that *is* what you experience. But I interpret your comments differently. What I see happening is you using Dennis as a Band-Aid for a gunshot wound. He covers the wound temporarily, but when he leaves, the wound is worse and more infected than it was before. Dennis is why we're not making progress here. I don't think it's inevitable for you to commit suicide. If I did, I wouldn't waste either your or my time here. I believe we can help you. I think we have in some very significant ways. You and I together *can* help Joan Dwyer if she can make the commitment to being here so we can work out her troubles for the long term rather than seek the temporary relief of being with a man in the present. Relying on Dennis to solve your problems and make you feel worthy is a step back to your life with Al and before that to your feelings of worthlessness your father impressed on you. You yourself said that being with Dennis was like reliving the divorce many times over, and that's exactly what brought you here in the first place. Do I think Dennis is bad for you? Right now I do. *Yes.* You got out of the hospital only three weeks ago, and already you're sacrificing yourself for his needs, ready to terminate therapy with me because he wants you to go to a doctor who's a friend of his. I think you need to be here on your own—just you and me instead of it being you and him and me and you always needing to discuss the latest thing he's done to you. You have to spend some time really thinking about why you're with him and why you're backing away from therapy. I'm here for you, but if I am going to continue making all the effort I have in the past, I need to know you're making it for yourself as well.'' Pam reaches for her water glass on the table by her chair and takes a sip, maintaining a poised, controlled appearance, trying to keep herself from shaking because of a sudden rush of adrenaline.

"But I love him." Joan shrugs, helpless. "It's not that simple."

Pam takes a second small sip of the water. "It sounds more like you're afraid of him."

"I think I'd be worse without him," Joan argues. "He does help take my mind off my problems."

Pam gives Joan a quizzical look. "Maybe your mind should be on your problems. That is why we're here, isn't it?"

"I love him." Joan attempts explaining again, pleading. "I *need* him."

Pam places the water glass on the end table, one last push at Joan for the day. "Sometimes we love and need things—*are addicted to things*—that are bad for us." She checks the brass clock behind Joan's shoulder. One or two minutes left. She continues, "We're going to have to stop here. You can call me tonight and leave a message if you'd like to talk." Cutting Joan off cold, letting her feel her doctor's disapproval so she'll come back repentant.

Joan stands, her hands trembling. Her eyes glaze over, and she makes a concerted effort not to cry, not to crumple under her doctor's stare. "You don't want me to see him anymore. You think I shouldn't."

Pam walks to the door and twists the brass knob, feeling its polished surface slide with the sweat on her fingertips. "I can't decide that." She swings the door wide and lays a soft hand on Joan's shoulder. "Please call me if you need to."

Joan is gone, has left the office, and Pam closes the office door, walks over to her desk and sits. She doesn't take notes on Joan's session today, hasn't taken notes on any of the patients she's seen this morning. Pam leans on her elbows, resting her face in her hands. She wants to cry, wishes she could but can't. To wrest Joan from Dennis and leave him womanless, with neither his mistress nor his wife—that is her goal. To prevent him from getting his way. Having the pleasure of a mistress for a few months, using her to hurt his wife, then expecting to dump her easily and have his wife back—this should not happen. Wanting both women, Dennis deserves no woman, and as much as Pam knows she loves her husband and is aware she could have him back if she wanted, she'd rather sacrifice their marriage and punish him. Dennis, so needy of being needed, will be alone, wanted by neither his wife nor his mistress, and if Pam can convince her patient to leave him, Joan and her doctor will have a stronger relationship for having worked through this very tough situation.

.   .   .

Dennis has a pile of work to do but knows it will be altogether useless for him to attempt to focus on three dozen cartoon drawings of milk shake cups, identical but for their mouth expressions. The cup's faces are all in various degrees of smiles, and Dennis is supposed to be deciding upon the top three smiles that best represent the *feeling* of the milk shake the client sells.

Dennis stares at the thirty-six cartoon drawings. Big grins, little smirks, several almost-sneers, some baring teeth, some shy, some coy, and he pushes the board away, angered and annoyed that this matters, that this is what he is paid to care about when all he can concentrate on is his life, the two women involved in it and how they've pulled him—or is it he who has pulled them?—into this state of despair.

According to Pam, he has never been any help to Joan Dwyer. According to Pam, he has only made Joan more unstable and proved to be an impediment to her progress in therapy.

"She *needs* you," Pam said. Only he no longer *needs* Joan, and how to bow out of this relationship without upsetting Joan greatly is the problem. Fearing Joan will attempt suicide if he leaves yet knowing he must leave her if he is to begin a reconciliation with his wife, Dennis can suddenly appreciate the dilemma Pam has been in for the past several months, can appreciate all she did to untangle their crossed lives. What did she do to try to correct the problem? What should he do? The best course of action he can think to take is to end his relationship with Joan and leave Pam to help her patient. Pam might then be more willing to have him back and refer Joan to another doctor, Dennis Perry and his wife having the chance to put this turmoil behind them, both the wiser and more committed to making their marriage a success.

Milk shakes smile at Dennis from across the desk. He, in his job, analyzes the smiles drawn on portraits of milk shake cups while his wife analyzes the needs and motives of the depressed and alienated.

She *is* the better—best—person to help Joan Dwyer, and the sooner he phones Joan, intimating that a break is imminent, the sooner Joan can get the help she needs from his wife, to get over her lover and get on with her therapy.

He dials Joan's number, and the phone has to ring only once before it's answered.

"Hello," Joan says.

Dennis stares at the smiling milk shakes, thirty-six smiling milk shakes. "Joan, it's Dennis."

"Are you coming over soon? I thought I'd make us dinner."

"I can't. Not tonight. I really can't."

"Andrea's going to be out for the whole evening at a friend's. You could stay over. You could come by as late as you want."

"I really can't tonight."

"Is something wrong? Did anything happen?"

Dennis shuts his eyes and leans on the desk. "I'm not sure— Do you think this is right for us?"

"What do you mean?"

He imagines her in the family room, the sound on the television muted. She stares at the silent picture on the screen. "I think we need to take a step back and see how this is affecting us both. What do you think?"

"I think everything's fine. Is this because I haven't called the other doctor?"

Dennis sighs into the phone. "No. I think you should stay with the doctor you have. I shouldn't have recommended another to you. That was my mistake." He waits for her to say something, to have some response. "Joan?"

"I'm here."

"What do you think?"

"I don't know what you want from me. I'm trying so hard, and I don't know what you want anymore."

He opens his eyes, squints at the light aimed over his desk, his eyes refocusing. "I don't know either."

"Please come over. We need to see each other."

"Not tonight, Joan. I'm sorry."

"When will I see you next?"

"I'll phone you later. I'll call you when I'm home from work tonight. How's that?" This is what it must be like to talk to a child, Dennis imagines, convincing her you'll be home soon and have not forgotten about her.

"Why can't you stop by? It's on the way. There's no reason."

"I can't, Joan. Listen, I have to go, have to get back to work."

"I love you."

Her need is the bait to keep him. "I know. Good-bye." He hangs up, breathes in and out, preventing himself from becoming emotional, for he's done what he had to do. The milk shakes smile, and Dennis, through staring unconsciously at this board these past few minutes, by instinct alone has whittled the thirty-six down to eight. He picks up a white grease pencil and places a check by each of the finalists on the clear plastic sheet overlaying the drawings. He will now attempt to narrow the eight to three.

Tim Boxer hands Pam his check for the past month's sessions. Pam casually places the check in her schedule book, to be entered into her billing account files later.

"So I think I've decided this," Tim Boxer says, ending the session. "I can't afford to be here anymore now that I'm paying the costs of the medication too, and since I can get some group counseling at the center, I guess I have to sacrifice this once I run up to my limit on my insurance."

"Do you know when that may be?"

"I think after next month. Probably by August."

Pam nods. "Then maybe we should start talking about how we should end this and prepare for that. If you know who you'll be working with at the center, if you'd like I could speak to him or her about our work here. But that's entirely up to you."

Tim Boxer stands, putting on his navy blue windbreaker jacket. "I'll think about it."

Pam stands, escorting Tim Boxer to the door. "If you'd like, we could talk about reducing your fee if you think that might help. But if it can't, then we can continue on and prepare for you to work in therapy elsewhere."

"Thanks," Tim says, zippering his jacket. "I'll think about that too."

Pam opens the door, Tim Boxer leaves, and she is alone, done being Dr. Thompson for the day, and as she is closing her office door, Jack Briden calls, "Pamela, come here for a minute."

He's trapped her, and Pam exits her office, walking down the hall to his. Jack stands at a bookshelf. "What's up? How are things going? I keep observing your patients in the waiting room hoping to find the woman you're torturing. When does she come in?" So casual, as if this were only office gossip and not her life on the line.

Pam sits in the chair opposite his desk. "Oh, Jack, how are things with you? I haven't seen Michael at all in the last week."

Jack lifts a book from a shelf and sits at his desk, folding the book open, leafing through its thin pages. "No, we are through. He tired of our therapy, said he wanted another doctor. Even asked me to refer him to someone."

"Did you give him one?"

He picks up a pad of paper, looking at the book, then making a note on the pad. "No. I told him to go to a bar and meet someone. That's all the therapy he needs."

"Do you miss him?"

Jack waves a hand, an awkward pause. "So, do you have another confession to make? What's been going on?"

Pam smiles. She would love to confess, and if she weren't so certain how truly awful and horrific she has been regarding Joan Dwyer's therapy, if she weren't so certain that every action she has taken in this endeavor is so entirely unethical and damning even by Jack Briden's standards, if she knew she wasn't going to pursue worse actions, she would happily confess it all in exchange for his compassion and understanding. She just isn't sure she can trust him not to report her to the APA. Now that his affair is over, Michael Flanting's having dumped him, she has nothing to hold over his head, not even a pathetic consensual affair to keep him from turning on her.

Pam stands. "I'm sorry about Michael. If you ever need to talk, I'm here."

He looks up from his book. "It's gotten that bad, huh? What is her name? *Joan Dwyer.* Let's get her the help she needs. We can put an end to this."

Pam smiles; she's afraid she'll cry. "I'll let you get back to your work." She leaves his office: one phone call to Joan before heading home for the night.

Box of freezer bags. Coil of rope. Black nylon shopping sack with black canvas handles. Joan stands at the kitchen table and places both the rope and box of freezer bags in the nylon sack. The answering machine is set to pick up, Joan not needing to be disturbed by a phone's ringing as she was before, and the thought occurs to her to switch off the phone's ringer, thereby leaving herself entirely undisturbed with the machine available to callers, letting them think all is fine and she is out when she is really down and dead. Joan switches the phone's ringer off and lifts the nylon sack by its thick handle, about to head into the living room when she realizes she'll most likely need scissors to cut the rope to a manageable length, and she reaches for the utility drawer by the phone, yanking its brass handle. A jangle as scissors bump against hammer, bump against stapler and screwdriver, and Joan takes the scissors, fitting her thumb and fingers through its holes. She leaves the kitchen, passing through the dining room, shopping bag in one hand while the other snaps the scissors open and shut, open and shut, slicing waves of the cool, air-conditioned air. She walks to the phone in the living room, unplugging its cord from the wall.

The sky burns red across her face as it sets in the west behind a cloud over New Jersey. Joan sits on the couch, unpacking the bag, tearing at the perforated strip running across the entire width of the freezer bags' slim box. A crunching, rhythmic tear like playing cards woven between the spokes of the two-wheeler with training wheels she rode through Central Park over thirty-five years ago, and Joan reaches into the box, withdrawing the roll of freezer bags with their efficient seamless edges. Four bags are torn from the roll, and the roll is placed back in the box, Joan setting the box away from her on the coffee table. She lifts the oval-shaped coil of rope and tears off the cardboard belt that cinches its middle, making it look like an eight. She unwinds an arm's length, dropping the coil in the lap of her linen skirt, and dropping the length of rope around her neck, the loose end hanging just above her breast. Joan snips once, and the cut end falls to her lap, meeting up with the coil. The leftover rope is placed along-side the box of freezer bags, and Joan places the freezer bags to her right, the cut piece of rope at the center, and the black nylon bag to her left on the coffee table.

She cannot please anyone—her therapist, Dennis, her children, Al, her parents—so Joan opts for pleasing herself; the only thing she wants is not to have to live another day of this life. A pampered, care-free girl grew up to become a spoiled, worthless woman. The only thing accomplished in her forty-two years was giving birth to Andrea and Todd, and that was less her doing than Al's and nature's. She lay there passively while Al fertilized the egg. She lay there passively on tranquilizers while drugs forcibly induced labor. Two children came out of her body, neither of whom want to have anything to do with the life from which they sprang, and Joan acts, selecting the freezer bags, inserting one into another into another into another—four becoming one—and pulling the four-layered bag swiftly over her head. The bag drops gracefully to her collarbone, and Joan takes a breath, satisfied with the bag's comfortable, loose fit, and when she exhales, the bag fogs up, steamy. Inhaling again, the bag is sucked gently into her open mouth, plastic wrapped over her lips and gums and teeth, the bag sealing itself to Joan's face with the moisture of her breath as its adhesive.

The view of the city is hazy through the plastic, like a foggy, misty day. Regine Pointer has always been jealous of the Robinses' apartment view, facing the open air of the city downtown and the New Jersey skyline, while hers faces the backs of other buildings. Regine Pointer living her entire life alone and independent and satisfied, whereas Joan Dwyer can't handle being alone for a few hours without swallowing medication or panicking herself into phoning her doctor. As she returned from therapy and lunch and entered the lobby this afternoon, Miss Pointer and Brooke were already waiting for the elevator, and when the car arrived, all three women entered and rode up together. Joan said hello to Brooke and Miss Pointer, but nothing more, not wanting to hear a callous comment from her neighbor's mouth, but as they got off the elevator, Joan turning to her door, Regine spoke out. "Being taken by a man does not make you any better than me," she scolded. "Don't put on airs because you've reeled yourself in a beau."

Joan offered Miss Pointer no reply. She only entered her apartment and took a Xanax. The phone rang, and she answered it. As close to a rejection as she could have received without his outright saying it, and Joan walked to the family room and turned on the TV, watching a talk show about daughters who had been sexually abused by their mothers as children but only remembered it as adults.

"I'm a survivor. *Not* a victim. Don't call me that," one pretty young woman in her twenties said. "I didn't blame myself, get depressed, and do nothing. I got angry and confronted my mother and blamed *her*! I took control and took back my life. I'm a survivor!"

Survivors. Regine Pointer and this young woman, and Joan sat there, never abused by her mother or anyone, feeling like a victim and feeling guilty for being so pathetic and suicidal, when compared with the lives of the struggling women on the TV show, her life has been a dream come true. *They should be the ones killing themselves, not me,* Joan thought, and before she could stop herself, she was heading for the Suicide Shelf.

Joan reaches to the table and shakes open the black nylon shopping bag, taking its two canvas handles and drawing it over the freezer bag. A snug fit, all light is erased, no more sunset, and Joan closes her eyes in a complete darkness, no shadows of light filtering in through the thin skin of her eyelids, no orange-red veil of veins pressed against her eyes.

Deep darkness, a bottomless well. Joan can see forever with her eyes closed, black with no shadings. Her breath comes shorter, only whispers of fresh air make their way through the bag's opening at Joan's neck, and the air Joan breathes quickly becomes thick and stale, her tongue tasting slick plastic, exhaling through her nose, lungs straining for a breath of clean air that does not reek with the smell of the mustard-garlic dressing that adorned the lunch of chicken salad she ate at the deli downstairs.

Joan leans forward, gropes the coffee table, fingers fanned and reaching. She locates the cut piece of rope, quickly winding it about her neck twice before knotting its ends once, then twice, secure. Joan settles on the sofa, her back against the sofa's back, hands clutched together, lungs straining for air, and Joan, inside her head inside these bags, feels a ripping through her chest, a burning tear reaching through her chest, up her throat, and into her mouth, plastic violently sucked against the roof of her mouth. Pressure increases, her chest exploding in pain, desperate, and she wants to resist the body's will to survive—*Sometimes we love and need things, are addicted to things, that are bad for us*—and Joan wants the need eliminated, but the pain is too much, too severe, her body bent forward, over her knees, hands pressed flat against chest as if to keep her lungs from exploding through her rib cage. That pain is all Joan can feel, all-encompassing, overwhelming, needing to be silenced, and her hands take over, the body winning out over her will, the pain too much, too severe. Her hands go to the knot at the back of the neck, fumble at its tight loops; a fingernail snaps; a knot loosens. Fingers claw at the rope, claw it from around the neck, and she desperately pulls the bags from over her head, mouth wide, gasping, inhaling deeply, eyes blinded by the red descending sun, pain easing from her body, lungs filling with air, relieved. The bags and rope drop from Joan's hands to the carpet, and she reaches up, slides a forearm across her chin, wiping spit into the cloth of her shirt, then smoothing fingers across her forehead, pushing back hair wet with sweat, sticky with hair spray.

Hoping to relax her way into a second attempt at asphyxiation, Joan goes to the liquor cabinet and selects the ingredients required to make a martini: the martini glass, the martini shaker, the vodka, the vermouth. She places everything on the coffee table alongside the rope, freezer bag, and nylon bag and heads into the kitchen for the ice and olives.

Standing at the refrigerator, door ajar, rectangle of yellow light slicing across her waist, jar of green pitted olives in one hand and full ice tray in the other, a red blinking is noticed from the corner of an eye, and how can a woman kill herself without knowing who has left this message on her answering machine? How can she bring herself to stick her head in a black bag, secure it with rope twisted into a complicated knot when she is still puzzling over that message blinking, waiting to be heard and, if unheard now before she kills herself, the message possibly left unheard for eternity?

Joan touches the thick glass bottom rim of the olive jar to the play button, giving a firm tap.

Joan takes a sip of the martini before answering her doctor's question, second sip from her third martini of the evening since listening to the message from Dr. Thompson, phoning her doctor back, leav-

ing a message, switching on the kitchen phone's bell, and plugging
the living room extension back into the wall.

Joan puts down the glass on the kitchen table, the kitchen dark but
for light spilling in from the living room, across the dining room floor
to a thin patch of light at the kitchen's entrance. Joan taps her feet in
the narrow shaft of light, her eyes caught on their pale shadows.

"Joan?"

Joan straightens, halts the toe tapping, brings the receiver closer to
her ear. "Hello."

"Maybe we should discuss this tomorrow at your usual hour."

Joan leans a hand on the table, maintaining balance as the doorframe tilts before her. "He said he thought it wasn't right. He said he
didn't want to see me anymore."

"He said that?"

"I think so . . . I don't know . . . He said he might call again
later." Joan pivots on the balls of her feet, stretching across the distance between the phone at the counter and the kitchen table, fasten-
ing her hand on to her drink glass and bringing it to her lips.

"You're not sure, then?"

Joan finishes off the martini. "I'm done."

"Done with what, Joan?"

"Everything." Joan plants the glass on the counter, then grabs it
up again, bringing it before her, eclipsing a living room lamp with its
cone. The lamp's light breaks out in shafts up and down the crystal.

"What does that mean, Joan?"

"I'm going to try my bag thing again. That's what it means."

"You promised me you wouldn't try that. You promised me we
could meet tomorrow."

Joan remembers making the promise at the start of this conversation, minutes later already regretting it. "Well, I want this all
done," Joan says matter-of-factly. "I want to be away from everything that makes me think. I want everyone to leave me alone."

"I know, Joan. I know that."

"I'm so tired of all this talking. So tired of caring when I don't anymore."

"Joan, we can—"

"He's gone. I'm done with him. It's too hard with him, and without him around it will make it easier for me to do this. I'm so sick of caring when no one else does. No one else can."

"Do you think you can put away the bags and rope and not try anymore tonight? Can you promise me you'll do that, or should I come over?"

Joan slumps into a chair at the kitchen table. "Don't come over. I don't want you here. I'm drunk."

"Then you're promising me you'll put everything away and go to bed?"

"That's what I'll do."

"And I'll see you tomorrow."

"Yes, we'll meet tomorrow." Joan pauses, then continues, an afterthought: "But that doesn't mean I'm promising not to kill myself ever. I'm only promising not tonight." She stands, walking to the phone console, wanting this conversation over so she can return to the living room, clean up the mess, and mix herself a couple more martinis.

"We'll talk about this more tomorrow."

"I'm going to go now." Joan leans on an elbow, resting at the counter.

"Phone me later if you need to. Call me at home. Do you have a pen to write down the number?"

Joan takes the pen and pad of paper she keeps by the phone. "Yes?" She writes the sequence of numbers her doctor tells her. Her doctor's home phone number.

"You have it, Joan?"

"I'm going to drink and go to bed," she informs her doctor, informs herself.

"I'll be seeing you tomorrow. Call if you need to, please."

"Good night, Dr. Thompson."

"Good night, Joan. Take care." With that Joan hangs up the phone, immediately going for another martini.

Ten minutes later, as Pam has a T-shirt half over her head, arms reaching to the ceiling, the phone rings. She pushes her head through the neckhole, marching to pick the phone up before the machine answers. "Hello."

Joan speaks in a low, tired monotone. "I think I have to do it tonight. I don't know how not to."

Pam stands transfixed, taken in by the brilliant night-lit view Joan has of the city before dropping her gaze to the coffee table and focusing upon the clutter of tools that have occupied Joan this evening: the alcohol, the ice cube tray with its scattered rectangular pools of melted ice, several crumpled plastic bags, and a short span of rope winding a path through the debris.

Joan comes from bolting and chaining the apartment door and seats herself on the sofa before the coffee table. She rests elbows on knees, eyes unfocused, staring at the windows. Pam peers over Joan's slumped shoulders, then walks around and takes a seat in a chair opposite Joan, waiting for her patient to say something. After several minutes of terminal silence Joan still sits frozen, face blank and lifeless.

"What do you think we can do to help you?" Pam breaks the moment. "I don't know what more I can do without your help."

Joan remains silent. Her eyes don't even register Pam's presence.

"You need more care than I can give you in three sessions a week."

"Then I'll come more often," Joan mutters in a flat voice.

"I can't be a baby-sitter for you. That's not my job. Our work is supposed to take place in my office during our scheduled sessions. It doesn't help our therapy for me to be here."

"Then let me do it without making me feel bad."

"I'm not trying to make you feel bad. I'm trying to help you understand why you feel that suicide is your only option when it clearly isn't."

Her eyes red and puffy, Joan faces her doctor. "I called. Isn't that what I'm supposed to do?"

"You called and made it clear that if I didn't come over, you would attempt suicide."

Joan slumps in the chair. She pulls at her eyelashes, which feel sticky with residue. "What do I do? He's leaving me, and I don't know what to do anymore." She pulls out an eyelash, flicking it across the room. "I thought it was right for me to . . . " Joan shuts her eyes, sighs audibly, opens her eyes, shrugging her shoulders. "Why don't you go home?" she says, resigned. "You can go home now. Thanks for coming over, but go home."

"I'm not going to leave before you assure me that you'll be okay for the rest of this evening."

Joan stands. "I'm going to bed now. You go home. I'm going to bed." She waits for the doctor to rise, but Pam does not, remains seated. "I'm going to sleep. You can go. Thank you," Joan repeats, anger growing.

Pam stares calmly at her patient. "I haven't finished speaking with you. I did not come over here to be dismissed like a servant."

Joan folds her arms over her chest. "I don't care anymore. I'm tired."

"Well, I'm not done," Pam protests.

"Well, I am," Joan says wearily, trying to maintain her balance.

Pam sits forward, speaking at Joan, her voice calm, controlled, soothing. "I think you're very afraid right now. You're afraid he's going to leave you and you'll be all alone. If we work together, I'm sure you will feel better about yourself and you'll understand that you are not alone but that there are people who want to help you, who love you." Pam reaches to the table, packing Joan's things away in the nylon bag: the rope, the freezer bags, the scissors. "I understand it will be hard without having Dennis in your life. You will have only yourself to live with, no diversions, only yourself with me to help, and I'm sure that scares you very much, but I will help you through this. I think I've demonstrated that I care about what happens to Joan Dwyer. Even when Joan Dwyer has not cared about herself, I have, and I will continue to in the future if she's willing to try to. I only hope she'll trust me enough to give us a chance at bringing her the kind of life she'd find pleasure in. You don't need a man to be happy and worthwhile, and I don't know if I can help you right now if you're with one. I think we've both seen that. It's pointless. I know we can give Joan Dwyer a life she'll be proud of on her own. And *then* if a man comes along, that's great, too. That I'll support.'' Pam stops, setting the bag on the floor, observing the effect her words have worked on her patient.

Joan wipes at her face with a hand, and Pam stands, going to Joan, taking her in her arms, holding Joan close. Joan gasps, breath hot on Pam's neck, Joan's arms limp at her sides. Pam holds Joan's head to her shoulder, rubbing her patient's back.

No message from Joan waiting to be heard in the basement apartment, and he's surprised, expected to come home and find some plea for him to see her tonight. Dennis pours scotch into a jelly jar glass with a cartoon painting of a pterodactyl, pouring the glass half full, half empty, no ice, and taking the drink over to the couch, where he reclines head on sofa arm, thinking through the receiving of no message from Joan on the machine. A good or bad sign, this no message? A good or bad omen? He said he might phone tonight, and he supposes he should, easing Joan out of their relationship rather than breaking it off severely and leaving her hanging. A call tonight, another in a few days, maybe—*maybe* see her one more time, and it will be done and things will be set for him to go back to his wife.

·   ·   ·

With the ringing of the phone, Joan stiffens in her doctor's embrace, suddenly too aware and ashamed of this intimacy. She raises her arms and pushes Dr. Thompson back, turning away, picking up the phone's receiver.

Pam watches Joan withdraw, so quickly does Joan regain her composure. Joan holds the ivory phone in one hand while laying the other flat against the tabletop. All poise and control. Joan's head tilts to the side. The shirtsleeve of the arm holding the receiver slides from Joan's wrist, halfway down Joan's forearm, at which point the cuff rests, filled.

Joan stands with her back to her doctor, embarrassed, as if she'd been tricked into all she felt before, as if the feelings weren't there in her waiting to come out when given the opportunity by her doctor, but as if she, Joan, was empty and her doctor had used this vulnerability to fill a very impressionable, unstable Joan with thoughts that caused her to lose control, break down, and cling to her doctor for safety. Only the ringing of the phone saved Joan from losing herself to her doctor's control.

"Hello," Joan says, sharp.

"Joan, hi. This is Dennis."

And Joan shudders, doesn't need this man to determine her emotions, moods, and thoughts. "Hello."

"How are you doing?"

Joan feels her doctor's presence, Dr. Thompson's influence, all that her doctor has said. "Are you calling because you feel guilty for our last conversation? Is that what this is?"

"I was only going to ask if—"

"Dennis, why are you calling me?" Joan breaks in, afraid to let him continue, to let him speak and seduce her. "Are you afraid I'll kill myself, so you have to check up on me? Is that what you're afraid of?" Joan pauses, keeping herself angry, not breaking down. "My life is not empty without you. It's not," Joan insists, her hand still resting on the table.

"I never said—"

"If you don't think this is right, then it's not. I agree with you. I only got out of the hospital three weeks ago, and already you're playing games with me again. I don't need you to check up on me to satisfy yourself. Please don't call anymore. There's no point. You can't help." Joan hangs up. Tears streak and sting her face, and she feels Dr. Thompson's presence behind her, at her back. Joan just wants to be left alone, finally, ultimately to do it, this time for good, no turning back or panicking, no reaching out for help, but just to draw herself together and get the inevitable over with. Joan keeps her back to her doctor, attempting to regain control, when she feels the crushing weight of Dr. Thompson's hand on her shoulder, her doctor's hand firmly gripping her shoulder, and Joan cannot help leaning into the warmth of the hand, the warm touch of her doctor, and Dr. Thompson turns Joan toward her, reaching out and pulling Joan into an embrace.

July

"All my time revolves around my visits here. All I do is spend my days thinking about therapy and then I have therapy and then I go home and wait until it's time for me to phone you and then we talk on the phone and I say good-bye and hang up and then sit waiting for therapy or my next phone conversation with you. My time is spent working on trying not to kill myself. I sit and think and want to kill myself and then use all my energy, focus all my energy on not killing myself." Joan tosses up her hands and laughs. "Is this how I'm supposed to live? Is this it? Because I can't do it for much longer. I'm sure of that. . . . Not too much longer. It's becoming more difficult to resist doing it when therapy seems to be doing so little and the time in between sessions feels longer and emptier." She places her hands on the chair's arms, then changes her mind, placing them in her lap. "My time here is useless, there's nothing left to be said. Almost as if I've died inside but I'm still around talking and walking and waiting and with August coming in a few weeks, you'll be on vacation and then what happens? What do I have then without therapy to wait for? Andrea will be away in Colorado. What do I do with my life then? I can't do it much longer." Joan shakes her head. "I can't. I won't."

Pam glances at the clock. "We have to end now."

Joan immediately stands, grabbing her handbag. "Here I go. Back into the vacuum of my life."

Pam rises. "You'll call me at home later?"

Joan walks to the door. "I don't think it helps anymore."

"Maybe not, but it doesn't hurt, so I'd like to keep in touch."

"If you want."

"What time should I expect your call?"

Joan pauses, her hand on the doorknob. "Nine, like always. Hooray."

"I'll speak to you then."

Joan opens the door and leaves.

Pam sometimes wishes Joan would kill herself, therapy with Joan is that unbearable, patient and therapist playing a waiting game of Can the therapist help the patient care enough to work at getting better before the patient loses all patience and kills herself? And Pam is worn through with the game, worn through with the worry and speculation over which day or night it will happen, when Joan finally gives up and hurls her body out a window or stuffs her head in a plastic bag.

Every night for the ten minutes leading up to the appointed time of the call, Pam sits by the phone, waiting for the phone to ring and let her know that Joan is still alive, not dead, and for the last ten minutes of the three therapy sessions Pam has each week with Devon Taylor, Pam waits with growing anxiety that the buzzer will not sound, indicating Joan's arrival and her need to be let into the office.

The day when Joan kills herself. Less a question of *will* Joan kill herself and more a question of *when*, Pam having adopted Joan's opinion that perhaps Joan is correct in saying her suicide is inevitable, unavoidable, cannot be helped or stopped. Pam sits through session after phone call after session after phone call, Joan's voice growing more angry and panicked and depressed with each conversation. Joan is filled with alternating bouts of anger and despair; in some sessions she is so despondent, her voice so flat, that she almost appears catatonic. On other days she is so furious and frustrated with her life, she seems ready to self-destruct under the pressure of an emptiness so deep it consumes her life and all those around her.

Dr. Pamela Thompson, a woman in the midst of having divorce papers drawn up, a woman left by her husband for another woman, refusing to take him back when he changed his mind. He begged her not to do it, crying over the phone, but she persisted. The life they had was gone and could not be re-created, and her anger at her husband and herself is so great that Pam doesn't believe either of them deserves the happy ending of a new and improved marriage. She told her lawyer to tell Dennis's lawyer to tell Dennis not to contact her anymore. The price he must pay, she loves-hates Dennis that much.

A call from Joan Dwyer at nine, Joan Dwyer being the person Pam has the most contact with. Pam speaks to Joan at least once every day, watching her patient drift farther and farther to the edge of the world, about to fall off, and if a person has stopped mattering to the world, if one has stopped mattering to oneself, if life is a lonely, desolate pain, a never-ending, bottomless, howling, raging storm of the mind, unbearable and unendurable, an endless parade of take-out dinners eaten alone in the stillness of an empty apartment, of going days without sharing one's feelings with another human being, of feeling life drain out of one's life as one awakens on a weekend morning only to find oneself stranded in bed with nowhere to go, no one to turn to and hold, nothing to look forward to but a matinee movie alone with a box of Goobers and a Diet Sprite, failing to exist for anyone's sake but one's own, and one's own sake is empty, *why go on*? Is life *that* precious? Pam knows all too well a person can be in therapy for years before finding any relief from depression. Years could pass before Joan feels any significant relief from the burden of her illness. Is it worth living through years of pain, day after awful day after awful day, all for the hope of one day feeling a tad better? Or is it better, more logical, to face up to life's realities, inventory and assess the situation, take life in for all it isn't worth, and then call it quits? Ending one's drag through life can be as noble an act as living it. The courage to kill oneself, to meet life and death head-on, can be as courageous as fighting off this consuming doom. Maybe Joan is correct. Maybe when she phones this evening, Pam will tell her patient that she shares her point of view. Perhaps suicide is, if not the only option, possibly the best, most practical, realistic solution. The enormous waste of money Joan spends on therapy with her doctor. She would be better off handing it all over to Andrea. Better spent on a shopping spree at Bergdorf Goodman.

"—and then like all the others, she got up and left right after. All business, no pleasure."

Pam looks to Bill Matson, her patient of the hour. She refocuses upon him as he finishes describing another of his rendezvous with a prostitute. The latest installment in the Bill Matson Chronicles: prostitutes ordered in to his apartment. "Did that surprise you?" Pam asks.

"No. Sort of. But what was different was that immediately afterward I knew I would tell you about it and I thought about what you would think of me when I did. It occurred to me that I'm always paying women to be with me. Paying them for sex and you for emotions."

"This is an emotional prostitution for you?"

"I don't feel much emotionally when I'm not here, so it's almost like I come here in order to feel things that I've shut down on the outside. This is my emotional satisfaction, like the girls are my physical satisfaction."

"But do you always leave satisfied? Is therapy that kind of an exchange? I don't give you the emotions, do I? They come out of you. They're your emotions to be felt wherever and whenever you can. It doesn't only have to be here. Maybe that's how you are now, separating your physical and emotional needs, controlling how these needs are met by paying for them like services, but hopefully the more you open up here, the more you'll be able to open up and carry your behavior over into the rest of your life."

"Are you angry that I'm comparing you to a prostitute?"

"How do you feel about it?" Pam asks. "How I feel about it doesn't matter."

She doesn't know how she's done it, but she's somehow managed to get herself to decide upon a movie and get herself to the theater on time for the show. This is the first night out Joan's taken on her own in so long she can't remember, and she sits in the fifth-row center of the movie theater, sipping at her Diet Coke, so proud of herself for deciding to do something and actually following through and implementing the plan.

The houselights dim and the coming attractions play and Joan thinks that maybe things had gotten so bad that they eventually had to get better, maybe that's what happened tonight: She hit bottom, almost drowning, and is now making her way up to the surface.

Joan sips at her Diet Coke, bubbles on her tongue, a rush of caffeine stimulating her nerves. The titles of the movie flash by, and Joan thinks that for the first time in a long time, maybe life isn't so bad, at least for the next hour and forty-three minutes she's sitting here safe in this movie theater. She has stumbled upon two hours not to think about herself but to think about something outside herself, and no matter what occurs once this movie ends, at least for the next two hours, all will be good.

·   ·   ·

Nine-fourteen. The phone has not rung, and Pam wants it to ring so she can answer it and get this call over with. Wants the call done with her patient Joan Dwyer. With Joan Dwyer for today and forever. A quarter after nine.

Pam sits by the phone in the den, but it does not ring. No call from Joan—ever-punctual, ever-dependable, desperate, needy, suicidal Joan. Pam cannot help thinking back to the last time Joan missed an appointment or call, and there was only that once that led directly to the hospital. She stares at the silent phone, guessing how long she should give Joan before phoning herself. It was Pam's phone call that awoke Joan from her previous pill-induced sleep, and at nine-thirty, Pam decides, she will phone and get this call done, her obligation to her patient fulfilled. In ten minutes. If Joan suffocated herself or jumped from a window, she could already be dead for all Pam knows.

Joan Dwyer dead. Pam breathes in the thought. How does she feel to have Joan dead? Pam pictures Joan with the plastic bag secured around her head. Pictures Joan lifeless in her bathrobe, sprawled across the living room couch.

Joan isn't phoning because she is dead, Pam is sure, and Pam sits and wonders if she should rush over to Joan's apartment this instant, attempting to save her as she's done before, or if she should wait and let Joan die as she's chosen to.

Nine-thirty. Pam's hand goes for the phone, hasn't fully realized how tense, how worried for Joan's life she actually is. She dials the number, listening to the phone's ring, then the machine picking up, Andrea not home to save her mother's life.

Pam speaks. "Hello, Joan. This is Dr. Thompson. I'm at home. I was expecting your call at nine. I hope everything's all right. Please phone me when you can. Thanks. Good-bye."

Pam hangs up, imagining Joan dead in the living room, dead because she had nothing to live for once her therapist coerced her into destroying the one positive relationship she had going for her in her life, her therapeutic relationship with Dr. Thompson not being enough to keep her going, and Pam, now living through the reality of her divorce with Dennis, *from* Dennis, wonders what the purpose of prying Joan away from Dennis was if she wasn't going to get him back and resurrect their marriage. Pam has as good as killed Joan, putting the bag over her head and knotting it tight with the rope. She hits redial. "Joan"—she speaks into the machine—"please, pick up if you are there. Please, Joan. Pick up. I need to talk to you. Please, Joan." Pam pauses, gets no response. "Good-bye," Pam closes.

She hangs up, standing, going to the bathroom for a Xanax before heading over to Joan's for the rescue.

As she approaches the door to her building, Joan notices Antoine is busy speaking into the intercom, buzzing an apartment for a woman with her back to the door. Joan opens the heavy door herself, stepping into the lobby. Antoine's eyes meet hers, and *"Ah,"* he says, and he hangs up the phone. The woman at his side turns.

"Joan," Dr. Thompson says, her voice filled with anger and relief. "Joan," Dr. Thompson repeats, reaching out, touching a hand to Joan's shoulder as if to make sure she is real, not an apparition.

Dr. Thompson smiles, anxious and exhausted, and Antoine says, "This lady here is waiting for you, thought you would be at home. Was very worried that you weren't answering and she asked—"

Joan steps away from Dr. Thompson, "No. I'm just a bit late. Thanks for trying, though. Have a good night, Antoine. We'll be going up now." Joan turns to her doctor, a strained smile spreading across her face. "Why don't we go up?" she says. "Sorry I'm late."

The apartment door closes behind the two women.

Joan walks away, leaving her doctor behind. "He must think I'm crazy, first seeing you dragging me out of here in my nightgown on one night and now you giving him the idea that I'm up here dead."

Pam stares, observing Joan as she heads into the living room, directly to the dry bar. Joan opens the cabinet, then walks across and out of the room. Pam walks to the living room, standing at the window. Joan Dwyer leaning out the window, jumping. A quarter-inch-thick pane of glass all that keeps one's life secure and intact, all that keeps one's world in place, and if the window were always up or broken, the glass raised or removed between the order of the apartment and the chaos—or is it freedom?—of the open air, letting oneself fall would be that much easier. Passing by an open window over and over so many times, one would eventually have to jump, one's resistance eventually worn by the permanent invitation.

Pam hears the sound of ice rattling against glass, and then Joan reappears with a martini shaker full of ice cubes. Joan goes to the dry bar. "I can't even wonder how many of my neighbors passed in and out of the lobby as you hassled my doorman. 'Crazy Joan Dwyer in Sixteen-B. Her psychiatrist had to come over here last night to save her from killing herself again. Second time in the last couple months.' I can imagine all that over coffee and croissants in the Rayburns' and Bickfords' and Tarrytons' apartments tomorrow morning. I hope Miss Pointer down the hall didn't see you." Joan pours the vodka and vermouth, placing the cap on the shaker, then lifting the glass and rattling it repeatedly. Ice breaks, the alcohol mixes, frothing, chilling, and Joan stops shaking the container, unscrewing its silver cap and pouring herself a martini glassful over three pitted green olives. She takes a sip and sits in the chair by the sofa. "I was having a good evening. I got myself out to a movie and was feeling fine. When I come home to this, it's hardly worth trying." She won't even look at her doctor. She looks out the window, waiting for a response, an explanation.

Pam stares at the side of Joan's face, fascinated with her patient's callous, self-centered view of the situation. "Do you really believe I dragged myself here this late at night to embarrass you? Do you believe that was my purpose?"

"That's what you've accomplished."

Pam sits on the couch by the arm closest to Joan. Joan sips her drink, looking away to the window, watching her doctor's reflection lean over the arm of the sofa toward her.

"I'd rather you didn't drink while we're speaking," Pam says.

"My drinking won't interfere with your talking."

"I'm afraid it might interfere with your listening."

"I'm listening. Don't worry."

Pam decides not to pursue the point. Maintain control is her primary objective; keep calm, soft-spoken, and firm. "Didn't you agree to phone me this evening at nine?"

"I had an impulse to go to a movie. I forgot."

"Have you considered how I might have felt when I didn't receive any call from you?"

Joan eats an olive, hates being scolded as if she's done something wrong. "You came to the conclusion that I had hurt myself. I understand that, but I didn't. You were mistaken."

"Isn't that a fair conclusion to come to, considering how depressed you've been, considering your history and the last time you broke an appointment with me?"

Joan takes a sip of her drink, sets the glass on the coffee table. "You thought I was dead or dying, so you came over to help me."

Pam says nothing, wanting her message to sink into Joan's mind and take hold. Let her feel guilty, and then she'll continue. She'd like to ask Joan for a drink but unfortunately knows better; she'll pick up a bottle of wine on her way home later.

"I guess I failed you. I'm sorry," Joan says, giving up some of her anger, taking on some of the guilt offered, and she looks at her doctor for the first time since entering the elevator. Dr. Thompson looks less angry than upset, concerned. "I was feeling better for a moment, and I forgot," Joan explains. "I'm sorry. I forgot about my call to you." She waits for Pam to forgive her, a pardon, and she sits, hands folded in lap, legs crossed.

"I didn't forget your call to me." Pam sits back. "I spent my evening waiting, and when the phone didn't ring, I was terrified. When I only got your machine here, I didn't know what to think. Wasn't sure what to do. But I did what I had to, and whether I embarrassed you or not wasn't important to me.''

Joan can't believe she forgot this, forgot to call her doctor, so unlike her. Her doctor so concerned and worried, and Joan's accusing Dr. Thompson of embarrassing her. "I'm sorry . . . I don't know what else to say.''

"Do you have an idea why you might have forgotten?''

"No. I think I just forgot.''

"Well, I think you were trying to push me away so it would be easier for you to kill yourself. You want to die, and I'm the only thing preventing you. You're not even a bit angry at me for trying to help you, for saving you before?''

"I don't know." Joan looks at her drink, afraid to take another sip, afraid of being reprimanded. "I don't know what I was thinking or feeling.''

Pam looks at the wreck of Joan Dwyer. Her continued relationship with Joan Dwyer destroyed any desire she once had of saving her marriage, and now Joan's severe suicidal behavior threatens to destroy her professional life, occupying too much of her time and thoughts with worries. Being a friend, a mother, a sister, a sitter, a nurse, a doctor, and sharing a lover—all too much for Pam to take, and maybe Joan isn't worth saving or isn't here to be saved anymore. Maybe she's already gone, her death inevitable, and Pam should stop caring, forcing herself to care. Maybe if Dennis had never met Joan Dwyer, he would not have realized all that was missing from his relationship with his wife. Maybe if he hadn't known he could have a woman like Joan, he wouldn't have resented his wife for not being like her. Pam doesn't know, and she cares too much to care, hurts too much to care and witness the pain she's inflicted on this already too pained woman. She needs to refer Joan elsewhere, this weight around her neck, and Pam looks at Joan, Joan sitting wiping tears from her eyes, sniffling, picking at her fingernails—*Joan Dwyer dead. Dead or at least out of my life*—and Pam straightens her posture, catch-

ing Joan's attention. "I don't think I can help you anymore," Pam
begins, and Joan winces as if hit. Pam continues, staring at Joan as if
Joan weren't there at all. Maybe this is for Joan's good, or maybe,
Pam admits, she's doing this purely to rid herself of Joan Dwyer and
end this chapter in her own life. Pam makes her speech, not bothering to take in Joan's reactions to the words, speaking to Joan as if she
were only a cardboard cutout. "The attention and treatment you require cannot be accomplished on an outpatient basis such as we've
been working in. Our therapeutic relationship is not healthy if I need
to be worrying about you at all hours of the day and night. It's not
good for either of us. I think I made a mistake in letting our relationship become too close. I thought I could work through this with you,
but I no longer find myself capable of doing it. It's affecting too much
of my life. This is not how therapy is supposed to work. I've let it get
off course, and I've come to realize how grave a mistake I've made.
You need more than I can ever possibly offer you on an outpatient
basis."

Joan searches for an answer, her mind in shock. She reaches for her
glass, holds its cone in both hands. "So you're saying that I'm too
needy and require too much attention, that I'm too much of a burden." Joan takes a small sip and places the glass down. "I understand
that, but I'll stop. I promise you I'll stop, just don't stop seeing me.
Don't say you'll stop—"

"You need to be in a *hospital*, Joan." Pam cuts her off, silencing
her patient. "You need a doctor with a support staff where you'll be
safe and watched. I can't do that for you. I can't be everything to you
as I've tried."

"You're sick of me."

"I'm trying to help you do what's best for yourself."

Joan sits stolidly for a moment, about to begin speaking, but her
thoughts are all jumbled. She is suddenly so scared of her doctor, her
doctor's suggestion. "Like for how long?" she asks, trembling.
"How much longer than Lenox Hill?"

Having said all she needed to say, Pam is at once calm and at ease, a professional. "This would be a long-term hospital. I have one in mind. It's a beautiful place, not a locked ward. An open hospital in the country."

Joan shakes her head rapidly, picking up her glass, going to the bar. "I'd rather kill myself. I'd rather be dead than be a mental patient. I won't become that."

"I think a hospital would be the best thing for you, Joan." Pam holds her gaze still, fixed on Joan's back. "I think it's what we have to do for you."

Joan pours the vodka. *"No! No."* Joan shakes her head, her eyes blurring with tears. She lowers the bottle to the bar, her shoulders shaking, choking back tears. *"I'm not that sick. I can't be that bad."* And Pam watches as her patient absorbs the fact of the hospital, as her patient realizes their relationship will eventually, inevitably end.

"No . . . " Joan shuts her eyes. *"Please, don't let this happen to me. No—"* And she lets out a loud sob, a gasp, gasping for air, her hands covering her face, her mouth open and gasping. *"No, please, no,"* Joan cries into her hands. *"No, please."* But Pam knows Joan's cries are less those of protest than of surrender.

August

Seconds after Dennis comes inside Roberta, he knows he'll have to fire the girl, doesn't want to have her walking around the office, typing his correspondence, arranging his appointments, when she has now become, at this moment, a reminder to him of a sexual encounter he presently, most recently, has the liberty of having because his wife won't have him and he's been left by—or did he leave her?—his mistress.

He pulls out of Roberta, rolling onto his back, wishing she would evaporate, vanish, his need for her gone, but Roberta doesn't know, isn't done, and she reaches over, playing with the hairs on his chest, her fingernails trailing a path to his navel, then playing with the hairs there. She's the third woman he's slept with this month, seventh since his last phone conversation with his soon-to-be ex-wife.

"It's going smoothly, isn't it?" Pam asked, and Dennis agreed. They established a time when he could return to what was once their apartment to pick up his remaining clothes and the boxes kept in storage in the building's basement.

"Since you've redone the place, it doesn't look or feel like I'm giving anything up by letting you keep it. It's not like it's my place anymore, so it's hard to miss what isn't there."

"I guess so," Pam replied. And before she could say good-bye, he asked, "So how is Joan doing?"

Her voice strident: "I cannot discuss Joan Dwyer with you. It's unethical. Good-bye."

"God, what time is it?" Dennis rolls away to the clock, twisting onto his side, a thigh sliding from between Roberta's scissored legs: 7:44 P.M. A palm at the small of his back. Why did he leave his wife and begin this pursuit? After a moment's thought, after Roberta has slid her hand down to cup Dennis's ass, he remembers. Remembers feeling neglected, wanting a child. And now he sleeps with women he doesn't care about once or twice a week, no loving wife or child in sight.

Seven forty-five. Not even dark. Another half hour to forty-five minutes of light left in the sky. Roberta and Dennis came to his apartment directly from work with a bottle of white wine, bought at the corner liquor store. Roberta's hand won't leave him. Dennis keeps his eyes fixed on the clock, watching another minute pass. His orgasm felt like nothing. He can't even remember having it, it's so negligible, forgotten after only five minutes.

Roberta kisses him on the cheek. "I love you," she says, needy, but he knows she doesn't mean it.

Joan sits on a sofa in the living room as the older cleaning lady with curly dyed red hair empties the ashtray on the end table, dumping it in a wastepaper basket. Another cleaning lady, the older woman's daughter, polishes the keys of the baby grand piano in the far corner of the room. The clumsy sound of low, then high keys, mixing to confusion. Joan sips an iced tea, listening to the conversation Ruth, a twenty-year-old patient, has with one of the psychiatric nurses sitting across from her on another couch. Ruth talks about trading in her brand-new Jeep Cherokee for a brand-new Corvette. "Do you think that's practical?"

Last night, while waiting in line at the nurses' station to receive medication, Joan and a group of other patients witnessed Ruth storm out of her bedroom, pick up a vase of flowers sitting on a table in the hallway, and smash it against the wall. "Will you please shut up out here?" she screamed before retreating to her room in tears.

"Your Jeep's only two weeks old," Donna, the nurse, comments.

"I know that," Ruth says. "But I don't think I want it. I could trade it in for the Corvette. I'd really like one in yellow. Yellow is a good color, isn't it?"

Joan has been at the Berling Center for twenty-two days. The average stay is eighteen months. Dr. Thompson recommended the small forty-patient hospital in Massachusetts' Berkshires. "It's an open hospital where you'll be able to have your own room and have a car if you'd like so you can do things in the area. You'll be in therapy four days a week. There will be lots of group meetings for you to attend. Arts and crafts facilities. They have a painting instructor. They even have a school for the doctors' kids, which patients can volunteer at. That would give you the chance to be around young children again."

"That might be nice," Joan replied, willing to go along with anything the doctor suggested, her will defeated. Five days later Todd and Andrea drove their mother up to the hospital with six large suitcases full of clothes and the television from her bedroom. "The man over the phone said the rooms are cable-ready but to bring your own TV," Joan informed her children.

"Fuck you!" Ruth exclaims, glaring at Donna. "I don't need everyone judging me! If you're not going to help, don't help. I don't need everybody criticizing me for wanting a Corvette."

"I wasn't criticizing you, Ruth, I just thought you ought to—"

"I don't need to listen to this." Ruth stands, marching from the room.

Donna smiles weakly. "So, how has your day been going?"

The nurses dress in civilian, everyday, ordinary clothes just as they did at Lenox Hill, and during her first days here Joan couldn't tell the patients from the nurses. Now, twenty-two days into her stay, Joan can distinguish nurses from patients, however seldom she may interact with either. Joan eats alone at the table in the corner of the dining room, sits silently at group meetings, and watches TV alone in her room most days and nights, venturing into one of the common rooms only when they are nearly empty. When Joan speaks, it is in therapy with her doctor or to a nurse when she needs her medication or is asked a question. She avoids most other patients, fearful of catching their diseases by osmosis, fearful of taking on their affects of hallucinations, paranoia, and delusional thinking.

"It takes awhile to get used to being here. You'll adjust, it just takes a little while."

The mother of the cleaning team dusts the fireplace mantel. The daughter polishes a brass lamp in the corner of the room. Joan looks back to the nurse. Where is Dr. Thompson now? Whom has she found to fill the three therapy spaces once occupied by her infamous patient Joan Dwyer?

Joan wants to phone her former doctor but knows she cannot. Their relationship is done. Joan wants to phone Dennis, tell him where she is, what she's come to so he can come to the rescue, but again knows she cannot. Their relationship is over as well. Al phoned on Joan's third day at the hospital to wish Joan good luck, sounding casual about it all, as if he'd always expected his ex-wife would eventually come to this, as if it were only a matter of time and he were just wondering when it would finally be. Todd and Andrea have phoned once a week for the past three weeks, giving Joan news reports from the outside world. Todd has moved into the family apartment, giving up his place with Emily, moving her too into the

Dwyer home. "I'll keep watch over everything while you're away, and this way we'll be able to save money by not paying rent." Andrea phones from Colorado and tells her mother of all the clothes she's buying in preparation for school. "I'm going to look great this fall, Mom. I'm going to look so cool!"

"What do you think you'll do today? Have you thought about assisting at the school yet?"

Nothing left in her life but her life, this hollow vessel that she is, and if only Dr. Thompson hadn't broken her will to kill herself, hadn't persuaded Joan that there is hope for her and this hospital is it, Joan wouldn't be living in a hospital today but would be gone, having had the strength to kill herself and end this pain.

Donna places a hand on Joan's. "Things will get better. You'll feel better. I promise you will."

Joan looks down to the hand holding her own. Her thin, frail fingers covered by the long, tan fingers of the nurse. She feels older than forty-two. Thirty to forty years older. All she has the energy to do is sit and stare at whatever passes into her line of vision. A patient and nurse sitting in the room, a robin on the windowsill, a cloud in the sky, a doctor in a burgundy leather chair, a program on the television. The nurse gives Joan's hand a light squeeze, and the touch feels good. Joan misses it when Donna takes her hand away.

"It helps to think of this not as an ending but as a new beginning," Donna says. "This is your chance to work through the past and then go on. It might be hard to feel it now, but by coming here, you've given yourself the chance to start again."

Joan guesses that if she hasn't killed herself yet and has gotten herself to the hospital and stayed, she may not kill herself, may never kill herself. Donna may be right. Killing herself would have been the end. What this is, Joan doesn't yet know.

The older cleaning lady switches on a vacuum, sweeping its brushed nozzle along the white curtains framing the bay window overlooking the front lawn. The vacuum sounds loud and gray. A gray noise, empty and wanting, and Joan listens.

.   .   .

As she has lived through this disorder, it has all been a struggle to survive, to keep her head clear and above water. Throughout it all Pam
thought she was thinking logically, but looking back, she finds she was
reacting quickly to the immediate circumstances. Only now, after it's
all over, in August and on her four-and-a-half-week vacation, does
Pam discover that while she thought she was saving everyone, the result is that she has only—and only barely—managed to save Joan
Dwyer. Dennis has been punished but spared. And Pam is losing, has
lost the life she was so anxious to preserve.

Too hot and sticky to leave her apartment, Pam spends her vacation in bed or on the living room couch, wrapped in the comfort of
chilly air-conditioned air. Dennis gone, Joan gone, her patients on
hold: no one in her life to think of her, no one to listen to her troubles or support her at her weak moments, no one to sit on a couch
alongside and share Chinese take-out food while watching VCR movies, no one to climb in bed next to and seek comfort from—with no
one—a life of her own making. Pam sits at home, watching the freaks
gracing the stages of TV talk shows all through the day and into the
night, Jack Briden's ultimatum before her. Program after program of
people in need, their lives destroyed by themselves and others, and
instead of being ashamed enough to hide their pains, they advertise
them for all to bear witness to.

Destroying Joan's life only to save and destroy her once again, putting her in a hospital. "I failed as a patient," Joan cried at their final
session, a session the morning of the day Todd and Andrea were taking her up to the hospital. "I failed like I failed at everything I've ever
tried in my life. You *should* let me die; you shouldn't try to help me.
Some people just aren't worth saving, aren't supposed to live, are
mistakes." Pam told Joan that that was the sickness talking, that the
sickness was making her feel this way, but with time and therapy at
the hospital she will view life differently.

They stood at the door. "Good-bye, Joan. Good luck. I think this

is the best thing you can do for yourself. I'm very proud of you."
Pam reached out to embrace her patient, but Joan flinched back,
turning away, having none of it.

"You must really hate me to send me away like this. To do this to
me." Joan wiped her eyes with the wad of tissues she clutched in her
hand, leaving the office, exiled from her life in the city to a mental
hospital in the country.

Pam has spent the last few weeks considering whom she hates,
who is guilty of all the crimes, who has committed all the sins, who
has broken all the laws, who must pay the price and be punished.

The day before he was to begin his August vacation in the Hamp-
tons, Pam went to Jack Briden in his office, letting him know that the
Joan Dwyer situation had been taken care of, that she had convinced
her patient that she needed to be hospitalized and thus Joan Dwyer
was being cared for and was out of danger.

Jack stared at Pam, his mouth agape. "What kind of doctor are
you, Pamela? Over the past three months you've worn this patient
down to the point where she was suicidal and had to be hospitalized?
Who do you think you were protecting by sending her away? Joan?
Yourself? You were certainly protecting your husband from ever getting to her again—that's what it looks like to me: You couldn't help
and didn't want your husband near her, so you worked her over until
she'd do whatever you thought was best for her. Correct me if I'm
wrong."

Pam had thought he would be pleased with her accomplishment,
had thought she had done well by Joan. "I think the hospital will help
her."

Jack rolled his eyes. "I'm sure it will be a help, but would she have
needed to be hospitalized if it weren't for your manipulations of her
therapy? Would hospitalization have been necessary if not for you?"

"I don't know," Pam replied. "It's possible."

Jack shook his head. "I don't think I can live with this. I don't
think you know right from wrong anymore."

"Jack, what are you talking about?"

He continued. "You're off all of August, right? By September you have to have reported yourself to the Ethics Committee or I'll do it for you. That's four weeks to think about it and decide. But either way, the APA's going to know. This is going to be reported. I can't take the chance you might do this to another patient. You need help, Pamela."

The panel on one talk show consists of women who rarely leave their homes. Women so fearful of others they are afraid to go out in public. One middle-aged woman with short black hair in a striped red and yellow dress speaks to the audience from her home via a video monitor set up at center stage. "I feel stuck inside my house and don't know how to get out," she says. "I love the movies, but I can't go out because I'm afraid so I have to wait until everything comes out on video. I rented *The Little Mermaid* when it came out, and when the little mermaid girl sings that song 'A Part of Your World,' that's how I feel. Like I'm not a part of this world but can only watch it going on and don't know how to be a part of it. That's my favorite song; it says so much for me."

To be brought before the Ethics Committee of the APA, her personal and professional life exposed, her judgments criticized by her holier-than-thou colleagues, Dr. Thompson no longer known for being a fine therapist who has helped hundreds of patients but as the doctor who destroyed the life of one Joan Dwyer because Joan made the mistake of having an affair with her doctor's husband. Even if they don't take away her license to practice, the disgrace of having the charges brought against her would be bad enough. Pam can imagine the story leaking out, going public, Joan Dwyer, Dennis Perry, and Pamela Thompson becoming public figures, tabloid names for all to enjoy. To turn herself in or let Jack do it for her. What difference does it make? In the end her career will be over either way.

Fail a husband, fail a patient, fail a marriage, fail a profession, making that which is personal professional and that which is professional personal. Destroying all others for the sake of preserving oneself. Survival of the fittest. Crime and punishment. And even if others eventually do forgive, Pam can't forgive herself. Jack Briden is right; she did use Joan's therapy against her; she did send Joan to the hospital because she could not bear to treat her anymore, could not bear the thought of Joan reuniting with Dennis. Everyone has to be punished: Dennis denied a wife, Joan banished to a hospital, and Dr. Pamela Thompson, the infallible, respected psychiatrist and loving wife, no longer exists. Pam feels she has been transformed back to the child of her past she worked so hard to bury: a fat, unwanted youth, starving for approval, hating herself and all those around her. There's no going back, no rearranging history and making what never worked work—her childhood, her marriage, her profession—and Pam switches off the television. Time enough to call it quits, knowing when the end has arrived, when to say good-bye.

Unlike Joan, Pam knows the pills and combination of pills required, knows and has the combination set and waiting at her bedside in a daisy-patterned Dixie cup next to a large glass of water, cool and clear.

About the Author

LAWRENCE DAVID is the author of the novel *Family Values*. He was educated at Bennington College and New York University's Tisch School of the Arts. He lives in New York City.

About the Type

This book was set in Perpetua, a typeface designed by the English artist Eric Gill, and cut by The Monotype Corporation between 1928 and 1930. Perpetua is a contemporary face of original design, without any direct historical antecedents. The shapes of the roman letters are derived from the techniques of stone-cutting. The larger display sizes are extremely elegant and form a most distinguished series of inscriptional letters.